DRAGON 2

BRUCE SENTAR

CONTENTS

CHAPTER 1

"I said to hold on to him!" Morgana yelled as two more red, puffy darts lodged themselves in the mortar beside the troll.

"Are you fucking kidding me?"

The world around me pivoted as the troll used me like a wrecking ball on the old, abandoned building. So much for luring it and its friend out into a trap. The wall bounced, or maybe that was my head, as the hulked-out para continued to thrash me.

"You should be able to hold a stupid troll. You're a dragon," Morgana spat. "How can you still not shift at all?"

I would have rolled my eyes if the world wasn't still spinning. It was totally an inappropriate time to rib me for my draconic shortcomings. She knew it was a sore spot.

The moment was broken as I was slammed into the ground again. This time, my leg came loose from his grip, and I had a moment of reprieve, like sleeping in a concrete tomb.

But then he picked me up to start it all over again. Luckily, he swung me at a new angle, and I got a chance to curl up like a ball, grabbing his wrist and making myself a smaller target.

I heard the staccato puffing of Morgana's dart gun behind me, watching as the little red dart tuffs peppered the troll's chest.

"Whew. Good going there. You really had him." Morgana chuckled.

I was more concerned with the troll's eyes as they rolled back up in its head; clearly, he was about to go down. I used my legs to kick off its arm to clear myself just in time for the one-ton paranormal to crash to the ground. Soon after his crash landing, he reverted to a pale, naked guy covered in tribal tattoos. I was even more glad I hadn't ended up under the naked man.

"Fuck," I cursed and grabbed his arm to haul him over my shoulder. "So, you said these are swamp trolls?"

I started moving back towards Morgana's reinforced van, throwing him in the trunk. Morgana had already deposited the lovely lady troll he'd been with in the back.

"Yup," Morgana replied, far closer to me than I'd expected.

I turned around to find Morgana right behind me. She was wearing her normal leather pants and a corset that pushed up her chest for the world to see. The drow vampire wore it like it was everyday wear. But she was also a badass mercenary and my guide into the paranormal world. Leather just fit her like grass was green.

But, as she stood there, she seemed to split into two Morganas, and then three. She said something in response to what I'd said, but it sounded miles away despite her being right next to me.

"Something's wrong," I mumbled, but my tongue felt like it had grown three times its size in moments.

The world spun as I took a stumbling step and fell into Morgana. My head landed on the open cleavage of her chest, and I nuzzled in ready to sleep right there.

"Oh my. The dragon has already come home to roost? I thought I had more time," she cooed and pressed my face deeper into her cleavage.

Then she let out a chuckle, and I felt a pinch between my shoulder blades and looked up to her holding a dart between her fingers.

"Haha, ah, that makes sense. Whoopsie? Let's get you some of T's antidote." She dragged me over to the side of the van and threw me along the center seating row.

The van looked beat up on the outside, but it was one of the most expensive cars in her garage, and that was saying something. It was armored and outfitted to be better than a tank. But it was still a waste next to all the premium sports cars if you asked me.

Morgana came back around to the side of the van and plugged my mouth with a vial. It tasted like death, but my senses came back to me in a rush, as if the world just seemed to light back up.

"Whoa." I sat up straight. "That stuff works well." I touched my cheek. It was still warm from being pressed into her chest, making me blush. Which, in turn, annoyed me. Dragons shouldn't blush.

The beast inside of me agreed.

My abilities from my beast were still limited as Morgana had pointed out. It was getting in the way of my work, too. Morgana had been harping on me about my inability to shift for the last few weeks; she was getting frustrated trying to train me.

"You wouldn't have needed that if you could shift. Because you ARE a several-ton dragon. That much tranquilizer shouldn't put you out like that."

There it was—right on cue.

"We've tried," I growled, and the beast joined me in frustration. It had been three months of trying. Finals were just two weeks away, and I still hadn't made any progress on unlocking more of my draconic heritage.

Sitting up, I was feeling jittery, so I went to walk around the scene of mayhem the two swamp trolls had caused, righting a dumpster as I walked.

"Oh yeah. Now no one will notice that something went down here," Morgana snorted. "Leave it and we'll get you back to your foxy friend. I'm sure she's still waiting at the bar."

"What can I say? We are two peas in a pod."

The vampire rolled her eyes. "More like disgustingly in love. I thought a dragon would have had his prick in a dozen waiting holes by now."

"First off, no one knows I'm a dragon besides you and Scarlett. Second, there aren't a dozen women after me."

"There are at least two, whom you are pointedly ignoring. At least Kelly isn't still hanging around the club trying to pin you down like some lovesick sheep."

I looked down the street, not wanting to talk about the situation with Kelly. She and the wolf pack had become so insistent that I come and compete for alpha that they had actually started causing problems with Scarlett and me.

At that point, I had completely frozen them out, and not because Scarlett had said anything, but because I could see how uncomfortable some of the girls had made her. They— well, they got too aggressive, and I was afraid that Scarlett was going to come in on them mobbing me naked at one point and misunderstand.

Kelly had gotten the message loud and clear, although she hadn't taken it super well. It had been radio silent from that point forward.

And then there was Jadelyn. Things between us had been... trickier.

We both were awkward around each other. It felt like something was bubbling just under the surface. But I had promised Scarlett that I'd wait until she was ready. Which would have been easier if I could have also avoided Jadelyn more easily. But Jadelyn was Scarlett's best friend and employer, so that was a no-go. Sighing, I re-checked the trolls and hopped into the passenger seat.

As I sat, I realized I needed to readjust myself. I was starting to get excited, which made little sense. Sure, I was thinking about attractive women, but not in that way.

"Morgana... are there any side effects of T's antidote?"

She coughed as she started the car, and her eyes flicked down to my crotch in a knowing way. "We'll get you back to Scarlett ASAP. Remember, if it lasts more than 4 hours... don't go to a doctor. Just find a brothel or something. Docs won't be able to fix T's special blue juice."

Turning in my seat, I fixed her with the biggest glare of my life. "You said it was an antidote."

"It functioned like one, right? But... he might sell them for other purposes too. A bit of a pick me up in several ways, you know..." She didn't even try to hide the smile that was stretching so wide I could see her fangs.

"Fuck me." I planted my head on the dash even as my cock became so hard I was pretty sure it could bend steel.

"If you say so. I'll grab a strap-on when we get back."

"Not. Funny." I took a deep breath. "At least we got the trolls. Why did this job have such a big bounty?"

Morgana looked a little more serious and watched me out of the side of her eye as she ran over a curb to get back onto the street. From there, she gunned it down the road. I was glad it was at least empty, and there wasn't anyone for Morgana to implicate if she crashed.

"You didn't read the job close enough."

"Huh? Stop the trolls causing trouble. Uno, dos. Two trolls no longer causing trouble."

Morgana pressed her lips into a thin line as she suppressed a laugh. "Of course you don't know. Right now, it is swamp troll migration."

"Swamp troll what?" I did a double take. "They migrate? Like birds?"

"Swamp trolls are very susceptible to the cold. They migrate from the great lakes region down to Florida every year, passing through Philly in the process," she explained.

I looked in the back of the car at the two naked trolls that looked like they would fit right in at a trailer park. "And this is a bad thing. Why? Can't they just hop a flight if it's such a big deal?"

"Swamp trolls... and well, most troll subspecies... aren't exactly the sharpest tools in the shed. Evolutionarily, they haven't needed to be. Their regeneration causes almost zero consequences in them doing dumb shit during their early development and learning."

"How dumb are we talking?"

"The stupidest shit. You wouldn't believe it. I've seen them take turns shooting each other in the face for fun."

That reminded me of a certain meme. I pulled out my phone and searched 'Florida Man'. "Like this level of stupid?"

"That's a troll," Morgana informed me with one look at the article about a drunken man ripping a urinal off the wall to take it to go.

"What about this one?" I flipped to another story.

"Troll. What is that?"

I looked at the meme with a new light. "Uh, a joke on the internet about stupid things people in Florida do... shit, it just hit me."

"Yep. Welcome to swamp troll migration. We need to get them through the city and on their way so they can do stupid shit in Florida and not here." Morgana chuckled. "Otherwise, our city may become the joke. Philly Man. I can see it now."

It was comical and terrifying at the same time. I definitely didn't want to spend my time cleaning up their mess in perpetuity. "Anything else I need to know about them?"

"Don't feed the trolls. They like to stick around if you feed them."

"Got it. So we are driving down to the south side and dropping these guys off? They won't just come back?"

"They operate a lot like any migrating animal. They'll wander down to Florida on their own from there. We just need to make sure they keep moving. Once we drop them, we can get you back so you can take care of your very noticeable problem."

My pants were stretched tight as they tented noticeably. I was glad that there was no one around and the trolls were knocked out, but the remainder of the drive to Scarlett felt like it took forever.

As soon as we got back to the bar, I left the trolls to Morgana, unable to handle it anymore. I ignored her laughter as I charged through the place, finding Scarlett and dragging her away in a hurry.

***

Scarlett fell backwards into the sheets, letting out deep breaths as she relaxed on the luxurious bed with dragons designed into the headboard.

Mine.

A greedy part of me, a part that I knew was tied to my dragon half, demanded that she never leave me. Even though we were just dating, my beast and I had sunk our claws in deep; she wasn't going anywhere as far as my dragon and I were concerned.

"Zach. I love it when you look at me like that." Her pink lips curled up into a satisfied smile. "You always have that look after we have a great time in bed; it's like the same look you get when you put gold in your hoard."

I guffawed. "There's a look when I put things in my hoard?"

We were in the suite that Morgana had given me in the space attached to her bar. Underneath this mattress was a spatial vault that held my hoard, and Scarlett had seen me more than once check on it or store earnings from my job with Morgana within it.

I had a nice little mound about the size of a laundry basket of gold and jewels at this point. It filled me with a little draconic pride every time I saw it.

She nodded. Her hair was matted to the top of her head and only her little fox ears bounced with the movement. "It's like a very dominant sort of contentment. I feel safe, loved and secure in so many ways when you do it."

"Good. You should be all those things. And mine. Most importantly, mine." I let my chest rumble as I nuzzled her neck and took a deep inhale of her cloves and vanilla scent.

"Yes, all yours." She stroked the back of my head and planted kisses of her own on the side of my head as her two fox tails softly batted my back.

I could feel myself rising to the occasion once again as her kisses trailed along me. Scarlett was soaked in sweat from the four sessions we had just finished, but maybe she could do one more. T's potion had really packed a punch, and I was still itching for more.

Prodding her with my newest erection, she opened up and lay back in the bed, sleepily smiling at me. Seeing her laying there content, spread for me, filled my heart with warmth. But, when I penetrated her lower lips, she winced. I quickly pulled out, my brow furrowing.

She let out a little whimper, then groaned and looked up at the ceiling. Her gaze was distant, like she was thinking over something difficult.

"Talk to me, Scar. We don't have to go again."

"I— shit." She pinched her eyes closed, and I sat up, watching and waiting for what she'd say next.

But time continued to pass in silence, and it began to grow awkward. I could feel my possessiveness flare up. It felt like she was pulling away. "Scarlett, spit it out."

She let out another frustrated groan, and in her hands appeared an illusion of a white flag that she started to wave in my face.

The whole act snapped me out of the possessive spiral I had been starting down. "Wha—"

"I surrender," she said, as if that explained everything. "I tried, I really did. But a dragon's libido cannot be tamed by a single kitsune, no matter how foxy I am. Zach, I'm sore as hell. Even with those tinctures I've been getting from Morgana, I can't keep up."

"Wait, what tinctures?" I frowned, trying to remember when she'd been taking them.

"Never mind. We can talk about that later. But, Scarlett, it's fine. We can slow down if you want."

She rolled her eyes. Apparently, that wasn't what she was trying to tell me. "I'm not talking about slowing down. I mean that I give in. I need help. You have my permission to play the field, my sexy dragon. No doubt you won't have any trouble finding others interested in you. We both know there's already a few."

"You want me to… find another girlfriend?" I was confused by her sudden change of heart. We'd known it would come eventually, but I didn't expect it this quickly. While my dragon was interested, the part of me that had grown-up human was adjusting just like Scarlett.

She looked confused. "I thought you'd be happy. Don't you want to just stick your dick in every hot girl you see? I mean, you have the stamina for it. Twenty-nine times."

"Twenty-nine?"

"Times we have had sex in the last week." She grabbed my face and stared into my eyes. "I love you, Zach. But I need you to stick that massive prick of yours into someone else from time to time. It's time you bring somebody else into this bed. Ideally, somebody who isn't a bitch."

I was shell-shocked. She hadn't given me even a little warning that she was close to ready to expand this relationship. And I'd been pushing everyone away because I was afraid that, with my nature, Scarlett would misunderstand.

Now... my mind short-circuited and re-booted several times like a computer with a booting error as I tried to reconcile the alternative path my life would go down. Twenty-one years of expecting a nor-mal, monogamous relationship that would eventually lead to marriage and kids was a lot of societal expectations to undo, even with my draconic urges.

Although if I was honest with myself, those draconic urges weren't even satisfied with the twenty-nine times we'd gone at it. The potion Morgana had given me had led to the most recent times, but even without it, I lasted beyond Scarlett every time. I just accepted it and went with what she could do.

But now Scarlett had thrown a flag on the play. The rules had changed, and I wasn't prepared.

"Zach... you got awfully quiet." Her ears had drooped, and her tails were just resting on my back rather than their normal lively selves.

"Thinking?" It came out as a question. "You just dropped this on me a little sud-denly. I don't even know what to do next. Do I just go hit on someone? Then what?

Tell them at some point that I have this other girlfriend who isn't going anywhere, and she'd be number two?"

Life as a human hadn't prepared me for starting a harem.

Scarlett started laughing so hard that tears squeezed out of her eyes. "Oh my god. It's not that hard. Just walk up to Kelly, or any of the wolves for that matter, and drop your pants. They'll be on you in seconds. Or maybe, just maybe, you could stop avoiding Jade. Or if none of them are interested, go to a bar and grab somebody else. I just ask that she's para so that she understands this a little more."

I blinked. "The wolves aren't like that."

She sobered up in a snap and gave me an incredulous look. "Do you realize how many gifts I've gotten from the college pack? How many of them are now my BFFs after realizing going through you was a lost cause?"

I paused. Had I really been that disconnected from it? I needed to lie down.

Rolling off of Scarlett, I plopped down in the bed hard enough to make the whole thing bounce. "Okay, you need to start sharing more. I froze them out because I was worried about my promise to you. As for Jade... well, let me handle that one. She knew the deal. Just send her your blessing so she's at least a little prepared for this."

"I can do that." Scarlett rolled against me and kissed my shoulder. "Never thought I'd be doing this, but I'm going to try to help you get another girlfriend. I'll be your wing woman." She chuckled.

"This is new for me, too. But I want you to promise me that, no matter how much of a break you want, this doesn't come between us. I love you, Scarlett, and even if I love another girl here eventually, you will always be my first. My love for you won't diminish one bit."

She snickered. "I'm okay if your physical love tones down a little." Her fingers found my hand, and she entwined hers in mine, holding onto me tight. "I love you too. Now let's get cleaned up. Finstein posted tonight that there's a pop quiz tomorrow." She rolled her eyes. "I hate it when professors do things like this to try to make their stupid websites important and force us to look at them."

"Bleh," I agreed. "At least I'm up to date on that class. I'm running a little behind in biology."

Scarlett made an unamused humming noise and tapped her lips like she was thinking. "Now if only you didn't find every reason to skip biology. It's almost like you were avoiding someone." She ended her 'thought' by leveling a glare at me.

"Message received. Talk to Jadelyn. But I need to study first."

Scarlett had said that she wanted to help, but I was the one that needed to step it up. Apparently, I was entering the dating pool once again.

"And before that, I'm going to cuddle and love on my favorite kitsune. No thoughts of sex. Just time with you."

"I'd like that." She smiled, rolling over onto my chest. I wrapped an arm under her and stroked from her bright orange hair down to the small of her back until we fell asleep.

CHAPTER 2

Scarlett was happily munching down a muffin at the table as I came back from the kitchen with an omelet the size of my head.

Morgana's bar, Bumps in the Night, was slowly becoming my home. It helped that her kitchen was open 24/7 and I ate for free. Between the free food and the awesome suite she'd created for me in the magical pocket dimension she called the Atrium, I didn't have much reason to leave. She'd taken her role as my mentor seriously.

"I see you got your muffin fix for the morning," I teased Scarlett.

Scarlett narrowed her eyes over the tasty pastry. She had a love/hate relationship with muffins. The hate was all about what they did to her hips. "I really need to go teach Morgana's chef about muffin making. These were in the oven for too long."

Reaching over and tearing a corner off, I popped it in my mouth to confirm. It tasted perfectly fine to me.

Her mouth dropped open like I had just committed the foulest of betrayals. "MY muffin."

"You can get another."

"No, I can't. Because then I'll eat an entire second muffin. Yet here I am now without a full muffin." She held it out as if asking me to examine the crime scene. "We can share a toothbrush, but a muffin?! That's a step too far."

I snickered at her mock indignation. Though, knowing Scarlett, it was a little true. But I enjoyed getting a reaction out of her. "Fine. By the way, you should probably bring some things over to the room here."

"Ha. I think that, if I brought much over to your little lair, you might stuff me in your hoard," she teased.

"My lair? You make me sound like some sort of villain that's kidnapping you to my evil lair." I started in on the meat packed omelet, though I'd added spinach in an attempt to be healthy. Or at least, that's what I told myself.

I was still eating far more than made sense. This omelet was big enough to feed a family of four. Thank goodness the chef knew I was a paranormal and didn't think much of it.

"You're a..." She looked around and leaned in. "You-know-what. You have a hoard, and your kind have lairs."

"Huh." I hadn't thought of it that way before. "Okay, it's my lair. But not an evil lair."

"Of course not. Unless we want to try that out with role play." She tapped on her muffin. "That might actually be kind of fun. Once I'm rested up and ready to go again, we should try it out. Because no doubt that, if we play like that, you are going to get real dominant and rough." She wiggled her eyebrows at me.

But I didn't really process what she was saying, because her father had walked in as she had started talking. His fox ears swiveled to us and the scowl that formed on his face as he approached told me he had just had the displeasure of hearing his daughter talk about sex.

The detective was a kitsune, like his daughter, and they had that same fox-orange hair. The difference was he had it covering his face in a thin beard that wasn't very well kept at the moment.

He looked tired and overworked to me, but then again, the way he ran around for the Scalewright family, I had a hard time imagining him taking a day off to rest.

"You know maybe we could—"

"Scar, your father just walked in," I interrupted her, knowing she'd already be embarrassed as she replayed what she'd just said.

"Shit," she cursed and looked over her shoulder. "Hi, Paps. Want some of my muffin?" She must have felt terrible about it to offer her muffin as a consolation.

The detective remained unamused. "You stayed here tonight. The Scalewright family is our responsibility to protect."

She waved off his concern. "I had two men watching the sorority house all night long. There's no problem."

He narrowed his eyes dangerously before giving up on his daughter and focusing on me. His face was all business. "Is Morgana here?"

"Don't think so. But I can take the request."

Technically, Morgana had made me a partner in her mercenary business. We split the profits 50/50 if we worked together, and I'd even started taking a few jobs on my own for full value.

"I want both of you on this." He pulled a manilla folder out from under his arm. Pausing, I hadn't noticed it when he'd walked in. Had he hidden it with an illusion, or had it just blended in with his tan jacket?

"What's this?" I took the folder; the tab read 'OTM Conference'. But before I gave it another thought, I asked, "Any news on the person you were looking for from the drug case?"

There had been someone who had used a human like a skin suit. Apparently, skinwalkers weren't real, but because of the only piece of evidence we had, I tended to call the mystery person the skinwalker.

"No, but these are just the people to have answers if you want them. We don't govern the magi."

Scarlett leaned over to read the folder's tab and swore. "I forgot it's in Philly this year."

I cleared my throat and raised my eyebrows, prompting her to look up and realize I had no idea what she was talking about.

She gave a sheepish smile. "Order of the Magi. Or OTM. They have a yearly conference in one of the para hub cities every year."

"Like magicians?"

Both of the kitsunes snorted in the same way that marked them as family.

"Please call them that," Scarlett laughed. "Oh, they hate the word magician; it makes them feel like stage performers. No, they lump themselves all together as 'magi' and then argue endlessly about what makes them all different."

The detective hid his smirk only a second after showing his amusement, returning to his typical neutral face. "It's a big deal. Thousands of them will flock here.

Market East will be flooded with them, and we need to keep disturbances to a minimum."

"So just have the council throw up their normal rules. Why do we have to babysit them?"

"They aren't part of the council," Scarlett stepped in to explain. "They are humans who use magic, so it is a little of a gray area when it comes to paranormal definitions."

The detective cut in, going with a more direct approach. "They *identify* as human and fall outside the council. They govern themselves, and not effectively." The way he said it sounded like he didn't quite accept that someone could choose to not be part of the paranormal community. "The convention starts on Saturday, and with your ability to see magic, we'd like you to do a sweep of the convention center beforehand. Make sure everything is clean before we let the magi in to set up."

"I have class today, and we are on another job managing the swamp trolls. I could probably swing by on Friday afternoon and do the sweep if that works?"

"You can't do it tonight?" he pressed.

I scrunched up my nose and leaned back, thinking about it. "I'll talk to Morgana and see if she can handle the troll sweep tonight on her own. No promises. Our usual rate works?"

Detective Fox grumbled about the cost, but he didn't put up a fight. He simply nodded and turned to Scarlett. "Daughter, please don't shirk your duties too long. Boys will come and go, but your bond with Jadelyn isn't going anywhere."

Scar rolled her eyes while looking away from where her father couldn't see it. "Got it."

I hadn't poked too much into the exact nature of her and Jadelyn's relationship, but it was odd. Both she and her father were the right hand of the current head and the heir to the Scalewright family. Her father had made it seem as if he had gotten her mother pregnant when he'd learned Jadelyn had been conceived in some sort of odd arrangement.

But it didn't feel like that between Jadelyn and Scarlett. Scarlett seemed like the closest thing Jadelyn had to a sister. She just also happened to manage her security detail.

Waiting until her father was gone, I turned back to Scarlett. "I'm not getting in the middle of any obligations, am I?"

"No. It's fine."

Normally, I let it be, but this time, I decided to press a little further. If I was to make inroads with Jadelyn, I should untangle their relationship.

"Is it really? We've avoided it, but what exactly are you to Jadelyn? Could you walk away?" I hated putting it out there like that, but I wanted to make sure.

"What? Oh god. No, it's nothing that bad. I'm not her servant or anything." She took a deep breath. "You should have asked earlier if you wanted to know."

She continued, "The Scalewright family is old money. Like barons and dukes. But it was in the renaissance period that they really boomed, taking an iron grip over the waterways around Europe. And then their business went crazy when colonization happened. As sirens, ships didn't sail if the Scalewright family didn't want them to."

"Right, but how does the Fox family fit in?" I pressed.

"Getting there." She gave me a sly smile. "The timing is important to understand, because a lot of how things work was built during those times. So the practices seem a bit archaic. Our family has been guarding them for generations. Tradition dictates that the guard is raised with the royalty they are supposed to protect, to form a bond."

It definitely seemed archaic. "And you don't resent that?"

"No. I went through a phase as a teenager where I did, and I had sworn to my father that I was going to quit. I even quit for a whole six months at one point." Her ears wilted at the memory.

"What happened?"

"Jadelyn got hurt. The guy who had replaced me did a shit job. So I came back, beat the shit out of him, and took the job back. She is like a sister to me. She treats me well, and the pay is fantastic. I own a small chunk of their company and get fat dividends." There was a big smile on her face.

I wasn't quite sure how I felt about it. I especially judged her father. But, as long as she was happy, I wasn't going to complain. "So, if you're making good money and have a lifelong job, why go to college?"

"Jadelyn's here, so might as well. Also, I like having options. Even if I never end up going into pharma or whatever with the degree, I'm smarter for it."

I nodded. I wasn't sure I would have made the same decisions, but I didn't need to. It had brought Scarlett into my life, and as long as she was happy, I didn't have to go all protective dragon boyfriend and kill a bunch of people.

I paused, realizing I really would do that for her.

"Let me scarf down this omelet and then we should head to our classes. I'll see you in organic." I pushed past the awkward conversation and dug into the meaty omelet with the gusto that only a hungry dragon could have.

***

I sat in one of the cafeterias during my break between classes, staring at the information within the Order of the Magi folder the detective had given me. But my concentration was broken when somebody sat down next to me. I quickly flipped the folder closed.

"Hi, Zach." Jadelyn smiled at me.

It was that same neutral smile she'd been giving me all semester, like she was always afraid she'd be seen as too forward. Although I appreciated that she was giving me space after the complexity her kissing me at the sorority party had caused at the onset of Scarlett and my relationship.

"What are you working on?" She glanced at the folder, and I saw a flash of recognition when she read the tab.

"Detective Fox handed this to me this morning."

"Oh, that's a big deal. I... uh... threw your name out for that actually, since you can see magic and Scarlett vouched for you. The other option was two dozen elves going around and casting spells to sense magic in a grid to check out the venue." She blushed before her straight, platinum-blonde hair fell in front of her face like a curtain.

"Oh." I hadn't realized Jadelyn was responsible for me getting this job. "Thanks for thinking of me."

There was a long awkward stretch of silence during which she pulled her hair out of the way. I wasn't sure how to work to ease the tension between us.

"So, have you talked to Scarlett at all?" I fumbled for a way to tell her that I was going to date other people now. Knowing how her kiss went over with me in the past, I figured Scarlett should probably give her the all-clear first.

Jadelyn laughed. "You realize she is both my roommate and we work on nearly everything together, right? So yeah, I've talked with her. But if there's something you're getting at, you should probably be more specific."

Taking a deep breath, I tried to let go of my nerves. "Well. You remember when you kissed me earlier this semester?"

The way her cheeks heated told me she remembered that well enough.

"Well, what she couldn't tell you exactly is what I am. But she knew that, because of it, I would likely have more than one girl around me. Possibly a harem." Just saying that word out loud was uncomfortable. I felt like I was butchering this.

Jadelyn nodded. "I got that picture already. But you are just with Scar right now."

I nodded, pausing before I continued. "Right, and that's all it was. But she changed her view last night. I'm officially on the market, I guess... for more. Scarlett and I are still together though."

"Uh, huh." She made a slow nod. "But what does this have to do with me and Scar talking?"

There was a bit of anger, or maybe hurt, in her eyes as she said it.

I realized that, after avoiding her for months, things might not be the same. She might not still have feelings for me. I hadn't considered that she wouldn't be ready when I was, and I deserved that for making her wait.

But I needed to dragon up and make my desire known. She could decide what she wanted from there. "Well, I'd like to ask you on a date, Jadelyn."

She cracked a smile and then slammed it back down into a frown. "You won't even tell me what you are."

"Does that matter? Even if I was a swamp troll, would that make a difference? Would that suddenly change it all?"

"There are some paras that just don't do well—"

I held up my hand to stop her. "What I am won't cause you any harm. I am, however, extraordinarily dangerous. Just not to those I care about."

She eyed me up and down. "Okay. I'll bite. I'm free on Saturday."

A relieved rush of air slipped out of me. I was glad she hadn't lost interest. "I can make Saturday work. Meet me at Bumps."

Jadelyn raised a curious eyebrow. "What am I dressing for? A dinner and then the club?" Her tone suggested that was boring, and she expected more.

I realized Jadelyn had enough fancy meals and clubs in her life. She was looking for something different. "Wear jeans you wouldn't mind getting dirty and shoes you can walk in for a while. And never mind on Bumps. I'll pick you up at the sorority?" I made a mental note to bug Morgana to borrow one of her cars.

"Ah. That would be lovely. I need to warn you though that a trip like that might warrant a security detail for me."

I hadn't considered that, but it made sense. "I'll work it out with Scarlett. Don't want to ruin my surprise just yet." I had no clue where we were going, but a hike and maybe a nice spot under the stars sounded like the perfect way to get to know Jadelyn.

She tilted her head. "I guess you dating my head of security does make things a little easier."

"Good. Then I'll pick you up Saturday at seven." I made an entry in my phone before changing the subject. "Do you happen to know anything about these magi? Gotta be honest, I feel like I'm studying up on a class I haven't gone to all semester."

"Like biology?" She gave me a telling look; she knew exactly why I'd been missing class.

I didn't even try to make an excuse and owned it. "Scarlett is too important to me. I was a little afraid of messing it up."

"Until now."

"Until she gave me the all-clear to explore my paranormal nature and seek other women."

I took a sip of my water as a way to hide my nerves. Talking about trying to form a harem both made a part of me smug with satisfaction and made my human instincts cringe. But it was something I was just going to need to push through.

Jadelyn made an innocent hum of understanding. "That's not quite the way she described it. More like, you are insatiable in the bedroom and need more than just one poor, sore kitsune to satisfy you."

My water came out in a spray. Thankfully, no one was sitting across from me. "You said you didn't talk to Scarlett."

"I said you had to clarify. Of course, we girltalk all the time." She smiled, full of cunning.

I had to remember that, not only was she a beautiful woman, she was also a business woman, training to take over a colossal business empire. There was about zero chance she wasn't an expert in negotiations. Of which angling for a date most certainly counted.

I buried my face in my hands. "Please. Spare me the details. The magi?"

Having won, she wore a satisfied smile on her face. "Sure, what do you want to know?"

Flipping the file back open, I skimmed through the first few pages. "So, I get the request from the detective. But what I don't get is exactly how they all divide themselves up. He switches between sorcerer and wizard like they mean more than just some generic terms. This didn't exactly come with an appendix for that."

Her eyes opened wide in understanding. Having been part of my unfortunate introduction to the paranormal society, Jadelyn knew I was new to all of it. I didn't know what those raised in the paranormal world their whole life knew instinctively.

"Okay, so wizard and witch are pretty much the same. Both of them are more into a ritual and academic approach. Lots of mixing, grinding and detailed drawings."

I nodded along; that made sense.

"Sorcerers are like the guys who don't need to understand anything. They just have a talent for it. They have something not human in their heritage, giving them an innate control over a limited part of magic."

When I nodded, she continued, "Then you have warlocks. They have magical potential like wizards and witches, but none of the understanding. So they rely on something more powerful than themselves through a pact to control their magic." She made a disgusted face when she talked about warlocks.

"We don't like warlocks?"

"We barely like any of the magi. They refuse to be part and parcel to the para councils. Yet they are probably the biggest danger to the secret of the paranormal world. Think about it, if the big secret came out, which side do you think they'd be on? Do you think they'd be hunted like the rest of us?"

"Oh." I understood then. "They know the secret but don't have the same risks as everyone else."

"Exactly. And that's how it went down in the 17th century. So we are forced to make sure things go smoothly at the convention. Even if they won't claim to be paranormal, we claim Philly and will make our presence known."

I smiled, enjoying watching her talk like a person of authority. I liked this side of Jadelyn far better than the woman who was tied up in an arranged marriage she didn't want. Ever since the engagement with Chad had ended, Jadelyn seemed to be taking life by the horns, and I found it way sexier.

My phone buzzed, and I picked it up.

'Swamp Trolls. Need back up. East side of campus,' Morgana texted.

"Shit. Got to go. More swamp troll fun." I waved the phone at Jadelyn as I stood. Not wanting to leave it there, I added, "Saturday. 7 pm. Dress for a hike."

"I'll be there. Be careful with the trolls. They are a great way to lose an arm. And I'd prefer you have both your hands available when we have our fun for the first time." She winked at me.

Her flirtiness caught me off guard slightly, but then filled me with a bit of warmth. I was looking forward to Saturday and seeing where things between us would go.

I gave her a smile and added, "Maybe they should be terrified of me."

CHAPTER 3

I stepped out of the cafeteria, moving quickly to get to the edge of campus. The monolithic buildings and manicured lawns of the college campus felt less calming than they once had now that I knew Philly had an underground society of the paranormal. I couldn't help but look at people I passed and wonder if they were something else.

"Roomie," Frank's familiar voice pitched as he hurried to catch up to me. "Why are we walking so fast?"

"In a rush. What's up, Frank?"

"Dude, you haven't been home in a few days. I'm just wondering which of the girls' houses you were bunking at, or are you hopping between them?" The way he smiled as he said it told me it was something he'd done before.

And I wasn't surprised. Frank had always had a way with the ladies and serious commitment issues as long as I'd known him. And we'd been best friends since freshman year. But, at the moment, he was breaking his pattern and focused on one woman.

Enjoying that I'd catch him off guard, I threw out, "Just one, but I have a date with a second here soon."

Frank's eyes nearly popped out, and he nearly missed a step before catching himself and keeping up with me again. "You're kidding me. Like you are actually dating two of them?"

I decided to make it a little more fun. "Yep. And they are roommates and best friends."

His face grew concerned. "Dude. That's bad, very bad. When they find out, they are going to carve your nuts off. And they will find out. Girls talk!"

Frank huffed a little as he worked to keep up with me, but he didn't say anything. I was already at an advantage with longer legs, even without the paranormal extras.

"It gets better. They know, and they are into it." I shot a winning smile at Frank, whose mouth had fallen fully open.

"No way."

"Yes way," I fired back.

"Do they have friends?"

"I thought you and Maddie were tight? You guys seem like you might go all the way and tie the knot."

There was no way I was going to offer something that would cause him and Maddie trouble. My roommate Frank had taken women as a challenge, something to win and then move onto the next one. He was good at it too, until he had finally scored my best friend and swore he was done with his promiscuous ways.

And I liked them together. Maddie kept him on his toes, too. During the first few months of them dating, she had been touch and go, and the vastly different approach had kept Frank working to keep dating her.

I found myself relieved that they had lasted this long, and that Maddie seemed able to manage Frank. Unfortunately, that also happened to include plenty of wall thumping sex, which was another reason I had been out of the apartment. Listening to two of my closest friends have sex wasn't exactly fun.

And it didn't help that I felt like I'd been lying to Frank more and more. I couldn't tell him about the paranormal, and so much of my life now resided in the paranormal world. There were strict rules on telling normies about the paranormal world, and breaking those rules often ended in both the para and normies deaths. The council didn't mess around with keeping the secret of the paranormal world.

Frank had gone quiet after my question about Maddie, and I became more worried. "Everything okay between you two, Frank?"

"Yeah." He sounded disappointed. "It's just starting to lose that flame, you know?"

I didn't really know. Scarlett and I had no such issue, but then again, she'd apparently been going out of her way to keep it going in bed. "Talk to her, Frank. Maddie took enough of a risk on you. Make sure she knows what you are thinking. Relationships are mostly communication. Chemistry is only a small part of all of it."

"Look at you dropping sage advice," he said as I crossed the border that marked the eastern edge of campus.

Almost on cue, a sporty black Ferrari spun around in traffic and screeched to a halt in front of me. The door flew open in a fluid motion, like it was a continuation of her turn.

"Get in," Morgana's Swiss accent demanded.

"Which one is this?" Frank asked, starting to bend down to get a look at Morgana.

"Not one of my girls." I grabbed the roof of the car and swung myself low. The sports car was so low that it felt like I was riding only inches above the pavement. "Catch you later, Frank."

"Bullshit. If she's not one of your girls, work your magic, Zach. I'm rooting for you. I mean, look at that car!"

I closed the door before he could get a look at Morgana and see her blue skin and silver hair. And if that wasn't enough, her red eyes made her clearly not human.

During the day, she relied on cars with windows that were illegally tinted to the point that it was almost impossible for me to see out of them at night except for the brief moments we passed by a streetlamp. She'd also been known to pretend she was cosplaying to try to cover up her different appearance, but she mostly tried to avoid being seen.

"Where to?" I was rocked back into the seat as Morgana floored it and the Ferrari purred under her. She zipped through traffic like she was playing a high-speed intense game of dodge the other cars.

"Shit, let me get my seat belt on." Fumbling, I put my backpack on the ground and got my seatbelt clicked in. But it only made me feel marginally safer. Despite riding with Morgana for a while, I wasn't any more comfortable with her insane driving.

"Market East. The convention center reported a troll sighting. Good thing it is empty today."

"Of course it is. The Order of the Magi's conference doesn't start until Saturday."

Morgana did a double take, and I paused, savoring the moment of being able to surprise her.

"Okay, how do you know about magi?" she conceded.

"Detective Fox came by this morning with a job to scope the place out. They hired us because of my ability to see magic," I confessed. "I told them I'd swing by tonight or tomorrow and check it out."

She shrugged. "If we are going there anyway, might as well check it out now. There's only one troll, so this should be easy." There was the sort of cruel smile she had when she trained me on her face. "That is, of course, if you can shift at all."

"Oh hell. You aren't going to help, are you?" I knew the answer as soon as I said it; her face had said it all.

"It's broad daylight, and neither my drow ancestry nor my vampiric affliction like the sunlight. Me being there will be hard enough on my reserves."

"At least you won't go poof like the stories."

Morgana made a distasteful grimace. "Baby vampires made too many public mistakes. I can handle the sun, but it would still strain me to do much more activity than a normal human. Plus, drow complexion isn't great with the sun."

I gave her an unamused look. "Really? Skin care?"

"Do you think blue skin is so that I protect myself from UV light? No, it's so I blend into the dark. We drow have little to no melanin in our skin; we burn easily, and it isn't pretty."

"I'll make sure to pick you up some sunscreen on the way home," I teased.

"Magic is much better and doesn't stink up my car. You can never get that smell out." Morgana peeled around the corner, her back tires sliding out behind her and bumping the curb before she expertly rebounded into her lane.

Yeah. A sunscreen smell in her car was too much, but hitting the car's rims against the curb was no problem.

I closed my eyes and tried my best to enjoy the ride. It was much better with my eyes closed when I couldn't see her nearly crash a dozen times a minute. She might have insane reflexes with her elven heritage and her vampire prowess, but it made her a terrifying driver.

When I felt her screech to a stop, I cracked open my eyes to see the large, modern convention center. It had white painted metal and a glass front—a slightly odd modern choice when the rest of the surrounding buildings were old New England style brick buildings.

The style wasn't my favorite, but in the middle of Market East, everything was well done. While it didn't fit, it was at least tasteful.

"Morgana, you are in the crosswalk," I sighed.

She laughed and pulled around to the side to the first floor of the parking garage and parked across several spots. "The report was twenty minutes ago, so be careful. Go find it."

"Roger." I pulled a hard case from the backseat and pulled one of my handguns from the foam padded case, along with a spare magazine. Doing a quick check, everything seemed in order. I held the gun at my side as I got out of the car.

The gun wasn't going to be able to do much more than be a minor distraction to the swamp troll based on the regeneration I'd seen them do before, but at least it was something.

Morgana got out of the car with her twin swords strapped to her hips. They slapped her leather clad thighs as she moved. She leaned over the top of the sports car, her larger chest squishing against the top in a way that would make a car show girl jealous.

"Remember, shifting is complex. You need to relax your body and tense your mind. It's kind of like when you tense your abs and relax your butt to poop."

I covered my face with my hand. "You did not just make that comparison."

She shrugged. "It's true. I don't shift, but I've talked to enough of them to understand it at least in theory. You could always go ask your little werewolf girlfriend about it."

"Not my girlfriend."

"Pretty sure she wants to be. She did beg you to be her alpha." Morgana emphasized alpha with a wink.

Ignoring her, I headed for the parking garage entrance to the convention center. "Scarlett told me about the tinctures you've been giving her."

Morgana froze mid-stride, pausing just before the door. "Am I in trouble?"

"I kind of wish you'd told me she was having that much trouble."

Morgana was my partner and Scarlett my girlfriend. I felt out of the loop for them to be working together like that.

"Not my place to get between the two of you." Morgana held her hands up as I held the door for her. "Everything okay?"

I nodded, then shook my head. "She is pushing me to date right now. I have a date with Jadelyn on Saturday."

Morgana couldn't help but flash me a smile before she read the mood and suppressed it. "Sorry?"

"Don't be. It's stupid. I feel like every other dude on the planet would be hooting and hollering for this sort of opportunity. And

I probably would have joined them when it was all just some sort of fantasy concept. But shit, Morgana, it's messing with my mind trying to break from what I expected my life to look like."

"I've told you before, but I'll say it again. You need to internalize that you aren't human." Morgana gave me a look like somebody would give a lost puppy.

The beast banged its head against the inside of my chest, hating the pity that Morgana had just thrown my way.

"Cut it out, Morgana. I asked her on a date. Just—" I let out a sigh. "It's difficult to adjust to not being human."

As if drawn by our conversation, a lumbering, brown swamp troll thumped around the center of the convention center as we rounded the next corner.

Poor sap. He wasn't getting the right timing. The conversation with Morgana had really made me want to pound something's face in. It helped that some anger had built up in me; my fire breath was churning inside of me, ready for something to burn.

Unleashing my breath as a way to vent, I cooked the stupid troll.

"Zach. That's not going to work," Morgana warned me even as my breath ended.

The troll was hunkered down, his skin shrunken and steaming, but as it uncurled from its crouch, its eyes fixed on me with hate.

Morgana tsked, leaning against the wall as she ever so helpfully added, "Their bodies are steeped in swamp water year round. You aren't going to do much more than steam some of it off and help them lose water weight."

The troll charged me, screaming as if to confirm her assessment.

I tried to draw on my beast, pulling it up toward the surface while also trying to relax my body and let the change happen.

Seconds ticked by and nothing happened. It was taking too long.

A one-ton troll tackled me to the ground, smashing the cheap laminate tiles under us.

"Oof. Didn't work, Morgana," I wheezed.

The troll, now on top of me, stank like rotting swamp water. As it moved and I got a deeper whiff, I decided it was closer to cooked, rotten swamp water as its burn blisters healed rapidly inches from my face.

"I didn't bring the tranqs. You are on your own. Dragon up, Zach," Morgana chuckled.

Once again, I tried to relax while simultaneously shoving myself into the shift, but once again, nothing happened, and the troll pushed off of me.

"Oh, fuck."

A meaty fist wrapped around my ankle, and the troll picked me up. I immediately flashed back to my initial encounter with trolls when I was swung around like a limp noodle. Not this time.

I still had my handgun, so I aimed at his forearm. He was only two feet away, so aiming wasn't the most important, but I liked to think that I did my best not to shoot my foot.

Unloading the magazine into the troll's forearm, I pulped it with all eight rounds.

The troll dropped my ankle, and I rolled away, fishing in my pocket for the other magazine and reloading.

My last encounter with a troll had taught me that center mass with a 9mm did jack shit to a troll. But at least this time, it had temporarily disabled his hand and freed me. That was more than I'd expected. But now I only had a second magazine if I needed to do that again.

As expected, the troll's arm healed before my eyes. Its swampy green skin covered the exposed flesh in seconds. Throwing back its head, the troll screamed in rage as its hands pounded the floor, shattering more of the tiles. Huffing like some sort of primate, it charged me.

Coiling the strength in my legs, I waited until he was close. At the last moment, I released the coiled strength, jumping high over its head. Even as it swung its arms up to try to snatch me, it only grazed the bottom of my boots.

Unable to stop itself quickly enough, the troll's momentum carried it forward and into a stumbling halt as it turned around, stomping its feet, charging again.

I considered my options. My fire breath didn't work, neither did the gun. That really only left a physical altercation. But, without shifting to gain mass, it didn't matter how strong or tough I was when fighting something almost ten times my weight. Out of most of my moves, that only left creative alternatives. I needed to find a way to use the space or something around us to shift things in my favor.

The troll came at me for another pass, and I jumped, but this time, my eyes landed on the high overhead light fixtures and, particularly, the metal cables that supported them.

Landing, I ignored the troll running for the wall and jumped up off a corner to snag one of the lights.

"What are you doing?" Morgana asked, watching from the side.

The troll, distracted by her voice, briefly considered her, but dismissed the drow vampire as a threat.

Normally, that would be a lethal mistake, but she seemed content to stay out of this one. I'd had enough of her tough love form of training to know that she'd decided that pushing me into a corner was a good strategy for helping me shift. I wasn't going to get any help.

"Getting a tool," I grunted, pulling myself up and getting a good grip on the wire before tugging.

Thankfully, it gave way easily, not meant to hold much weight but more just to balance the light fixture. Unfortunately, as it gave way, I lost my support as well. I managed to land on my feet, but my knees protested the impact they took.

"Great, but how is that going to help? Maybe, and this is just an old vampire's opinion, you should shift and just kick its ass? You are a dragon," Morgana gave me her version of a pep talk.

I worked to not roll my eyes at her and keep my focus on the troll.

The troll's first through third charge hadn't worked, so in its infinite wisdom, it tried again. Fourth time's the charm, right?

Looping the metal wire, I jumped once more at the charge, but this time, I swung the wire down like a jump rope, catching the troll under the chin.

As it caught, it ripped me out of the air. Working to keep a firm hold on the wire, I slammed my back against the troll's back as I held on for dear life.

"Oh, we are troll riding now?" Morgana teased. "That actually looks kind of fun."

The troll didn't appreciate my impromptu harness and thrashed, its big bulky arms trying to swing behind its back to grab me, but it just didn't have that sort of flexibility.

Trading the two ends of the cord between my hands, I shifted to my front and got my knees under me. Yanking back, I attempted to strangle the troll.

We weren't supposed to kill them, but I wasn't even sure I could kill a swamp troll. Given their bulk and their regeneration, I had a feeling even Morgana's grenade launcher wouldn't take it down for long.

The troll thrashed as I pulled back with all my strength, my knees digging into its spine. I pulled until I was bending the troll backwards, its arms flailing as it failed to reach me on its back.

Even then, the metal cord only scraped the tough hide on its neck, so I pulled harder, getting one foot under me and doing one of the toughest lunges of my life.

It strained, and one of the filaments of the metal cord snapped off, curling in warning that others might be about to go soon. The troll was grabbing at its throat, trying to get a finger under the metal cord.

In my own determination, I gave one last yank and the troll's back crackled as it fell limp under me, crashing to the floor. With its tension gone, so was the tension on my cord. I tumbled off to the side, rolling away as the troll flopped to the ground like a dead fish. Slowly leaning forward to look at it, its eyes were still very much alive.

The crackling of bones sounded as it let out an angry gurgling noise.

"I think you broke his neck. He'll be back on his feet here shortly," Morgana reminded me.

Grabbing a chunk of the broken floor, I walked over to the troll. "This isn't personal. I just need you to go to sleep for a bit." It wasn't a tranquilizer, but rocks to the head tended to work just as well. Looking up from the mess I made of the convention center, I glared at Morgana. "You didn't even bring the tranquilizers?"

"Nope. I mean, we could both escape if we needed to."

I huffed, puffing my hair a little. It was getting longer than I'd like. "At least help me with him. I have no idea how he's going to fit in the Ferrari."

"No need. A cleanup team from the council is coming. I just assumed this would make a mess."

Even as the troll shifted back into a human form, it was still a large round man. The Ferrari had almost no trunk space.

"Since we are here, I guess I should check this place over for magic." Bending down, I took the metal cord and hogtied him as best I could with the stiff metal cord. Wouldn't want him waking up while I had my back turned.

Finished with the troll, I focused on the shifting that I could do. Sure enough, my eyes shifted, and the world became far brighter and more detailed than viewing it through my human eyes. My dragon eyes allowed me to see traces of magic.

"Oh, there are enchantments here. One right there." I pointed to the center of the wide-open entry hall.

Morgana stepped over and wove a minor spell. As she did it, the enchantment I could see became visible to the naked human eye. "That's just a ward to keep away pests."

"There are good enchantments here too?" I realized it wasn't just going to be finding and destroying each. Someone would have to interpret them.

"Yep."

"Fine. Let me go get the duct tape from the car. I'll mark everything with tape, and we can just have the council come by and do the final check. They'd like that better, anyway." I stepped over the unconscious troll with a bit of pride.

Taking down a troll had been work, but it made me far less anxious than knowing I was about to start dating multiple women at the same time.

CHAPTER 4

There had only been a few enchantments I'd found that Morgana had marked, saying that someone more specialized than her had to come and inspect to determine their safety.

But we had found out why the troll had been drawn to the convention center. One of the enchantments put out a smell like freshly baked cookies. It was one of the enchantments that Morgana had said needed further inspection.

The place was massive and there were no small number of small enchantments here and there throughout it. Morgana tagged along once the cleanup team came to retrieve the troll and tried to teach me a few of the enchantments. I wasn't sure I was actually getting much of it.

"Why are you teaching me this?" I asked.

"Since you have magic, you have the ability. It will just take years of study for you to be able to use it."

I grumbled. "Let's master shifting first. When I can turn into a several-ton dragon, we'll see what I still need magic for."

That earned me an eye roll. "Subtlety has its uses."

"That's what I have you for." Bumping her hip, I elicited a small smile from the vampire. "Besides, what fun is subtlety when I can just smash everything."

Walking back to the massive entryway, we found a man arguing with a mixed group of sirens, elves, and something that looked very human.

I sniffed the air and caught the scent of a dog. The human-looking paranormal must have been one of the omega wolves from the incident with Chad. Many of them had been scooped up by the council and put to work on mundane tasks, such as cleanup.

"This is a mess. Why the hell are you even here?" The businessman waved his arms angrily, and my eyes that were still shifted caught just a hint of magic coming out of the sleeves of his very expensive-looking suit.

"Excuse me. Can we help you?" I interjected, stepping up to the group casually. "Also, please stop waving about your magic."

He fixed me with a look, his eyes going to mine and giving a distasteful snort. "I hate the ones that can blend in."

I was about ready to sock him across the jaw, but I realized whom, or rather what, I might be dealing with. In front of me was a very well-kept looking blond man with a square jawline and a business suit that probably cost more than my yearly grocery budget, but I was fairly sure he was a magus.

That subtle magic washed off of him and tried to cling to me.

I recognized what it was trying to do immediately. A subtle feeling of warmth towards this man tried to rise up, and I threw against it all the hate I had of manipulators. It shattered whatever goodwill his charm had tried to instill in me. But, in that brief exchange with his magic, his focus had already passed me. He stared wide-eyed at my partner.

"Morgana! In the flesh. I didn't know you'd be here." He opened his arms to hug her like a best friend.

She put out a hand on his chest to keep him from touching her. "Don't touch."

Even the magi knew Morgana on sight, but it made sense. She was the only elven vampire I'd ever heard of. And the elves would keep it that way if they could. They hated that she was a living example that elves could indeed be turned into vampires, something they claimed was impossible.

"Prickly as ever. I remember when I was a kid that you came to do a job for my family." He spoke with a familiarity, and I was unsure if it was something that he did with everyone or if he was seriously crushing on Morgana.

"I don't have time for this. Do as my partner says and drop this stupid charming spell."

He gave a boisterous laugh. "It's a potion that I mixed with cologne. It's harmless, and I can't just dismiss it. What are you doing here, anyway?"

"We were hired to come here and deal with a pest problem." I nodded towards the man now in the back of a car that had somehow moved inside the building.

"What's that?" He eyed the unimpressive looking chubby man.

"Swamp troll. Big fuckers when they are awake and testy," I said with a little pride at taking it down with my bare hands again.

"I thought they'd be bigger," he said dismissively. "Oh, where are my manners? I didn't fully introduce myself. I'm sure my name will jog your memory, Morgana. I'm Jared of the Nashner line." He did a little flourish of a bow.

Morgana just stared impassively at him. "Have I taken a job for the Nashner line?" She tilted her head in thought. "Can't think of it."

I took far too much joy in watching the man deflate.

"Of course. The famed Morgana must be so busy. Even the premiere sorcerer house of Poland is below her memory." His voice reeked of bitterness. Clearly, he was not happy about being forgotten.

"Well, nice to meet you. But we are off. Our job is done, and we have more work to do."

"Wait. I can't let you go like that." Jared grabbed my shoulder, and I had to fight the reflex to bend and throw him over my shoulder onto the floor. Luckily for him, he let go as I twitched, clearly sensing me suppressing the urge.

He laughed nervously. "Please, it's not often one gets time with Morgana. I can't waste this opportunity. Given the troll problem it appears we have in town, I'd love to hire you to do security for the event."

Morgana did a slow turn. "I work exclusively with my partner, and I'm not sure the convention wants to pay my going rate."

"Of course. You are worth your weight in gold. As one of the sponsors, I can guarantee you'll be paid just fine."

"The convention is three days long. Two kilograms a day sounds about right," I said. It had taken me a while to get used to doing business in gold, but I'd learned how to calculate our rates.

"Two kilograms?" Jared asked.

Morgana clarified, "Gold. Six kilos for each of us for the three days and we'll do daytime security."

I nearly lost my poker face. I had priced us at one kilo each. Two was just exorbitant.

Sweat prickle up on Jared's face as he made a slightly pained expression. But, after all his bluster, there was no way he was going to chicken out on the price. That just wasn't how a peacock like him worked.

He'd end up paying over six hundred thousand dollars for three days of security, and that kind of price made me nervous. I had a feeling Morgana did remember his family, and she was not a fan.

"Perfect. A drop in the ocean," Jared said with a flourish, spreading his arms wide as he plastered on a smile.

But apparently, Morgana wasn't done. "We take payment in advance—here's my cashier's number."

She reached into her bra and pulled out a piece of paper and pen. I now knew that Morgana used her spatial magic to create pocket dimensions on her clothing. I'd wondered before how she stashed it all; her clothing was far too tight for the number of things she pulled out.

Jared took the paper, so I wrapped a hand around her hip to lead her away. She leaned into it, and her sinfully curvy body pressed against me in a way that made me hot under the collar, even though I knew it was just a show for Jared.

Damn Morgana. Despite how youthful she looked, Morgana had lived a long time, and she knew what she was doing. Swaying her hips and pressing against me, when we were just out of earshot, she laughed gleefully, like I'd just whispered a joke.

I could feel Jared's eyes digging into my back. And she was so convincing, I found myself leaning a bit harder towards her.

She smirked up at me, clearly noticing my subconscious falling into the flirtation with her. Looking down, I realized my hand had wandered to her butt as we approached the car.

I squeezed her rear in slight revenge, but she only laid it on thicker. "Mmm. Yes please, harder dear."

"Damnit, Morgana." I slapped her ass, and she only moaned in my ear, teasing me further. "Stop it. Scarlett asked for a sex break, and I might just bend you over the hood of your car if you aren't careful."

"Maybe that's just what I want," Morgana whispered in my ear, eliciting a slew of quick daydreams before she dashed them away with her classic throaty laugh, bringing me back to reality.

She gave an extra little wiggle, turning and pushing me up against the side of the car. My breath caught, my brain spinning at the idea of being with Morgana, but also having trouble not being interested. Morgana was sexy, but she had also been my rock in the paranormal world. My brain told me not to mess up what we had, but the beast in me was roaring to take her.

As my brain spun and my body felt paralyzed between Morgana's and the car, she let out a throaty laugh.

"You should see your face. That was almost as fun as screwing with Jared." Morgana backed off me, walking over to the driver's side.

I reached down, adjusting myself before climbing into the car.

Pulling at the collar of my shirt, I could have sworn some steam escaped. "Yeah. Well, I wasn't entirely joking." Taking my seat in her sports car, I turned down the temp and blasted myself with cool air.

Meanwhile, the beast was hammering away in my chest, telling me I should just do it.

Me and Morgana, though? That just seemed preposterous. She was like a best friend, a very, very hot best friend. But something about the idea that it could potentially happen felt like it would ruin what we had going on.

Wanting a change of topic, I decided to get to the bottom of Morgana's dislike of

Jared and away from the flirting. "So, what did his family do? Some big old family grudge? They kill some elves and are on a blacklist?"

I pulled on my seatbelt as she pulled out of her completely illegal parking job.

"They are on an elven blacklist. But no big scary grudge. I do hate his father though, and he felt like the spitting image of him just now." The way she angrily revved the engine told me it was going to be a terrifying ride back to campus. She liked to take her anger out on the road.

I was nervous about having her diving deeper into her anger for the drive, but screw it, I was curious. "You have to give me more than that."

"Sorcerers have innate magic, which is inherited from a paranormal ancestor. You know that much, right?"

"Yep. Jadelyn explained it to me." I at least remembered a lot of what she'd said.

"Well, Jared's father had hired me at one point. He was sketchy on the details, but he offered me lots of money, so I showed up. When I got there, I learned their family line was pretty thin, and their magic was dwindling."

"Okay, and I'm guessing something happened that made you angry enough to double their rates?"

"Yes. Think about it. How would his father ask me to help increase his family's inherited magic?" she asked, and my mind went off racing for the answer as it hit me smack in the face.

"He didn't. Fuck. Please tell me you didn't."

"Of course I didn't!" Morgana shot me a hateful glare for even thinking she might. "I got there, and he propositioned me like a whore. I slapped him in the face and stormed out. It was one of the few times I've reached out to the elves on my own since they disowned me. I told them what he'd done, and they happily banned him and all their associates from relations with the elven kingdom."

There was a smug, satisfied grin on her face.

"Damn right. He deserved that. You don't think he'd try that again?" Even below the cologne, I had gotten the sense there was quite a bit of magic power in Jared. I was fairly certain I could take him, but it had made me want to take him down when he'd put his hand on me.

Morgana must have noticed the same potential in Jared. "Based on his magical potency, I'd guess that I wasn't the first person he'd given that offer to. Jared must be the kid of something paranormal if I had to guess."

"Why even work for his family, then? We can decline the request," I offered.

"No, we'll go. If he tries anything, though, I'll just take his head." She jerked hard on the wheel and floored it as she shot into traffic.

Thinking about the opportunity to question some of the magi about the skinwalker loose end from the drug case, I made a request. "Try to be civil. For me? I want to see if I can't get some answers from them."

The same part of me that was satisfied when I killed Chad demanded I do something about this skinwalker. I felt a raw need for the skinwalker to pay for what he had done to our community. The beast agreed; the skinwalker needed to die, preferably brutally so.

If the Order of the Magi had any information I could use, then I'd rather Morgana not ruin that for me.

"Answers?" she asked.

"Detective Fox still turned up nothing about the mysterious skin suit that showed up at the drug facility. I was thinking that the magi might have a few leads."

Morgana sucked in a sharp breath that had nothing to do with her driving. "They are a pretty insular group. You might point them in the direction and then never hear anything while they deal with it themselves. That sort of magic is the kind they'd do an

execution on one of their own for partici-
pating in."

"At least that would deal with the problem. The idea that someone could skin
someone I knew and pass unnoticed gives
me the creeps."

"You think someone could mimic me?"
She gave a mock gasp. "I'm almost insulted.
They wouldn't be able to mimic my magic,
though. One way you can always tell. They
also wouldn't be able to drive as well as me."

I let out a deep laugh. It was true; nobody
could replicate Morgana's driving. "Do you
think it is a terrible idea to ask around?"

"No, but you better make some friends
before you do. The magi don't like paranormals. You saw how Jared looked at your
eyes."

I shrugged. It hadn't bothered me much. I
couldn't care less what Jared thought of me.
And it wasn't like he was going to be my best
friend after Morgana had made a scene of
being with me. The beast roared up at the
idea of being considered less than by Jared,
but I tempered it down. If I followed my
draconic instincts, I'd be killing assholes left
and right.

I looked at the clock and hissed. I had my
organic chem pop quiz in twenty minutes.
Morgana caught the noise, and I explained,
"Can you bring me around the south side
of campus? I have to get to class."

"No problem." Morgana made a hard right. "Have you thought about giving up school?"

"Not yet. It feels like it is so close to being over. Why bail out now?" Even as I said it, I knew I wasn't going to use much of what I was learning in school as a mercenary with Morgana. And I already had enough gold bricks to live a simple, happy life somewhere.

"We've taken on the conference job and the troll job. Both of these are going to take most of your time this weekend. I don't want you hiding in the corner studying while I do all the work." She scowled over at me.

"Excuse me? You just stood there while I had to wrestle a swamp troll to the ground. You owe me."

"Fine." The tires screeched to a halt. "Get out and go take your stupid test. I'll catch up with you later tonight."

I rolled out of the car, knowing better than to linger. Morgana didn't even wait for me to close the door, using her acceleration to slam it closed as she peeled out.

Students were giving me wide-eyed looks.

I shrugged it off, knowing they were caught off guard by her crazy driving and nice car. I hooked the backpack over my shoulder and started towards organic chem with long strides, pulling out my phone to check the time.

Shit.

I turned my walk into a dead sprint, weaving through the science buildings while trying to keep my speed down to normal human levels. When I reached the heavy wooden doors of the right building, I winced as I heard the handle crunch. I was still getting used to managing my strength under stress.

My feet pounded up the steps and through the hall and I rushed into the room, seeing Scarlett sitting alone, her eyes on the door, waiting for me.

"Take your seats. The quiz begins now. You have fifteen minutes."

I rushed to the front and snagged a quiz and sheet to record my answers on from Professor Finstein. He gave them to me, but they came with one of those you-should-be-more-timely looks. Luckily, ever since I'd helped him with the projector at the beginning of the semester, he'd been friendly to me.

"Cutting it close," Scarlett whispered as I sat down.

"Troll. I'll tell you later." I fished out a number two pencil and started in on the test, filling in the stupid bubbles. One glance at the clock, and I was heads down, reading the questions and filling in the bubbles hastily.

I tried to focus on the quiz and not have my brain wander through the chaos of the past day. Beating up trolls, spending time with my beautiful kitsune girlfriend, going after more trolls... my life was becoming much more chaotic. Throw in classes and I had to admit I was pretty proud of myself for balancing all of it. Despite Morgana's thoughts that I should drop school, I was pretty proud of combining my paranormal and human lives together.

But it was about to get messier as I started navigating multiple relationships at the same time. Not to mention investigating the skinwalker and figuring how to finally shift into my dragon form.

"Five more minutes," Professor Finstein called out.

Shit. Working to crank out the final questions on the quiz, I ignored the big paranormal to do list that was building up.

CHAPTER 5

"More trolls?" Scarlett asked as we headed out of class.

"Just one. It was at the convention center, so I did double duty and looked around the place, marking up all the enchantments with Morgana." I kept my voice normal and neutral; it drew less attention than whispering. "Met my first magus."

Scarlett pulled us away from the crowd. It was the last day of class for both of us. She'd picked the direction, which looked like it was about to go back to her sorority.

"How'd that go?" The slight apprehension in her voice confirmed that paranormals were not the biggest fans of the magi.

"He was a dick. Hit on Morgana, who then charged him double for us to work security for the event."

She raised an eyebrow. "Working for both the council and the magi as security."

I grinned sheepishly. "It's honest work."

Scarlett snorted. "If you didn't just like to sleep on your gold, you'd be rich."

"I like it better as gold, and I think it still makes me rich. Just dragon rich, not dollar-bills-in-hand rich," I teased.

She just smiled and shook her head in response. "That's okay. I can buy my own things for my freeloading boyfriend who would rather sleep on his gold."

"Hey now, I gave a single brick away for Morgana to convert for me." It had been like pulling a tooth, but I had done it. I didn't want to live off other people, either. One kilogram of gold had been enough for me to stay at college for over a year. That was enough converting gold into cash for now.

But I wanted to move off the topic of having to decrease my hoard. "So, you told Jadelyn."

Scarlett looked surprised. "You already talked to her? That was fast." She actually looked a little hurt, but she turned away from me to hide it.

"She caught me at the cafeteria during lunch today," I clarified.

"Oh. That means she went and found you after I told her." Scarlett had a smirk on her face when she turned back. "Do I need to give you two the room when we get back?"

I rolled my eyes. "No. But I do need your help. I asked her on a date. Going to Bumps seemed like it encroached on our time, and to be honest, I don't think she'd like me trying to take her to a fancy restaurant. So I told her to bring hiking shoes and jeans."

"Oh?" Scarlett looked intrigued. "Can't say I've ever seen Jade go hiking before."

"I'm thinking about some sort of picnic off of a hiking trail nearby. But you see, I have this challenge. My date has this really strict bodyguard outfit that watches over her. They're a major pain in the ass." I enjoyed the mock glare I got in return before I continued, "But I was thinking I should probably include them in the planning."

Scarlett's face had changed into work mode. I could already see the wheels turning in her head as I laid out my plans, thinking about how they would ensure Jadelyn's safety.

I'd let her and the team pick out which of the trails would be best for their needs as long as it fit my plan.

"Yeah. We can do that. No problem at all. Actually, I should be saying thank you. It'll make my life ten times easier if you keep doing things like this. It might even get my father to like you a little."

"He better start liking me. I'm not going anywhere." Giving my girlfriend a quick squeeze, I pecked her on the cheek and enjoyed watching her give me a blushing smile.

She sighed. "Jade doesn't stand a chance."

I hoped so. Because even walking next to Scarlett, breathing in her amazing scent, was making my head slide back into the gutter. I needed some relief. Although that would likely take some time with Jadelyn. She didn't seem like a sex-on-a-first-date type of girl.

"Hey, there's Kelly." Scarlett pointed through the window of the dining hall.

I followed her finger. Sitting inside the dining hall in the corner by the windows was the pack, or at least the females of the pack. All of which happened to make up the majority of our college's cheerleading squad.

It was as if Kelly sensed Scarlett pointing; she turned and locked eyes with me.

"Shit. I should probably go talk to her." I ran a hand over my face. This one was going to be harder than Jadelyn. When I looked back, Kelly was still watching me, a bit of sadness in her eyes.

"Chasing so many skirts," Scarlett teased. "It's okay. Catch up later?"

"Yeah. Not chasing her skirt, though. I need help with shifting."

Scarlett hummed like she didn't believe me, but she didn't challenge me on it.

Pinching her rear in return, I got a little surprised yelp out of her before I kissed her and let my hungry hands rove up her hips, pulling her closer. I groaned into her mouth as my other hand came around her back. I started to pick her up.

She broke the kiss with a smile and patted me on the cheek. "Down, boy. Go talk to your favorite werewolf. I'll be here for you later when you come back with tongue lashes."

Giving her the eye roll she wanted, I put her back down and headed into the dining hall, trying to ignore the fact that Kelly had been watching us the whole time.

The dining hall was vast; it had to be given the number of students that it served. But, instead of joining the packed line for food, I made a left and headed straight into the seating area. It was always loud during the food rushes. Over a thousand students were packed into the area grabbing food after classes.

Weaving my way through the press of students coming and going, I made my way over to where the pack was sitting. The females in the pack were all stunningly gorgeous. And there was something about them all being next to each other that multiplied that even more.

Kelly sat in the back of the group, perched up against the window. Her straight brown hair was pulled back in a tight ponytail, and she had quite a bit of her sun-kissed skin on display, with her t-shirt wadded up to show off her toned abs.

Kelly watched me, and as I approached, the others broke off their conversations as they noticed me as well. It was like a pack of wolves sensing another predator nearby.

I tried to ignore the awkward silence as I approached. It seemed eerie to have an entire section of the hall silent as the rest boomed with noise.

Kelly crossed her arms as I pulled up at the edge of their group. Nobody moved or made any attempt to clear a way for me, despite clearly knowing where I was headed.

I knew I'd blown her off. I had expected her pack would be protective of her as a result. "Kelly, have a minute to talk?"

She snorted. "Now you want to talk?"

As if an extension of Kelly, all of the girls crossed their arms and gave me the same stern look. It was a bit intimidating to have that many women mad all at once.

I had hoped to have a more private conversation, but I also knew that nothing in a pack was really private anyway. So I gave up.

Knowing that, as werewolves, they responded best to alpha attitude, I packed it on. "Yeah. Now I want to talk. Have a problem with that?"

I didn't love being a bit of an asshole, but I got all of their attention.

Kelly bristled and narrowed her eyes. "Are you about to pick a fight here? 'Cause let me tell you, big bad, the bitches of the pack aren't pushovers."

I kept eye contact with her, not backing down from the challenge. "You're mad, Kelly. I get it." I got a scoffed grunt in response to that. "But my answer hasn't changed. I need your help with something else."

After their pack's alpha, Chad, had nearly gotten them all killed, and I'd had to take him out, the pack had been in disarray. Some of them had wanted me to be their new alpha, but others saw me as an outsider.

I knew I wasn't meant to lead the pack. One of the roles as the alpha was to create the future generations. All the other men in the pack were sterile.

And the idea of sleeping with the pack females and then those females going back and having pairs, relationships with the beta males rankled me in a way that just thinking about it threatened to have my fire roll out of my mouth and torch the whole football team. Dragons didn't share.

I'd explained all of this to Kelly, leaving out the dragon part, but she still didn't seem convinced.

Kelly's posture shifted slightly, although she still clearly had her guard up. Curiosity finally winning out, she asked, "What is it you need my help with?"

Taking a deep breath, I admitted what was hard to say in front of a pack of shifters. "I can't shift."

There was an audible gasp across the females, many of which quickly had faces filled with pity. For a shifter, not being able to shift sounded like a death sentence.

Kelly quickly repeated back what I'd said, not seeming to believe it. "Can't shift?"

"I should be able to, but... whenever I have tried, the shift doesn't come. Obviously, I didn't know I was paranormal for a long time, so it's not something I've been doing since birth like most of you."

The girls parted, sympathetic looks on their faces. Two grabbed my arms and drew me into their group. More than a few of them gave me comforting touches, and they pressed in around me.

"What's happening?" The sudden shift had me off balance.

"It happens sometimes. After a traumatic event, sometimes a wolf gets stuck as a human. People say it's worse than a kidney stone," Kelly explained, getting down off her perch and sitting in front of me. "Tell us what you are?"

The werewolves enjoyed touch, and that became clear as they worked to console me. Hands snuck up my shirt and caressed my chest while someone ran their nails along my scalp. My body was instantly relaxing, enjoying the press of soft womanly curves around me.

It was hard to focus on talking to Kelly while it was happening, but I managed to reply to her question. "Sorry, Kelly. I can't tell you what I am. It is too dangerous, especially when I can't even shift. Once you know, you'll understand why I need to be able to protect myself."

"Join the pack. We'll protect you if that's what you need." She came forward until she was almost sitting on my lap. "You could have this every day if you were our alpha."

I groaned. It was tempting, especially at that moment. "Can't. I'd kill all of your beta males. Really. What I am won't play well with others. I'm far too territorial."

"We deal with bone-headed alphas all the time. Sometimes it just takes a softer touch to get them in line."

That snapped me out of it. "Is that what this is? A soft touch to get me in line?" Anger roiled in my gut. "You think this is a joke?"

"No," Kelly said unconvincingly.

I let my eyes shift as I leaned forward. "Any woman I touch is mine alone. I'll rip the guts out of any man who touches what is mine." The beast was pissed off at just the idea as it thrashed in my chest.

Kelly must have seen something in my eyes because she backed up, looking confused. "You really would."

"Yes. I'm not joking around here, Kelly. And I'd like your help learning to shift."

She tsked and waved the girls off me. They complied instantly, and I wondered for a second why the hell she wasn't alpha. It seemed like she practically ran the pack from what I'd seen.

"Fine. Let's go see what we can do." She turned to the girls. "Tiff, go make sure the boys aren't killing each other on the field today. I'm going to go take a walk with our far too possessive shifter here."

Kelly snagged a thin leather jacket from the corner and threw it on as she got up with the balance of a world class gymnast. "Come on."

"Thank you, girls," I told the rest of them. "You almost had me." A part of me had almost given in. But I knew what I'd said was true. I couldn't be their alpha, not without killing all the other men.

Kelly was tossing her hair out of her jacket as we walked. "So, you're not going to tell me what you are?"

"If you can help me shift, you can see for yourself." I winked.

She grumbled something low enough that I couldn't hear her before looking me in the eye. "Know that I can't be with you if you are going to be that possessive. And, if you want to be with me, you have to be alpha. I've decided that's the only one that's going to touch me after the whole Chad debacle."

"That makes sense. You want to be there to help keep the new alpha on the straight and narrow. How's it been going?" I already knew it had gone to shit, but I tried to leave it open so she could share what she was comfortable sharing.

Tossing her brown hair again, trying to get some of the stray strands out of her jacket, she looked away. "After you so kindly declined any involvement, the boys decided among themselves that they were going to fight for it."

She let out a deep sigh. "Every practice is a bloodbath. The boys are tearing each other apart. None of them have claimed alpha for more than a two-week stretch. They just don't have enough power behind any of them to rein the rest in."

I nodded. If they were all too closely matched, nobody would be able to retain the alpha position. "Why don't you become alpha? You even seemed able to rein Chad in."

Kelly scoffed. "That's not how it works. And I couldn't exactly impregnate all the girls. That's sort of a vital part of the pack."

I got her point, but I still didn't quite buy it. She was tough enough and had the leadership skills. Who cared that she didn't have a dick? Technology, or heck even magic, could find a way to fix that problem. There had to be a way to solve the beta male infertility issue.

"You are certainly the better leader and keep everyone in line. It seems like you're the alpha, even if you won't claim the title." I looked up, realizing we were headed in a random direction. "Where are we going?"

"To my car, then out to my dad's old bunker." Kelly pointed to a several-year-old SUV.

I swung around the side and hopped in, feeling a little awkward that I didn't know the fate of what had happened to the bunker since her father had lost his mind in it. "Is your father's old pack still using it?"

"No, they abandoned it. Won't go near it now that dad is dead." She visibly wilted as she pulled out and started towards it.

"Want to talk about it?"

"It would have been fucking nice if you had been there to talk about it when it happened," she snapped. "Not even just the alpha stuff—you completely ditched me."

I sighed and leaned back in the seat. "You wouldn't drop the alpha crap. I couldn't even have a conversation with you."

The tension rose for a moment as both of us relived the reason we hadn't been speaking recently, but eventually Kelly deflated and focused back on the road. "Fine. But

I'm not sorry. We needed an alpha. I needed an alpha."

"Trust me. When you see what I am, you'll think twice about it." Dragons weren't exactly known for being team players. There was a reason they were always keeping damsels in towers.

Kelly gave me some serious side eye as she drove through traffic. "Going to keep hanging that out there?"

"I need something to entice you to help me figure this out. Morgana has me chasing swamp trolls all around town and dropping them off on the south side. Made me fight one today alone in hopes it would encourage me to shift. I'm a little afraid of what tactics she'll shift to next."

Kelly laughed. "I want to see that; have me come join you next time. In past years, the packs would help with swamp trolls. A few wolves could take one down." She seemed to realize something. "In fact, you are probably dealing with so many because the packs aren't helping. Shit, I wonder if we need to get the college pack to help with herding them out of the city."

I hadn't realized the packs had helped in the past, but it made sense. The migration happened every year, and there would have been some process already in place to keep them in check. But Chad had seriously damaged the local packs; they were all still working to get organized again. It was lucky that Morgana and I could fill in.

"It's fine. Morgana and I are running around every night taking care of them. When she isn't pushing me, we use tranquilizers that an old elf makes."

"Now that makes a lot more sense than trying to take them down physically, but seriously. If we can't crack this today, I'd like to come with. Mostly to see you get your ass kicked." Kelly laughed, and though I didn't love the idea, seeing her rise out of the melancholy mood was nice.

"Okay. Come see my ass get kicked tonight. If nothing else, some coaching on controlling it would be nice. Morgana can try to help, but she's not exactly an expert on this."

Shifting wasn't something you could read up or pass on secondhand information. Having a werewolf around to help me might be just what I needed.

Kelly let out a mad cackle as she drove. "Oh boy. I'm going to film this, savor it for years to come. Swamp troll kicks cocky alpha around."

I sighed. "Not going to be your alpha."

"You can't deny you are worth being an alpha. Just because you won't be the pack's alpha doesn't mean you aren't one."

"Whatever." I shrugged, already knowing she was going to keep pushing. We'd work through it one way or another.

CHAPTER 6

B eing back in the bunker had an ominous feeling.

The front door had been replaced, but that was the only clean up that seemed to have happened since the battle that had raged inside. The old warehouse, which had served as the werewolf pack's den and housed an entire bunker underground, was a complete mess. The rampaging pack of werewolves had done a number on it.

Claw marks ravaged the concrete walls, and every door was a few inches wider than it should have been, carved away by scratching werewolves. We'd managed to make it out ahead of the drugged and angry wolves as they'd gone crazy hunting for the drug's source.

A winding staircase had once been in the warehouse, leading down to the underground bunker, but all that remained was a mangled pile of twisted metal.

"Yeah. This place is pretty fucked up." Kelly stepped up to where the stairs used to be and jumped down, shifting as she fell silently. She landed in a crouch, part woman, part wolf.

I followed her lead, but without the ability to shift, I landed far heavier. "I can see how it brings back bad memories."

The anchor chains that they had used to secure Brent, Kelly's father, were busted nearby. And two of the prison cells were obliterated as well.

Human things like the kitchen area and the recreation area were smashed. Cabinets weren't more than pulped wood, and what I assumed used to be a pool table had been thrown into a shower. Only a green velvet liner hinted at what the pile of wood and broken glass used to be.

"Perfect place for you to let loose, though. Not like you can wreck it more than it already is." Kelly prowled in a circle around me; only a few aspects of her wolf were out. "Strip. You didn't bring extra clothes."

She reverted to being entirely human as she stepped out of her clothes, even taking off her bra and panties.

I was caught off guard and found myself staring. It was hard to look away from her graceful body. But then I had to remind myself that she was off limits; she'd go to whoever was her next alpha, and that wasn't me.

Forcing myself to turn away, I stripped out of my own clothes, throwing them in a pile to the side along with my book bag.

"Okay wh— What are you doing?" I realized Kelly had moved close to me; I could feel the heat from her core at my side. Naked and mouthwatering nipples hung like they defied gravity, pressing just barely into my side. I could feel them drag along my skin.

She took a deep sniff of me, and I couldn't help but get her scent as well. The sage and mint, no, thyme, smelled like harsh nature.

Her closeness and my recently pent-up libido were having a reaction as I started to rise to attention.

"Oh, good. You do think I'm hot." She peeked around my shoulder, smirking like she'd won something. "Was starting to get worried by how you blew me off."

"Come on, Kelly. Obviously, you're gorgeous. You're also fun and smart as hell. But you're off limits. I don't want to kill your eventual alpha, and I already told you, I'm possessive," I reminded her—and myself.

Mostly reminding myself that I couldn't take the naked, supple-bodied werewolf who would totally roll on her back for me.

Damnit.

Her hands landed on my shoulders, softly trailing down my arms. A part of me began to wonder if she'd brought me down into the bunker with the plan of seducing me instead of helping me learn to shift. The thought cleared away some of the fog from my attraction to her, and I turned back, ready to get down to business.

But she was one step ahead. She danced back, a playful smirk on her face. "Come get me, big boy."

She partially shifted and jumped, her foot swinging up. She caught me in the jaw, knocking me to the side.

I stumbled a few steps and rubbed my jaw. She'd gotten me completely by surprise. "Is that what we are doing? Morgana has tried it; you can't anger me into shifting. It doesn't work like my br—" I cut myself off, having almost given too much away.

"There's more? Still holding back, I see. You know, hiding what you are might be part of the problem." Kelly bounded in again, coming at me in a full tackle.

I was still stronger than her, but in her partially shifted state, she was twice my weight. Catching her tackle, I lifted her off the floor.

Unfortunately, she countered the move, throwing her weight to the side. I had to stomp out to the left to keep upright, but then she twisted in my arms and curled away from me. I fell forward on top of the naked werewolf.

Kelly had a big grin on her face before she grabbed me and rolled herself on top, pressing her still very human breasts to my chest. "What's wrong, big bad alpha?"

Annoyed and knowing that I could be rough with her, I pulled back my arm just enough to have six inches of space before slamming a fist into her chest.

The shocked look on her face was worth it as I launched her off me. I might not have the mass, but I was far stronger.

She landed in a three-pointed crouch, her other hand holding her chest as she wheezed. "No wonder you could wrestle Chad. Fuck, you are strong."

The beast was feeling hot tempered and demanded that I smoke her with a breath of fire.

I had to remind the beast that it was just practice. We weren't killing this one.

She jumped to the side, then looked confused. "What was that? You just held back," Kelly demanded. Her instincts were sharp.

"You would have died. Chad did."

Kelly prowled around to my side, circling me. "They talk about that night. The night you killed Chad. Most of them were out of their mind, but none of them saw clearly what you did. First, you were wrestling him in the rain, and by the sound of it, you were hanging onto his back. Then there was a bright flash of light and steam rose everywhere. No one saw it clearly."

"So?" I stepped back so I could keep an eye on her and circled opposite of her in the wrecked bunker. "What do you think?"

"Fire makes sense. Flash of light, sudden steam in the rain. His corpse was a burnt-out husk from the waist up. So you used fire. Is that what almost happened? You wanted to burn me to a crisp like Chad?" she mocked. "Don't think it would be so easy. I'm nowhere near as dumb as he was."

I backed up as a sign I was done fighting. "You have a death wish if you want me to use that. Cut it out."

Kelly sprang forward. She wasn't going to stop.

Not amused in the slightest, I caught her wrist and leaned back as I swung her into the wall. Her forearm snapped, and she gave a small cry before she rolled away, clutching it.

"You are strong. Guess I'm not really enough to force you. If Chad didn't force you to shift, I doubt I'm going to." Kelly shifted back and set her arm with a wet crunch before picking through the broken wood. "So, what do you know about shifting?"

"You go from human to beast, with a sliding scale in between. Morgana said it was like taking a shit; you have to learn to relax one part and tense another."

Kelly looked up as she found a solid piece the length of her forearm. "That's not a bad way to put it. I've heard other shifters say the same thing. But do you know where the mass comes from?"

"Mass?" Even as I said it, my science education was sending off alarm bells. Obviously, this was magic, but how hadn't I tried to put science to it? "Where is the mass?"

"Think of it like this. You are the full creature you could be. That's why you are probably packing away far more calories than a human would your size."

I thought about it, admitting, "Ate four pizzas the other night, felt like I could have eaten more."

Kelly whistled. "You're big, aren't you?"

"A lot bigger than a werewolf." I'd put the wolves I'd seen maybe up to six hundred pounds, except for the alphas. The full size of a dragon from what Morgana had shown me was utterly massive. The oldest lived in Dubai, and she guessed he might top sixteen tons.

However, I was far younger. Morgana had guessed I'd be two or three tons if I could shift.

Kelly eyed me speculatively. The wheels in her head trying to figure out what I was with the pieces to the puzzle she had.

"Right. So all that mass has to come from somewhere. You aren't magically making it and shedding it every time. It is with you and, more importantly, connected to your body at all times. Some wizard might make a dozen theories about how exactly it works, but know that no one really knows, and it isn't likely that a wolf will let a wizard poke and prod him to find out."

"Okay, I'm following you. So it's like a jacket in your backpack. With you, but not always on. How do you put it on? That's the big part I need."

She made a sound of understanding as she tried to tear up the felt.

"So stubborn. Let me help." I came over, and with two hands, it was far easier for me to tear off strips.

"Since you are over here." She held out her arm and used the wood as a splint. "Help me out?"

At least this was something I knew how to do. Even though I'd given up my EMT job, this was pretty basic. I set the splint and wrapped her arm from top to bottom with several strips of the felt.

"Okay. So I've never shifted. How do I do it for the first time?"

"Most young wolves startle into their first shift. The sudden tension when they were otherwise relaxed leads to it."

"Don't think I'm relaxed in a fight," I commented, still annoyed that both she and Morgana seemed to think of trying to fight as the best way to do this.

Kelly suddenly jumped in my face. "Rawr!"

I reached up reflexively to put a hand between us, feeling the soft curve of her chest land in my palm. It must be male nature, because despite all the jokes about it, I gave them a small squeeze before I even realized what I was doing.

She yelped in surprise and jumped back before a sly smile spread across her face. "Oh, is that the kind of surprise you want?"

"No. God, that was an accident." I looked at my hand as if it had betrayed me. "Also, that didn't work. Anything else you can tell me about shifting?" I tried to ignore what had just happened.

"When it comes, it comes. You'll probably do a wonky partial shift for the first time. After that, it'll get easier."

"Like taking a poop?" I joked.

But she nodded seriously. "Exactly. Or like riding a bike if we want to act like adults. It's a coordinated thing, but once you get it, you get it."

I let out a big sigh, which was interrupted as my phone started ringing.

Morgana had sent me a gif of someone fanning their money out. 'Jared came through and paid us. Gold or cash?'

I texted back quickly. 'Gold please'

'You are going to have to give up some of it eventually.'

Smirking, I sent back 'Never!' before putting the phone away.

"What's got you so happy?" Kelly watched me and started to step around to take a peek at my phone. She was a nosy one, wasn't she?

With no reason to hide it, I told her, "Morgana and I got paid for a job this weekend. She charged him double and made him pay up front because she didn't like him."

Kelly let out an appreciative whistle. "Who's the sucker?"

"Some rich Polish magi family."

"The Nashners?" Kelly's eyes popped a little.

I hadn't realized they were that famous. "Are they a big deal? Morgana made them sound like chumps."

Kelly hid her face as she snorted. "To Morgana, they might be. But to the rest of us, they are stupidly rich and decently famous sorcerers."

I shrugged. If they were chumps to Morgana, I doubted I owed them any more respect. "Doesn't matter much to me. Pretty sure I could roast them too. Which is good to know because he was a dick."

Kelly slugged me in the side of the face with her good arm.

It caught me completely off guard as I wobbled to the side. "What the fuck."

She shrugged. "Trying to startle you into your shift."

"Ouch. Maybe try tickling or something." I rubbed at my jaw. Thankfully, she hadn't been shifted for that. "That's a mean right hook."

"Thanks. I've put down more than a few presumptuous wolves with that one." She shook out her hand and rubbed at her knuckles. "You are tough too. Strong, tough, you can summon fire. Shifter... hmm," she puzzled aloud.

It made sense. She thought I had fire, but she didn't know I *breathed* fire. Of course, like Morgana had said when we were first figuring it out, that was a pretty narrow list of creatures, all of which were very rare.

"Hell hound? I've seen one in a pack before. Nasty bitch. I could see a male not fitting in a pack."

"Nope. Nice try though. I'd eat one of those for breakfast." I was pretty sure they'd make a nice spicy snack, and the beast agreed. "Come on. Let's get back. I need to run by my place, and then it'll be time to head out to hunt trolls with Morgana... if you are still interested?"

"Yep! I may not get you myself, but I can watch a swamp troll clean your clock at least once."

"That interested in seeing me hurt?" I half-joked.

She nodded eagerly. "Call it revenge for ghosting me. After the first hit though, we are square."

I laughed. I figured it was getting off easy, and I could use the help to figure out my shifting. "Fine, but if I don't get nailed tonight, we are square either way."

"I think you're right—you'd make a terrible alpha. You're too tough for me to hen-peck back into line." Kelly teased me before she shifted back to fully human, walking over to wiggle back into her tight jeans.

***

Unlocking the door to my apartment, I ducked inside to drop off my stuff and get a change of clothes.

Kelly was right behind me as we headed into the apartment, and I got the distinct impression it was to snoop.

"Hi, Zach," Frank greeted me. He and Maddie were cuddled together on the couch. "Hi, Scarl— oh shit." He aborted his greeting with a terrified look on his face.

Maddie was a little more tactful. "Hello, I'm Maddie. This is Frank, his roommate."

"I'm Kelly. And I know about Scarlett. I even got naked with him today, and he didn't boink me. Trying to not be offended." She let out an exasperated sigh and looked away, towards the kitchen.

Frank, who was out of Maddie's field of vision, began mouthing 'what the ever-living fuck'.

I wasn't sure if he was disappointed at me for not having sex with Kelly or just completely jealous of my situation. So I did the proper response and just gave a helpless shrug.

"Just dropping off some stuff, and then we'll be out of your hair," I commented.

"Your place smells nicer than I'd have thought," Kelly stated, turning to Maddie. "I'm betting they have you to thank for that."

Maddie said something in return, but I was already going down the hall and dropping off my bag, opening my closet. I wanted something that said troll hunting, whatever exactly that was.

Stripping my shirt off, I tossed it on the bed to deal with later and slipped out of my nice jeans. I opted for a darker pair that was already a little banged up from catching a chupacabra last month.

My wardrobe was far different from when I had started the semester. Along with awakening my dragon half, I'd had a massive growth spurt. Frank, and then later Scarlett, had been pivotal to helping me restock my closet with things that fit better.

I was standing there in my boxers, jeans in hand, looking through the rest when Kelly spoke. I nearly jumped out of my skin.

"Go with the green shirt. It's ugly enough. You won't miss it when you shift on accident."

"Holy crap." I clutched my chest. "I'm going to kick your ass."

"Didn't work that time either." Kelly shook her head.

I realized she was still trying to startle the shift out of me. It was an odd sense of both being thankful for it and hating every time. But I opted for a grudgingly thankful grunt.

"One of these times, this is going to work. Then I'm going to scare the crap out of you." I took her advice and picked the green band tee, grabbing a bomber jacket I didn't really like too. "Care to turn away?"

"Nope. I like the view." Kelly smirked. "Plus, we were just naked together."

I rolled my eyes. "Thanks for giving them the wrong impression."

"I am?" She tilted her head in mock confusion. "Pretty sure there's enough chemistry here to make a chem class out of it."

"Sure, but there's also the whole not-your-alpha thing," I reminded her. "Unless you want me to tear your next alpha apart when he ogles you."

"Still not convinced you are that bad. But who knows, maybe you'll surprise me."

I let out a dark chuckle. I had a feeling that I would surprise her when she found out I was a dragon. It would definitely be a highlight of shifting to see the look on her face. I couldn't wipe that smirk off my face just picturing the moment.

CHAPTER 7

I was still sporting a wide grin as Kelly and I pulled up to Bumps in the Night.

"Could you stop smiling?" Kelly pouted. Her last several attempts to startle me into shifting had completely fizzled.

"Nope. I'm looking forward to your complete surprise when you find out what type of shifter I am." I smiled as I slid out and into the club. The dinner portion of the club was open, and the warm, dimly lit front room was filled with well-dressed couples out on dates.

Grabbing Kelly's hand, I pulled her to the side and around the screen towards the back where Morgana's club stretched further back than should be possible given the building's size. Morgana's unique spatial magic was able to stretch the space.

One of the servers got a good look at me and bowed before heading off to find Morgana. I made myself at home by the bar in the empty club area. Grabbing something fancy looking from the top shelf and two low ball glasses, I showed Kelly the bottle.

"I'm actually more of a tequila girl," Kelly replied as she stared at the bottle in my hands.

"Let me see what I can do." I looked back, grabbing a shot glass and a bottle of tequila. Coming back around the bar, I held it up for her approval.

"That'll work." Kelly took the shot and the bottle, knocking back several shots before settling with a single glass she was going to sip.

"Careful, we still are going out tonight to hunt trolls." I took the bottle back and put it on the shelf.

"Werewolf metabolism. I'll be fine in thirty minutes. Plus, I'm not the one hunting trolls." She sipped at the shot.

I only poured myself two fingers to enjoy. I didn't want to lose my edge.

As I poured it, Morgana sauntered around the corner, her hand running against the wall as her hips swayed. She often kept to the shadows, or at night in her club when the black lights came on, I'd seen her dance on the stage with no one realizing her skin was blue.

But around the club, she kept herself distant from other men. It had only taken one time for me to understand why.

She had danced with me and Scarlett one night only for men to come crawling over her. Morgana could handle herself and warded off dozens of men, but at the same time, it had to be exhausting.

"Grab me a flute, and there's a bottle of sparkling red in the fridge."

By red, Morgana meant blood. Well, what she really meant was champagned blood. It was her special drink of choice.

I opened the fridge and let my eyes shift so I could see in the dark behind the other bottles. Spotting my target, I pulled out a fancy gold-encrusted bottle.

While vampires might be low-key about many things, when it came to their favorite blood, they were not. Pouring Morgana a flute, I put it back to keep it fresh and raised my glass. "To another night of hunting trolls and making gold."

We clinked our glasses, and we all took a sip.

"Am I getting gold?" Kelly asked.

"No," I replied, maybe a touch too quickly. It had been instinctive when it came to splitting my gold.

Morgana swirled her glass with a look of idle thought. "I don't know. Maybe we should take a cut out of Zach's portion to pay for your time. That only seems fair."

I let out a low growl.

"I'm missing something," Kelly said.

"Yes, you are." Morgana smiled. "This one is a little touchy about his gold. Doesn't even cash it in. He just sleeps on it."

I froze; Morgana was dropping far too many hints. But Kelly didn't seem to figure it out, simply sipping on her drink.

Kelly replied, "I just think it's cool to have real freaking gold." She slugged back the rest of her shot and put it on the counter for another. "Hit me, barkeep!"

Turning back to me, she added, "My dad always kept a stock of gold. Rainy day funds and all." Her eyes seemed to zone out as her voice trailed off, and I had no doubt it was bringing up sad memories.

I poured her another glass, working to change the subject before she went too deep down memory lane. "Morgana, any news on the trolls?"

Her eyes slid off Kelly with a cocked brow. "Nothing yet."

"I'd expect something soon," Kelly added. "Dad always said when the restaurants started throwing out their scraps, trolls seemed to pop up all over, hungry."

"When are they human besides after we knock them out? I feel like they are in their shifted state more than most paranormals." I turned to Morgana. "Also, we are bringing tranquilizers this time."

Before I forgot, I wanted to guarantee that for my own safety this time. I'd managed to wrestle the single troll, but two or even three would be a train wreck.

"Pretty much anything sets them off," Kelly explained. Apparently, the pack's history in dealing with this had taught her a few things. "Anger, hunger, anxiety, heck, even just a bunch of flashing lights can overwhelm them and send them into a rage. That's why we get them down to Florida where they can enjoy soaking in their swamps for the rest of the winter."

Morgana nodded and her phone chirped. "You asked for this. Just remember that." She pushed off the bar and raised her glass. "Bottoms up."

I drained my glass and smacked it on the counter. "Where to?"

"Butcher shop. Looks like it's a fancy one, but luckily, it is para-owned, so they called it in when they found two trolls eating in the alley garbage." Morgana tapped on her phone as she headed deeper into her club and out to the parking garage.

"Sweet mother of god," Kelly gasped as she walked through the door into Morgana's garage.

I remembered my first time seeing Morgana's cars. Row after row of cars that were worth six figures could really shock your system. "Yep. But we'll take that van."

"Van?" Kelly scoffed. "Why would you take a van?"

Pulling a tranquilizer revolver from the armory, I snagged a kit of darts and the little loading tool. "First off, the van is the most expensive car down here. Second, most of these don't have the trunk space for a troll."

"Do I at least get a gun?" She eyed the armory of guns resting on the wall.

"Nope. You are just here to teach me, right?" I fired back what she'd said earlier as I dragged her away from the armory down the row of Jaguars, Lamborghinis, Ferraris, and other beautiful cars, ending up at the van.

The van was a beat-up looking old mini-van with now both side doors mismatched from the rest of the paint job. The first had already been there when I had started working with Morgana. The second was a result of a drunken minotaur we had wrangled a month ago. He hadn't appreciated our help and had kicked out the other side door.

The van had a top-of-the-line engine and drive system, and it needed it. Under the rough exterior was armored plating; the van was the next best thing to a tank. But it was heavy and drove like a runaway bull.

"Buckle up." I got in and secured myself.

Kelly had yet to experience Morgana's driving. She was in for it.

Kelly shrugged and hooked her seatbelt. "Not like a car crash would kill me anyway."

The way Morgana drove, I thought it might, but I'd let her experience the pleasure of Morgana's driving herself.

Morgana chose that moment to floor it, spinning out of her spot, jostling me as she ground the gears, the car still in motion and gunning it forward as we flew recklessly by millions of dollars' worth of cars.

Taking a peek in the rearview mirror, I caught Kelly already looking a little green and bracing herself against the door.

Morgana tore out onto the streets, and it was a miracle that she wasn't pulled over a dozen times as she gunned it through the city streets, using signs and road rules as suggestions.

***

When Morgana finally screeched to a stop in front of the butcher shop, Kelly scrambled out of the car and puked in the gutter. "Who taught you to drive?"

"I taught myself. Back when cars had steam engines," the drow vampire reminded us both of her age. "But I don't have a license, if that's what you are asking."

"No wonder," Kelly grumbled before picking herself up and checking to make sure she hadn't splattered on herself. Satisfied, she turned back to us. Her ear twitched as a metal clang rang out. It sounded like a dumpster being turned over.

Pedestrians were still walking down the street, and more than a few pointed and gawked at Morgana.

"Amazing costume, can I get a picture?"

She waved him off. "No, I have to get going."

He looked disappointed but rejoined his group, and I heard the distinct click of a phone camera. Rude.

"I bet you are going to be on the front page of some cosplay website, Morgana." I led the way, ducking into the alley next to the butcher shop.

There was a sharp intake of breath as a rotund man startled as I entered the dark alley. Further down, there were two trolls trying to fit into a dumpster at the same time, and not succeeding. They banged it against the brick wall of another building.

"You own the butcher shop?" I asked the man who held a cleaver low, as if it would do anything to protect him from a troll.

He nodded, and his eyes went wide when he spotted Morgana and Kelly, who filed out behind me. "Thank god. Can you take care of them?"

His focus was on Morgana, but she pointed her chin at me.

"He's going to take care of them. It might get a little messy though. Why don't you head back in. We'll take care of it."

"Thank you. Thank you," he quickly sputtered, ignoring Kelly and hurrying back into the back door of the butcher shop.

I shot Morgana a questioning glance.

"Vamp. He collects the blood for sale."

I paused. That was the first fat vampire I'd ever seen. I thought there was a rule they all had to be thin and broody looking. "Okay, then let's deal with these two."

Morgana eyed me as I pulled out the tranquilizer pistol and loaded it from the bandoleer. "That isn't how you are going to figure out your shifting."

"Well, I was thinking that maybe we shouldn't let them cause a mess tonight. I take lefty, you take righty."

The girls shared a look.

"What? There will probably be another one tonight. If it is in a less risky spot, I'll fight them."

Kelly turned to Morgana rather than talk to me. "We could get some hotdogs from the butcher, I bet. Lure these guys somewhere else."

"Hello. Not the plan. Plus, we are in the middle of a shopping area with a ton of pedestrians out on a Friday night. No way we can just lure these two dumb trolls around with hotdogs."

Kelly's eyes shifted over my shoulder, and I could feel the back of my neck prickle. Acting on instinct, I ducked, and a whoosh of air sounded above me. A trash bag sailed just over my head, nearly hitting me.

"Duck," Kelly said late. The smirk on her face told me that she might have done that on purpose.

"Thanks for that." I turned and faced the two big, green problems that had spotted me and were now coming my way. Dart guns hadn't exactly been a focus in Morgana's shooting range, but I at least knew the basics. Thankfully, swamp trolls made big targets.

Squeezing the trigger several times, three red, puffy darts found their way into the troll's chest.

But it didn't take it down. The troll was still coming, taking a big sloppy swing at me as it tripped over its own feet.

Ducking inside the swing, I came up on its side and landed a sharp punch in its kidneys. The already wobbly troll took two steps to the side as it overreacted to the hit.

I knew an opportunity when I saw one. With it leaning away, I dove into a tackle and took the huge troll down before I rolled away just in time for its meaty hands to slap its own chest.

"Want to put a few more in it for good measure?" I called out to Morgana, who already had her rifle at the ready and shot a dart longer than my hand into the troll. The mixture T had come up with was potent, but it was better safe than sorry. I didn't want one of these waking up in the trunk of the van on the way out of the city.

"Careful. Here comes the second," Morgana warned.

The other troll was pulling itself up out of the dumpster, an old, moldy hunk of meat hanging from its mouth as it turned to appraise us, still chewing. Its eyes really didn't seem to hold much of a spark of intelligence. They were like two little, beady, black marbles, lifeless. But they managed to see the other troll on the ground and its neanderthal brow furrowed.

It took a lumbering step to square itself against me, and I popped out the cylinder of the revolver, seeing three more of the darts still ready. Popping it back in, I looked up at the troll. I had it.

This troll was a little more cautious as its dumpster dinner date lay passed out on the ground, shifting back into its human form.

"Kelly, you want to get that one out of the way?" I asked, keeping my eyes on the active troll. This one was acting differently; the previous trolls had all been impulsive and animalistic.

While this troll very much looked like a troll, it seemed to be more intelligent. It looked at the gun in my hand and grabbed the lid to the dumpster, ripping it off and sending the dumpster grinding along the alley. Then it held up the lid like a shield.

"Oh, great." My little darts, while full of potent tranquilizer, weren't going to punch through that. So instead of shooting, I set off at a run towards the troll as it brandished the shield in front of it.

Jumping, I used the shield as a step, launching myself up and over the troll as I twisted and tried to get a line on it.

But the troll spun with me, keeping the dumpster lid between the two of us as it grinned victoriously. It stomped and charged, even before I hit the ground.

I couldn't do much midair to change where I was going to land. So I was forced to watch as the troll caught me on his makeshift shield and carried me forward, plowing me into and over the lip of another dumpster. The dart gun clattered to the alley floor as I wheezed for breath.

"Yuck." Glaring at the troll from inside the dumpster, I tried to figure out a plan.

But I didn't have long to think, because the troll grinned as its big meaty hands grabbed the sidewalls of the dumpster. Its shoulders bulged with effort and the troll's tongue popped out like some sort of piston under too much pressure as it used its hands to crumple the side walls inwards.

They groaned as the metal bent in towards me.

Oh, hell no. I wasn't about to get trapped in here like a bug inside a wrapper. But the problem with being thrown in a dumpster, aside from the stink, was that you didn't really have any solid ground to get traction on.

To be able to get myself out, I had to flail my arms and half-crawl, half-swim across the trash bags to get to the lip of the dumpster that was already closing in around me.

As I got my hand on the lip, the troll smashed down the lid of the dumpster on it. It was everything I could do to not scream and pull the hand back.

"Listen here. Get out of my city," I growled angrily.

My comment only pissed off the troll further. It picked up the dumpster and started to shake it.

I clung on to the lip of the dumpster.

One garbage dragon shaken, not stirred, coming right up.

I felt like I was in the middle of a drink mixer, being mixed in with the garbage. I was definitely getting thoroughly coated in the stuff while he did it.

"Morgana. About now would be a great time to put a few darts in this guy," I called from inside the dumpster mixer.

Either she didn't hear me, or she was content to let me work this one out on my own. I was so going to give her a big stinky hug after this was done, then go sit in her precious van to stink it up.

Thoroughly mixed, the troll set the crumpled dumpster back down and opened the lid to take a peek.

I had held on through the whole thing, so as soon as I saw that lid lifting, I threw my dizziness and aches aside. This was my chance.

Throwing myself up and out of the dumpster, I clung to the troll's face, grabbing his chin and throwing my body weight to the side.

His head snapped to the side, but its over-developed lats bulged and prevented me from breaking his neck.

I groaned, annoyed that it hadn't worked. I just couldn't catch a break.

Getting a firm grip on its chin and digging my knee into its shoulder for leverage, I put my full strength behind it and twisted hard.

This time, the troll's neck made a satisfying wet snap as all the tension left its body and it tumbled to the ground.

It lay there, not breathing, but I could already hear the crackle of its neck healing. It would be fine.

I shot a glare at Morgana. "Thanks for the assist."

Walking over, I grabbed her gun out of her hands and shot the troll point blank with a large dart. Then I handed the gun back to her. "Do you two think this is a joke? That thing could have really hurt me."

Kelly wrinkled her nose. "You reek. But besides that, you are perfectly fine. It was the right call."

Whirling on Kelly, I fixed her with a stare worthy of a pissed off dragon. "You are supposed to be here to help me figure this shit out."

The only warning I had was the groan of sheet metal before the sound of something big flying through the air behind me caused me to spin back around just in time to see a dumpster flying my way.

Fuck this. Fuck them. Fuck trolls. Anger rolled through me at having to deal with even more troll shit. It was time to put this idiot down for good.

I snatched the dumpster out of the air with one hand, my claws sinking deep into the metal frame as I took a single step backwards to brace myself. The dumpster came to a halt midair in my grip, though the contents continued forward and spilled out behind me.

I hoped they both got a trash shower.

But as I thought that, I paused, my eyes trailing over to my right arm, which had not looked like that a moment ago.

Chapter 8

The dumpster came to a groaning halt in my very large, now-clawed hand.

I froze, staring at my right arm, trying to figure out if I was hallucinating. It was huge, covered in scales, but in the darkly lit alley, I couldn't tell what color. But I knew how it felt.

My arm felt incredibly strong, my fist and clawed hands tore through the dumpster's exterior like it was paper.

Tossing the dumpster to the side, all I could do was stare at my hands.

They somewhat looked human. I had five digits, but they were off. My thumb had moved closer to my wrist, and my other four fingers had spread out. And all five of them were tipped with razor-sharp claws. Given the test they had just done, they were at least sharp enough to tear through the thick metal of the dumpster.

Finally, remembering I was in the middle of a battle, I looked up at the troll. It stood there, neck healed with a dart in its shoulder, but it wasn't giving any signs of going down.

Behind me, I heard Kelly gasp. "You're huge."

Looking down, I realized that, while the rest of me was still human, I was enlarged like I'd seen some werewolves swell when they were partially shifted. Based on my surroundings, I'd guess that I had gained another foot of height, and my body had swelled with more mass.

My right arm still dwarfed me though. It hung down, the claws scraping the concrete.

A grin spread across my face. I couldn't wait to see how I matched up now against a troll. I also wouldn't mind a little payback for coating me in garbage and smashing my hand with the dumpster top.

Charging the troll, I swung with the biggest right hook of my life.

Even as it blocked, my blow was heavy enough to send it staggering back. I wasn't on par with the size of a troll, but I easily weighed as much as an average werewolf right now, which was a far cry better than earlier in our fight.

My massive right arm grabbed the troll by the shoulder, my claws sinking into its flesh as I wrenched it to the side and smashed it against the back wall of the butcher shop. Based on the man's earlier reaction, he was likely shitting himself as he heard the fight continuing to unfold.

But I couldn't be more excited. Even able to shift this much, I was able to take on a troll. I couldn't wait to celebrate.

The beast pressed up in my chest, trying to get me to let out a roar of victory, but I clamped down on that. It would draw too much attention here with normal pedestrians on the other side of the buildings.

A new tactic formed in my mind, and I decided to test it out.

I held onto the troll's shoulder and jerked it away from the wall, tossing it on top of the overturned dumpster. It collapsed under its weight.

"Let me know how you like being wrapped up in a dumpster." I grinned as I used my right arm to bend the dumpster over its side, trapping its arm. Then I switched to the other side, pinning the troll like an overstuffed burrito. "Now maybe we can get you to calm down, and you'll pop right out."

The troll didn't seem to appreciate that. It struggled, and the dumpster started to give, so I went back to work, wrapping it up good and tight in the warped dumpster.

"Gun please, Morgana." I held out my right arm.

"Yeah?" she asked with a smirk, handing me the gun.

I didn't think, instinctively reaching to take the dart gun from her. But my claws sank right through the metal, ruining the gun. "Oh."

She snorted with laughter. "You owe me a new one. But that was still worth the look on your face."

Reaching forward, she snagged out some darts and strolled over to the pinned troll, manually stabbing them into him.

I stared at her. "That works, I guess."

Kelly had managed to push through her shock and was circling me. "Huge. What are you?" She peered at my arm. "Some sort of ancient crocodile? Oh wait, a dinosaur?" She fumbled for her phone, and the bright white flashlight came on, illuminating my arm in the dark alley.

I hadn't seen the color before, but it was clear now. Under the bright light, my arm glittered with gold scales. They were bright in the center and darkened toward the edge of each.

Kelly's jaw hung open, and she just stared for a moment before she fell into a crouch and covered her mouth.

"No way. No freaking way," she gasped. Her eyes were still locked on my arm as she dealt with her own realization.

"The color gives it away?" I asked Morgana.

"Yeah, gold isn't exactly a common color in the animal kingdom." She rolled her bright red eyes. "Kelly, you are going to have to keep this a secret. Now that you know, you also know what it would mean if word gets out." Morgana fixed Kelly with a stare.

"He's a dragon." She seemed like she was on the brink of hyperventilating. "He's a freaking gold dragon."

Realization lit up in her eyes. "The talk about gold. Oh shit, territorial. Dragons are possessive, yeah, okay. Things are starting to make a little more sense." She rocked on her heels as she pieced it all together.

Happy I didn't have to hide it from her anymore, I decided to let her process while I figured out how to get clothed. I was currently standing naked in the alley, my clothes shredded and hanging off of me did little to make me modest.

"Morgana, pull the van up to the alley and we can get these guys loaded up? And then maybe take me back home so I can get a shower and a change of clothes?"

I saw Kelly's eyes flick up to my hips in interest, but I ignored her. I had a feeling she was also piecing together the strong dragon libido that seemed to be a well-known characteristic.

"No. You aren't getting in the van." Morgana shook her head.

"Come on. I'll scrape off a little gold from my hoard and we'll get someone to do a full cleaning. You won't have to smell me past tonight," I promised. Now that I had shifted and the problem had been dealt with, I wasn't feeling particularly spiteful. Although, I was ready to be home and clean.

I turned to Kelly. "How do I shift back?" I held up my massive right arm. "And now that I've done this, how do I fully shift?"

That seemed to snap Kelly out of her thoughts. "Do not shift all the way right here. You'd squish us both. How big are you?"

"I have no idea. Raised human, and only recently figured out what I am."

Kelly let out a mad, cackling laugh. "Chad picked a fight with a dragon. Oh my god, the sheer idiocy." Tears squeezed their way out of her eyes as they pressed shut, and she held her stomach as she lost it. She was definitely becoming hysterical.

Apparently, me being a dragon had been too much.

"Wait. Scarlett knows?"

"Yes. Morgana, Scarlett, and you are the only ones. Well, Chad might have realized it at the very end, but you know, I kind of smoked him."

Kelly's eyes went even wider, and the blood drained out of her face. "I was baiting you to breathe dragon fire on me this afternoon."

"Yup."

"Thank you?" There was a little fear in her eyes now.

"I mean, I'm not some loose cannon you have to worry about. I'm not going to go around killing and pillaging all of Philly."

She looked to Morgana for verification.

"He's fine. Relatively harmless, at least compared to most dragons." Morgana said.

"Is their reputation that bad?" I asked. All I really knew so far was that the king of dragons apparently lived in Dubai.

Morgana winced. "Yes. They have a violent reputation. Everyone talks about the Bronze King in Dubai, and he's mostly just an unrepentant cad that likes to collect every kind of woman he can get his claws around. Others? They've smoked entire cities in anger."

"I might have a little ball of anger in me, but I can't imagine going that far." I paused, my mind starting to go down the rabbit hole before I pulled it back. "But, Kelly, back on topic. How do I shift back? As cool as this arm is, it would be way more convenient to have my human one back."

"Just relax, let it all go."

As she said it, I realized a part of me had still been tense, like a ball of tension in my shoulders.

Taking a deep breath, I worked to release that tension. As I did, I could feel the shift as my bones reorganized themselves. It felt like the pressure right before you popped a knuckle, a little painful, but followed by a sense of relief as everything settled back to where it was supposed to be.

I smiled down at my now human hands before looking back up at Kelly. "Do me a favor? Grab one of the trolls. Morgana, car please. I want to get out of here."

Morgana gave me a smirking salute before heading off to the van. "Yes, boss."

Kelly still stood there, staring at me.

I added, "This doesn't change anything, Kelly. I'm still me."

Kelly gave me an incredulous look. "This changes fucking everything. I don't think you appreciate how big a deal you are. Not just Philly, but the entire global paranormal world will ripple when it comes out that you are a dragon. And you're not just any dragon. You're a fucking gold dragon."

I thought about Morgana's investigation into my last name, and how she thought it meant I might be related to the once true king of dragons. Logically, a gold dragon sounded like a big deal. But was that it?

The beast pressed against me in my chest, almost like it was telling me there was still more for me to discover about myself.

I took that as a good sign and just let it be. Being able to shift my arm was a win for now, and I didn't need to paint a larger target on my back.

And I was more hesitant now than ever after hearing about the violent reputation. The last thing I needed was having the current king of dragons getting pissed; I was not ready to fight a dragon with hundreds or thousands of years of experience on me.

"Can you keep this quiet? I'm trusting you." I stared into Kelly's eyes, seeing my own slit eyes in their reflection.

"Yeah. But I get why you can't be our alpha now." She sagged. "Dragons have harems, and they don't share their women."

I nodded. "For what it is worth, I'm sorry. You and the other girls are lovely, and I was definitely tempted, but..." I gestured to myself. "Dragons don't share like a pack does."

Morgana's van pulled up as close as it could to the alley. Kelly and I quickly each grabbed a troll and threw them in the back. I climbed over the trunk into the back seat while Kelly went around and got in the passenger seat.

"Okay. Time to get rid of these two. Then back out for more." Morgana kicked the van into gear, and I could see the moment of panic in Kelly's eyes as she scrambled for her seatbelt and held onto the oh-shit handle for dear life.

***

I slumped into my seat in biology the next day. Even my lumpy, book-filled backpack seemed like a welcome pillow. Maybe I could just rest my eyes for a few seconds before class started…

"Psst. Class is starting," Jadelyn hissed in my ear.

I jumped up, blinking. "Huh?"

Jadelyn was sitting next to me, her signature white jeans blindingly bright along with her straight, platinum-blonde hair. It made her seem almost too immaculate, like she was untouchable. Then again, she was pretty much a modern-day princess.

"It looked like you could use a little rest. I saw a report this morning. Seven trolls last night. You helped more than a few paranormals too." She looked impressed, and I slid my bag to the floor, rubbing at a drool spot.

Something about how she said we'd helped several paranormals stuck out to me, though. I knew the butcher shop had been a vampire, but had the others been paranormal run businesses too? What were the odds of that?

I filed that away to think about later. Morgana could help me look into it.

"Thanks, I look forward to swamp troll migration being over and being able to sleep again," I grumbled, pulling out a notebook and clicking my pen to the ready. "But enough of that. Are you still good for our date tomorrow night?"

She gave me a winning smile. "Yes! Scarlett told me you made her life easier, and she's helping out. Truthfully, that she's involved makes me far more comfortable."

"Of course. Scar is your head of security."

Jadelyn regarded me with a searching look. "That isn't what I meant. It makes me more comfortable going out with her boyfriend."

Oh. OH!

"That too. I thought you would have known that Scarlett is pushing me to date other women." I lowered my voice on the last bit, still concerned with what the general population might think.

"She told me. But having her involved in planning our date means something. So, care to tell me where we are going? She wouldn't spill."

I smirked, and Professor Vandal cleared her throat. "Oh look, class is starting."

She jabbed me playfully with her pen. "You're lucky I need to pay attention to get good grades in science."

She opened up her own notebook, which was almost painfully organized. There were tabs carefully separating meticulously structured notes. Most of the tabs were business and finance classes, but there was a little heart next to biology.

Pretending I didn't see that, I focused on Professor Vandal as she started pacing up at the lectern and going through her lesson. Class was another lesson that felt redundant from high school, but that was about par for entry-level college courses.

As class wrapped up, Jadelyn gave me a friendly hug and an excited wave before promising to be there tomorrow.

As I walked out, I realized that for once I had some free time. With no plans for the afternoon, I decided to take a catnap before heading out with Morgana once again for swamp troll clean up.

***

With my new ability to partially shift, the trolls weren't nearly as much of a problem, and I could actually do something when Morgana told me to hold them down.

Though I still struggled to initiate it, my right arm came when I needed it. Kelly had said it would just be awkward partial shifts at first.

Throwing one of the most recent trolls into the back of the van, I shifted back. This time I was prepared with a pair of baggy sweatpants, and I had taken off my shirt beforehand.

"Morgana. What are the odds that this place is paranormal-owned?" I looked at the clothing store we were behind.

"Low. Paranormal makes up a very small fraction of the city despite our prevalence in your life recently," she replied easily.

"Jadelyn said something to me today. That last night, we helped a number of paranormals. It got me curious."

I could see the wheels turning in Morgana's head, but she replied, "Not our problem. Tell the council and they'll likely get Detective Fox to look into it. If he thinks it is a problem, then he'll hire us."

Based on the way she was now eyeing the business next to us, I had a feeling she would look into it on her own. I'd piqued her curiosity.

Not calling her on it, I moved over and nudged the troll into the trunk, making sure I didn't smash her foot with the lid. "Okay. We need to get ready for tomorrow, don't we?"

Morgana let out a grunt of acknowledgement. She was clearly oh-so-thrilled with the idea of spending more time with the magi. So much so, that I was worried we'd have a few dead magi before the end of the convention.

But I pushed on. "So. Anything I need to know before I dive into this convention?"

"Be careful of warlocks. They have a screw loose. All of them, if given the opportunity, would love to dissect and study you. So please, do not shift." She waited to make sure I acknowledged the request.

"Got it. Don't shift. Can I shift my eyes to see magic, though?"

She paused. "Sure. Just no arms. The gold scales give you away. The eyes should be finc. What else?" She tapped her lips.

"Can you explain warlocks a little more?"

"Wizards and witches train, sorcerers have natural talent, and warlocks are like someone who took out a loan on power, skill, or both. Which also means that warlocks can be forced into things to keep their magic because of this loan. I should say that not all of them are necessarily evil, but the way they gain and maintain power often opens up corruption." She paused with her hand on the van door. "Their patrons are powerful, often unique paranormals."

"Demons?" I asked.

"Demons, angelics, old forgotten deities, or even powerful Faeries."

These caught my attention. We hadn't dealt with many of these paranormals yet, and I had yet to see many of them.

"Are those all here in Philly?"

"No. Most of them live off plane. Heaven, Hell, pocket dimensions, and of course, the Faerie Realm. But there is a big connection between our dimension and the Faerie Realm here in Philly." She noticed my interest in that particular group.

"Got it. So they're a bunch of heavy hitters. What do they get in return for helping the warlocks cheat with magic?"

"A worker drone. They sort of translate that magi's intent into magic for the warlock and bolster the human's magic, and in return they have control and can get the magi to do what they want. It isn't like mind control, more like a geas."

"That sounds... terrible."

"Yeah, it's not ideal. The warlock knows what they are bargaining for, at least contractually, though application can get tricky, especially with the Faeries. There was this one deity that became popular a while back, Akhlut, that was popular among warlocks."

"Why is that?"

"He's an old god of the Inuit. Pretty much forgotten, but came from a simpler time. He just wanted small tributes in exchange for power." The way her lips curled up told me there was a punchline to this one.

"Fine, what was the tribute?"

"Socks." Morgana burst out laughing.

I didn't get it. "Socks?"

She nodded and got herself back under control. "He had magi doing small calling spells to steal individual socks from mortals because he didn't want pairs. Oh, and they had to be used."

Something clicked in my head. "Wait. Like these warlocks were stealing socks? Just single socks?!"

"Yep, as tributes to Akhlut, some of those warlocks stacked up quite a bit of favor and power. But not all patrons are so simple—most require much harder tributes."

I was still reeling from what she'd said and had to ask a clarifying question. "Do socks go missing in your dryer?"

"No?" She sounded confused. "There are wards on my bar. Most para have things like a simple ward to prevent unwanted spells and guests."

Getting in the car and leaning back, I couldn't believe it. "That the paranormal world doesn't have missing socks in the laundry might be the weirdest thing I've heard yet."

Morgana chuckled as she started the van. "Just wait until you hear about the hydra mating rituals."

CHAPTER 9

It was Saturday, the day of the convention, and I was ready for whatever trouble the magi would bring. Getting out of one of Morgana's nicer cars, it felt like a normal event.

Men in business suits and women dressed in a sensible level of wealth poured out of the parking garage alongside Morgana and me.

"What were you expecting? Pointy hats?" she asked, seeing my expression.

"Honestly? At least one pointy hat would be nice. Though, I do see a few robes."

There were a few attendees who either couldn't be bothered with decorum or wanted to stand out, fitting the more typical robed old man with a long beard stereotype. They seemed like the type that just was too old to give a shit.

I instantly liked them.

"Well, each and every person here has magic. It's an advantage over other mortals, so it's no wonder they end up more well off." She waved her hand vaguely at a group of suited up men drinking and showing off their expensive watches. "Human nature includes a strong portion of avarice. Paranormal aren't above it, but something about the shared threat that looms over us unites us when needed."

I wasn't quite sure how to take that; up until recently, I had considered myself human. But it was fair to say that there were several people I'd known who would quickly choose wealth over most anything else.

I did love my hoard, but I needed to be better than that.

The beast agreed, and a sense of wanting to punish those that harmed others washed over me. I struggled to call it justice, but to the beast, it was a sort of primal justice that made it feel proud.

"It's fine. We are just security, right?" I asked as Morgana skipped the line and showed her phone to the desk.

We were given a set of badges with yellow 'security' labeled down the side. Then they waved us through.

More than a few of the pompous magi gave us strange looks, and more than a few of the men watched Morgana's tight, leather-clad ass. My beast rose up again, wanting to fight, but I pushed him back down.

Morgana was our partner in this mercenary business, and she was the kind of woman that would make it known if she wanted something else. At least, that was my view on it. Morgana wasn't exactly subtle about most things.

If she had any interest, she'd let me know.

"Morgana!" An overly enthusiastic Jared came up, strutting in his gray suit with a subtle pink pinstripe.

I could sense the same charming perfume on him and gave a snort to clear it out of my nose.

Following him was a small group, but they didn't seem to give him much regard. I noted an older man just about as disgruntled with Jared as I was. There were two others, and based on the way the crowd parted around them, I knew they were highly regarded.

"Everyone, this is Morgana. She's here for security." He waved towards my partner, who was currently grumpy because she was weakened due to the daylight. But the small group lit up as Morgana was introduced.

"Professor McGregor," the old man stated, grabbing Morgana's hand with both of his own and shaking it forcefully. "A pleasure to meet you. Might we get a demonstration of spatial magic?"

"I'm here as security." She picked up her badge for emphasis. "Hopefully, my magic isn't needed."

He seemed disappointed and, unlike the others, had no problem showing it.

"Candice." The woman next to him paused before adding her last name, like it meant something. "Burnadesh."

It probably was somewhat well known in the paranormal world, but it meant nothing to me.

"Florita De Leon," the other woman introduced herself. She had an odd set of piercings that looked like they were made from real animal bones. There wasn't anything obvious, but something about her made my skin crawl.

"Again, just security. This is my partner, Zach," Morgana introduced me.

All of their eyes slid off of me as if I didn't matter. My pride wanted me to show them just how much they should respect and fear me, but I held it back. It was easier to just be security.

There was a commotion of excitement in the crowd of magi, everybody flocking to an area where it sounded like somebody had just arrived.

Morgana and I made our way closer in case we needed to calm the crowd, and I quickly saw what was causing the commotion.

The Paranormal Council had arrived.

Jadelyn, her father, and even Sebastian, were in attendance. Their guards, including the fox father-daughter duo, were trailing behind them.

What caught me completely off guard was a woman with green hair like summer grass and golden eyes like the summer sun. She blazed with so much mana that, even without my eyes shifted, I felt like I could see it radiating off of her.

Morgana leaned in. "That's the Summer Queen. Even the Faerie come out for the magi conference, mostly as a show of power to help keep them in line."

"It's November though, shouldn't it be the Winter Queen?" Even I knew about the legends of the fae and the courts of the seasons.

"You're partially right. Winter is in season, so she is currently ruling the Faerie realm. Her daughter rules the fall before her, just like the Summer Queen's daughter, the Spring Queen, does for her." Morgana gestured to a less prominent version of the Summer Queen, who was standing behind her. "The Summer and Spring queen have time to be here."

I remembered what I'd been told before; the Faerie were the third of the factions that ruled the council. Until now, they'd just been a name, almost a rumor. The power those two wielded made it clear why they could remain prominent without showing their faces.

Rupert, the patriarch of the Scalewright family, noticed us standing to the side and tossed me a scowl.

I took that to mean that he must know about my date with Jadelyn tonight. Now I had two disapproving fathers to deal with, and they were close. That boded well.

Where detective Fox looked like a disgruntled detective, Rupert was cut like a marble bust of Poseidon come to life. I had to admit it was a tad more intimidating than the detective, but that wouldn't deter me at all from pursuing Jadelyn.

Jadelyn perked up and pushed through the throng of magi that had come to rub elbows. "Zach."

"Didn't know you'd be here," I said as I felt the weight of dozens of eyes on me. Those that had just fawned over Morgana were trying to reevaluate me now that another of the more eligible paranormal females was talking to me.

Jadelyn gave me a broad smile. "I knew you'd be here."

The weight of the onlookers' gaze turned fiery hot as I went from interesting to competition. I knew that Jadelyn was now once again an eligible bachelorette, possibly the most influential one in the para world.

These magi and para around me had hopes of courting her. Too bad I had claimed her already.

My beast rose up, possessiveness spiking around the thought of these men desiring her, but I pushed it down. It wasn't the time.

"Then you have me at a disadvantage. I know pretty much no one here." My eyes drifted over to Scarlett, who was hanging back with a smirk.

Jadelyn grabbed my arm and pulled me along with her. "Then let me show you around. As a lost one whom I introduced to para society, I feel responsible that you understand the relationship between para and magi."

I let her pull me along, tossing a look back at Morgana, who only gave me a wink and a thumbs up. "Then lead on Jade. I am here working security though, so I might have to step away," I said.

"We could use the extra security anyway." Jadelyn smiled around at the crowd.

I nearly laughed at her statement. Not only was everyone in the paranormal group powerful in their own right, but the Summer Queen standing near me felt like a nuclear fission test about to go off. She radiated power at levels I hadn't felt before.

The Summer Queen noticed my attention and raised a green eyebrow in question. I wondered if I wasn't supposed to feel her power like I was. Focusing back on Jadelyn, I listened as magi came up to her.

No sooner had the group paused than Jared pushed his way forward, grabbing Jadelyn's hand and pulling it up in an old-world sort of handshake that felt like he was ready to kiss it.

"Well hello. You are even lovelier in person." His eyes shifted to me. "You just seem to be everywhere." His statement wasn't unpleasant, but there was a subtle undertone of warning within it.

Jadelyn was quick to respond. "You know Zach? He's amazing, isn't he? We are courting, and I think I might have found the one."

More than a few people nearby suddenly coughed, including her father.

"Courting?" Jared asked, surprised. "I thought you were Morgana's partner." He said it with a smirk, clearly believing he was about to expose my infidelity in front of everybody.

"She's my business partner, at least for now. Never know with my type; we are capable of loving many women." I shrugged helplessly.

There was a gap of silence that lingered before being broken by the giggling of the Spring Queen.

A young man stepped forward and pointed a stick at me. Doing a double take, I realized it was actually a wand.

"I challenge you to a duel for the right to court Princess Scalewright."

I couldn't help but notice the smug smile on Jared's face as he took a step back.

However, Jadelyn cleared her throat. "As he is my guest currently, I invoke my right to defend him."

"What?" I growled, not liking her stepping in front of me.

"Please?" Jadelyn looked into my eyes and Scarlett came to my other side.

"Take her up on it," she whispered in my ear. "She needs this."

I relented and nodded, taking a step back.

"Thank you. I'm sure you could handle this, but Scar warned me not to let you fight." The lovely siren patted me on the arm and stepped away from me. The entire crowd seemed to give the group space.

Scarlett looked a bit reluctant at Jadelyn fighting, but she clearly thought it was best. And she was probably right. I wasn't sure I could completely keep my shifting from happening, and having my arm shift would tell everybody what type of paranormal I was.

"You are new, a lost one?" A woman in a plain, white button down and tight pencil skirt asked as I joined the ring as it formed.

"Yeah, I'm a lost one. I stumbled into this about four months ago when I figured out I wasn't human. Is this a duel?"

She smirked. She was kind of cute, but in a very plain way that made her sort of forgettable. "Yes, it's one thing that both para and magi society could agree on. Duels are used to resolve conflicts. In this case, the conflict is over you."

I grumbled once more at the idea of someone else fighting my battles, and the beast agreed.

"I'm Zach." Holding out my hand, I introduced myself as Jadelyn squared up against the twerp with a crooked twig as a weapon.

"Sabrina. I'm new too, but to the magi." She blushed. "It's really hard to make friends when everyone has known each other since they were kids. I heard you were new and wanted to see if I could find someone to commiserate with."

I understood her struggles more than she knew. "Yeah, everyone is kind of set in their ways, aren't they?"

That earned me a smile. For some reason, I just felt comfortable about Sabrina.

She focused back on the fight. "She's about to kick his butt, isn't she?"

"Pretty sure. If not, I'll just tear him apart." I let out a low growl that rumbled in my chest.

She looked over at the two combatants. "His wand is far better done than the rest of his equipment," she commented.

I let my eyes shift to see both of them. Jadelyn was wrapped in blue mana, while the twerp was wrapped in a sticky, black fog. There was something about the black fog that felt familiar.

Since Sabrina seemed to be making herself comfortable, I decided to see what she knew about the duel and fighting. "So how do you think this is going to play out?"

"The guy has a decent stock of enchantments, but we have no idea what sort of spells he might have, or even what type of magus he is. Your girl is a siren, everybody knows that. She'll cast like a water sorcerer." Sabrina tried to work out how the battle would unfold.

I had to admit, I was a bit excited. I knew Jadelyn had magic, Scarlett had told me that, but I'd never seen her in a fight. She was just so above everything else in life, an untouchable princess, that I hadn't even considered her training to fight.

But, based on the way Jadelyn squared her feet and loosened her arms, she'd had training.

"Fair enough. I'm biased, but Jadelyn looks like she knows what she's doing. The guy has some unknowns, but I don't see her losing."

There was one thing nagging at me, though. It had all unfolded so quickly that it didn't feel entirely natural. And if it was a setup, then the twerp might just be prepared to fight Jadelyn.

"I think you are right. Not that much will come of this; if it goes too far, someone will step in," Sabrina agreed. "But it should still be an exciting duel to watch."

Snorting, I didn't think she understood just how dangerous a duel could become. "Is that how magi duels work? Because para duels end in death."

"No! Really?" Sabrina gasped. "There's no way anyone here is going to let harm come to the heir of the Scalewright clan. Even I know who she is."

Sabrina seemed genuine, but I wondered if it was the perfect time for someone to attack her. An accident during the duel would be a blow to her father and their clan. As big as their business empire was, they had to have a host of enemies.

I watched the two fighters circle each other. I expected Jadelyn to wait for him to make a move, but she let out a clear note. Suddenly, it was like a fog bank had rolled. Our knees were quickly hidden beneath a dense, wet mist. Scales dotted her neck and shoulders, even creeping up at the edge of her jaw.

"Oh, she's taking control of the field," Sabrina commented. Seeing my confusion, she continued explaining, "She has sorcery of water, but it's not that great when fighting on dry land. She could probably pop some water lines around us, but instead, she just spelled in a fog bank to give her some water and moisture to work with. It's super smart."

The magus jerked his hands forward and shouted something guttural, causing the fog to part around his hands. Casting, I watched as he shot two bursts of wind towards Jadelyn.

Luckily, she seemed capable of handling the attack. She lifted her left arm, and a shield, similar to the one she'd given me before my duel with Simon, came out of a bracelet on her arm.

After dispelling the wind attack, Jadelyn sang a note while swaying her right hand like she was conducting an orchestra. Three arrows of water formed before firing forward like they were launched from a high-pressure hose.

The magus fumbled but managed to shout and blast the three arrows with a jet of fire that reduced them to steam and robbed their momentum.

"People always underestimate water," Sabrina said. "They forget just how powerful it is."

I looked at what she meant, seeing Jadelyn forming three more arrows and firing them again, only this time one at a time.

The wizard had to defend not against a single attack, but one spell spaced such that he had to cast three more jets of fire.

"She's going to wear him down like that," I realized.

Sabrina nodded with excited eyes. "Pretty, established and powerful. You have a winner there."

I felt pride prickle in my chest as my beast tried to claim her. But I tried to settle him once more. We hadn't even gone on a date yet. Although, I was getting the distinct feeling that he wouldn't let me subdue him much longer.

"We'll see tonight how we are together. It is actually our first date," I replied to Sabrina, ignoring the battle with the beast.

"Oh!" she replied. "Well, I hope you woo her. That father of hers looks like he hates you right about now, though."

Over on the other side of the duel, Rupert had a neutral, stony expression. But from time to time, he'd look away from the fight and over in my direction; I couldn't miss the anger he had towards me.

No doubt in his mind, I was to blame for her currently being embroiled in a fight.

But, from what I'd seen so far, Jadelyn could handle herself. She currently had the wizard pinned down with a steady stream of water arrows.

As the magus became more frustrated, the wand Sabrina had mentioned before came into play. He flicked it forward and black lightning raced out of the wand.

A hand caught me even as I was trying to take a step forward. "She's got it."

The mist sank inward, capturing the black lightning in a bubble. The spell writhed and crackled as the energy of the spell bled out of the bubble slowly.

Jadelyn let the bubble hover before she pushed it at the wizard.

"I surrender," he yelled, watching the bubble with terrified eyes.

"Oh, you don't even want to see what kind of magic you tried to use on me?" There was a cold anger in Jadelyn's eyes. If that spell was half as dangerous as it looked and had hit its target, I might not have had a date tonight.

To use something so lethal against her had been an attempted execution, but Jadelyn simply hovered the bubble in front of him. "Someone apprehend him. I want to know where he got that wand," she commanded.

The wizard went from backing up slowly to pausing, something seeming to light up in his eyes and his face becoming horror struck.

"No, please, I don't want to die." He yelled a bit more before he threw himself into the bubble. The black lightning tore at his body, wrapping itself around him as he screamed and disintegrated before our eyes.

Sabrina hissed beside me. "That did not turn out like I expected."

"No. I think that went rather poorly." Scarlett corralled Jadelyn along with several other of her shadows and cordoned her off from everyone else. My girlfriend caught me watching and gave me a smile and a nonchalant wave, like this was just another day at work for her.

I realized that it actually might be. The two of them had kept Jadelyn's life out of mine. Someone coming to attack her, then committing suicide, could be typical for them, but I sure as hell wasn't used to it yet.

CHAPTER 10

Watching Jadelyn duel, I struggled to stand by and do nothing.

Jadelyn's life had been in danger and the protective part of me that was my dragon was in a fury that I had stood by and just allowed it to happen. It didn't make sense to be so protective already. We hadn't even gone on our first date, yet I found myself struggling not to rip someone's head off seeing her in danger.

"You okay?" Sabrina asked.

"I think so. Just need to calm down. Watching that did some things to me."

Sabrina grabbed my arm and pulled me so that I wasn't blocking the flow of traffic. "It's hard when we watch someone we love fight."

"I don't—" I paused. There were certain feelings between Jadelyn and me, but l-o-v-e was an extreme. Although, my reaction was stronger than just some crush. I wasn't sure what I'd call it.

Sabrina smirked. "Come on. They dragged her to the opening ceremony, which is now about to start. It'll take your mind off it."

I grunted and let Sabrina pull me along. "I'm working security."

"Uh huh? Do you have a post you are leaving?"

"No?" We hadn't been given any formal instructions. It seemed like they were leaving it up to our judgement. Or rather, we were an afterthought.

"Then come do security over here. You can stand at the back and be just as broody there as anywhere else. I'm sure no one will cause trouble with your grumpy face." She laughed.

I paused, and Sabrina was jerked back when I planted my feet. "Why are you doing this?"

"Trying to make a friend," she answered, her laughter dying as her face turned serious. "I wasn't joking when I said it was hard being new to the magi."

Nodding, I started up again, dragging her along. "Okay, I guess I could use some friends too. Being the new para wasn't easy, not until Morgana took me under her wing. I get it."

"What kind of para are you?"

I gasped in mock horror. "Did you really just ask me that?"

Her face turned red instantly. "Sorry! I didn't know I wasn't supposed to ask."

Laughing, I nodded at the booths by the entrance of the area and picked up a pamphlet. "I do need to operate as security, or I won't feel right. They paid me to work here."

"That's fine. I'll sit in the back by the edge here."

We made our way to the far-right corner of the space. It was a large gathering hall, filled with cheap plastic chairs. The crowd seemed to be flooding its way in as two magi worked at the front to get the microphone at the podium and a projector up and running.

"Please, fill in towards the front. Plenty of seats up front!" an announcer was calling out.

Sabrina found a seat towards the back, and I positioned myself up against the wall, crossing my arms and generally looking threatening.

Across the way, I could see Scarlett's bright hair and the very distinct green hair of the Spring and Summer Faerie Queens up front and center.

Once the crowd had largely filled in and there was just a trickle of remaining attendees, Jared, along with the old wizard and a young witch, stepped onto the stage.

I shifted my eyes, wanting to be able to be alert. Based on what I could see, the young witch appeared to be an old woman covered by an illusion.

The old wizard stepped forward, bumping the microphone and getting everyone's attention. "We welcome everyone here to the two hundred and thirty-fifth gathering of the Order of the Magi. Wards are up to keep those who don't know our secret out, so feel free to openly discuss your gifts within these walls! It's such a cherished time for us to come together and share our knowledge; I encourage you to take advantage of it."

He cleared his throat. "Let's get the boring stuff out of the way."

The PowerPoint moved to the next slide, and I snickered. For a big, bad group of magi, this seemed oddly mundane.

"For legal purposes and potential feuds, the OTM does not sponsor any spell craft that may be learned here at the conference. We must all do our due diligence before using magic. OTM does not sponsor nor promote any particular entity for pacts, though information about them may be available at related booths..."

He droned on through a number of legal platitudes, covering his and the organization in the case that someone had an accident related to the information disseminated at the conference.

It felt typical, like I was in a corporate affair. But it made sense; the magi were people and likely had their own lawsuits and grudges.

"Now, for those who might be attending for the first time, we welcome you. We will begin as we always do by honoring our history." The old wizard stepped back, and the witch, Florita, stepped forward. Unlike the wizard, she had a haphazard number of small charms dangling from her person.

"We the magi draw our lines back to the days of old, when paranormal creatures walked the world unobstructed by global news and cameras at every corner." Her eyes slid happily to the council's group.

The slide shifted to an image of a dragon. "Praise to the dragons who shared their knowledge with our ancestors and gave humans magic. The dragons watch over us." She bowed her head in reverence.

I was startled at that last part, looking around at all the somber faces as the entire crowd nodded, bowing their heads and repeating after her. Only the paranormal remained quiet.

They were literally worshiping the dragons.

"For those who haven't studied the ecology of magic in our world, dragons pump the very source of magic into our world. As such, they are sacred. Praise be to dragons, for they not only gave us magic, but they continue to sustain our ability to perform it."

The crowd murmured 'praise be to dragons' and nodded along. Even Sabrina was following, and for some reason, a chill went through me watching it.

Caught between my surprise at their reverence and my swirling thoughts on dragons, I lost track of what they were saying as the witch led them through a small history lesson. I was pulled back into the moment as she stepped back and the crowd went quiet.

Jared came forward then, putting his hands on the top of the podium leaning into the microphone. "Now that our history is done, what about the future?!" He asked the question with enough excitement to energize the crowd.

"Magi are a force to be reckoned with in the world. There is so much we can give back to our communities. So much we can achieve. We can use magic to help heal the world!"

A loud throat clearing caused him to pause, pulling the whole room into silence.

The Summer Queen spoke, "While maintaining secrecy, of course."

He echoed her. "Of course. But still, so much can be done, hidden under the guise of technology."

I didn't have to see the paranormal groups' faces to know they weren't fans of this idea. There was a palpable tension in the room as he continued his speech full of vague messages of hope for what magic could do. It was meant to be inspirational, but it might have just put a target on his back with the council.

The session wrapped up, the crowd sufficiently energized.

Jadelyn and the others were immediately mobbed as soon as it ended, and I wondered just how bad that would be if they all knew what I was. Shuddering at the thought, I moved on.

"Want to hang out for the rest of this?" Sabrina asked, coming back over to my side.

"Sure." It wasn't like I had a better plan than wandering the convention. "So what was that about dragons? You guys worship them?"

She wrinkled her nose. "Lots of lip service mostly, not a lot of action. But dragons did give humans their first experiences with magic. Every influential family has a story about their great great great grand-pappy having been taught magic by some dragon."

"Why though?" I frowned. I wondered why the dragons would take the time to give magic to humans.

"To defend their land? Maybe use the human mages to make gold? I don't know; I'm not a dragon." She emphasized the end like it was the most absurd concept, and it was everything I could do not to smirk.

But, based on the way she talked about what the dragons taught them, it sounded more like someone teaching their pet rat a trick rather than really imparting knowledge. Dragons no doubt treated humans like pests running about, especially if they didn't have much in the way of weapons back then.

"Ever heard of a family taught by a gold dragon?" I fished, wondering if I could glean any insight about my potential family from their lore. Although, I wasn't positive that color was hereditary, but it would make sense.

She shook her head. "Not that I'm aware of. I feel like someone would be shouting it from the top of the convention if they were trained by a gold."

"That big of a deal?"

She scoffed. "Yeah. Golds and reds are the top dogs of the dragon lore. But I haven't heard of any of them in real life. There's less than thirty dragons in existence, and only a few of them are commonly known."

"The bronze in Dubai," I agreed, having heard of him from Morgana.

"Yep, in one of my mentor's books, they say it is because of him that we even have a rough estimate of how many there are."

Our conversation was interrupted as a hooded man with a pentagram shoved a pamphlet into my hands as we strolled by. "Ozak the black is looking for new warlocks. It's far easier than studying, and you can tap more power than a sorcerer."

I brushed him off, but I looked at the pamphlet. "Holy shit. This is a demon, and he's recruiting warlocks with pamphlets? How is this okay?"

Turning it over, I saw a contract of sorts written out in fine print right next to a picture of a happy man surrounded by wealth. I nearly laughed aloud at how the clause about potential for accidental death was right next to the gleeful image like the fast speech warnings after a drug commercial.

Sabrina spoke like an old man, "You youngins have no respect for the way we used to do things. Phones have ruined all the young magi. You just buy things without looking because you want them now." She spoke normally, "He blames consumerism and instant gratification on people turning into warlocks. But I want to learn the actual magic theory from him. The right way."

It made me laugh. "That's your mentor's take on it?"

"Yeah. He's a crotchety one."

"Mine too," I threw out, thinking of Morgana's insistent need to push me.

"Excuse me?" Morgana cleared her throat. I paused in my step. Of course, she happened to be around at that moment and her pointy blue ears picked up our conversation.

Sabrina's jaw dropped as I felt Morgana lean against my side. "M-Morgana?!"

"The one and only." She did a bow and added a small flourish, enjoying the attention.

Looking around, I realized most people were staring at her as they passed, and there seemed to be a small fan club hanging in the wings. A few were taking selfies with her in the background.

"Oh my gosh. I've read the accounts of the battle of Bastov." Sabrina's eyes were wide as she stared at Morgana.

I turned to my partner. "What's the battle of Bastov?"

She waved it away. "That was four hundred years ago, and I was a baby vampire with a grudge. I had a mean streak back then." She raised her eyebrow as she said, 'back then,' daring me to challenge that she still did.

Sabrina nearly choked. "Mean streak? You snuck out of a besieged city and killed hundreds, leading to a break in the siege. Some of the accounts say that was one of the first steps in pushing back the Church's crusade across Europe."

Morgana shrugged. "They had it coming. Don't let the Church fool you. Several hundred years ago, they were more militant than petty tyrants. It was either believe or die."

I still hadn't gotten the scope of what happened back in the 18th century. Morgana had been there and apparently was turned during what became a bloody war between the Church and the paranormal.

"You know, I still don't know much about that time period."

"Boring war. It's always the same. Two sides fight, thousands upon thousands of the less fortunate die, all just because of the two dick bags that started it. The end." Morgana gave me a level stare that told me to drop the conversation.

She really hated to talk about that part of her past with me. I wasn't sure if she was trying to hide something from me or just not relive it. Could it really be that gruesome?

"But how did you get tangled up in it? Don't drow live underground?"

"Inside mountains," she clarified.

Sabrina was more than happy to pick up and add some details. "Her people stayed behind thinking they were safe, but they were smoked out by the Church's forces. Morgana fled and was turned, only to become a hero for the paranormal."

Morgana leaned in close to Sabrina. "I fled and sought help only to be turned into a tool or an abomination, depending on who's talking."

I already knew about how she was caught between the elves and the vampires. Elves refused to believe that they could be turned, so in their warped logic, that held true if they claimed she wasn't an elf. Vampires, on the other hand, wanted to raise her up to snub the elves.

A complicated situation, to say the least. One that I knew was best to avoid. "So how about these warlocks, Sabrina? Any of them like to wear skinsuits."

Morgana gave me a look that told me it wasn't the smoothest transition in the world, but I was curious. And it got us off the sensitive topic.

"Eww. No. Skinsuits?"

I pulled out my phone and opened up an email from Detective Fox. "Like this."

She gagged a bit as she saw the photo. "Oh my. That's... disgusting. Was someone in that?" She looked away from the picture.

"That's the theory. Morgana and I take on work among the paranormal community, and this showed up when we were taking down a corrupt group."

Scrunching her face together, Sabrina seemed to toughen her resolve before looking back at the photo. "That's bad stuff. If you send it to me, I can talk to my mentor?"

Morgana stepped in. "Do you think he'll have an answer soon?"

Sabrina waved her hand around her. "He's here somewhere. I'm sure I'll find him at the closest pub once this is done. He's probably in some back room smoking and talking with a bunch of other old men."

"I'd love at least something to go on." I included the image in a message and handed my phone to Sabrina. "The mess that they caused killed dozens and then stranded two wolf packs."

She took the phone but kept her eyes on me. "This thing killed two wolf packs?"

"No. It manipulated an alpha into doing it," I clarified.

"Oh." She looked down and after a moment of hesitation, started typing, ending with the little sending whoosh before handing it back. "I'm not going to get roped into anything dangerous, am I?"

Taking my phone back, I gave her my best reassuring smile. "No, we'll take care of any information that comes from this. But given you're asking around about a killer, probably best to only ask people that you trust?"

She opened her mouth to argue and then thought better of that idea. "That makes perfect sense. I'm just going to show this to my mentor and see what he says."

Somebody new stepped in front of us. Taking him in, my guess was he was another warlock.

"Maxakeen the Pink invites you to explore the pleasures of her patronage." He shoved a pamphlet in my hands that Morgana promptly plucked out.

"Oh look, Zach, this one is a succubus. Right up your alley. Maybe you should think about it" Morgana teased.

I snatched it out of her hands only to see succubus porn on the inside folds. My eyes widened, and I had trouble looking away. But it was more out of curiosity than lust. I promise.

"See, that really does interest you."

Sabrina took the pamphlet from me and tossed it into the trash. "Don't bother. They all want something, even if it is years down the road or seemingly minor." Her cheeks were flushed, and I had a feeling she'd gotten a glimpse of some of the images inside.

"Or they just want his seed. His copious amounts. Did you know his girlfriend has been taking tinctures to heal herself down there because Zach here is so vigorous? She even is trying to get another girlfriend for him who can share the load with her. Who knows, maybe a succubus could really take the edge off Zach," Morgana teased me, watching Sabrina's reaction.

Sure enough, Sabrina's ears were blazing bright red. "You have multiple girlfriends?"

"Just one at the moment," I scowled at Morgana. "But yes, I am also starting to pursue Jadelyn."

Sabrina covered her mouth before uncovering it just a little to whisper. "You have a... harem?"

"Yes, he does, darling. His girlfriend is in desperate need of help," Morgana teased.

Sabrina stood there, flustered for a moment, before she just turned and bolted.

I sighed, watching her go, before turning back to Morgana. "Happy now?"

She gave me her toothy vampire grin. "Very."

"Well, don't go scaring all my new friends away. My love life is none of your business. Unless you're offering to get involved?"

Sabrina had been plain and immediately in the friend zone. I had been hoping she would be someone I could commiserate with about normies and not make it sexual. Morgana just had to stick her nose into it and make it weird.

"Don't offer what you aren't willing to put up." Morgana arched one of her silver eyebrows and smirked.

"Oh, stop being such a damn tease, Morgana." I swatted her away. "I was making a friend, and you scared her off."

Morgana just kept smiling. "Oh, I'm almost positive she'll be back."

But she didn't come back for the rest of the convention. I spent the remainder of the conference patrolling the place, looking intimidating. It was some of the easiest money I'd ever made.

A few times as we walked around, some young woman would get the nerve to walk up and try to talk to Morgana. When she didn't outright kill them, there'd usually be a mini stampede, and it would take forever to get moving again.

I listened to all they called out and said, learning more about her. Based on the crowd, she had a reputation of being both a bloodthirsty monster and also a badass role model for young women.

How exactly those two paired together was beyond me. Maybe if Sabrina came back, she'd lend me the book she had read about Morgana's battle.

CHAPTER 11

I pulled up to the sorority house in one of Morgana's BMWs and shot Jadelyn a text. As soon as I hit send, she popped out of the house.

Smirking, I knew that meant she'd been eager and waiting for me. Behind her, the door was filled with her sorority sisters, all gawking and gossiping.

I got out and gave Jadelyn a hug and a peck on the cheek before walking her around to the passenger side and opening it for her.

"Thank you."

"Just giving those girls something extra to gossip about."

She blushed and scooted into the seat. "Yes. Although I'm not sure opening the car door is going to make many headlines once they recognize you as Scarlett's boyfriend." She sighed.

I got a good look at her as I got back behind the wheel. As usual, Jadelyn looked almost as if she'd been carefully sculpted and then freshly dressed by a tailor. Every-thing fit perfectly as she stretched out her long legs in the car and gave me a sultry look for my inspection.

"Like what you see?"

"I do." Squeezing her thigh first, I moved my hand to the gearshift and shifted into reverse, heading out of Greek Row.

As I drove, I couldn't help but notice her boots were spotless, like they might have never seen a hiking trail before. "When was the last time you were on a hike?"

She watched me rather than the road. "I wasn't always so busy. Back when me and Scar were kids, we spent a lot of time to-gether. That meant we went through the same early survival and combat lessons."

"Oh. You fight?"

"No. Not anymore. When I came into my magic, that became the focus, along with learning the family business. I'm afraid those combat lessons have been lost for the most part." She said the last part with a sad note to her voice, like she often did when referring to her family obligations.

"You did great in that duel today. Did Scar manage to find anything on why?" I asked.

Jadelyn shrugged. "Suspicion that he was a warlock. Not much else. But let's ditch that topic. I want to know about the man in the car with me."

As I turned, I saw two black SUVs pull out with me. Scarlett waved from the driver's seat of one of them before she leaned over the wheel and gunned it around me, leading the way.

"Not much to tell. I led a pretty basic human life before all this, but I'm an open book. Ask away."

She grinned mischievously. "Is what Scarlett said true? Twenty-nine?"

"Twenty— oh." I realized what she was talking about and sighed, deciding this was where she could tell if I was going to be completely open with her. "If I'm honest, twenty-nine didn't even wear me out. We only stopped there because I didn't want to hurt Scarlett."

Jadelyn rubbed her legs together as she squirmed in the seat. "So, you know I was engaged. Sirens are a little different when it comes to relationships."

I worked to keep my face on the road and not look at her, but she definitely had my attention. I was kicking myself for not asking Morgana or Scarlett more about sirens.

"Tell me more. Last thing I want to do is make a misstep in the courtship of my favorite siren."

There was a pause as she looked away. "I have no experience. None whatsoever."

I paused. That was definitely not what I was expecting. Realizing she was holding her breath, waiting for me to respond, I quickly added, "That's perfectly fine, Jade. I didn't have much experience before Scarlett."

"No, it's more than that. It is a siren thing. Our virginity is important." She turned back, her face still flush. "It ties in with our song. We form a bond with our first."

"Oh. Like..." I struggled to come up with any comparison.

She laughed. "There isn't really anything like it. We call it a siren's wedding when she sings a man into the ocean. Because after that, she's committed to the man."

My brain swirled as I processed that. "So you are only ever going to be with one guy?"

A hand squeezed my thigh, and I took a glance from the road. Her face was serious and her eyes sincere. "Yes. And that's why I really have to thank you for handling the Chad situation. My dad was pushing that one and... I'm glad that I'm not stuck with him."

"You're welcome."

"No. Not just a 'you're welcome'. What you did was amazing. Not everyone would go to those lengths; a wolf pack alpha isn't something most want to deal with."

The beast rose up in my chest, declaring that it was our job to take care of things like that. This was our territory.

"You're growling." She patted my leg, looking me over carefully. "Scarlett still won't tell me what you are, you know."

Scratching the back of my head, I pulled onto the off ramp and headed for the park.

"Yeah," I blew a breath out. Telling her was hard. "I want to tell you, but it will change things."

"Scar gave whatever it is the 'all clear'. Even told our dads to cool it."

"Really?" I hadn't known she'd done that. I hadn't even known that their dads were asking about me.

"Yep. Threatened her dad in front of mine. Something like 'once what he is comes out you are going to regret giving him a hard time'." Jadelyn gave me a big grin. "So I'm pretty curious myself."

"Unless they do something terrible, it's not like I'll cause trouble. They're the fathers of two of my favorite women." I pulled into a parking spot. "We're here!"

My paranormal identity was a crisis I wasn't yet ready to take on. From learning what Scarlett and Morgana had told me about dragons to seeing them literally worshiped at the magi conference, I definitely wanted to keep my identity as a dragon on the down low.

And I also wanted a chance to get to know Jadelyn and feel a connection before I told her. I needed to know that she was with me

for me and not because I was some powerful creature.

I reached to open the door and hop out.

"Hold up. Wait for someone to give us the
signal." Jadelyn didn't make a move to get
out and instead stared out the window.

In a few moments, a man in a suit listened
to his earpiece before giving us the okay.

"Is it always like that?" I asked.

"Sort of. Places like our home, Morgana's atrium, and the council meetings
are pre-secured, so there isn't the hassle
of guards. You probably don't notice them,
but I always have two shadows on campus,
and there's a team watching the sorority
house."

She talked about having a constant sur-
veillance team and a security detail like it
was a decision between which cereal for
breakfast. Clearly growing up that way, she
didn't know any different, but it seemed
stifling.

"I'll be honest with you." I closed the car
door and hurried around to help her out.
"That isn't something I can relate to. If we
start dating, will I have to do something
with them?"

Jadelyn paused, her winter coat rubbing
as she brought her hand up to her chin in
thought. "Not sure. Your place in the Atrium is about as safe as it can get. I might
not be able to spend much time at your

apartment, though, without a lot of extra hassle."

I shrugged and took her hand, pulling her down the path. "I don't spend much time there anyway. The place Morgana gave me is pretty sweet."

Jadelyn gave me a serious side eye look. "You have no idea how expensive that place is, do you?"

"No? Morgana made the space, right? So it is just a bit of work for her."

She stopped and gave me an exasperated look. "For her to even connect a place to the Atrium, we are paying her millions. Not only is her creating a place for you connected to her space more than just 'a bit of work', it is exorbitantly expensive. Even with my wealth, I would hesitate to spend that kind of money."

"Oh." I hadn't even considered that it was a big deal that she'd set up the space for me.

But the part that surprised me most was that she'd given me the room after a few days of knowing and training me. "How long would it typically take her?"

"Weeks? Months? I'm not sure. She made a big deal of it the few times she made things for us."

Surprised, the wheels started turning in my head, but I filed it away and decided to focus on Jadelyn and our date. "Guess she just takes being my mentor that seriously.

But enough about her. I'm more interested in the beautiful siren walking with me in the woods. I've met your father. What's your mother like?"

We kept on walking. "Supportive. Always there helping my father in the background, making sure I had everything I needed. She doesn't leave the house often, but she's very much a part of home, you know?"

Then she paused and winced. "Shit. You didn't know your parents. I'm sorry, that was insensitive."

I brushed it off. I had gotten used to the fact that many others had a more standard childhood. "It sucks for sure. But I was raised by an older couple, and I get what you mean. When I'd come home to my mom baking cookies, I was always filled with a warm, gooey feeling."

"Exactly." Jadelyn recovered. "Always cooking or doing something to make home better."

"Sounds like a great mom." My eyes tracked a homeless man on a nearby bench. He was covered in rags and his hat was hiding his face. I gave Jadelyn a questioning look.

She waited until we were a little further away. "The security team is going to try and be as unobtrusive as possible. He seems harmless, and I trust them."

"Far be it from me to make a decision for them," I said, but something about the homeless man had been like an itch. It kept nagging me as we walked.

The trail pitched into a steep incline just ahead, and we both had to lean forward as we walked, stopping the conversation as we focused on the trail. It was warm for this late in November, but I found the cool air and the crunch of fallen leaves refreshing on our hike.

I only caught her security detail twice during the hike. They hung back, giving us privacy yet clearly working to make sure Jadelyn was safe. I couldn't blame them after the duel earlier in the day.

It wasn't until the hill leveled back out and the trail swung around the hill that we started to get a great view.

"Beautiful." Jadelyn breathed in deeply, taking in the view.

From the hillside, the sun was still hanging in the sky, but it was low enough that it was starting to be tinted dark orange. We only had an hour of light left.

"There's something serene about a nice view on a hike." I wrapped an arm around her. "Maybe because you work for it, but they are just a little more special."

"I like this one." She leaned her head against my shoulder and relaxed. "But it's special for other reasons."

Giving her a quick squeeze, I let go. "Come on. The spot we're going to isn't far from here."

"More than just a hike?" she teased.

"Dinner too." I grabbed her hand and pulled her along. It wasn't that much further around the bend until we came upon the little viewing platform. There was a small fire pit and a couple of benches around it.

Most importantly, Scarlett had gotten the milk crate I'd given her here.

"Tada. Your table is ready." I made a big sweeping gesture.

"Thank you." Jadelyn took my hand as I made about as much pomp and ceremony as I could before depositing her on the bench next to the crate. "What do we have here?" She picked at the contents, taking out the tin foil and holding up a bag of frozen burger patties.

"Dinner." The firewood was already stacked. I just needed the matches. But as I dug around in the crate, I came up empty. "It looks like we might have lost the matches."

"It's fine. We can get one from the security team; they might have a lighter."

"Oh, no. I think instead I'll show you a little secret," I teased, stepping over by the fire pit.

She didn't answer, instead leaning her chin on her palm to watch.

Thankfully, while I might have been having trouble with shifting, my fire breath was well under control. Cupping my hands around my mouth, I blew out a small stream of fire right into the center of the pit, which roared to life as the dry wood caught quickly.

It was dragon fire, after all.

Jadelyn leaned back and clapped excitedly. "Ooh. Fun trick."

"Thanks. Now for the main course." Pulling out several plastic containers with carrots, potatoes, onions and mushrooms, I placed them in front of Jadelyn and pulled out two peelers. "Care to join me in the excitement that is hobo dinners?"

She took one of the peelers with a gleeful smile. "How do we do this?"

"Well, just take what's in the plastic container and peel it back into the container. I washed the vegetables before I gave them to Scarlett. And then we'll cook them." I started with the mushrooms, which were the hardest, letting Jadelyn take the potatoes.

"Easy enough." She started to peel the potato while poking around in the crate. "Mmm s'mores."

"Don't ruin all my surprises," I teased. "This isn't too rustic for you, is it?"

"Not at all. It's nice. Very different from dates I've been on before. Those were always nice dinners and exclusive clubs." She looked a little lost in the fire as she talked about her past dates. "You know when we first met, and Simon said those things about me—"

I put a hand up to stop her. What that pompous elf had said wouldn't have hurt her back then if it didn't have a grain of truth. He'd insinuated that she was just her father's whore, essentially being used for her potential marriage to lure in allies. But I didn't see her that way at all.

"Don't worry about it. I'm glad I was able to win the duel with him and keep your honor intact." I winked at her.

She smiled as she went back to peeling. "Thanks. You know, you startled a lot of the council with that duel."

"They can be as startled as they want. Doesn't mean much to me."

"Not many would say that. They can make almost any para's life a living hell if they want to. I have a feeling that, if Morgana wasn't protecting you, the elves would be harassing you right now."

I just grinned. "They may regret that in the long run anyway. I welcome them to try."

She shook her head in disbelief, and we settled into a comfortable silence as we filled up the plastic containers full of peeled veggies.

I got to the onion and looked at the peeler skeptically. Thinking of the fire, I concentrated on my finger, turning it into a razor-sharp claw and carefully cutting the onion in half.

"Are you trying to give me clues?" She looked at the claw. "Also, that's incredibly sharp. It looks like one of those knife sale videos."

"Just getting used to what I am and what I can do." I used my claw to quickly tear the onion apart. It wasn't pretty little cuts, but then again, we were making hobo dinners and everything else was peeled.

"Okay, now the fun part." I took out the foil and laid it down beside me on the bench, measuring out a square. But then I remembered how much I'd been eating and doubled the size from what I'd done before I knew I was para. "You don't have to make yours this big. I just eat a lot."

Jadelyn laughed and made her much smaller foil square. "I'm guessing we add the food?"

"Yep. Break up one or two patties for some meat. Don't forget the onions, they are critical. Otherwise, everything ends up chewy."

"Yes, chef," she teased, sprinkling in her own ingredients before pulling the ketchup and mustard out of the crate and adding a small dollop in her foil.

"You can't overdo the ketchup. Here." I took the bottle and hosed down my own dinner as an example before moving on and doing the same with mustard. Wrapping up my foil and doing my best to keep it as flat as I could, I then helped Jadelyn with hers and stuck them both deep into the fire before sitting back down.

"That was fun. I've never made something like that before." She took the opportunity to lean against me again.

Next to the fire, I was feeling a little warm with my coat on. Taking it off, Jadelyn joined me, and we draped them over our shared backs. Getting closer to Jade was a pleasant bonus.

Cuddled up and enjoying the warmth of each other as the fire crackled, we watched the warm sunset.

"Things like this are nice from time to time," Jadelyn broke the comfortable silence. "I don't often get the opportunity to just relax."

"Is it always so busy?"

She leaned back against the bench, pulling me with her. "Busy, but not bad. Dad and the company take a lot of my time. It often seems like there's really not any time for myself."

She sighed before continuing, "Then there are things like Chad and all he took out of me to make things work between us. So far you are different, though; you give me something like this and I recharge here with you."

I nodded along with her, although I couldn't really understand. She was an heiress being prepped to handle a multi-billion-dollar shipping company on top of everything else a woman her age dealt with.

It couldn't be easy. All I could do was just be there and do my best to support her. "I'm here if you ever need me. You just need to tell me what I can do to help."

She turned to me, completely dumbfounded by my response. "What you can do?" She repeated it, processing the words as if it was completely outside her expectations.

Strange how a sincere offer to help could make her stumble.

"Yep. I just want to help. And honestly, you probably know better than I do how I can accomplish that."

Jadelyn relaxed, and her eyes widened as she processed that. This might have been the most surprising part of the date so far for her. "I don't know. But just knowing that you put that out there means a lot." She turned to face me to make sure it really sank in. "Thank you."

I kissed her on the cheek and continued to enjoy the sunset with her. Our hobo dinners added to the ambiance, the juices trying to escape from the foil and filling the air with delicious aromas.

Even Jadelyn was sniffing the air. "I didn't expect them to smell so good."

I laughed. "What were you expecting?"

She shrugged. "Honestly? With burger patties and roots, I figured it would be bland."

I did my best to look offended.

Jade just laughed and smacked me on the shoulder in response. "I'm sure they are going to taste great."

"Just wait. Hobo dinners have something special to them," I assured her. "There's something about being cooked over a real campfire that brings out the flavors."

She smiled, nuzzling in closer. "Where'd you learn to cook like this?"

"My father had a penchant for spending time outdoors. Though if I'm honest, I'm mostly a city boy at heart."

Jadelyn laughed. "You might as well be a wilderness survival expert compared to me."

One of the dinners started to leak and the sound of sizzling filled the air. I got up and headed closer to them.

"Are they done yet?"

"You sound like the eager kid at the camp-fire. Not yet—they need a bit more time." I used a stick to curl the corner back closed.

She pulled me back to the bench after I was done checking on them. "I'm eager to try something new, and something cooked by you."

A grin plastered itself on my face as I leaned forward. "Why don't we do something then to pass the time?"

"Oh yeah? How should we do that?" She smiled and tilted her face to mine. I couldn't help but stare at her pink lips as she closed her eyes and gave me all the permission I needed.

Wrapping my arms around the back of her neck, I pulled her close, and we shared a tender kiss. Her lips were soft and inno-cent, unlike my voracious Scarlett. Jadelyn didn't kiss with tongue, instead rolling and nibbling with her lips, pulling and tugging at mine like she was encouraging me to deepen the kiss.

It was soft and sensual, and it was taking everything I had to keep the beast from ripping off her clothes and taking her right there on the bench. But based on the beast's response, it had already claimed Jadelyn.

I pulled back before he got too greedy.

"You really are possessive." Her eyes searched mine.

"Yes." I wasn't going to deny it. Dragons did what they wanted.

"Sirens only claim one man; it's nice to feel you latch on so strongly as well." She trailed off at the end, and I knew she was thinking about Chad and the other women he'd been with, even when they were in a relationship.

"You should know, I'm very possessive and protective. It is in my nature."

She gave me a squinty eyed look. "How possessive are we talking?"

"Like a dragon with his gold," I joked, trying not to give it away in my look that there was more to it.

She laughed, completely unaware of how close to the truth it was. Jadelyn leaned forward, kissing me on the cheek. "I like that."

Then she kissed me again, distracting me from the fire.

We stopped enjoying each other's lips minutes later to the sound of the foil crinkling under the fire's crackle.

When we broke apart again, she gave me a lip biting look. "I can't go all the way, but I can do some things." Her eyes were filled with a fire that had my body aching for more.

I was about to respond when I caught a whiff of something burning. I looked at the fire before turning back to focus on her.

What she was suggesting was far more important than the food.

But she caught the same smell and slapped me in the chest. "We will continue this later. I'm hungry!"

I gave her one last kiss, promising to pick the discussion up later, then got up to see the corners of the foil charring black. I grabbed sticks to navigate them out of the fire and a smaller stick to peel back the hot foil. Fishing a plastic fork out of the milk crate, I pulled the first morsel out, steaming in the cool November air and held it out for Jadelyn.

She took a dainty bite off the fork, careful not to burn herself. "Yum. That's actually really good." She leaned around the fork to give me a kiss.

I pulled both meals away from the fire with my bare hands. It didn't even cross my mind until she pulled away and noticed it with a raised eyebrow. I'd used the sticks earlier because of habit, but I didn't need them now, did I?

"Fire really doesn't bother you, does it? I mean, I guess I should have realized that after your duel with Simon."

Waving her comment away, I focused more on the plump pair of lips before me. Leaning forward, I was halted when I heard shuffling steps behind us. I quickly pivoted, keeping Jadelyn behind me.

The homeless man we'd passed on the way in was stumbling towards us, sniffing the air in a way that didn't quite seem human.

I didn't want to look like an insensitive ass, but I also didn't want to have my date interrupted. "Hey, man, if you want, we can drop off the rest of our food after we're done."

But the homeless man didn't acknowledge me as he staggered into the firelight. Something rippled beneath his skin before he took one large whiff of our food; at the smell, his pale pink skin started to turn into a thick swampy green hide.

Oh shit.

CHAPTER 12

Jadelyn spotted the troll at the same time, started to try to push around me. "Zach, watch out!"

Like hell I was going to get out of the way between her and a swamp troll. While it was still bubbling up to its full size, I moved, tackling it to the ground as more shouts started in the surrounding woods followed by gunfire.

Whatever was happening in the woods, the security team would handle it. I needed to focus on the troll. It was the immediate threat to Jadelyn.

I grabbed the swamp troll and got my feet under me, pushing him like a sled out and away from Jadelyn. No matter how well she could handle herself, a swamp troll liked to throw around its weight, and I needed to get it away from her.

Scarlett shouted something, and I didn't need to be a genius to know to get off the troll. Gunfire sounded and blood splashed off the troll as its body twitched.

"Zach, we'll handle this." The look of guilt on her face got to me. This was the second time today Jadelyn had been in trouble, and both times had involved me.

The swamp troll rolled to the side, the gunshot wounds already closing. It stood, wiping the drool from its face. But it didn't look at any of us; its focus was entirely on the hobo dinners.

Grabbing the closest one, I threw it to the swamp troll, hoping that would stall it.

Sure enough, the ugly brute swiped it off the ground and bit into the hobo dinner, foil and all.

Morgana had said not to feed the trolls, but at least it kept this one busy for a second while I figured out a plan.

Seeing the swamp troll distracted, I gave it a running leap, landing on its back and grabbing its head before twisting with all my strength. I snapped its neck, sending it to the ground like a puppet with its strings cut.

But even as this swamp troll went down, more shouts and gunfire from the forest told me we had a bigger problem.

"Scar, I can handle a single troll. Make sure your team is okay."

She gave me a sharp nod before giving Jadelyn a look that I didn't understand. "I'll be back shortly."

As soon as she left, Jadelyn clued me in. "She wants to make sure I'm okay, but she has a job to do."

"Don't worry. Not much is going to get past me."

As if I was summoning bad luck, a troll climbed up over the ledge next to the campsite.

I caught him before he could pull himself all the way up, and my fist caught him in the jaw, snapping his head back and causing him to tumble back down.

Twigs cracked back the other way as several more swamp trolls came into the firelight.

"Zach. Let me help."

Before I could object to her getting involved and potentially getting hurt, Jadelyn sang a note and mist appeared around us. The moisture clung to her clothes, and scales started to dot her neck.

The beast rose up inside of me and I could feel it pushing for me to shift, to protect Jadelyn. But for now, I held the shift back, wanting to keep that as a last resort.

As I watched the approaching trolls, a glowing light sprang up behind them. It encompassed us and them in a large circle. I studied it, trying to figure it out.

"What is that?" I asked Jadelyn, but I had a sinking feeling I knew the answer.

"A barrier spell." Jadelyn looked pissed.

"I'm guessing that it isn't from you or your people?"

Jadelyn squared her shoulders. "No. Looks like help isn't coming anytime soon. Scar is going to be pissed."

I looked at the barrier; the bright light of it blocked my view of the outside, and I knew it would block others from seeing in.

That meant that it was five swamp trolls versus Jade and me. And help was cut off. If I held back, one of us was going to get hurt, and I wasn't going to let that happen.

I positioned myself between Jadelyn and the trolls, ignoring her protests. Part of me wanted to throw the food at them to see if that would solve the problem at hand. But I knew better. The number of trolls and the barrier spell? This was a setup.

Water arrows shot over my shoulder, taking chunks out of the troll in front as the other trolls screamed and charged.

I pushed my beast forward while trying to relax, practicing the technique to shift that Morgana and Scarlett had taught me. "Come on. Come on."

It was like a word at the tip of my tongue; it was just right fucking there but it wouldn't come.

Growling, I took my anger out on the first troll to reach me.

He swung with a meaty fist that would have knocked my teeth out, but Morgana had me trained better than that. I caught his arm with both hands and leaned back, pulling him off balance before rolling all the way to my back and planting my feet on his chest to launch him over me and slam him onto his back.

But I knew that would only keep him busy for a second, and there were other trolls to deal with.

A second troll came at me, but out of the corner of my eye, I saw the other three charging Jadelyn. She was forming more water arrows, but it did about as much as a high caliber gun. It wasn't enough to take out a troll.

It was like that moment was frozen in time. Seeing the three trolls moving towards her, I could already play out the battle in my head. If I did nothing, Jadelyn was about to die.

Everything slowed down, as if moving through molasses for a second, before everything started to shrink. I had to reach the troll about to get to Jadelyn. There was no other option.

My claws sank into the troll's shoulder, and I slammed its head into the dirt like a child throwing a doll. Falling to all fours, I drove the troll into the ground and my jaws snapped forward, grabbing the next closest troll in my maw.

Blood squirted over my face as I bit down, then thrashed the troll until its arm came loose.

My attack had accomplished my top goal. None of the trolls were looking at Jadelyn. Satisfaction rolled through me before anger burned through at them, for even daring to try to attack my mate.

I pushed up from the ground and stood back on two legs, a large tail behind me helping counterbalance my massive body.

I was massive. Jadelyn came up to my hips, the trolls to my stomach. I'd taken on a hybrid form. My claws flexed and my tail swished behind me as I focused on my new appendages for the first time.

I was surprised that I was able to use them so well this first time in my full hybrid form. But the answer to how it was possible came as I focused inward. The beast rode shotgun in my mind, translating much of my thoughts into actions. The bundle of instincts was in full use, but that didn't mean I had any loss of control.

Just... my intent translated differently. I could also feel my brain going a mile a minute, and strange urges kept popping up. If my body was two stories tall right now, how big was my brain? Were dragon brains anything like humans?

I shook my head. All the new sensory inputs and what felt like a supercomputer in my head were making me lose focus. It was time to deal with these trolls.

Gleefully growling, I bared my teeth and let loose a roar that shook the earth. It was playtime.

Snatching one of the trolls up by their feet, I remembered the first time one of the swamp trolls decided to use me as a wrecking ball. I smacked the troll on the ground, spinning around, using my tail to knock the others away from Jadelyn.

She was precious and weak compared to me. She needed protecting.

Feeling a hit, I looked down at a troll trying to beat me with its fists. It drew my focus back to the trolls.

The one in my hand was beaten and bruised, bones poking out of its arms in different directions. The scent of its blood tickled my nose.

Snack.

Before I even realized what I was doing, the beast translated my hunger into chomping down on the swamp troll and tearing it in half, tossing the torso up in the air before catching it and chewing the bones to dust. It slid down my throat, a satisfying mouthful in a way I hadn't experienced before.

They were herby in a bad way, like hay that had been left out too long and started to stink.

The trolls ran. They finally seemed to register me as the predator I was. But something about them running triggered something in me. My instincts went wild, and I darted forward, catching one in my mouth and thrashing it until it tore in two. I moved methodically, grabbing and tearing apart the remaining trolls.

They were like microwave burritos—absolutely terrible, but they at least satisfied the hunger. I scanned around, looking for any more threats, when my eyes settled on Jadelyn. My mate lay against a tree staring wide-eyed at me.

Prowling back over, I loomed over her and huffed her scent. She smelled like lilies, layered with a bit of a salty brine smell. Lilies and ocean breeze. But what made me unhappy was the sour scent of fear wafting off of her.

My weak mate shouldn't fear me. I growled.

"Zach?" Her voice shook.

Huffing, I blew her hair back as she continued to look at me wide-eyed and the sour scent of fear lingered.

I tried to send mental notes to my beast that we need to be less scary. Leaning in, I nuzzled her, and she clung to my scaly snout.

"Holy shit." She stroked the side of my nose, and I gave her a warm rumble of contentment. "You're a dragon, a gold dragon."

I nodded and accidentally tossed her a few feet in the air, only for her to land and wince in pain. I surged up around her protectively, wanting to end the pain. There were still trolls in the woods, and we were surrounded by this barrier, but it wouldn't last.

She was too weak; I needed to protect my small mate.

Something churned in me as I looked at the barrier. I felt trapped, claustrophobic.

"Zach." Jadelyn applied pressure to turn me towards her. It wasn't enough to actually move me, but it got my attention. "It's okay. I'm okay, and we are safe thanks to you."

I huffed, pleased to find that the sour smell of her fear was fading.

She summoned a globe of water and splashed it against her face. She was beautiful; scales framed her face and her ears changed to fin-like structures that curved out of her blonde hair.

"See, I have scales too." Her voice tickled my hind brain in a way that made me sigh.

Of course you do, you're a siren, I thought to myself.

Then it hit me. She was trying to keep my attention, trying to calm me with her voice.

If my mate was trying to help me, then I should help her.

Opening my jaw, I hovered my teeth over her shoulder as I smelled her scent sour again.

But her expression became one of steely resolve. "I trust you."

My teeth pierced her shoulder, and there was a flash of warm magic inside my mouth before I let up. I only took a few drops of blood, licking them up as I tasted my mate. But I marked her; she was mine. No one would hurt her now.

Jadelyn looked down at her shoulder and her ruined shirt. Her hand traced the shimmering design that was imprinted high on her right chest. "I love it. What is it?"

I huffed her again, her hair blowing back. Protection for weak mate.

"I love it. But, Zach, can you shift back?"

Focusing, I knew that I had managed to shift, but never had I talked with anyone about how to shift back. A part of me panicked, wondering if I was stuck.

My mind ran a mile, no twenty miles a minute, and I reared back. Looking around once again, I felt the claustrophobic feeling began to intensify again. My body readied itself for a fight.

Jadelyn's clear, crisp song wafted into my ears and calmed me, but I shook my head, torn between my instincts and my logic.

I didn't need to be worried. No one was going to mess with a dragon. But my instincts were new and far more powerful than I'd expected. My dragon brain was dumping adrenaline, or some draconic equivalent, into my system in preparation for a fight.

Then suddenly the world went dark.

I realized that the darkness was a result of the barrier spell coming down. I instinctively picked up Jadelyn, spinning around as the gunfire started.

Curling in on Jadelyn, I protected my weak mate from the gunfire as it peppered me and bounded off my scales. It was like standing out in a hailstorm. It hurt, but did no lasting damage.

"Cease fire!" Scarlett was screaming at the same time as Jadelyn was shouting for everyone to stop.

The gunfire slowed, and I breathed a sigh of relief that I didn't need to kill all of them.

Scarlett and the detail were well enough trained to stop when told. I leveled an intimidating glare at the mass of suited up security detail. All of them stood there frozen, their guns trained on me.

After I determined it was safe, I unfurled around Jadelyn, but my claws stayed on her and kept her close in case I needed to protect her again.

"What, you couldn't recognize me, Scar?" I retorted, but it only came out in a guttural growl. Apparently, the beast didn't do so well with speech.

The detail jumped in their own skin and flashlights focused on me as they all tensed.

Scarlett stepped between her men and me, turning to them and trying to keep her voice calm yet full of authority. "Do not. Under any circumstances. Shoot the fucking gold dragon. None of you will live if you piss it off. Am I clear?"

"Yes," they said in unison, but they held onto their guns as if those tiny toys would offer any protection from me.

I laughed inside at the thought. I wasn't going to lie; it was awesome to be a badass dragon.

"Are you okay, Jade? Come, let one of our guys check you out," Scarlett called over.

"I'm fine, but I don't think I'm going anywhere at the moment."

Scarlett tilted her head in confusion, her little fox ears flopping in the way I found adorable. "Why?"

I growled at both of them talking as if I wasn't here.

Jadelyn laughed. "I don't think Growly here is going to let me go. But, Scar, everyone's phones, tablets, anything need to go on lockdown. I want nobody able to communicate until we resolve this."

Damn right. My little weakling mate wasn't going anywhere until I knew it was safe. My back flexed with wings I didn't have, but my instincts told me I should be able to fly. That only caused me confusion.

"Shit," Scarlett spat before turning around and taking a bag off her back. "Everyone—phones, radios, even your damn smart watches. I want everything electronic in here, now. We are dark until we debrief."

Jadelyn pulled my attention again with her hand on my chin, turning me to look at her again. "Well, this was a surprise."

I tried to talk again, but all that came out were more growls. This was starting to get a little frustrating, along with my inability to shift back.

Scarlett pulled out her own phone, typing in a short message before shoving it in the bag as well. "Okay, Jade. My dad knows we went dark, and no one has a line outside. Now, what do we do about him? You are in there, right, Zach?"

I snorted, blowing her ears back and got a whiff of her cloves and vanilla. My first mate. I nuzzled her into the ground as she clung to my snout.

"Okay, big boy. I hear you." She laughed as I gave her a happy rumble. "Can you talk?"

Lifting off of her, I shook my big head.

Jadelyn spoke around my arms. "Scar, we have a few things to talk about after this. A gold dragon?"

"I know." Scarlett grinned so wide I thought her mouth might split. "What they say about a dragon's sex drive isn't the half of it. Welcome to the club."

"Nothing about what he is leaks out." Jadelyn looked up at me to reassure me. "If we have to kill the whole detail, we'll do it to keep your secret."

I growled and looked at the group of tasty treats.

"As a last resort." Scarlett got in front of me. "Fuck, for your first shift, you are pretty high strung."

Jadelyn jumped in my clutches. "This is his first shift? Shit, shit." She focused on the security detail. "None of you even think about running. See this big guy? He's running entirely on instincts right now. I saw him tear apart and eat five swamp trolls. Do. Not. Run."

Damn right I ate five of them. The detail looked tasty too.

"Okay. We need to get him to shift back." Jadelyn patted the side of my head. "As wonderful as it is to be wrapped up by him. I think we need to get out of here."

Scarlett was still appraising me. "You know. I'm damn thankful that you didn't shift into this during sex. Pancaked fox isn't a good look on me."

That's what you are worried about? my throat rumbled.

"Of course you would have crushed me." Scarlett laughed.

I'd never do that, I grumbled.

"Not on purpose," she retorted.

Jadelyn looked back and forth. "You can understand him?"

"Just the gist. He is my boyfriend. Even if he can't speak, I understand him enough at this point to know what he's trying to say."

I nodded excitedly and pointed to Jadelyn. My instincts were driving me not to shift back until she was safe.

"Sorry, love. I have no context for what you just tried to communicate."

An exasperated puff of flames came out of my mouth, and everyone jumped. Even Scarlett jumped back and put a hand on the weapon at her hip. It looked like they were all still on edge.

But I couldn't blame them. I could only kill all of them and leave no evidence if I decided to throw a tantrum. There was extra weight to my actions, and I needed to be more careful.

Scarlett pulled a swatch of fabric off the ground, and I realized it was my pocket. She pulled my phone out of it. "Hold on. I'm calling Kelly."

"Kelly knows?" Jadelyn's surprise showed, and Scarlett blushed before turning to speak into the phone.

"Hey, girl. I got a biiiig problem right now."

"What's wrong?" I could hear Kelly on the other side of the phone.

"I have a big, golden problem right now. I need help. Pronto," Scarlett hissed.

Something thudded on the other side of the line, and Kelly's voice became clearer. "Wait. Shit. He didn't."

"He did, and he isn't changing back. We are in Blue Bell Park on trail three."

"On my way."

Scarlett hung up. "Okay. I guess we'll wait. Not feeling like shifting back?"

No, I growled. My tiny mate wasn't safe yet.

CHAPTER 13

The sound of somebody jogging towards us on the trail had everybody on edge. I watched carefully, still protecting Jadelyn.

Into the clearing barged a wide-eyed Kelly in a skimpy dress. She looked like she was about to go out to the club. She slowed down, taking in the scene around.

"Oh, wow," she said, her eyes looking up at me as the campfire reflected in her eyes. "He's huge."

"Yeah, and not shifting back," Scarlett retorted, sounding a little annoyed at me.

"Look at him. He's guarding her. Why is he guarding her?" Kelly asked, looking around and seeing the blood for the first time. Her eyes locked on something, and I followed her line of sight.

A single firefly blinked red. My brain got confused seeing the red. Focusing harder on it, I could make out a drop of blood coating it and tinting its light.

In the heat of the moment, I hadn't realized how violent and bloody I'd been with the trolls.

"They were attacked by multiple swamp trolls," Scarlett informed Kelly, leaving out vital details of the barrier spell.

Growling at Scarlett for leaving that out, I frowned. Something told me it was important.

"Look at him." Kelly gestured to me. "Whatever happened, he doesn't think it is safe for him to let go of her. You aren't going to get him to shift back until he thinks it is safe."

I nodded my head rapidly. Yes, Kelly. Tell them.

My mind was already catching back up. In the shock of my transformation and everything that had happened, my mind hadn't focused on an important aspect.

How did anyone know to put that barrier spell here? That meant someone had planned this; someone had lured the trolls here and the only people that knew about this spot and our date were still in the clearing.

I let a low threatening growl rumble out of me as I turned towards Jadelyn's security detail. Scarlett, Jadelyn, and Kelly weren't a concern. I trusted each of them.

But these others? I should just toast all of them to be safe.

"Stop." Scarlett must have seen my intent, stepping and positioning herself between the detail and me.

I looked over at Jadelyn and used a claw to draw a circle in the dirt before pointing to the two of us and making two x's inside the circle and then five dots.

She gasped, clearly catching up.

"Scar, we've been so wrapped up in the big guy. Who made the barrier?"

I could see Scarlett's eyes dart back and forth rapidly as she thought through it. Then she cursed. "Everyone, guns down. We have a problem." Scarlett turned back to me. "We'll handle this. Do. Not. Kill. Them."

Puffing smoke in her face, I disagreed with her strategy. Killing them was the smart option. It made sure we didn't leave any loose ends.

"What's going on?" Kelly asked.

Jadelyn explained, "We were attacked by swamp trolls, like Scarlett said." Her eyes wandered to the blood on the ground. "But at the same time, a barrier spell went up around us, trapping Zach and I in with the five swamp trolls and keeping Scarlett and the others out."

Kelly looked at the blood. "I'm gonna guess that is what's left of five swamp trolls?" She turned back towards me. "And what's hanging from his muzzle."

It's not a muzzle. It's a snout. I growled and hovered over her.

Kelly put her hands up in surrender. "Sorry? Can't he speak?"

I tried to tell her that of course I could, but it came out once again in a growling mess.

Kelly laughed so hard she had to hold her stomach. "Oh, this is great."

While this was amusing, I was more interested in the security detail and which one had betrayed Jadelyn. Scarlett was already investigating, though, pulling them aside one by one.

My eyes roved over the security detail, and instinctively I could feel that something wasn't right. There was something my draconic senses were picking up on that my human mind couldn't. My mind seemed fast, but I knew I was processing more through my instincts than I was consciously.

I tried to puzzle through it, but I still couldn't. I waited for Scarlett to finish interviewing each of her detail; it didn't take long.

"This is my crew. There's no one new. They are all vetted every two weeks. None of them are a problem," Scarlett reassured me.

She was clearly trying to calm my dragon, but my instincts were telling me something else. I leaned into those instincts, letting them guide me as I eyed the group.

One of the detail in particular caught my attention, but for the life of me, I couldn't have explained why.

"That one." Kelly followed my focus.

"Can't be. That's Daryl. He's been with us for eight years. His wife is friends with my father. There's no way."

My own sense of unease was growing as I glared at Daryl, looking for some sort of excuse.

These instincts had been right before, such as with Chad. I thought back to Jared and then even the hobo walking into this park.

Each time my instincts had picked something up and I had ignored it, it came back to bite me. So I wasn't about to do it again this time.

I growled, thinking over how to handle this.

Scarlett grabbed my chin and tried to pull me down. "Do not kill one of my men."

Nudging her to the side, I towered over Daryl, getting his scent. He smelled like rotten flesh mixed with fear. The fear was to be expected, but what was that putrid smell clinging to him?

Jadelyn, still in my arms, took my concern more seriously. "Daryl, use your magic."

I looked down, surprised. Something clicked. Skinwalker?

"He's a siren like me. I want to see his magic; it's a precaution in case there is an illusion on him."

She wasn't thinking skinwalker like I was, but the test would work just the same. I focused back on Daryl.

He held up his hands. "My magic is nothing like yours, Miss Scalewright. I don't want to embarrass myself."

I growled; there was no reason for him to evade this if it saved him from suspicion and my jaws.

If he was the skinwalker, he had now tried to attack Jadelyn twice. Once through Chad and his pack, and now again. Was he after Jadelyn?

My mate.

An angry growl threatened to erupt into a roar.

"Daryl, just use your damn magic before he causes more problems," Scarlett demanded.

But, instead of following her orders, Daryl backed up, looking over his shoulder.

"Daryl. Don't run," Scarlett warned, but it was no good. He turned, running at a dead sprint.

It was like a trigger for my instincts. I uncoiled around Jadelyn and pounced over the group. He had a dozen yard lead on me and ducked into the woods, like it would save him.

I was a predator on the hunt. The few small trees snapped like twigs as I crashed through them with two bounding strides. My claw catching him and knocking him to the ground. He was pinned under my claws like a mouse caught by a cat.

Things got interesting as his skin split and a naked man shot out, like a banana comically squeezed from its peel. Still on the ground, he spun up a magic circle in the air.

Scarlett's face was lit up by the crackle of a stun gun as she slammed it into his neck just before I could catch him in my jaws. There was a sick satisfaction in watching him twitch and jerk to the clicking of the stun gun.

I snapped at his still body. He'd be done causing problems in my belly.

"Easy, Zach. We want to keep him for questioning." She waved and two more men came forward; one grabbed him, cuffing the naked man, while the other stuck a syringe in his neck. "We'll get what we can out of him."

I huffed. Eating him would have been far more satisfactory, but I could see the logic in her move.

Jadelyn was by herself now, but now my instincts weren't going crazy telling me to protect her.

"Are there more?" Scarlett asked.

I felt better, but there was no harm in double checking. Knowing what to look for this time, I sniffed, looking for the scent of rotten flesh on all the guards. I cleared them one by one before finally feeling like I was able to relax.

Kelly patted my side. "I think it is time for you to shift back."

I tilted my head for her to continue.

"It's pretty simple once the stress is gone. You seem comfortable enough. Now just relax and let it slide away."

Laying down on the ground and curling up like a massive kitten, I closed my eyes and tried to relax.

The beast was there, still riding along with my thoughts. I slowly pushed it away to float back to my chest.

Leaves and twigs prickled my side as I opened my eyes, finding myself naked in a forest with people who were the correct size surrounding me.

Kelly let out a soft whistle. Her eyes were focused between my legs. "Damn shame you won't become my alpha."

"I can always kill all your beta males if you'd like." Chuckling, I pushed off the ground. The date had been more of an ordeal than I would have liked. So much for a relaxing picnic.

"No thanks. I kind of need them to have a pack." Kelly clicked her tongue after giving it one last look.

"Offer stands."

Kelly chuckled. "Glad to see you're back. I'm going to call it a night. Please don't come anywhere near my pack. I'll work to get them off the idea of you."

I didn't miss that she referred to it as her pack in a way that still made me feel that she'd make a better alpha than most of the men.

"Thank you very much for your help," Jadelyn interjected herself. "I apologize for disturbing your evening and then kicking you out. But we have some things we need to deal with."

Her torn clothing and the scar on her shoulder made me remember what I'd done.

I had marked her as mine, and my dragon had done some sort of magic. I needed to get more information from Morgana right away about what it meant and how the magic worked.

Kelly didn't mind and gave me a winking salute before running off into the darkness.

Scarlett was pulling her phone out of the bag and calling someone. I assumed it was her father by the way she spoke. "We had a problem, one of our own. Jadelyn was attacked on her date, but everything was resolved. We have the suspect out cold. Prep a cell for a magus, and we need a debriefing for my whole team."

There was a curt affirmative on the other end of the phone before Scarlett hung up and looked at the rest of us. "Pack it up. We're going back to the Scalewright manor. Each and every one of you is going to get interviewed. We need to understand how they got Daryl and clear everyone for duty."

"When you are asked what happened"—she pointed to me—"what he is needs to stay between us. Do I make myself clear? Once we leave here tonight, even amongst yourselves or to me and Jadelyn, you don't mention what he is. For purposes of debriefing tonight, you can describe what happened. He and Jadelyn were cut off from us by a barrier spell with five trolls. When the barrier came down, he had taken care of all five trolls, and Jadelyn was fine.

"He wants to keep what he is a secret, and you owe him at least that much. If it was any of us trapped in that barrier with Jadelyn, we would be dead. Any questions?" Scarlett finished her speech with her hands on her hips.

I kind of liked the authoritative, badass vibe she was putting out.

"He's really a dragon? I thought they had wings."

Not backing down, I spoke up, feeling just a small twinge of awkwardness standing there naked. "That was my hybrid form. I'm much bigger if I went full dragon."

There were a few nervous gulps in the group.

"Any other questions?" Scarlett pushed.

"What do we say about Daryl? He was sniffed by a dragon and found out?"

Scarlett paused for a moment. "Just say Zach was able to detect it. Leave out all details pertaining to his paranormal species." When there were no other questions, she clapped her hands. "Move out. Jadelyn stays with the big ugly, unless one of you thinks you can guard her better."

Her eyes went back to my naked form. "Someone get him a spare pair of clothes too."

In the end, one of the guards gave me a pair of sweats from his SUV and I found myself driving with Jadelyn in the car and four SUV's hovering around me in traffic.

The streetlamps strobed through the front windshield as we rode quietly in the car.

It was Jadelyn who spoke up first. "Thank you. For saving me, and for trusting me with what you are."

"I didn't have much of a choice."

"You didn't have to save me, and you could have killed the security team." She trailed off before stating quietly, "You are a gold dragon. Who are we to try to tell you what to do?"

I glared at her out of the side of my eyes. "It seems what I am has changed how you talk to me." That bothered me; it was exactly what I didn't want.

"What you are demands respect," she replied carefully.

"I'm still me. I'm the same guy you were just having a date with before you knew." My hand tightened on the steering wheel and the leather creaked.

She paused for a moment, considering what I had said. She let out a sigh as she nodded her head, seeming to realize she'd been treating me differently.

As her face softened, her hand began trailing along my thigh and her nails grazed me through the sweatpants. "Then where were we before the interruption?" Her voice had softened a bit. "Ah yes, I was explaining that a siren can't lose her virginity until they are sure the man is the one for them. But they can do other things."

"Jade." My voice carried a warning tone. "Don't do this just because of what I am."

Her nails dug into my thigh. "Listen up. This was going to happen before I learned you are one of the most powerful creatures in the world. Do you know how many times in my life I've second guessed someone's friendliness for someone wanting me for my wealth?"

I opened my mouth to tell her that it was never about that, but she pushed on through.

"No. I know you didn't give a crap about that. You didn't know when you met me. At that point, you were outside the whole sphere of the paranormal."

"Then what?" I growled.

"Learn to trust yourself and make up your mind. I went on a date with you, and I was about to give you a blow job before I knew anything. Can you relax? Do you trust me that I'm not here for your gold scales?"

Blowing out a breath, I realized just how much I was planning to push her away once she knew. "Yeah. I can and I do."

"Power is a burden." She let her hands wander to the inside of my thigh again, and this time I was filled with anticipation as I started to tent in my pants. "I get it, but let me still be just a girl on a date with a guy that she really was hoping to hook with a great blow job."

I relaxed in the seat as she worked to get us both back in the mood with soft touches. Breathy sighs escaped her as she felt the size of me.

Her fingers finally began undoing the tie to my sweatpants, pulling them down. I felt the cool air on my erection before she wrapped it in her warm, soft hand, pumping it gently. Her seatbelt clicked, and she crawled over the center console.

I couldn't help but appreciate the beautiful blonde as she bit her pink lips and her sapphire eyes drank me in hungrily.

"This only works if you can keep your eyes on the road." She put a firm hand on my chin and turned my head back. "Plus, half the fun is watching you struggle not to be distracted."

Her head ducked down, and the top of her head bobbed as she kissed along my hips and feathered the shaft with soft, fluttering kisses.

The anticipation was killing me, and I pushed my hips up to her. "You make it hard to focus."

"Would you like me to stop?" Her voice was muffled as she spoke next to my skin.

"I'd like you to start."

One hand left the wheel and tangled with her hair, pushing her on my erection. I let my eyes dip for a moment as her lips wrapped about my cock and she drew me into her mouth. Her hand came up without looking and found my chin, pointing it back at the road.

A satisfied sigh forced its way out of me as I leaned back in the seat, enjoying her while I tried to focus on the road.

She started slowly at first, working herself up and down the shaft, her tongue licking the underside and finding a sensitive spot that made me gasp. Like a kid with a new toy, she ground her lips against that spot, licking and suckling at it until I couldn't help myself and started thrusting up into her.

I banged her head against the steering wheel, but she didn't stop. Instead, she grabbed my hips, trying to force them down as she continued to assault that one spot she'd found.

"Fuck," I groaned. I wanted to do something rather than just receive.

Keeping one hand on the wheel, I slid the other down her back and around the curve of her ass until I found the faintly warm cleft of her sex. Even through her jeans, I could feel the heat. Something about that reassured me that she was into this and it wasn't for show.

I used two fingers to apply pressure at the top, rubbing and stroking her clit through her jeans.

She formed a seal around my cock and drew me in deep before her throat vibrated with a moan that had me twitching and ready to blow. But she pulled back to look up at me and make sure my attention was still on the road. It was, despite how badly I wanted to pull over and take her right there.

Jadelyn wasn't an experienced expert, but she made up for skill with enthusiasm as she bobbed wet and fast on my cock with wet slurping noises, wanting to drain me dry.

I had to stop rubbing her and brace with both hands on the wheel. "I'm cumming."

She drew me deep into her mouth once again as I painted the back of her throat. My body relaxed in post sex bliss while she sucked and pumped the last bits out of me. I could feel her shiver against me as she took down my seed.

Coming up for air, she sat back with a satisfied smile as she tossed her hair and adjusted her top back to her carefully sculpted look. Somehow she managed to tame her post sex hair.

"That was great. I wasn't expecting just how pleasurable your seed was."

"It was?"

"It's magic." She smiled and leaned against me. "Not quite as good as an orgasm, but pretty darn close. Not to mention, dragon seed supposedly does wonders for a para's health."

Her talking about it made me wonder if she wanted more, and I felt myself rise back again.

"Oh my. Already?" She shook her head. "No wonder Scarlett said you were insatiable."

"She did?"

"Yeah, that's part of why I wanted to do that before we even went on the date. I know about her needing a break, and I had to admit I was curious. And to be clear, it had nothing to do with you being a dragon. Just about a man I was interested in and I knew needed the release."

I glanced over at her smiling, once again noticing the tear in her top and the scar underneath. "About that." I nodded at the mark. "I'm sorry, but I think I went a little overboard."

She moved aside the tear and looked at the pale scar that would have blended in with her skin if not for the hint of magic I could see in it. "I kind of like it. Feels like you marked me."

"Pretty sure that is exactly what I did."

Jadelyn shrugged. "I trust you."

It held more meaning than just the scar; it was also about what we talked about earlier. I wasn't here for her money or any other ulterior motive.

The feeling was mutual; somehow our connection made me sure it wasn't just about me being a dragon.

"I trust you too." Pausing, I took a deep breath. "But now that we've gotten that out of the way, what's the plan when we get to your place? And help me prep for meeting your parents. I wasn't prepared for that tonight."

"Even a dragon is nervous meeting the parents." She laughed. "Well, it will be intense. I have no doubt Scarlett and my fathers are going to descend on us like hawks and try to get to the bottom of the attack tonight. Be prepared. They aren't going to be nice about it. And you're one of the new variables, so they'll probably be extra critical. Also, my mother is going to want to meet you. I'll do my best to keep them both in check, but try not to kill my father?"

I laughed. "For you, I'll do my best." Taking the exit ramp, I followed the turns as Jadelyn pointed them out.

CHAPTER 14

"Wow," I said as we pulled into the large circle drive in front of Jadelyn's house. House was a bit of a misnomer though; mansion was a far more apt description.

As soon as we came to a stop, the four black SUVs surrounded the BMW. I ignored the SUVs blocking us in, surveying the enormous home. It was a massive stone structure, very stately, with water features dominating the front. I probably shouldn't have been so surprised that they had several fountains, a large, attached pool house, and what looked like an outdoor lagoon.

"You guys really like water." I felt like an idiot the second that came out. Of course they did. The Scalewright family were all sirens.

"It's fine. Everyone mentions it the first time they see the place." Jadelyn stepped out of the car.

As her feet hit the ground, a team from inside the home immediately hurried out and escorted her into the house while one other took the keys to the BMW from me. I was left to trail along behind her as Scarlett and her team unloaded their prisoner.

I walked up, my neck craning to take in the front entryway. It was a large, three-story-high square room with a large glass ceiling and a garden under it basking in the moonlight.

Jadelyn stopped, and the bodyguards nearly ran into her. "Make room. He stays with me."

They gave me wary looks before parting and doing as they were told.

"That's not necessary daughter." Rupert strolled forward, his shoes echoing in the large room. "We need to talk to everyone involved tonight."

"Father." Jadelyn turned and bowed slightly, but the bow felt a little stiff, even to me.

Detective Fox showed up on Rupert's heels. "I see once again you're there when she's in danger. Almost suspicious." The detective narrowed his eyes at me.

I growled at the insinuation, but Jadelyn jumped to my aid. "Both of you watch it. I won't hear a word from either of you against him."

Rupert looked like he'd been slapped by his daughter's outburst. "Excuse me?"

I knew she had been in her father's shadow for some time, but the way he reacted told me she had been docile and following his lead. I had a feeling that might be about to change.

"You heard what I said. I stand behind him, and if you both don't get with the program, you'll regret it," she threatened.

Her father's expressions shifted from surprised to upset in an instant.

For a moment, I thought he was going to shout, but instead, he just pulled back his shoulders like an animal making its presence known. But then he quickly pivoted, and his glare was directed at me. "What have you done to my daughter?"

"Who has done what to my daughter?" a mature female voice rang through the hall, almost as if it had been sung. "I came as soon as I heard."

An older version of Jadelyn glided into the room. She was wearing a green dress, somewhere between formal wear and nightwear. She moved straight to Jadelyn, wrapping her up in a hug. Jadelyn's mother was beautiful for her age, and I had to admit I was excited that Jadelyn would retain her beauty for years.

On her side was another woman in tight-fitted exercise clothes, five fox tails splaying out behind her. She was clearly Scarlett's mother, but she had light brown hair instead of the fox orange that her husband and daughter shared.

"Mom, dad is being unreasonable. This is Zach." She stepped aside and gestured towards me.

"The Zach?" she asked, her words dripping with meaning that made my newest mate blush, but Jadelyn didn't hesitate.

"Yes."

Her mother's gaze was hard and critical in a way that only a potential mother-in-law could mimic. "Handsome. Is he all you thought?"

"And more," Jadelyn said before moving on the other side of her mother and away from her father.

"Well then. Husband, it sounds like we should be treating him like family and not some sort of pest to be dealt with. Don't you think?" Her voice dripped with meaning, and I got a good feeling that things didn't happen in this house without her approval.

As much as Rupert walked around like a king among the council and the world outside, here in the home, it was clear who was in charge.

"Yes. Besides, he already claimed me," Jadelyn stated proudly, and I nearly face palmed. Why did she have to add fuel to the fire?

Rupert's face went red instantly, and his wife's hand on his chest looked to be the only thing preventing him from boiling over.

"Let us handle him. Use that anger where it belongs: on the situation with those that thought they could take a shot at our daughter," she said.

I wasn't sure whether to be grateful or terrified. She'd helped me avoid the wrath of Jadelyn's father, but both mothers turned and fixed me with critical gazes. I had a feeling they weren't going to be a walk in the park. They were already judging if I was good enough for their daughters.

"Fine," Rupert spat. "Girls, come with us. Let's get this all sorted out."

Scarlett barked orders at her men, who filed on ahead as they all moved deeper into the mansion. Two men brought up the rear, carrying the unconscious warlock. She flickered back for a moment, kissing me on the cheek and giving me a wink before darting back after her father, none the wiser for her slight detour.

Jadelyn gave me a pat on the shoulder. "It'll be fine. Once they get to know you, they'll defrost a bit." She finished her statement with a nervous laugh that failed to put me at ease.

I was hoping I survived long enough to make it into their good graces.

But it was time to face the music. I turned my focus to their mothers as everybody else left the entryway. "I guess I'm all yours."

Scarlett's mother had her hands on her hips as her tails waved agitatedly behind her. "Follow us."

"Uh oh," I joked, but neither of them laughed, making me more wary.

They both turned and walked side by side through the home quickly enough that, even with my long legs, I was forced to pick up the pace to keep up.

After enough turns to get me lost, they soon stopped in a parlor filled with stiff but comfortable looking furniture, arranged in several groupings meant for a larger party.

They picked one that already had a tray of cookies and milk set out, along with a stack of plates and cutlery.

Neither of them offered me the food as they sat down and crossed their legs. Jadelyn's mother folded her hands neatly in her lap while Scarlett's mother laced them together and held onto her knee.

"Introductions are in order. I'm Claire," Jadelyn's mother started. "And this is Ruby."

Claire Scalewright and Ruby Fox. I tried to cement those names to memory as I worked to not break out in a sweat. Somehow, talking with two potential mothers-in-law at the same time was more nerve-wracking than going up against a group of swamp trolls. Sadly, I couldn't just eat them to get out of this.

As they both let their eyes rove over me like they were picking me apart, I decided I would definitely rather fight a dozen swamp trolls.

"Pleasure to meet both of you." It came out formal and stiff, but I thought it was a safe response.

Claire only hummed as she looked at me, pondering. "Let's start with the simple part. What happened tonight?"

I quickly explained the date and the situation we found ourselves in with the encroaching trolls. I added a description with the barrier spell and my following suspicions that led us to apprehend the warlock.

I kept to the script and left out everything about me being a dragon, like we'd all agreed upon in the clearing.

They both let me speak, staying silent at every pause. When I was done, they waited, completely still, as if to confirm that was all.

"So... you just happened to take out five swamp trolls? By yourself?" Ruby's eyebrow raised; she clearly wasn't convinced.

"Yes?" It came out like a question.

"So, you weren't involved in this in any way?" Ruby pushed. "Your date was just an opportunity that this person exploited?"

"Yes, Ma'am. I was just on a date and protecting my woman—" As soon as those words left my mouth, I regretted it.

Both of their body languages shifted as they leaned forward, like predators about to pounce.

Jadelyn's mother definitely wasn't happy.

" — my date." I smiled and tried to correct myself, but she wasn't buying it.

"You called her your woman, as if you already laid claim. She said you marked her?"

"Maybe?" I hesitated, not even fully sure what I'd done or the full significance. And it wasn't like I could describe it to them without outing that I was a dragon. This definitely wasn't how I had pictured the conversation going.

"It would seem we need to be a little more vigorous with you if you are going to be as bold as to call my daughter your woman." Claire seemed a little angry, and Ruby put a hand on her thigh to calm her down, but when she turned to me, there was an intensity in her eyes.

"Have you claimed my daughter as well?"

"Yes," I said that one with far more confidence. The beast reared up like he was ready to fight her if she contested it.

I wasn't exactly comfortable as the two women turned to each other and started talking as if I wasn't there.

"He is dating both of our daughters."

"The nerve," Claire agreed. "It seems he's quite dangerous too—five trolls."

Ruby nodded. "He's all my daughter talks about. Maybe he bewitched them both? We don't know what he is. It's entirely possible."

"The bastard seems to have won the hearts of both our girls. I'd hate to see one of them end up brokenhearted," Claire replied.

I cleared my throat. "Excuse me. I'm right here."

Claire looked at me dismissively. "Of course you are. I haven't told you that you can leave."

That was all it took to push me over. "Listen up, both of you. I'm in your daughters' lives, and there isn't anything that is going to separate me from them."

Ruby and Claire both stared at me, faces blank, before Ruby spoke, "I wouldn't rule it out so quickly. We could make your life quite difficult." Her eyes continued to bore into mine as she waited for my reply.

Recognizing the challenge for what it was, I gave her a wicked smile. "Bring. It. On."

The haughty look on Claire's face evaporated into a smile. "Oh. I like him. He passes?"

"Yes. For now." Ruby eyed me up and down, but her eyes held more of a smile in them. "I can see why Scarlett is so smitten.

Well mannered, but enough of a spine you can't push too hard. He passed that test."

I was annoyed that they'd made me think they didn't consider me worthy, but I moved past it. Here, I needed to be on my best behavior.

"Both of your daughters are absolute gems, and I'm honored that they've decided to be with me." I went with a safe reply.

"Yes. But if you want our husbands off your back, you need to truly convince us," Ruby clarified.

It seemed that both of them already had an idea of what they were looking for from me, so I cut to the chase. "What do you need?"

Claire took the lead in the conversation. "Truthfully, we know quite a bit about you already. But what you are has been a large question mark. One that we need to know in order to give you our full support."

Ruby jumped in. "We trust our daughters and that they have made an informed decision while keeping it a secret on your behalf, but we can't be in the dark if you want our support."

I looked back and forth between the two mothers. Their intentions seemed good, and my instincts were quiet; nothing about them was sending warning bells off. While it wasn't ideal to have more people know, I understood why they were asking, and

I knew they'd feel more comfortable with me dating their daughters if they knew.

Deciding to trust my instincts, I nodded before spotting a security camera in the corner of the room. "I can't have this recorded."

Ruby grabbed a butter knife off the table and threw it over her shoulder directly into the lens of the camera, shattering it and showering sparks to the floor below. "Good enough?"

I could see where Scarlett got some of her spunk. She might be more dangerous than her husband.

"This is sensitive. I can't have it leaking out. Do you both promise to keep this even from your husbands?" I pressed.

"This is between us three, for the purpose of knowing that our daughters' hearts are safe," Claire reassured me.

Deciding to just rip the band-aid off, I stated, "I'm a dragon."

Claire and Ruby sat there, stunned for a moment. "Impossible."

I wasn't sure what to say to that. It was the truth.

Ruby seemed to recover first, skepticism showing on her face. "Prove it."

I really didn't think I needed to, but clearly they weren't going to believe me without seeing it.

Sighing, I stepped away to a larger, open space in the room and started taking off my clothes. It was awkward undressing in front of my mothers-in-law, who were both checking out my body like they were assessing my viability for their daughters and future grandchildren.

Steeling myself, I focused inward. Telling myself it was just like riding a bike, I shook out my arms. I could do it again.

I relaxed my body and flexed the beast, pushing it upward and outwards to the surface. This time, it came far easier than ever before.

I could feel my bones crackle and my muscles expand as I flooded my body with new mass. It wasn't so much painful; it was more like the pressure in your knuckles right before they pop.

When it was finished, it had that same satisfying feeling.

I opened my eyes to find myself towering over the two mothers as I crouched on all fours in my hybrid form. It had felt like I'd need to really push to move past this, but I could feel the full dragon form lingering at the edge of my awareness.

Claire sat with a neutral expression, but her eyes betrayed her. "Impressive." She breathed. Both of them looked like they were seeing a unicorn.

"Gold. You failed to mention that," Ruby added, standing up and touching me to confirm it wasn't an illusion.

My point proven, I shifted back and slipped my clothes back on. "I hope you can both understand now why I'm keeping this a secret."

"Oh, yes." Claire nodded, her eyes shining with excitement. "Cookie?" She gestured to the treats that had been laid out on the table.

I took the gesture as her form of acceptance of me. And I wasn't about to turn down food; after shifting twice, I was ravenous. One cookie was followed by two and soon four, then six.

"Our kitchen staff is still here. How much do you normally eat?" she asked, pulling out her phone.

"Lots. Maybe enough for four? Mostly meat if you can." I didn't want to impose and order too much.

She tapped on her phone. "Eight meals will be on their way." She smirked, clearly not buying that four would be enough. "You look like a growing young dragon; be sure to eat your fill anytime you are here. Make yourself at home."

I shook my head. She was already mothering me.

"A gold dragon. I can't believe I'm even seeing one, let alone considering my daughter marrying one. She knows, right?" Claire asked.

I nodded. "Tonight I had to shift with the five trolls. She didn't know before then," I clarified.

Ruby was just as mystified. "I assume Scarlett has known for months?"

"Yep."

"My little troublemaker found herself as the first mate for a gold dragon." She shook her head in disbelief.

Given their previous apprehension towards me calling them my women, I thought mate was a little too far for tonight. "I don't know if I'd call them my mates."

Claire's face became stern again as she started scolding me. "You marked my daughter; the least you could do is take responsibility. How would she ever wed someone else, now that she's been marked by a gold dragon? No suitor would touch her."

"Scarlett was first, and you've been with her for months. No doubt you've marked her too," Ruby added with a touch of pride.

I could stare down five trolls, but my future mothers-in-law? I folded instantly. "It isn't that I am not committed to them, but I'm still new to this and taking it slowly."

Even as I said that, the beast head-butted me from inside my chest, demanding I speed the fuck up. The possessive instincts of mine wanted nothing more than to sink my claws into both of them and not let go.

Claire burst into laughter. "Sorry. It isn't every day you get a chance to make a dragon nervous. We'll work this out with our daughters. But we do want to move this forward. You have our support."

Ruby nodded along, but added, "Our husbands will find out eventually. If you walked into my husband's office here at home, you'd think he was a serial killer and you were his obsession. He has an entire wall dedicated to researching you after you started dating Scarlett."

I had no idea what to say to that, so I just sat there.

"Our husbands will find out. But do me a favor?" Claire asked.

"Anything." They had given me their blessing and would support me in pursuing their daughters. I was happy to help how I could.

"Let us be there when they find out. Oh, the look on Rupert's face. It'll be priceless when that 'bastard' he's been ranting about shows him up. Neither of them has been able to stop talking about you at dinners. Our girls are driving their fathers insane." She sighed before shifting her focus. "What do you know about siren marriage?"

"That it is sort of a... uh... one and done sort of deal." I struggled to not say virginity around Jadelyn's mother.

"She hasn't already given herself to you, has she?" Claire asked for clarification.

"No. Nothing. She told me that was off the table." Like hell I'd tell her mother she just gave me road head on the way here.

"Do you know what happens to a siren when they take their first love?"

"No, ma'am." I leaned forward, interested.

But Claire shook her head. "I'll let my daughter explain it. That is something between you and her. Though, if you marked her tonight, I expect she will want to expedite the process. I hope you are ready, young man."

Ruby looked shocked, but then her thoughts quickly turned inward as her eyes lost focus. "What about Scarlett? Are you going to solidify things with her as well? If you are going to marry Jadelyn, you should at least support Scarlett as your first mate."

I found myself cornered by the two mothers as they shifted gears, pushing their daughters onto me. They were mine as far as my dragon was concerned, so it didn't bother me too much. In the end, I was glad I had their support.

I looked over at Ruby. "Do Kitsunes have a particular ceremony in your culture?"

"Most paranormal culture has informal rules for weddings since many relationships don't conform to the tax standards here in the states. But if we were to even let you do something informal with the girls, we would have to do some formal affair, given the Scalewright family. There are expectations," Ruby said.

Claire nodded in agreement. "Unfortunately, with our family status, we are expected to make an announcement if Jadelyn's marital status changes. But I want to get back to the fact that my daughter's now marked. Can you explain that in more detail?"

"Yes, my daughter at least deserves the same," Ruby said.

"I wasn't sure what happened. Tonight was the first time I transformed. When I was feeling protective of Jadelyn, I did it on instinct."

"That makes it even better," Claire said excitedly. "That you felt so protective tells us a lot."

I wasn't sure if I'd be able to do it again, but I would certainly try. Scarlett at least deserved that much. She was first, and I cared about her deeply right now, possibly even more so than Jadelyn.

Both mothers seemed excited at the prospect and giggled, chatting away as I just sat there

"I'm glad I have your blessing, but what about their fathers? Any tips?" I was not looking forward to trying to win them over.

But Claire waved off my concern. "We will handle them. But I meant what I said. This will only stay quiet for so long, although you can depend on us. One of these days, they will find out." She paused until I nodded. "Good. Now come sit over here with us."

The two women parted and made space for me between them on the couch as a servant came in with a tray of food.

"We've heard about you from my husband's investigation, but we'd like to hear it from the source as well. Tell us about yourself." Ruby leaned in, and they both started to barrage me with questions as I dug into the food.

CHAPTER 15

Half an hour and several thousand questions later, Rupert, Detective Fox, and the girls came back into the room.

I'd just finished off another plate of food, stacking the empty plate on the leaning tower of dirty dishes that had accumulated. A maid swooped in, grabbing them and cleaning up my extensive meal.

"Please don't stop there if you're still hungry," Claire doted on me. "Would you like some lobster?"

Both men eyed me with a mixture of annoyance and admiration. I doubted they'd seen many people eat eight full meals and still order more.

But the surprise fell off their faces, a scowl taking its place on Detective Fox's face. "It's time that we interview him as well."

Scarlett's tail bristled, and I knew she was a moment away from picking a fight with her father.

"No need," Claire declared, patting me on the shoulder. "Zach here might as well be family. And I expect him to be treated as such." She gave her husband a meaningful look.

I enjoyed watching Scarlett's mouth drop open as she stood behind her father, but the expression on the two husbands was even better.

"You can't be serious. This involved the safety of our daughter; we cannot leave any avenue unexplored." Rupert quickly regained himself.

Jadelyn stepped forward and pulled me off the couch. "That's right. As I said before, Zach saved me tonight. That alone should be enough for the both of you." In front of both of their parents, she kissed me on the cheek and pulled away, blushing bright red.

I wrapped my arm around her and held her tight, the beast in my chest flaring up, prepared to fight for her.

Claire spoke first, cutting off the husbands. "Daughter, why don't we wrap up for tonight. It's been quite eventful, and I'm sure you could use some rest. Tomorrow, Ruby and I would like to have a conversation with you two."

"Of course." Jadelyn nodded, bolstered by her mother's support.

Rupert glared at me, as if he was trying to figure out what magic I had worked on his daughter and wife.

But I ignored him, wanting to know what they'd learned from the prisoner. "And the warlock? Did you get anything useful?"

Since neither of the men readily spoke, Scarlett jumped in. "He'll still be unconscious for a few hours. Once he wakes up, he'll get the works. But from the interviews, it sounds like Daryl's daily habits shifted two days ago."

I didn't like the sound of that. "Just in time for someone who might be coming to town for the Order of the Magi conference."

They looked at each other. Clearly, they'd considered it but hadn't wanted to say it.

"When you get more information, give me a call, Scar?"

"You'll be the first call I make."

"It isn't unlike our family to have conflicts with the magi," Rupert spoke up. "This needs to be handled delicately. This is not some mid-forest brawl with a few trolls."

"Five," Jadelyn clarified, and it sounded like it wasn't the first time.

"Unfortunately, no one else saw all five, and there were no corpses." Detective Fox and her father seemed unwilling to give me full credit, but that was fine. The fewer people puzzling about how I took down five trolls, the better.

Instead, I focused on the conference. Warlocks hadn't seemed all that ostracized. "Warlocks seemed relatively accepted at the conference, but it sounds like that is new?"

"Yes. Only certain kinds of warlocks were condoned in the past." Detective Fox made a distasteful expression. "It would seem that things have loosened up significantly since the last conference in Philly."

Jadelyn explained, "All the way back to the beginning of magi. Warlocks are not only those you would think of with dark rituals, demons and old gods, but those you might describe as clerics or priests that worship angelics."

I realized where she was going before she even got around to it. "The Church. They employ warlocks."

"The Church," she agreed, saying the name with the same gravity that I'd heard every time someone mentioned the paranormal conflict back in the 18th century.

That added a new layer of complexity to all of this. It also explained why the Scalewrights wanted to handle this carefully. I would try to be more discreet, but if anyone came after my mates, I wasn't going to play nicely.

"I understand." I locked eyes with both of their fathers, conveying my feelings.

"Since it seems there's nothing more to gain for now, why don't you go home?" Rupert dismissed me, but his wife had another idea.

"Yes. I think our daughters should show you out."

Jadelyn and Scarlett didn't miss a beat. Each of them grabbed one of my arms and pulled me away from the tense parental situation. I wasn't about to put up any resistance; I was happy to put some distance between us.

"Don't worry. With mom on your side, he should lose most of his bite in a day or two." Scarlett snuggled in close to me. Her smell of cloves and cinnamon wafted in the air, calming me.

"So, are you going to tell us what you did to our mothers?" Jadelyn asked.

I smiled down at her, shrugging. "They grilled me, but in the end, they said I couldn't earn their blessing until I told them what I was. So I told them, but then they didn't believe me. So..."

Jadelyn's eyes went wide. "You showed them?"

I nodded. "My instincts told me they were trustworthy. I'm starting to trust my instincts more. And let's face it, I needed their support or things were going to get much more tense with your fathers."

"Thank you," Jadelyn said, leaning against me. "I know you guard your secret. To share it with them for me and Scar means the world to me."

"It does." Scarlett's tails happily beat against me.

We walked quietly through their home. I pretended not to notice the security around the house who were watching us like hawks. I kept my senses open, but no other sign of a skinwalker presented itself.

Scarlett pecked me on the cheek to get my attention, and I turned to get a full kiss, but then I paused. I wasn't sure how okay they were with me showing the other affection when we were all together.

"Good luck. I'll give you two a moment." Scarlett's hand trailed off my arm, like she was reluctant to let go before she stepped away.

A guard pulled up with Morgana's BMW and got out, giving Jadelyn and I one look before moving away and giving us some privacy.

"Was that okay? I'm new to the whole two girlfriends thing."

"I'm your girlfriend now?" Jadelyn cocked an eyebrow.

As she trailed off, I thought briefly about what her mother had implied. Jadelyn might push past girlfriend in a hurry; I needed to get my mind wrapped around if I was ready for that yet.

"I mean, after..."

She put a hand to my mouth. "Don't say it." Her eyes shifted to the guards at the front door. "But yes. Sorry, I just wanted to tease you. I'm happy to be your girlfriend. As for the kiss with Scar... it was different?" Jadelyn tried, after struggling to find the right words. "I didn't hate it. Obviously, I knew it would happen eventually. But I can't say I wouldn't have rathered it was me."

I let my arms wrap around Jadelyn, pulling her close and tilting her chin up. "Like this?" Holding her tightly, I kissed her passionately, without a care for the guards watching.

She was hesitant at first before she threw caution to the wind and started shoving her tongue into my mouth and raking her hands through my hair like she couldn't get enough of me. She held nothing back.

When we broke apart, I was breathing heavily, and feeling a little dazed by the raw passion she had exhibited.

I rubbed my messy hair and looked sheepishly to the guards, who were studiously focusing everywhere but at us.

"Thank you, Zach. For the date, for saving me, and most importantly, not letting what you are get to your head. Unless you run to the ends of the earth, I want a second date." She smiled, a joke on the edge of her lips. "Scratch that. Even then I'll hunt you down for that second date."

I gave her one more kiss. "Until next time then."

Getting into the BMW and driving away, I had a grin plastered on my face. Somehow, despite being attacked by a bunch of trolls and interrogated by my girlfriends' mothers at the same time, I was giddy. I had two amazing budding relationships and I was no longer as freaked about dating multiple women. I couldn't wait for that next date.

***

As I pulled into Morgana's garage at Bumps in the Night, I pulled out my phone to find a number of texts.

Sabrina offered some answers to what she'd been able to find out tomorrow, saying it was too much to text.

Easy enough.

Morgana's, however... I skimmed through the multitude of references about me getting it on with Jadelyn.

After rolling my eyes, I texted back, 'You must have not had any trolls tonight; you seem bored. I'm back from the date.'

She shot back immediately, 'Down at stage three.'

I locked up the car, proud that I had brought this one back in one piece.

I wasn't surprised she was prowling her club since the trolls were light that evening. It was her business, and she was always snooping around, making sure she knew everything that went on within it.

Bumps in the Night was not only a fancy restaurant early in the night, but it descended down several layers, each one increasing in its depravity. I was glad she was only at the third stage. I wasn't going back down to the fifth stage.

The first level housed dinner and live music until the lights went down. Then the tables were cleared for a dance floor. The second was EDM music on a dark dance floor. And the third, well, Morgana called it a burlesque show, but it was a black light lit room with a number of stations for women to dance around a crowded dance floor.

Music pumped loudly enough to give everyone that feeling of privacy, while more than a few drug deals happened.

It was clean enough, only the relatively recreational drugs. Morgana made sure of it.

Down on the fourth floor... well, I wasn't likely to go back down there.

When I entered the third floor and tried to scan for Morgana, it was understandably hard. A blue elf should stick out like a sore thumb, but here under the blacklights, no one noticed.

Try as I might, I couldn't spot Morgana's silver hair. It usually lit up like a beacon under these lights. After several minutes, I grew bored, and the center stage caught my attention.

I sighed. I should have looked there sooner.

Morgana was strutting back and forth on the stage in nothing but garters and a corset. Her hair expertly covered the tips of her ears, and under the blacklights, she looked like a tan woman with blindingly bright blonde hair. I could tell what she was at first glance, but I assumed others that didn't know what she looked like must gloss over the details.

Her lithe, graceful form pranced around on the stage, and her alien, elven face struck me as beautiful but different. She grabbed the center pole and leaned back, her eyes finding me in the crowd instantly.

The smirk on her face told me she was having fun as she showed off her flexibility to the hooting and hollering of the dancing crowd below.

I rolled my eyes, and she bent off the pole, doing a somersault that got the crowd going. She ended her dance, leaning against another pole as she popped off one of the clasps holding her stockings and slowly, sensually ran a finger under them, teasing them down.

I had to admit that I wasn't immune to her show. Most men would notice her and have trouble looking away. But I didn't want to see Morgana that way, so I grabbed a drink at the bar, on the house, and wandered over to Morgana's favorite corner. I parted the thin chain that somehow everyone in the rowdy crowd respected.

She watched me go and only danced to the end of the song before strolling off stage, another performer taking her place.

As she walked through the crowd, bodies turned. Everybody's attention still locked on her until she slid down into the booth beside me.

"You didn't take your siren for a spin all night long?" she teased, getting comfortable next to me. It was quiet in this corner, though I was unsure if that was magic or the engineering of the foam padding around us.

"And I thought you'd be out hunting trolls."

Morgana shrugged before signaling for one of her servers to get her a drink. She sat back, popping the laces on her corset which had been even too tight for her.

"Nothing tonight." She accepted a flute of dark liquid, likely her favorite blood, from a server as dancers started to crowd the table.

With the chain gone, it seemed this space was open season.

"So, how was the date? Did your little princess love the great outdoors?" Morgana cut to the chase. She was one of the few people in my life that I could confide everything in, both normal and paranormal.

"It was great; she loved it." I started out.

"Of course. You kept her off her game. Took her out of her natural habitat of nice dinners and fancy parties. It was smart. You said you were making... hobo dinners? Ha. I wanted to see her eat like a homeless person." Morgana laughed and relaxed, savoring her drink.

"Just because it's called a hobo dinner doesn't mean it is what homeless people make. It's a common camping meal though. She loved it, though we didn't get to eat more than a bite." I had fun leading into the big reveal of the trolls, but was cut a bit short by Morgana leaning over and sniffing next to my shirt collar.

"You smell different. And not just because you had a lovely lady with you tonight. You smell... fantastic." Her eyes glowed red in the darkness for a moment before she pulled back and downed her entire glass.

Unlike the refined Morgana I was used to, she made a jerking gesture to a server and held up three fingers. He was back in a flash with two glasses and another flute. I watched Morgana down the two glasses and wave away the waiter.

"What was that?"

"Tell me what happened." Her casual demeanor was gone.

She didn't seem in the mood for story time, so I cut to the chase. "Trolls attacked us, warlock trapped me and Jadelyn. I went full hybrid transformation, and then I tore apart five trolls." I gave her the short highlights.

I wondered if doing my full hybrid shift had changed my scent?

"Is everyone okay?"

"One of their security team is dead, but the warlock was wearing his skin."

She frowned. "Sounds like you are going to end up going down the rabbit hole after this one."

"Damn right I am," I growled.

Morgana leaned in again and sniffed at my neck. "It must be a side effect of your transformation. Your blood smells heavenly. Smelling you makes me hungrier than you can imagine. I'll have to stay topped off; otherwise, you might tempt me." She gave a dark chuckle and leaned back against the leather booth. "So it was an eventful night. You had a nice date and got your full hybrid form. Roaring success."

She took another big sip. "So, did you two celebrate after? Make it to first base?"

Rolling my eyes for her own satisfaction, I gave her the more detailed play-by-play of the night. She asked a few questions, but mostly listened.

"She gave you a blow job, didn't she?" Morgana teased. Apparently, I wasn't doing a good enough job hiding it after my third drink. "Ha! I knew it."

"You didn't tell me sirens can't go all the way."

"Yes. They have that nasty little problem. But don't worry, when you bag her for good, it will be totally worth it." She took a sip of blood. "How I wish I could get one for myself."

"Care to share?"

"No, I'm told it is one of those things you just have to experience to fully understand. Besides, where would be the fun of ruining the surprise?"

"I'd have to get married for that. Knowing what I'm getting into would be nice."

Morgana leaned against me. "Don't be like that. It isn't as if this is the end. You'll have dozens of weddings for your bevvy of beauties."

I raised my eyebrows at dozens, nearly spitting up my drink. "I just got used to two, Morgana."

She ignored me, continuing on. "And I'll get to host all the bachelor parties."

"What?"

She gestured around at the club. "Who do you know that would give you better bachelor parties? Not to mention, you haven't really made friends broadly in the para world."

About to argue back, I realized that she wasn't entirely wrong. Frank and Maddie were my best friends, but since I'd learned I was a dragon, I'd been distant from them. And it would be hard to explain to them that I was getting married to a Siren and possibly a Kitsune at the same time.

"Fine. You can plan my bachelor's party. IF there is one."

Morgana rubbed her hands together greedily.

For now, I was just going to try to roll with it. Despite my still very human up-bringing, I was a dragon and was always meant to be a dragon. I'd struggled most of my years fighting the instincts that roared, sometimes literally, inside of me. It was nice to finally be able to follow them.

Morgana's eyes flicked past me as I felt someone drunkenly lean up against me.

Our booth had steadily been encroached upon, and this wasn't the first of the night. But something about this one put Morgana on edge. I could feel my new neighbor rub up against me, and the humid breath of someone's mouth close to my neck.

Before I realized what happened, Morgana was there, grabbing a woman's throat and pulling her off me. Morgana dragged the woman by the throat to be only inches away from her own face.

"Am I invisible?" she asked.

The frightened girl shook her head. "N-no."

Morgana hissed and showed off her fangs. "It sure seemed like you were ignoring me. Coming in and trying to nibble at someone sitting with me?"

That's when I realized what was going on. This was another vamp in attendance in Morgana's club.

"Sorry, he just smelled so good. Won't happen again," the vampire promised.

"It better not." Morgana punctuated the threat by snapping the vamp's neck and tossing her out of the booth. A server came and grabbed the vamp under the arms, hauling her out like an overly drunk patron. She'd recover; I'd seen Morgana recover from worse.

"Was that necessary?" I asked.

"I think you need to be a little more careful with how you smell now. Wouldn't want you surrounded by hungry vampire hussies." Morgana lifted her drink with a smile before she draped herself over my lap. "Better yet, let me ward them off."

I ignored the tightness in my pants at having her on my lap, focusing on my drink instead. But what really bothered me was feeling my beast flare up protectively over her. I grumbled back at him, telling him this one wasn't going to happen. He already had two women we needed to figure things out with. But the beast continued to push.

Morgana wiggled a little, and I wondered if she knew and was messing with me.

"You're not making a move are you, Morgana?" I did my best to try to keep it light.

"Of course not." She batted her lashes before a smirk spread across her face. "Besides, you couldn't handle me. And I don't want to get hooked on that tasty blood of yours."

I nodded, not entirely convinced. But for now, I'd just ignore it and enjoy the night. Morgana wasn't one to shy away from what she wanted, so there was no need to over analyze.

CHAPTER 16

The night out with Morgana had been fun, but as I stepped out into the morning sunlight outside of the convention center, I regretted the last couple of drinks.

"Welcome to my world. The sun is a bitch." Morgana laughed, stepping out of the car with ruby red shades that matched her eyes, once again in her classic leather outfit. Only this time, she seemed to be a little bolder.

Her leathers seemed cut even more sexually than usual; though, how I knew that, I couldn't quite put a finger on it.

"Is that what the shades are for today?"

"That and I can eye roll all the magi all I want without them seeing."

I laughed at her joke, but she didn't join me.

"I'm serious. I plan to give Jared and his cronies eye rolls all day. Call it my harmless revenge for being out here in the daylight."

"That bad yesterday?" I asked as we got our badges.

Morgana sighed, hesitating for a moment to take her badge before grabbing it and following me in. "They all want to see me perform my magic like a monkey performing at the zoo. I'm too old for that shit."

I felt for Morgana. She was an anomaly in her world and had worked hard to carve a respectable name for herself instead of becoming an outcast. She was better than being used for a moment of entertainment for the magi. I had a feeling it had been part of what had factored into the rate she'd given Jared.

"At least they have no idea what I am. I have no doubt they'd want similar things from me."

"That would be fun to see." Morgana smirked. "A whole lot of trouble, but then again, we might be able to get you an orgy of lovely ladies willing to worship you on their knees." She emphasized the word worship, clearly enjoying herself.

I stopped and glared at her. "By the way, a warning would have been nice. I caught the intro and their feelings on dragons."

My chastising only seemed to encourage her as she smiled even wider. Ignoring her, I pushed past her and into the convention.

As we strolled into the convention center, it was already in full swing despite being early in the morning. People of all shapes and sizes in all walks of life were going booth to booth checking out what each offered. Occasionally, two people would run into each other, and the result would either be shouts of anger or sparks of joy hugs.

I turned to Morgana. "So after last night, the Scalewright family will be fully on board with tracking the skinwalkers. Apparently, all it took was a troll attack on their daughter."

Morgana nodded. "I expected that after what you said last night, but did your little fox give you any more information?"

Scarlett had given me a quick update, but she also seemed to be waiting to see me in person to run through the full details.

I knew Jadelyn and her family were going to try to speak to the magi today, and I hoped that might also provide more information we could use.

From the detail Scarlett had given me, this was not a singular person that was responsible for the attack, but instead a group. Because of that, the Scalewrights didn't think that they could handle this on their own quietly enough to not warn the magi's beforehand.

If the paranormal went after a group of the magi in the middle of the conference, there was a risk they would be starting something larger than we wanted. Though I disliked Scarlett holding back information from me as if she thought I would go rogue and do something myself.

Of course I totally would. My dragon half was champing at the bit to get a bite out of whoever attacked my mate.

The Paranormal Council rolled in like yesterday. They moved as a group, creating a stir as they parted the crowd. As they moved, Rupert flagged down the magi leadership, quickly pulling them aside to a private conference room.

With the suddenness of their arrival and the immediate urgency with which they all departed, the magi quickly began to whisper, gossip and theories stirring all around me. I smiled, enjoying being in the know.

But I didn't want to miss the information. I darted forward with Morgana on my heels, ducking into the room before the door closed.

Rupert's eyes locked with mine as I moved into the room, but he quickly looked back to the magi, which I took as acceptance of my presence. I slid along the edge of the room to observe.

The Spring Queen stood next to me, giving me a questioning look with those piercing golden eyes of hers.

"You didn't cause another incident, did you?" She said it with only a slight quirk of her lips, so I took it as teasing. She didn't wait for an answer before turning back as the conversation began.

The Faerie were a strange culture; I didn't have the time or energy to understand them right now.

I eyed Rupert, who looked stern and composed at the moment. But I'd had a number of interactions with him at that point, and I could read him. He was a lidded pot about ready to boil over. This case was personal.

"We have evidence of a serious problem involving a group of magi here in Philly."

The lady with the heavy accent, Florita, scoffed. "What does that have to do with us? This is your city." The way she said it was full of disdain.

Rupert's un-amusement was palpable. "While the Order is convening in our city, it is both of our problems. The last thing I need is for a larger fight to break out between our two people."

"You mean it would be an inconvenience given that there are enough of us that you can't just blow us out like a candle?" the old wizard grumbled. It sounded like the paranormal had used a heavy hand in the past when dealing with the local magi issues.

Jared stepped forward, surprising me. I hadn't thought of him as a peacemaker. "Of course. The sensible thing here is for the magi to handle this amongst ourselves. That way, no one gets the wrong idea.

These magi you are referring to have committed criminal offenses, I assume?"

"They attacked the Scalewright family last night. One count of premeditated homicide and several counts of attempted murder." Detective Fox spit a little as he declared the charges. "I would hope that's enough for you to take this seriously."

By the looks on the magi leadership's faces, it was clear that they understood the gravity of the situation and it had soured their day. This was not something that could be swept under the rug without a bigger shitstorm down the road.

"If you have enough information to go after this, I assume you have someone in custody?" Jared clarified.

"Yes. Though he's not in a condition to do much at the moment," Detective Fox sneered.

The magi grimaced but then schooled his face. "Either way, he should be handed over to us. We'll deal with him, and we'd like to question him ourselves."

The Summer Queen raised her hand, and the two groups facing off broke their tension like a cut string. "It might do you both some good to have a neutral party take care of this." Her eyes shifted over to me and Morgana.

Jared looked at the two of us, his disdain for me showing in his face. "You think he's neutral in this?"

His accusing tone was enough to make my beast rear up in my chest.

"No. We have gotten with the times. We have an internal group that takes care of this sort of thing now," Jared added.

Rupert grunted, clearly not happy, but accepting the outcome. "We expect updates and results of your own interrogation. As you are well aware, these magi are guests in our city and you are responsible for them. We will let you handle this yourself, but we expect it to be taken care of. If not, this is our city, and we will step in." Rupert's tone turned heavy at the end, the threat hanging in the air.

It didn't make the magi happy to be threatened by Rupert, as was evidenced by the thin pursing of Jared's lips. But none of them said anything. I was not looking forward to the political aspect of being a part of Jadelyn's family. I had a feeling they wouldn't love my approach to conflict—just wrecking whatever wronged me with fire, but it was a pretty effective approach.

Conversation over, I turned to head out with Morgana, but Jared stopped us. "I don't want to see him"—he pointed at me—"anywhere near this. I know you use him and Morgana as mercenaries."

I paused, my dragon roaring at the idea of not being involved in hunting down the people who had attacked Jadelyn.

But Rupert gave me a clear look that told me to stand down. It took a lot of self-control, but I suppressed the desire to snap back.

"Fine." I stared Jared down, giving my best eat shit smile. "I won't go after the warlocks for now while you work to track down and fix the problem. However, we do have active jobs. I can't promise that, if they are causing other trouble, we won't run into them."

Rupert stepped forward, backing me. "It's true. They do a number of services for the city's paranormal community. We can't hamper them in that. But you will not pursue the magi, we have your word?" he asked.

"Scout's honor. I'll just stick to my current jobs," I promised, already having another idea on how to go about this.

Both sides seemed amenable to my promise, and it seemed the matter was resolved. The conversation changed, with Jared taking point now hunting down the cabal of warlocks.

The meeting officially wrapped. It had been a faster conversation than I had been expecting between the magi and the Paranormal Council.

As we headed out, Jadelyn grabbed my arm and pulled me along to the side. My arm slithered around her hips, and I held her tightly before a throat cleared behind me.

"It seems I'm not going to get rid of you," Rupert said grudgingly, although there was a slight acceptance in his eyes that hadn't been there when we had walked up the night before. "My wife and daughter have impressed upon me that you should be treated as family and will probably become family. But I would like to remind you that our family has a certain prestige to uphold. I expect that, if you are treated like family, then you won't embarrass the family name."

He said it like a statement rather than a question, staring me down as he finished.

But I was more stunned by what sounded like acceptance. I had a feeling it was the closest I was going to get to it from him.

I held back any snarky replies and gave him a serious nod. "For Jade, I think I can manage that." I looked over, seeing Jadelyn blush as she squeezed my side in thanks.

Rupert seemed satisfied enough as he gave me a nod, breaking off with the rest of the council before turning back and calling out over his shoulder. "By the way, my wife is planning an event for you two. Well, two events. One sooner in private and one more public at the end of the year."

I paused, realizing what he was suggesting. It hit like a sack of bricks. Something told me they were already planning the siren wedding. I wasn't afraid of commitment, but this was fast. I tried not to show it, but Jadelyn must have sensed my reaction. She started rubbing my shoulders comfortingly.

She leaned in, whispering in my ear. "It's okay—we can talk later. Maybe even get some privacy."

"That sounds perfect. And I'm not against it," I hurried to clarify. "Just struggling to wrap my head around how sudden this all is."

She gave me another one of her brilliant smiles and pulled me along. I kept my eyes out for other men that might try to duel me for Jadelyn like they had previously. If I had to fight to keep my women, I would. I had no intention of giving any of them up.

As Jadelyn and I broke off from the group, Morgana swooped in like a shadow. "I see you two lovebirds are having a blast."

"Something like that. Shame the magi wouldn't let us go after the threat directly."

"I warned you before: the magi are an insular group. It was unlikely they would let you, me, or even the Scalewright family deal with one of their own," Morgana reminded me.

"Then why involve them?" I looked at Jadelyn. My beast was ready for pure, unadulterated violence in response to the attack on one of my mates.

Jadelyn blushed and refused to meet my eyes. "This is what we have to do. From the information we gathered, we know it is a group of warlocks working together. If you were to go after them..." She read me like a script. "...it would become a larger issue. There are too many to do this quietly."

She sighed, still looking away. "I'm sorry, Zach, but for now, you need to stay out of this one. You need to protect our two groups' relationship and your secret."

She wasn't wrong, but I hated being left out of the loop. "Morgana and I could at least do some information gathering."

"And I'm sure you'd gather information—along with a pile of corpses." Jadelyn shook her head. She knew me well. "So, for now, we'll let the magi do their best to handle it on their own. But if they fail... then other blunter tools can be used."

I put my hand on my chest in mock outrage. "Do you hear that, Morgana? We are the hammer."

"You certainly like to pound things," Morgana said, barely containing her laughter at her own joke. Jadelyn sputtered, trying to hold in her own laughter.

"Zach?" Sabrina's voice cut through my annoyance.

"Sabrina." I waved her over. "This is Jadelyn. That's her security team." I pointed over my shoulder. "And you've already met Morgana."

Today, Sabrina was wearing an undyed robe that looked like it belonged in a monastery. It seemed like she was trying to hide all of her curves.

"It is an absolute honor to meet you." Sabrina grabbed one of Jadelyn's hands with both of her own and bowed slightly as she shook it.

The siren didn't miss a beat, quickly shifting into her gracious public persona. She smiled sweetly back at Sabrina. "Pleasure is all mine. How do you know Zach? Are you looking to join his harem?"

I nearly stumbled. "What the heck, Jade?"

She poked me in the nose. It was cute, but it barely distracted me from my annoyance. "From what Scarlett has told me, you need more. And women around you will become part of your strength. So, I'm taking applications. Unlike the situation with Chad, I'm going to be proactive."

"Applications?" She made it sound like it was her harem, not mine.

"Do I get to throw one in?" Morgana asked with a smile.

"Of course. You practically have your application in already. I'm surprised you haven't taken him for a spin one of those nights you secluded him at your club in the name of 'work.'"

Morgana's face made me burst out in laughter. Her head was reared back like a surprised animal as she struggled to find a comeback. "It is work. Waiting for the call is part of the job."

"Chill. She's just joking, Morgana." I patted my partner on the shoulder as I chuckled, but I didn't miss the rapid silent communication that occurred between Morgana and Jadelyn with their eyes.

"Anyway." Jadelyn drew the word out to find a change in topic. "We were talking about Sabrina."

"Zach, I talked to my mentor—" Sabrina started, but I waved my hands to get her to stop. Last thing I needed was her to show Jadelyn that I wasn't giving up on the warlocks just yet.

"We can talk about that after. It seems Jade would love to get to know you."

My siren mate took that as approval, and she pulled Sabrina a little further ahead to talk.

It looked like Jadelyn was going to start actively recruiting. I stood dumbfounded a bit, trying to wrap my head around every-thing that was changing so quickly.

"Didn't want the princess to hear what Sabrina had to say?" Morgana asked curiously.

"Of course not. We are forbidden from looking into it, remember? However..." I smiled wide.

"We are still one hundred percent going to track them down?" Morgana gave me a wicked smile of her own and held up her hand for a fist bump.

I bumped her fist and then clarified, "No, nothing like that. But we are hired to keep the swamp troll migration moving smooth-ly, and it would seem that someone might have manipulated them. We can't have that, now can we?"

"Of course." Morgana smacked her fore-head. "We have to solve the troll problem. And maybe Sabrina will know something about that magic used."

I smiled, feeling like I had successful-ly worked my way around the rules quite nicely.

"But, in reality, you are breaking your word to the princess." Morgana got serious.

"Well, maybe they shouldn't have at-tacked MY princess. Now I know why drag-ons kept them up in tall towers," I grum-bled.

Jadelyn had pulled Sabrina so far ahead that they were stopped between two booths.

Both of the booths were similar. White seemed to be the main color, with holy symbols covering their posters. "Morgana, just how bad is the Church?"

"Bad?"

"Like, do they still secretly do terrible things?" I'd grown to dislike the idea of the people who once attacked the paranormal world at large.

"It depends. They give many people hope. And they certainly do good deeds. How do I describe it..." She paused before speaking again. "You have an organization whose roots are based in executions, starvations, and deceitful land grabs to force worship. And has amassed such a critical power that it marks itself in almost every aspect of modern life. But since then, it has become the single grandest outpouring of charity in the world. It ends up being a mix. That sort of power brings more than a few that would misuse it and continue to harm the lives of those who don't conform. But it also does good for the world and its people."

I understood her point. "The aspect that holds the power does have a dark side, but it's not all bad. I get it. Everything isn't quite so black and white."

"No. You misunderstand. I'm trying to get you to think holistically and start to make up your mind. As people are trying to convince the Scalewrights or the magi leadership of what to do, your opinion matters. One day in the not-too-distant future, you'll have the power to do something about it." Morgana's voice was heavy. It felt like she was speaking from experience.

I think I was starting to understand why she hid from her own past. From the way some of these people around Morgana gushed over her and from the snippets I'd learned of her time during the 18th century war, she no doubt had to make some tough calls.

"What did you do?" I asked quietly, wondering aloud.

She scowled at me for a moment before relenting with a sigh. "I learned that organizations are much like fighting a hydra. Cutting the head off is about the worst thing you could do." She paused. "I'm not ready to go deeper into it."

"Of course. You've given me more than enough to think about." I picked up one of the pamphlets promoting an angelic patron for warlocks. Even a dragon couldn't make a decision without knowledge. "Let's wander and collect some reading material for me. How can I make decisions if I'm uninformed?"

Morgana smiled. "Knowledge is a certain sort of power. Let's see who we can dig up some dirt on."

CHAPTER 17

It wasn't until after the convention that Jadelyn separated from Sabrina.

"I really like her," Jadelyn said as I walked her to the dark SUV that would take her and her security team home. "You could really use the help of a wizard. They might not be great in a pinch, but a prepared wizard is a terrifying thing."

"Are we really pulling in more so soon? I thought you'd be more interested in talking about... plans between you and me," I hedged, knowing that I needed to breach the conversation, eventually.

"Yes." She fidgeted, blushing heavily. "About that. My father refused to hold anything public because of the skinwalker threat. But my mother pushed him and won't settle for anything less than a small private... event early next week. Tomorrow?"

"And we're talking about a wedding, a siren wedding? No one will tell me exactly what to expect." I looked at the men waiting in the SUV and wanted a moment of privacy with her to talk rather than talking in the public parking garage.

"Hey, can you guys get out of the SUV and give us a minute?" I asked them.

The security detail was quick to comply. Everyone, even the driver, got out and took up points around the car as I slid in and pulled Jadelyn with me.

"Everything okay?" she asked, sounding scared.

I let out a heavy sigh. "It is." Grabbing her hands in mine, I turned, so that we were facing each other. "Look, this feels fast. I've known you for four months, and we've gone on one date. Now you are offering to give yourself to me in a way that we can't undo." I looked down at her hands as if they'd hold answers.

"You've marked me. That feels more permanent than a wedding ring. Plus, this is what I am choosing to do. My heart was made up before the date. The date was just a sort of confirmation for me. The fact that you are what you are only makes me want to nail you down even more before a dozen others join when they see how amazing you are." She tilted my head up to look into her eyes.

"Zach, you are a good man. You are amazing to my best friend, supposedly a fantastic lover, and I have no doubt you'll be able to provide and protect as many women as you could want. I trust my judgment with men the same as I do with the family business. Either I'm all in or I'm out." She paused, taking a breath before her eyes softened and she nearly whispered, "The question is, are you all in?"

"I—" I paused. Saying this without conviction was useless. Jadelyn deserved better than that.

I put my thoughts together and then I started again. "I am worried more about you than about me. This sounds permanent for you. Not that I would ever walk away, but everything we have together is so fresh. I don't know what the future holds. I want to know that you will continue to be happy in this relationship."

She smiled brilliantly. "I want this. As far as the future, no one ever knows what it will hold. But this feels right, natural. And your beast must agree. Honestly, knowing that the beast wanted to mark me makes me even more confident in us being together."

I pulled her close and kissed her, suddenly feeling hungry for her.

Jadelyn broke the kiss and put her lips next to my ear as she sang a soft, sweet song that lit something inside of me.

Pushing her into the back of the seat, I rocked the car as I growled with pent up need, letting my hands aggressively wander her curves.

She sang a few more of those dulcet notes into my ear before she gave up in a fit of giggles. "Take your pants off. I'll help you blow off some steam. You really are pent up; I didn't expect such a strong reaction."

***

Jadelyn was fixing her lipstick, putting a fresh coat on as the security guards remained outside the vehicle. They seemed to be pointedly ignoring what had just happened in the car behind them.

"I see why Scarlett needed help. Which means we do need to find you more women. I'm not sure Scarlett and I will be able to keep up on our own." Jadelyn rolled her lips together and checked them in a compact mirror.

"Lost myself a little there." I was a little embarrassed. After no sex for a few days, it appeared my stamina had declined sharply. But I at least made up for it in recovery time.

"That's okay. I meant to rev you up with my song, and I enjoyed every minute of it. There's something about the look you give me. And there's a thrill of knowing that I can bring you to that state." She smiled and planted a kiss that was still wet with lipstick.

I didn't need a mirror to know there was a big pink lip print on my cheek right now. "Marking me yourself?"

"Call it a siren's mark if you want. Or maybe a little revenge for when you made me choke on it the first time. I've never had semen come out of my nose before."

"It has quite a few magical properties," I said as if that solved things, scratching the back of my head. I'd gotten a little carried away.

Jadelyn patted me on the thigh. "Yes, it does. Scarlett told me a bit of what to expect, but experiencing it was something else."

At that, I frowned. Was there something I was missing? But I pushed past that for now. "I think we've kept everyone waiting long enough. I'll talk to you later. Tell your mother to set a date, and I will do everything in my power to be there for it."

"Will do." Jadelyn smiled as I left the car and flipped open my phone, finding several texts from Morgana and Sabrina asking where I was.

Heading back into the convention center, I wandered around until I met back up with Morgana and Sabrina. "Sorry about Jade, Sabrina. I had no idea she was going to be so pushy."

I went to say more, but Sabrina held her hands up for me to stop. "I should be thanking you. Getting a chance to talk to the Scalewright heiress for so long... many magi would kill for the opportunity. But I was surprised that you wanted to put off talking, though. You seemed so interested in the skinwalker."

A guilty smile crossed my features. "I promised not to go hunting down the cabal of warlocks that were involved with the skinwalker."

"Then what are we doing?" she asked, now more confused than ever.

"There is another problem I'd like your help with. We've been tasked with making sure the swamp troll migration passes through Philly, and someone seems to be luring them off route." I looked around, wondering if the convention wasn't the place to have this conversation.

Sabrina didn't quite understand what I was getting at, but luckily, she seemed more than eager enough to help. "Okay, if you think I can help."

Morgana must have picked up on my discomfort. "Why don't we find another place to talk this through?"

"Bumps?" I asked. It wasn't as if Morgana could openly hang out in many places.

"What's Bumps?" Sabrina asked, looking between the two of us.

"Morgana owns a bar here in town. You'll enjoy the ride if nothing else," I snickered.

My partner didn't find my joke quite as funny as I did. "If it is such a problem, then you drive. Try not to sink this one at the bottom of a river." She tossed the keys at me, which I caught before they hit me in the face. With her aim, they were meant to hit me in the face.

Shrugging, I led them both out to the parking garage. "Sure."

For the last several days, she'd driven a different Ferrari. It was a mind-boggling display of wealth if you asked me, but then again, Morgana could do what she wanted.

She was old enough that no doubt a few early investments of hers had to have blossomed into some insane wealth.

"Nice car," Sabrina commented as she squeezed herself into the tiny backseat.

"Wait until you see her garage." I buckled up and pulled the car out of the garage. I drove at a pace that I hoped would teach Morgana a few things about how sensible people drove. "So, Sabrina, what did you manage to find out?"

She pulled out her phone as if it was filled with notes as she started to scroll through it. "There are a few things, but the strangest thing was when I asked my mentor about the spell. At first, he seemed to recognize it, but then he had doubts, almost like he was trying to convince himself he didn't know the spell."

"Do you think he's involved?" I asked.

But she shook her head vehemently. "No. He's a crazy old coot, but he'd never do something this dark."

Morgana turned around in her seat, and I realized she didn't even have her seatbelt on. Crazy woman. "Do you think he could know someone that might be involved?"

Sabrina's eyes lit up with understanding. She took a moment to consider it before giving a small nod with a shrug. "Yeah, that might just fit. But I have no idea who. You have to understand, my mentor is pretty much a hermit. He met up with a bunch of other old men here at the conference, but before then, I don't think I've ever seen him talk to another person, at least not willingly."

Right now, it was one of our only leads, but I still had to be careful. I didn't want to break my word. Gray space I was fine with, but openly breaking it wasn't something I would do.

For the moment, I abandoned the idea of following up with her mentor and instead continued with the approach we'd already planned on. "Sabrina, do you have any idea about the troll problem part of it?"

"Troll problem?" she asked.

"We can't go directly at the problem, but we can go from another angle. We are on a job to take care of the swamp troll migration. Someone, very possibly the same group, is manipulating the trolls off their migration. It's causing trouble in the city."

"What do you mean by manipulating? Are we talking about charms, compulsion, what?"

"That's what we don't know." I turned to Morgana. "Maybe you can explain?"

That earned me an eye roll from both of the women.

"Really?" Sabrina sighed.

"I'm not well versed in magic. Just a brute," I joked.

"Okay, well, there are many schools of magic, but it all really just boils down to intent and method. If you're talking about coercion in some way, then that requires the controller to have something in continual contact with the troll," she explained.

"We can rule that out then." I thought back to the trolls at the park. Once they had transformed, everything on their person had been destroyed. I had the displeasure of seeing their troll junk and was certain there wasn't anything still on them. "They were as naked as the day they were born, not even a magical signature lingering on them."

Sabrina paused, losing whatever thought she'd had as her eyes grew wide. "You can see magic?"

"It's a talent." I shrugged.

"That's an understatement." She eyed me more seriously for a moment before continuing on. "So if they weren't wearing something physically or magically, then that leaves simpler types of magic."

Taking a turn towards the club, I focused on the road for a moment and Morgana picked up the conversation. "It wouldn't take much to set off a troll if you could just get them there. Maybe a calling of some sort?"

Sabrina considered that. "Depending on the range, the size of net needed, that could require significant power," Sabrina explained. "Maybe something even simpler?"

"Like what? Some hotdog smelling enchantment?" I joked, but both of them seemed to take it seriously.

But I knew we were running out of information to use to narrow it down. "I don't think we have enough to narrow down how they're doing it. Maybe we should instead focus on where they are doing it?" I redirected the conversation.

Morgana pulled out her phone and started tapping away, dropping pins on a map.

"Assuming this is the same group, we know who is doing this, but we don't know why." I looked at Sabrina in the rearview. "Is there anything bubbling in the magi community that would explain why a group would go after paranormals?"

She shook her head. "Nothing new, just the normal grudges. My mentor seemed to think that the paranormal and magi were getting along just fine when we came to the city."

Morgana let out a small grumble, seeming far less confident in the two groups being civil. "The magi and us are always at the brink of something."

"I always thought magic would have made life simpler, but it sometimes feels like it has only made everything more complex," Sabrina lamented.

"It isn't so much magic, but any form of power. It makes people do stupid things." Morgana and Sabrina shared a moment of commiseration.

The rest of the ride was quiet as Morgana made small noises on her phone, mapping out the troll attacks we'd worked so far.

When I rolled into Morgana's garage, I peeked in the rearview to catch Sabrina's jaw drop open.

"This must be the nicest club in the world. Everyone who goes here drives one of these?"

I laughed. "No. These are all Morgana's cars."

Sabrina's baffled expression focused on Morgana. "Why?"

"'Cause I can. Plus, this isn't that excessive. I've had my eye recently on a gold-plated BMW."

"Gold-plated?" I perked up before I squashed down whatever urges I had for gold. "I mean, if you do something that excessive, I quit. Wait, first I'd steal it."

Morgana rolled her eyes and strolled into the club. Sabrina was hot on my heels.

"So what is this place like?"

"You'll just have to see. It has a bit of everything and is bigger on the inside."

Sabrina's eyes were wide as we stepped into the first layer of the club. She was looking around, clearly trying to figure out the puzzle that was the inside of the building. "This place is huge."

"Yup." I moved through the empty dining room. It was still too early for customers. Instead, paranormals were out in the open, moving about to get the place ready.

When we came down into the second level of the nightclub, there were even a few goblins working on the lighting around the stage.

Sabrina watched them with interest, and I realized she probably hadn't had the chance to see many paranormals before.

"How does she hide all of this? No one notices that it's bigger than it is supposed to be?"

"Pretty sure the guys on the lower levels are too drugged out to notice. Otherwise, there's a big paranormal crowd that uses the club. They obviously get it." As much as I'd love to share in the revelation of Morgana's club with another, I wanted to focus on the task at hand. "Morgana, can you share the map you've been making?"

Morgana swayed her hips as she walked over to the bar and sat down. I took my preferred spot behind the bar and started to pour our group a round of drinks.

Morgana spun her phone on the bar top. "Look, I marked out where all the attacks have occurred this last week."

I looked at the pins on the map, hoping to see some sort of clear pattern. But it just looked like a giant jumble.

But then I thought about the other night and my mind started to be able to sort them. But when I thought about the attacks and looked at where they fell, I started to notice a pattern. Each day's attacks seemed like it had a pattern.

"Can you sort these out by day? Maybe color code them?"

Morgana nodded and started to sort them while I finished pouring us drinks, making sure to pour Morgana her favorite champagne blood.

She finished and put the phone back down. Plain as day, there was a rough line of pins in a different color for each night.

"Now we just need to figure out which way they are going tonight," I said, looking at the pattern.

Sabrina let out an excited squeal, pulling out her phone and flipping through it. "Here. Look." She pulled up a picture of a worn map. It had a much older Philadelphia depicted on it, but the lines followed the patterns of Morgana's pins. "This is a map of the ley lines. My mentor showed it to me before we came."

"Either of you care to explain what those are? All I know is what's in movies," I said.

Sabrina and Morgana were already excitedly pointing and scrolling onto the map.

Sabrina looked up at my question. "It's not that different. Many cities have a network of ley lines. They are sort of magical veins that run beneath the surface of the world."

"More than that," Morgana added, tapping where they roughly converged in Wissahickon Park. "Where the ley lines converge are connection points to other worlds. That's where the Faerie Realm connects to Philly." She pointed to where they came together.

"That makes total sense." Sabrina nodded, looking at the map. "So they are using the ley lines for whatever they are doing."

The idea of a portal to another world was bigger than I could fully process at the moment, so I ignored it, filing it away for another time. "Any other big portals around here?" I asked.

"There's one that leads to hell in DC," Morgana said casually, as if it was common knowledge.

"Is there one to heaven in the Vatican?" I joked.

Morgana nodded. "Yes. Though both hell and heaven have multiple portals throughout the world." She didn't seem to get my joke.

"Never mind. That's for another time. Let's focus on our troll problem and the cabal of warlocks causing problems in this world." I focused back on the map. "Can we predict which one is going to be used tonight, or does it tell us anything about what they might be doing?" I looked to Sabrina for answers.

"The whole point of ley lines is that they are constant sources of power. It might mean that whatever they are doing is large enough that they don't want to use their personal reserves. But obviously it limits where they can operate."

Limits where they can operate... "Why don't we wait and see which one they pick for the first troll sighting of the night, then we push ahead further down the ley line and see if we can't catch them in the act?"

Morgana and Sabrina thought it over.

"It is a sound plan, but it still puts us on the defensive. What do we do about the first troll?" Morgana asked.

"Bring Kelly?" I suggested. "Drop her off with a tranquilizer and have her put it down on her own?"

"That just might work. Call Kelly, and while we wait for the first call, let's test out your new changes. We have a few hours before the trolls will be active." Morgana was all smiles. It was that evil, vindictive smile that told me she was going to put me through my paces.

"Training?" Sabrina asked, looking between the two of us.

"You don't want to watch. I just get the crap kicked out of me by an old, blue granny." My head jerked back as Morgana yanked my ear.

"What was that?"

"Oh look, time to do a little training." I smiled over my shoulder. "Sabrina, do you want to stick around?" I felt bad leaving her here.

But Morgana made up for it. "I have a library if you'd like to look through it."

Sabrina's eyes practically shone. "Yes, please."

CHAPTER 18

I changed out quickly into a set of sweats I kept at the bar, deep within Morgana's twisting corridors. It was starting to feel like I almost lived with her.

"Ready?" Morgana came back after dropping Sabrina off.

I released a sigh, having changed quickly enough for her not to catch me with my pants down, literally. The two times she had, she'd made me fight like that, in the name of preparing for everything.

"Yeah. What did you have in mind?"

Morgana prowled the space. It was a wide, open room with a matted floor meant for combat practice. Practice weapons were arranged along the walls, and those were not-so-soft although at least not deadly. I should know. She'd whacked me in the back of the head with all of them at least once.

"I want to see you shift."

Nodding, I reached, starting to take my shirt off, but then moved to keep her in my line of sight. She loved to attack when I least expected it when we were in the training room. "Don't try anything."

"Oh, please. It was just that one time."

"Twice. You did it twice," I growled.

"Who knew dragons were such drama queens?" Morgana waved away my concerns, sticking her tongue out at me. Her blue tongue. That always caught me off guard.

Throwing off the rest of my clothes, I stood there comfortable in my nakedness for a moment before shifting. I pushed the beast to the surface, my bones cracking and popping into the new configuration.

But, of course, Morgana wasn't going to wait for me to finish.

A heavy blow hit my head even as I was shifting, and I staggered to the side. The movement halted my shift midway. It was so goddamn uncomfortable that I almost shifted back. But I realized that was exactly what she wanted.

Pushing through the shift, I came out of my shift a pissed off dragon-hybrid. I was a big, scaly beast capable of standing on two legs, or prowling on all four. But I didn't have wings, nor would I fit through any doorway. Even in the large training room, I couldn't stand on my back legs, or I'd be too far above Morgana to fight her.

Pausing, I realized I'd lost where she was when I finished my shift.

My head jerked back as someone land-ed between my horns and started pulling. Frustrated, I was more than happy to fight her in my hybrid form.

I curled in on myself and slammed my head against the floor, working to throw her off. But Morgana simply ran down my spine, smacking me with whatever practice weapon was in her hand.

Rolling onto my back, I tried to crush her, but she jumped, leaving me on my back as she was flying down, sword in two hands, to stab my stomach.

Damnit.

But a golden blur caught her right in the chest. My tail had swung based on instincts I didn't know I had, sending her flying against the wall with a wet crack.

Rolling back on my feet, I stood up and grunted as I went to check on her. My tail had crushed in the side of her chest, and it looked like she'd broken her neck against the wall. Both of those were popping back into place, though.

She took a deep breath. "I might have deserved that."

Of course you did, I grumbled, but it came out as guttural nonsense.

"Oh. My. God. You can't talk." She clutched her still healing chest and fell over sideways, laughing.

Not funny, I huffed, which of course only made her laugh harder. Hard enough that she sputtered up blood from her crushed chest.

I grabbed her hair with my jaw and tossed her into the air again. She landed back in the center of the mats. But that still didn't stop her from rolling around laughing at me.

Rolling my dragon eyes, which I could still do clearly, I stretched and let my beast come back down from the full dragon hybrid form. I stopped when I was still covered in scales and had put on a few hundred pounds, but my throat was human.

"Cut it out, Morgana."

"He talks!" She gave one last chuckle and rolled to her feet. "But seriously. Be careful. Your size isn't always an advantage. If I were using my magic there, you would have been dead a dozen times over."

"What do you recommend?" I asked, curious. For all the shit I gave her, she was an expert in fighting, and I knew many would kill for the chance to train with her. Although, they probably were less aware of her somewhat brutal methods.

"This right here isn't bad." She stepped around me, looking at it. "A little showy, though. You look like a knight in golden armor."

My face was human, but she was right. Scales coated me like a suit of armor, and a wicked-looking crown of spikes curled from my brow to protect my skull. "It doesn't feel that bad."

"Yeah? Think you can fight like that?" she asked. "I think your hybrid form is too big to be useful in most places. Almost anywhere indoors, it isn't going to work."

I grumbled, but she was right. I liked being a big fucker, but this form was more likely to be of help. Now, I stood at maybe seven and a half feet tall with another two hundred pounds of weight on me. A small doorway would be a challenge, but otherwise, there wasn't going to be much in the normal world I couldn't operate within.

"What are you going to call it?" She asked.

"I feel like a knight in gold armor, so this is me as a dragon knight." I gave the pseudo form a name.

She nodded. "I like it, and you get to pretend to be a knight in shining armor when you save yet another girl. Or a guy, you know you could save a guy for once." Morgana tried to deadpan, but her smile quirked ever so slightly at the edge.

I rolled my eyes. "Come on. Enough talk. I want to get used to this form."

Morgana came at me quickly, with the grace and speed that only an elf turned vampire could have. Compared to her, the rest of us must have seemed like bumbling toddlers.

Still, she wasn't able to crawl over me anymore, and I had enough training to handle her first flurry of punches. Changing tactics, she moved to try to sweep my legs out from under me.

I hunkered down, putting my weight on the leg and stopping her cold. Then I grabbed for her, but space bent away from me and she was out of my reach. She twisted and turned over me like I was a stripper pole, ending with my head in her hands. She pulled me in the direction I had been leaning.

I toppled over onto the ground, but not before sinking my hand into her arm and pulling her down with me. "It never ends well when we get down on the floor together."

She might be agile to the point I couldn't hit her, but down on the ground grappling? My strength was king down here.

"Who knows, maybe this time it'll end just right." She winked and bit her lower lip.

It distracted me only for a moment, but that was all she needed. The world turned upside down, and she rolled me, springing to her feet and escaping with a husky laugh.

"Keep your head on. Never know when you're going to have to fight something pretty." She waited for me to get to my feet.

"Yeah, well, let's see if I can't make you less pretty." I made a tight fist, eager to get a score on Morgana.

The elven vampire had hundreds of years of experience on me though, and by all accounts, was a war hero three hundred years ago. A war that she still hadn't told me much about.

I dodged another hit as I asked, "Morgana, what is 'the Church'? You've mentioned it, but you never went into detail. Is it the Vatican?" Sometimes Morgana opened up better when she was fighting.

She wove under a punch, and I met her next attack with the hard horns on my head, sending her stumbling back with a bloody fist that healed instantly.

"No, not exactly. What we call 'the Church' and any practicing religion here isn't the same. Though they were once the same." She came back at me with another hit. "They might be loosely connected, but remember, paranormals are the bad guys. We are the bad guys."

I took a chance and let her get a solid hit to my chest, bringing her closer. Wrapping my arms around her in a hug, I crushed her to me. It stung to take that blow to the chest, but once she was in my arms, she wasn't getting out. Already, the bones in her shoulders were starting to strain.

"Submit."

She slapped me twice, and I let her go. Morgana stumbled back, wheezing as her shoulder popped back into place. "That was good. Didn't expect your chest to be so hard."

"I might not be fully shifted, but these are still dragon scales. But don't dodge the question. I want to know more about the Church."

She sighed, panting a bit as she relented. "Think back to hundreds of years ago. Who do you think peasants called when vampires were eating people in their hamlets? Or when some other 'monster' showed up that everyone was afraid of." Morgana air quoted the word.

"Monster?" I asked, offended.

"What do you think we are? Stories about dragons don't often have them being kind, merciful creatures, now do they? No, you kidnap princesses, hoard gold and rampage villages." She looked me in the eye. "Regardless of what you stand for to yourself and the rest of the paranormal community, know that they see all of us as monsters."

I frowned. We certainly had some extra skill sets, but we weren't monsters, especially not in the sense that we were innately dangerous. But it made more sense for why the secrecy of the paranormal world had to be kept. I wanted to rebel and deny that the people I grew up with wouldn't think of us as monsters, but if I were honest with myself, I had a feeling they would.

A right hook caught my chin while I wasn't paying attention, and I stumbled to a knee.

"Quit moping. Stand up and fight. At the end of the day, you are what you want to be. I don't see Scarlett or Jadelyn running from you screaming. Sabrina, who's crazy shy, seems instantly comfortable around you. Hell, you have the entire wolf pack drooling over you. Don't throw yourself a pity party just yet because some idiots would consider you a monster."

She waited for me to recover. "The Church is a relic of a bygone era. They used to hunt us down with crosses and cross-bows. The best among them were warlocks wielding powerful artifacts blessed by an-gelics. Now they, like us, must live in secret."

I got back up, raising my fists to go anoth-er round. "Then I just have to be better than them."

"There we go." Morgana got back into a tempo, really starting to work me and put me through my paces while I held onto my dragon knight form.

She was a challenge like no other. Some-how, I knew that she had put herself through a crucible stained with blood to have the instincts she did when we fought. The distant echo of hatred that was in her voice when she talked about The Church was clear.

I wanted to know so much more about her past and what had really happened back three hundred years ago, but I had a feeling that she'd crack my jaw if I asked any more then.

So I did the next best thing. I taunted her to help distract her from going back through her memories. "Is that all you got? Pretty sure your age is getting to you, Morgana. That was weak."

She stopped on a dime and spun, her heel lashing out and catching me hard enough in the ribs that I knew I was going to have a wicked bruise tomorrow.

But I grabbed her leg and drove her body to the floor as I went all out on her, letting her push me as hard as she could.

Every time I forced her to use her magic, I counted it as a win, because someone who wasn't Morgana would have been dead each of those times. That, and her using magic was cheating. I mean, she could bend space. In a fist fight or even with simple weapons, that was a cheat code.

She worked me on the mat until I was too tired to hold my dragon knight form and reverted back to being human mid strike. Morgana didn't miss the chance to pull me off balance and flip me on my back with a wet smack as my sweat-soaked back made contact with the floor.

"Not bad. You lasted pretty long."

"Hard to hold that form. Human and hybrid dragon feel natural, but that one takes effort," I grunted, my lungs straining to pull air in.

"No, I mean it. Good work. But you could use your shifting a little more when you fight. More than a few times if you'd changed your size on me, it would have been easy for you to take the advantage and pin me." She tossed me a water bottle while she popped open another one of her champagned blood bottles.

I'd seen her have more than a few of them before, but that was in the dark club. Here it was clearer. The dark glass bottle was decorated, oddly enough, with angel wings.

Taking a heavy pull from the water bottle, its plastic crinkled as I sucked down to hydrate myself before coming up for air. "I think that might be a little more advanced than I'm ready for."

Morgana hummed to herself as she took a satisfied sip of her own beverage. "Something to look forward to then." She looked at my nakedness. "We need to get you some clothes that stretch too. Think you can keep your scales under your clothes? That might be a nice surprise if anyone tries something on the street."

I paused in my chugging. "Think I'm going to need that?" I asked.

"Can't be too prepared, but I think those scales could stop a low caliber bullet. Think of it like a bullet-proof vest," she offered.

That... made sense. I might be tough, but I didn't think I was bulletproof. Now I could be if I learned to use my shift correctly. My powers were coming in hard and fast, but it still felt like I was just scratching the surface.

Taking another swig of water, I tried to casually pry a bit more on our conversation from earlier. "Morgana. Can you tell me what really happened three hundred years ago with the Church?"

She looked up at me, her eyes growing more serious than usual. "I told you. People died. Lots of them. For no reason except someone leading the Church saw an opportunity to press an advantage. It wasn't even about killing paranormals—it was about giving the populace of Europe a shared enemy." She drained her glass and poured another.

She'd said that part before, but she rarely ever went into detail about her role within the fight. If she had played such a pivotal role in the war and was such a dangerous enemy of the Church, why the heck was she out in the open? Shouldn't they be hunting her down?

"Why isn't the Church coming after you? After everything I've heard, it's public knowledge that you beat their asses back. They should be coming after you."

She paused, her freshly filled glass halfway up to her mouth before she put it down and looked away. She turned back, weariness across her face. I'd seen her fight time and time again, and she never looked tired. "There's a truce."

"A truce?" My mind whirled at the idea. She wasn't part of the elves, and she wasn't part of the vampires. If there was a truce, it meant that she alone was able to hold off the Church? While she was no doubt amazingly skilled and a kick ass mercenary, she was just one person. I hadn't seen anything from her to suggest she was that powerful.

"There's a truce between the Church and I." She swirled her glass and sipped from it.

"You're going to have to give me more than that," I growled, not liking being in the dark.

"Suffice to say, I can't harm them and they can't harm me."

Now she was just being evasive. "I know what a damn truce is, Morgana. Why?"

"Because I'm a big, spooky paranormal and I leaned into my reputation. Don't worry about it. Even if you pick a fight with the Church, I'll back you." Morgana smiled around her glass as she drank deeply, enjoying her special vintage of blood.

I wasn't quite sure what to think. There were clearly more layers to peel back to get to the real Morgana than I thought.

I went to ask another question, but my phone vibrated in my pocket. Morgana smiled, knowing she was off the hook for the moment.

Pulling it out, I confirmed what we'd both expected. "Kelly is here."

"Then go get cleaned up. The last thing you want is to be smelly and sweaty around her. She might try to rub as much of your scent off of you as she can. Stupid werewolf." Morgana cursed the last bit into her glass as she drained it. "I need to start setting up a few things."

CHAPTER 19

Kelly had planted herself at the bar top. I found myself once again tending bar in the otherwise empty lower level. She motioned to me for another drink. I shook the tequila bottle, trying to remember how full it had been when we started.

Morgana was off managing something in the club while we waited. Sabrina had sat down on a couch, and after procuring an old wooden broom handle, had been working away at it with a knife. And that left me bar tending for a very thirsty werewolf.

"I mean, I know that Chad was an ass, but I kind of miss him."

"Okay. That is the official signal that you've had far too much." I opened up another bottle, but I put it on the shelf.

She rolled her eyes and played with her once again empty glass. "I'm not that far gone. Werewolf metabolism and all. But evil voodoo and killing other alphas aside, he was good for the pack."

"Things have gotten that bad?" I asked, leaning over the bar to listen as I considered if I should let her have more. I eyed her while she gave me her sweetest smile. I grunted, relenting.

Seeing my decision, she held her glass back up with a smile. "We can't even hold a practice right now. Every time they line up for a play, at least one of them ends up shifting and trying to tear another apart. Then the whole team shifts, and a brawl breaks out. It always ends with another one limping away pretending he's the victor and the new alpha."

"Why isn't he the new alpha?" I asked, pouring the drink and idly wondering how much this bottle cost. At some point, I wondered if Morgana would take it out of my cut.

"Because he didn't really win. The other wolf didn't really submit. Being alpha is more than just coming out on top of a dog pile. It is about being the fucking boss." She punctuated her statement by taking a lime from behind the counter and doing another shot. "I could whip their butts into shape, but they need a real alpha. They're all too close to each other's power, and none are strong enough."

"Well, I still think you'd make a great alpha." I refilled her shot glass. This time, thank heavens, she sipped it.

"Not how it works. The pack magic wouldn't even accept me if I tried."

This wasn't the first time we'd had this conversation; I knew her mind was set. But I still thought she should at least try.

Morgana came back around, still on the phone and looked at me with a question as she covered the phone. "Blonde or brunette?" she asked.

I blinked, not sure what she meant. Then I remembered she was officially planning my bachelor party. Rolling my eyes, I arched my brow as I said, "Maybe I like silver hair."

Her cheeks blushed purple for the first time ever. But she recovered quickly, giving me a thumbs up. "Works."

Then she sauntered off, her swords slapping her leather clad ass, making it ripple in ways that made my imagination swirl.

Kelly snorted into her drink, breaking my attention. I turned to her as she laughed harder. "Holy shit. You play a dangerous game."

"It's our thing. There's nothing really there," I told her, but I didn't hear the conviction in my own voice that I'd expected. "Besides, I never knew drow vampires blushed purple. That was a new one."

"Uh huh. That girl would suck you dry if you gave her the opportunity." Kelly paused and looked into her drink with a frown. "I meant that she'd suck your cock dry. Not the whole vampire thing. Although maybe that too. But not dead." She caught herself in her ramble.

"Sure she would," I humored Kelly. "She's trying to plan a bachelor party for me."

Kelly looked up from her drink. "You're getting married?!" Her mouth hung open, and she even looked a little angry. "Holy crap, how did I not know this?"

"A siren's wedding," I clarified. "It isn't that big of a deal, though. Her family is going to do something more formal later, but she doesn't want to wait. Either way, it isn't the end of the line for me given what I am." My eyes shifted over to Sabrina, but she was still fully engrossed in whatever she'd been working on.

"That makes perfect sense. Are you still not willing to add a few dozen wolves to your harem?" she said it lightheartedly, but there was just a touch of seriousness in her tone. I knew that Kelly was interested in me, but it just wasn't going to work with how the packs worked.

I changed the subject rather than have the same discussion yet again.

"Hey, Sabrina, what are you working on?" I pretended to be more curious about the broken broom handle she was whittling away at than I actually was.

It took her a full two seconds to register that I'd been talking to her before she looked up. "A blasting rod. It's just a simple tool for wizards to channel mana through and generate a spell. Sturdier than a wand. We can't all be sorcerers throwing around the elements like it's breathing."

Kelly laughed. "Hehe. You said breeding."

I put my head in my palm. "Kelly, she said, breathing. I think I do need to cut you off."

She swiftly turned back, pleading, as she clutched her glass. "I was just kidding."

"Sure you were."

She held the pathetic pose a few more moments before she could see I wasn't going to budge. She dropped it, sighing. "Well, if you are going to be like that, then I'll just go for the throat. I can't believe you are marrying Jadelyn already."

I did my best to keep my face neutral as she poked a sensitive topic. "It was her decision to push it forward, and I'm respecting her wishes. But I'm in this."

"That makes it so much better," Kelly said sarcastically. "So, did she know what you were before or after she proposed?" The way she said it was laced with an unsaid accusation.

"Enough, Kelly," I warned, and wrenched the glass out of her hand.

"What? I only said what everyone else would be thinking." She didn't let up, leaning forward into the bar.

"You should learn to keep some thoughts to yourself," I growled, leaning forward myself, putting my face right in front of hers, both with our own scowl.

Morgana came back just at that moment, her face set. Knowing those pointy blue ears of hers, she'd heard everything Kelly said. She looked between the two of us, holding our eyes before she finally spoke.

"Since you seem to be intent on interpreting my relationship with Zach." She gave Kelly a vicious smile. "Then I'll return the favor."

Turning on her heels, Morgana said plainly, "Zach, Kelly is jealous of Jadelyn."

"No. I'm not," Kelly emphasized, turning and almost throwing herself at Morgana before thinking better of taking on the drow vampire.

Morgana put her phone down on the bar. "Keep it up. You certainly sound like someone who isn't invested." Her voice filled with sarcasm. She stared Kelly down, nearly challenging her.

"Cut it out. I don't need two catty girls in my life, now or ever. It's a bad look on both of you."

Kelly immediately jumped in. "She started it!"

Morgana eyed her before calmly responding with more tact. "He knows that's a lie. You were sitting here spouting off before I came down. Bitter bitch."

"See. This is what she's like when you aren't around. Might as well be a tame puppy around you." Kelly threw her hands in the air.

As Morgana's phone vibrated again on the bar, I snatched it and moved around the bar before giving them one last look. "Sort it out. I don't want to listen to the two of you bickering in the car tonight."

I stepped away from the bar before the two of them imploded. "This is Zach with Silverwing Mercenaries." She rarely used her last name, but her mercenary company had it.

A bored sounding woman on the other end of the phone perked up. "Oh, I thought I had called Morgana."

"You did. This is her phone. She is..." I looked at Kelly and her, who were still facing off, on the verge of a shouting match. Neither woman was close to backing down. "... indisposed at the moment. I can take whatever it is. I assume this is a call about a troll?"

"Yes, it is. Do you have something to write down an address?"

"One moment." I juggled Morgana's phone onto my shoulder and pulled out my phone, ready to type with both thumbs. "Hit me."

She rattled off an address, and I repeated it back to make sure it was correct before sending it to Morgana. Her phone blipped in my ear in response.

"Thank you very much. Do you work for the council?" I asked, wondering if I should save her number.

"Yes, I handle messages for them. Technically, I work for Detective Fox."

"Oh," I hissed in sympathy. "Sorry about that."

She giggled. "It's not that bad. If you aren't dating his daughter, he's a very nice man, Mr. Zach Pendragon." I wasn't completely surprised she knew who I was, but it still caught me for a moment.

"Should I be worried? Sounds like you might be in the know."

She went quiet on the other end of the line for a moment. "It was a pleasure to meet you, Zach. I've already heard so much about you." She hung up.

I wondered what had led to her pause. Had someone else been in the room?

But I already knew that the detective had done some sort of detailed investigation on me. Maybe she had been involved in that. Beyond not wanting to spread what I was and deal with the complications, I really didn't have much to hide.

Kelly and Morgana's voices were picking up around the corner, and I stepped around, ready to break up the standoff. I really wasn't used to Morgana acting this way, but I figured Kelly's werewolf nature might be invoking some sort of territory competition or trying to set up some sort of pecking order.

"You two. Time's up. Put whatever this is aside. We have a troll to catch." I tossed Morgana back her phone. She snatched it out of the air without even breaking eye contact with Kelly.

"We were just finishing." Morgana pulled back a strand of silver hair that had escaped her ponytail and reset it.

Kelly looked awkward as she stepped away from Morgana and spoke to me. "You make a really good alpha boss when you need to be. We're done."

"Good. Morgana, I already texted you the address. Sabrina? Do you have the ley line map for us again?"

Our phones all went down on the bar with the new address, comparing it to Sabrina's map.

"I don't know anything there," Kelly said.

Morgana grunted and pointed to a neighborhood that was half an hour from the troll attack, next to Fairmount Park. "It's a gated community and exclusively elves."

Of course, the snooty elves lived in a gated community.

"There's something else," Sabrina added. "The convention center is on the same ley line."

I stepped back from the bar, considering the two options. Attacking the elves would be like attacking a fortified bunker. I had full confidence that an all-elf gated community was like a giant turtle shell of enchantments. And each and every one of them had magic of their own.

It was far too big compared to what they had targeted so far. It was too big of a leap.

As for the convention center, there had already been one troll there before, so maybe it had some sort of benefit. But so far, the magi hadn't been their primary target. Changing it up so suddenly didn't make sense.

The convention would still be running the next morning, but it would be reduced since many would be leaving town in the morning. What good did it do them to attack it tonight?

"I'm not sure it is either of those. I just can't get what we know so far to mesh with either of those options. There has to be another target."

"Then we'll just have to go there and wait to see what we find." Morgana dangled a set of keys from her hand. "Because whether we like it or not, there is a troll we need to take care of."

"Dibs on the biggest tranq gun you guys have." Kelly bounded off the barstool towards the garage.

I walked out with Morgana, grabbing the pistol I favored. "Let's drop Kelly off and then do a few circles around the elven community. Even if I don't think that's the target, maybe their information is flawed. They could think they are hitting a single elven household." I was grasping at straws, and I knew it.

"Can do." Morgana grabbed a bandoleer of syringes. Apparently, after losing her favorite dart rifle, she had opted for a more personal approach. She was pretty good at close combat. Her blades slapped against her leather-clad thighs in a reminder of just how dangerous she could be.

Kelly was already running over to the van with a massive dart gun and darts half the size of my forearm. It was complete overkill. T's special tranquilizer could knock out an elephant with just a small dose.

Rolling her eyes at the werewolf's antics, Morgana strutted out to the van with Sabrina on her heels.

Morgana slid behind the driver's seat of the van as Sabrina hesitated, taking a moment to summon up some courage before she got into the van. Clutching the carved broom handle with white knuckles, she buckled into the van and chanted wards onto the seat belt.

She hadn't ridden with Morgana yet. My only guess was that Kelly had scared her before we had come down from sparring.

I just got in the passenger seat and clicked my seatbelt, trying to find my happy place and center my breathing. Of course, Morgana's driving made that near impossible as she gunned it into reverse and then peeled out of the garage.

If I didn't know better, she was driving more aggressively than before. It only took cracking open my eyes and seeing her watch Kelly in the rearview mirror to understand why.

Kelly was braced against the side of the car, clinging onto the oh-shit handle with her leg wedged under my seat. She squealed as Morgana took yet another tight turn, causing a small smirk to spread on Morgana's face.

Oh yeah, Morgana was enjoying this.

Sabrina was chanting additional wards on her seatbelt and clinging tightly to her new tool.

Morgana made a turn, hitting the location of the ley line and continued following it. Unfortunately, that meant cutting diagonally across the city blocks, meaning she was zigzagging down the streets to keep with the ley line as best as she could.

"Keep your eyes open, Zach. We need to figure out the next target," Morgana reminded me.

Damnit. Shifting my eyes, I did my best to look down alleys and at pedestrians for signs of magic use.

"Calm down, Morgana. How do you expect me to see anything when you are going so fast?" I grumbled, partially angry seeing Sabrina behind me looking like she was giving herself last rites.

Morgana pouted, but slowed down just enough so that I wasn't getting whiplash trying to scan everything.

When we got to the address of the first troll, Kelly didn't even wait for Morgana to come to a complete stop before tumbling out of the car with her large tranquilizer rifle. She tossed us a salute as she dashed into the alley. Not long after her exit, we heard something thudding.

"Look at her. She finally has some work ethic. Pretty snappy exit," Morgana commented as Sabrina pulled the door closed behind Kelly.

"Yeah. I'm sure that's why she got out in such a hurry," I humored Morgana.

In response, Morgana floored it once again, and I found myself pressed into the seat as I tried to scan the streets. Unfortunately, nothing stood out.

I was able to spot the elven community before we were even close. The place was lit up with magic like a Christmas tree. Magic glowed in every color, nearly blinding me as we approached.

"Holy crap. Why were we even worried about this place?" I said.

"That bad?" Morgana asked.

"Thousands of wards. Even if a couple rogue warlocks were causing trouble here, I wouldn't be able to sift through all of this and find what they were doing." What sort of idiots would try to attack this? It would be like thinking it was a bright idea to go hold up a gun store.

I pushed past all the bright lights and got a good look at the community. It was beautiful, like a slice of utopia. The area was filled with white picket fences and open yards, broad gardens, and houses with a tendency to let vines claim at least part of their exterior walls. Enormous trees towered in the yards, with more than a few elaborate tree houses built amid their boughs.

"Okay, let's do a lap and make sure. I'm going to make a call," I directed Morgana, and she accommodated, slowing down and starting a lap.

Grabbing her phone, I called back the last number. "Hello, can you do me a favor?" I asked Detective Fox's messenger.

"Sure?" She sounded hesitant.

"We are tracking the troll, and we've noticed a pattern the last few nights. It leads me to be concerned for an elven neighborhood next to Fairmount." I started to read off the address, but she cut me off.

"I know the one. Sebastian lives there."

"Good. Could you pass along a message to him or someone else in the neighborhood that can put it to use? I just want them to be on the lookout for a troll tonight. Their wards are so bright that I can't hang around here and keep an eye out without going blind."

"Sure..." I could hear her scratching pen on paper. "Is that all?"

"Yes. And thank you. We'll focus on keeping the trolls away. You haven't gotten another call yet?"

"None. And you're welcome. It's always nice to be appreciated."

"Hey, you keep things running. You deserve to be appreciated. Have a nice night and call us if you hear of another incident." I hung up after letting her say goodbye.

Morgana had slowed to a slow roll and watched me. "Are you courting another woman?"

"No. God, not every woman I meet and am kind to is a sudden romantic interest." I kept scanning for any threats.

Morgana responded, "You know she has the hots for you."

I knew she wasn't talking about the lady on the phone. She was talking about Kelly.

"Yes. She wants me to be her alpha, but I can't be. I'd tear her pack apart. There's no way I could do what was expected of me and let the girls go back home with another man, even if he was a beta." I looked out the window as Morgana sped up, wanting a different conversation topic. "So. Where to?"

"Let's check out the convention center." Morgana seemed satisfied with my answer, changing the topic. "Cheer up, buttercup. There are plenty of girls out there."

I didn't let my thoughts linger on why she seemed so focused on Kelly and my relationship. We had warlocks to find.

Chapter 20

We were a few blocks away from the convention center when I spotted a red glow down an alley. My dragon eye recognized the spectrum of color as magic and not just some tinted light.

"Morgana, pull over here," I quickly called out.

Morgana's van screeched to a halt, and I jumped out, rushing into the alley before the warlocks could get away. Car doors slammed behind me; I knew the girls were tight on my heels.

I raced into the alley, quickly spotting three young magi. They seemed to be loitering around, flicking spells off to impress each other. One of them had fire streaming from his finger as he held a cigarette over the flame. His arm was frozen halfway to his mouth as we sprinted into the alley.

His eyes quickly slid off of me to Morgana behind me, clearly assessing her as the larger threat. One quick look over my shoulder, and I saw her hands itching on the pommels of her blades.

The three young men dropped everything, including the cigarette on the ground, at the same time as I heard the ring of Morgana's blades.

"It's just pot. Please don't kill us." A magus wearing glasses held his hands up, but then had to put one down to readjust his glasses.

There was a small enchantment on the wall behind them. I squinted at it before giving up and asking Morgana, "Can you check this one out? Right here." I pointed at the wall.

Instead of Morgana, Sabrina stepped forward. With a wave of her hand, the ward became visible.

"That's just for us to hide out here so we can do a little magic," the one who had dropped his cigarette stated. The cigarette definitely smelled like stinky weed.

"It's not every day we get to hang out with other magi, and we don't like the hotel and all the old farts." Glasses seemed to be pleading with Sabrina.

"I know. They just talk about the golden days all night long, don't they?" Sabrina made conversation while she looked at the ward. "This is really sloppy work. I almost couldn't recognize it."

"See, we weren't doing anything that needs those." Cigarette pointed to Morgana's naked blades with a trembling finger.

Morgana eyed them once more before seeming to decide it was time to put them away. She stuffed them back into the sheaths on her hips. "I think they are harmless." Morgana sighed. "Not who we are looking for."

There was a collective exhale from the group at Morgana's comment.

This was just a group of young magi hiding out from the watchful eyes of their elders. I leaned into my instincts to make sure, and they were quiet. These guys weren't up to anything besides maybe a little recreational drug use. It was a false alarm.

"Well, we certainly don't care about that." I pointed to the still burning cigarette. "Better pick it up before you start a trash fire here."

I started to turn, but then realized maybe they could still be of some use. "Look, there are a few warlocks causing trouble in the city." Taking out a little notebook I kept, I scratched my number on a page and handed it to them. "Call me if you see anyone doing something strange around the convention."

"Sure. Whatever, yeah." Glasses took it and spoke like he just wanted us to leave. I had a feeling he wouldn't call if he saw anything, so I went to impress the importance upon them.

"I know you want to throw that away as soon as I leave. But don't. The warlocks causing trouble could bring a world of hurt down on all magi in the city. Call us if you see anything. They already attacked a group of high-profile paranormals; the last thing we need is them to cause a larger problem."

That seemed to get their attention, and this time he put it in his pocket. I felt like I'd had a little more success.

We stepped away from our false alarm. "What do we do?" Sabrina asked. "Wait for another call?"

"That's all we can do," Morgana grumbled as she paused at the door to the van.

I hated the idea of waiting for another call, but our only other option at that point was continuing to scout along the ley line. We could completely miss them altogether again.

Frustrated, I reached for the van handle, but then screams broke up the quiet night.

I was running before I even realized it, heading just down the street towards the sound. I saw the hotel next to the convention center. Similar to the elven neighborhood, it was covered in wards, but unlike those, these were all separated and disjointed, as if done individually by hundreds of people.

I realized that was the exact difference. The magi no doubt had each put their own small protections on their rooms. And it didn't seem to be doing them much good.

A public trash can shot into the hotel lobby, taking out two magi as it flew. I winced, hoping they survived the metal trash can that was yeeted into the crowd. I knew from experience that trolls could put a ton of force behind something like that.

Taking in the scene, I grimaced. It wasn't just one troll. At least a dozen were transforming in and around the hotel.

"Shit." Morgana came up next to me and cursed.

She was right. I had dismissed this possibility earlier because they hadn't gone after magi before, but it looked like the convention was their target after all. Only it wasn't the convention center, it was the attendants in the neighboring hotel.

The magi were quick to react, lobbing lightning and fire at the trolls, but the hotel lobby was catching fire faster than the trolls. Both of those elements did little to stop a rampaging troll. I already knew that after having tried to cook one with dragon fire.

Frost worked much better. All the excess water in the swamp troll's body didn't freeze well. Seemingly in response, a single frozen lance crashed down among the trolls, freezing and shattering an arm. It did much more damage than the dozens of fire and lightning spells.

"This feels close to what I promised not to do now that it involves the convention. But given that we have magi that can't seem to save themselves, I need to go help." I watched Morgana to see if she agreed. This was potentially inviting trouble, and I wanted her to make that call.

Her blades rang out as she drew them again. "I'm ready to carve up some trolls, if that is what you are asking."

"I can't shift here, Morgana."

"Don't worry. I was starting to get bored. This'll be fun."

As if the dozen trolls weren't enough, more were spilling out of the nearby alleys as they continued to be drawn to the hotel. This was more trolls than we'd ever seen before.

"Where are these coming from?" I asked.

The trolls almost seemed to multiply before me. Despite the magi's best efforts to hold them back, the trolls were pushing into the lobby. Whatever tactic was being used to lure the trolls, tonight it had been dialed up to eleven.

I wanted to jump right into the action, but with spells flying all over the place, getting close was too dangerous.

"It looks like our troublemakers have really outdone themselves this time." Sabrina clutched her blasting rod in front of her, ready for a fight.

I looked at the rod in Sabrina's hand, worried that she'd brought fire to a swamp troll fight like so many of the other magi. "You sure you want to use that? You can always hang back. I promised you previously that you wouldn't have to fight."

But Sabrina shook her head. "No. I'm here, and I'm going to fight. Just because I don't want to doesn't mean I can walk away from this. Plus, I spent all the time making this. I want to give it a try."

She held out the end of the broomstick that had been carved, or rather butchered, by a small knife. Intricate carvings were broken up by cracks in the wood as she held it aloft like her prized possession.

"This thing is going to pack a punch." She sounded excited, like a kid with a new toy.

I figured Morgana had thrown me into more than a few fights in order to learn, and I could do the same for Sabrina. I just needed to make sure she didn't get hurt.

"Cover my back. Follow me." I approached the carnage out in front of the hotel.

Car alarms blared as one of the trolls smashed in the hood of a nearby car that had parked out front of the hotel. I looked around, realizing that it was quiet outside of the immediate battle.

Why the heck weren't people a block over screaming, and where were the cops? It wasn't as if the area was unpopulated.

Yet somehow, as I looked down the cross street, everyone was minding their own business, as if the hotel didn't even exist. I realized one or more of the wards around the hotel must be keeping people from noticing what was happening. They'd likely put it up to help keep them covered as they talked or worked any magic.

But I knew that, if the fight continued to spill out, even magic had its limits.

The magi were being pushed backwards in the lobby, and the front of the hotel was clear of haphazardly flying spells for now, but more trolls than I'd ever seen were in the area. And they could wreak havoc, as was proven by the three trolls pounding on the nearby car in an effort to silence the alarm that seemed to be annoying them.

"I think catch and release isn't viable tonight. We need to stop these trolls, however we can." I looked Morgana and Sabrina in the eye before I turned back, gritting my teeth and charging into the three trolls still walloping the car.

I didn't like the idea of having to kill the swamp trolls, but we didn't have many other options. This needed to be contained.

Sabrina all of a sudden came from my left, surprising me as she leveled her blasting rod at the first swamp troll we encountered. It lit up with a white glow and then started to pour out a jet of mist, coating the swamp troll's two arms as it tried to block.

Immediately after, its arms froze and crumbled into swampy slush under its own weight. The troll was just as baffled as I was.

"Damn, that's got some kick," I said, impressed.

Sabrina blushed. "I was just trying to help. Swamp trolls are weak to frost magic. That's just basic information in the bestiary."

Morgana patted her on the shoulder. "That was great work. Keep it up. We have more where that one came from."

Encouraged, Sabrina hit it again. This time she focused on its legs, reducing the troll to the squirming torso as little baby hands started to regrow from its arms. I tried not to look at the tiny hands; those things were creepy.

Feeling better about pulverizing them, given their regeneration, I looked at the others.

The car that the trolls had been smashing sounded pitiful; its alarm was waning into a sad beep as the crushed vital components attempted to sound.

As the car quieted, the other trolls looked up and saw the state of their third.

One of the trolls that looked up had tusks that curled up, nearly poking itself in the eyes. Tusky was a big fucker and proved it too by grabbing the smashed-up car and hauling it over his shoulder.

"Get back!" My clothes popped at the seams as I shifted just enough to take on more mass, doubling my weight and charging into the car just before Tusky threw it.

The geek in me was curious about what would happen when an unstoppable force met an immovable object, but it looked like I'd have to wait until another day. Because, as the sedan crashed into me, I barely kept my feet under me as I crashed back into the pavement. My shoes were torn up as I slid backwards on the pavement.

Sabrina gave me a small smile. I looked over my shoulder to try to check on Morgana, but she had disappeared.

Tossing the car to the side, I got a glimpse of the blur that was my partner as she twirled between the trolls, slicing and dicing at them. Those cuts served their purpose as a momentary distraction right before she cut at their joints, slowing them down, but certainly not stopping them.

I dove back at Tusky. "Morgana, keep the other one disabled. Sabrina, take it down."

Tusky looked up at me and swung for the fences, his big meaty hand sounding like a plane passing over my head as I ducked just under it. I came back up with a hook that caught his chin, just damn near perfect.

His head snapped to the side, and the lumbering fool took a few unsteady steps to the side before he shook it off.

But I was already there, following up on my hit by driving my fist into his gut and pulling him over to the side. I tossed Tusky on the ground and went down with him.

He thrashed, but I got a hand on a tusk and pushed his head back to the ground. Two big meaty hands came up and tried to stop me, but I shifted my fingers to claws and tore out his shoulders.

I smiled, looking down at him. That ought to keep him down long enough for Sabrina and Morgana to finish him off. Looking over, Morgana had gone for a similar tactic, and Sabrina's blasting rod was freezing his limbs off.

They finished up and came over to help me out with Tusky. "So, how long do you think this'll keep them down?" I asked casually as I did my best to keep the thrashing troll still.

"An hour, maybe two," Morgana said. "But this is going to cause a fucking mess. I am happy to be the mercenary and not the one cleaning this up."

The hotel itself had its glass front smashed in, and the front desk had been pulped to toothpicks. Uncomfortable lounge chairs lay strewn about, burnt to a crisp. The little grab and go snack alcove looked like something far too big had shoved its way in and forcibly enlarged the area. Half-eaten candy bars littered the floor.

Thankfully, it seemed the magi had been smart enough to use the stairwell as a bottleneck. For now, they had held the trolls from advancing up the stairs, but I wasn't sure how long they could hold it.

A few trolls were already trying to haul their huge butts up the side of the hotel, and though they were struggling, with enough sheer effort, one of them was bound to figure it out. Two of them working together would certainly be able to reach a second-story window.

"We need to figure out what's attracting them and stop it," I told the girls as Tusky became limbless. Watching his torso wiggle as he glared, I felt a little bad for him.

"Stupid magi, loving their flashy attacks. When will they learn that fire and lightning don't kill everything?" Morgana looked at the hotel lobby. "Not like our crack wizard here." She pulled Sabrina close, giving her a squeeze. "Now, what do you say we figure out what's drawing the trolls here?"

"Gosh. Thanks," Sabrina hazarded as she adjusted to Morgana's familiarity. "I think a lot of the magi just don't know the difference between a swamp troll and the far more common forest troll. At least, I hope that's what's happening. As to the root of this problem, I don't know. Whatever is drawing them here, it would work better if it was ground level or below ground. It is hard to tap a ley line on upper stories."

I nodded, grateful for that information. It saved us a lot of hotel searching. "Into the basement then." I pushed forward, glass crunching under my shoes as we made it to the lobby.

"What are you again?" She eyed my bulky form.

"Something big and dangerous." I winked, shrugging off her question as we found a maintenance only door that seemed like our best bet to get us into the basement. When I tried the door, it was locked.

"We need keys," Sabrina said. "I'll go—"

But she cut off as my hand turned into claws and I tore out the door handle and the lock. I smiled over at her. "Oh look, my bad. It was open the whole time."

She started to say something, then thought better of it.

Prying the door back, we started to step forward before pausing. Down the hall, we were met with an eerie red glow and shouting. It looked like others had beaten us here.

CHAPTER 21

I could hear men shouting from further down in the basement. I didn't give any time to pause and listen. Whatever was causing the trolls to come to the hotel needed to be stopped. Immediately.

Barging down into the basement, it wasn't much more than a boiler room with several cages of supplies.

But what caught my attention was the massive glowing magic circle. Around it, an old man was shouting at three younger men, or rather one in particular.

"Fool, get rid of this. I can still get you out of this," the old man said.

Only one warlock seemed like he was part of the conversation, the other two were bent down chanting. He was a scrawny man with a hairline that looked like it had abandoned him too early.

"No. It's you who doesn't understand. This power is real. It's power to make a damn difference while it counts. I don't have decades to practice. Unlike you, I'm not content to sit on my ass with magic and do nothing while the world crumbles around us," the younger man said.

"That's not what's happening." The older man stood straight with strength that seemed to defy his age.

"It is. Those of you with power aren't using it. Instead, you all let the world rot around you. We are going to make a difference." The younger warlock raised his hands in a grand gesture, as if there was more to see than a glowing magic circle in a rundown boiler room.

Sabrina stepped forward. "Old man?"

The old wizard turned, noticing our group for the first time. But his eyes zeroed in on Sabrina. "Good. You get to see the folly of your predecessor. Sabrina, meet Charles, my previous apprentice." Her mentor had a high-handed tone. It seemed that even in the face of the current problem, he was grumpy, but he was collected.

Not pleased about being completely ignored, I strode forward, ignoring the apparent reunion. I moved towards the magic circle, assuming whatever was causing the trouble was tied to it. Enough lives had already been lost.

"And what do you think you're doing?" The old man finally paid me some attention, scolding me like some child.

"Ending this the swift way." I'd seen Morgana snuff enchantments out with her hand before. And on tougher materials, she'd done it with her blades. Enchantments could be taken out by force, which happened to be my specialty.

But as I reached forward, a barrier blocked me. Annoyed at the defense, I hurled a strengthened punch at the barrier. Unfortunately, all it did was send back my own force plus an electric shock, driving me backwards.

"The hubris of youth. To think you expected to do better than me with a simple punch? If it were so simple, I would have destroyed it before I even talked to the imbecile." The old man turned back to the young warlock, his once apprentice. "Still hiding behind that? Come on, get out here."

I was starting to understand why Sabrina enjoyed mocking her mentor at the convention. He really was a crotchety old coot. It made me appreciate Morgana a little more, even if she liked dangling my life by a thread and call it training.

"Then what do we do?" I asked, looking at the magical circle. "You have magi dying above us; this isn't the time for a lesson."

"Before you hastily interrupted me, I was trying to appeal to my former apprentice's morals. That's assuming he has any left after whatever pact he's made with the being behind this." Sabrina's mentor turned his focus back to the warlocks.

"Give it up, old man," Charles scoffed from inside the circle. His boldness made more sense; he considered himself safe inside its barrier.

The old man rumbled something under his breath before speaking up. "I will not have you using an ounce of the knowledge that I gave you for such stupidity." He threw out his hand, a spell coming to life and hitting the magic barrier. The force sent a rumbling through the hotel, across the foundation.

The red circle pushed inwards, straining. For a moment, I thought he was going to do it. But it wasn't enough. The barrier rebounded from his spell. He quickly held up a bracelet that glowed bright, sucking the spell into itself.

A small dinging sounded as a piece of metal fell and hit on the floor.

"Borrowed power like this comes at a great cost, Charles. What was the price for this?" the old man taunted the young warlock and prowled around the edges of the barrier, scanning the floor and the markings underneath the warlocks.

I turned to Morgana and Sabrina. "Ideas?"

"If my mentor can't do it, I don't stand a chance," Sabrina said, shaking her head. We both focused on Morgana.

Morgana tilted her head back and forth before shaking it. "There's a lot of power built up inside of there. Even if I could bypass its protections with my spatial magic, I'm liable to just kill everyone in the hotel when it blows."

"Who is your patron?" the old wizard growled, clearly growing frustrated.

I would have thought that was private information, but either old gods wanted to be known, or Charles just felt that secure.

"Nat'alet. Good luck finding anything on him."

Who? I certainly had never heard of him.

I frowned and focused past Charles. The other two warlocks in the circle still had their heads bowed as they chanted. Was there more to this than they had already done?

"Some forgotten god. Think about it, Charles. Use that brain that I know is in your head. Why would he do this? What do you possibly have to offer him?"

Charles nearly stepped out of the circle, clearly getting annoyed at the interruptions from his former mentor. His movements were agitated and erratic. "I have so much to offer. He agrees with us. Nat'alet wants to help save the world, and the first step is getting rid of old men who hoard their power and watch the world wither."

The old man snorted. "A desperate old windbag is using you, Charles. He could be some trickster god hiding behind a false name, but you ate it up hook, line and sinker, didn't you? You were never very motivated, always expecting that one day everything would land neatly in your own lap."

"Shut up!" Charles screamed, seeming to come unhinged. He lunged like he was going to try and choke the old man, but it seemed the barrier worked both ways. Charles rebounded off of it, stumbling back, surprised and nearly falling over the other two warlocks.

"Pity," the old man said and turned away from the warlocks. "Sabrina, come here and give me a hand. It seems we need to try for a harder application of force."

"Don't you see?" Charles recovered and held his arms out wide in a grand gesture. "We are going to restore magic to the golden days you always talked about."

"If it were so easy that a couple of piped up young warlocks could solve it, we would have done it ages ago." The old man shook his head as he pulled out a stick of chalk and bent down, starting to scratch at the ground. "You are too stupid to realize when you've been conned."

Charles' face only filled with even more conviction. "No. We are capable where you were not. We didn't grow up in an easy, carefree life; we will solve this with a simple solution."

Charles crouched down on the old man's level as he worked. A smile split his face. "You see, the decrease in mana that has been plaguing you old men is fixable. We just need to give it time to recover. Magi need to stop using it, and since you won't on your own, Nat'alet has offered to help. Killing magi and paranormal to stem the loss of mana."

Okay, this warlock was looney. He wanted to kill everyone using mana to let it restore on its own? It would work, but it was a hell of a drastic way to go about it. And morally wrong in so many ways.

"And what does your patron get out of all of this?" the old man asked, drawing a neat circle in a practiced flourish.

"He's the god of balance. It helps him to realign such things. That's how we know what we are doing is good; the world needs balance." Charles' eyes caught the red glow of his magic circle, and in the moment, he seemed manic, lost in his own delusion.

As I watched his face, his motives became clearer. He may believe he was doing it for balance, but there was pain and anguish behind his eyes. He wanted to hurt his former teacher, hurt the other magi. This was a way to get back at them for some sort of slight he had felt.

I hadn't missed 'former' used when the old man referred to him as his apprentice. No doubt there was a story of loss behind that.

He wasn't about to listen to sense, especially not from his mentor. I'd only seen mania like this from overdone villains in movies, but it seemed very real at that moment. There was a conviction in him that any amount of words wouldn't shake.

Charles stood staring down his former master as the man continued to chalk out complex diagrams on the ground. "As you've said before, a prepared wizard is unstoppable."

The old man didn't even bother looking up. "If you're done, I have real magic to do. Hopefully, you can piece together at least a few of the symbolic relationships among this. I do hope you haven't given up magic theory entirely. Because you certainly aren't a wizard anymore."

At that, Charles gave up and spun around, crouching in a huddle with the other two and joining in their chanting. It looked like the gloating phase was over. He must be at least a little scared of what his mentor could do.

I looked at the barrier again, wondering what would happen if I fully shifted and attacked it. But if it exploded, while I was pretty durable, the hotel might not be. We'd likely end up buried in rubble.

Morgana held a hand on my shoulder, clearly reading my mood. "He seems to be quite the expert. Let's let him work."

"I just don't like being on the sidelines. There has to be something I can do."

But, before another option presented itself, a light came from behind us, and another party entered the boiler room.

I almost didn't recognize the man with the large two-handed sword wreathed in white flames hanging off his shoulder. I definitely hadn't been expecting him to be wearing a red and gold tabard emblazoned with a cross over his expensive suit.

Morgana cursed under her breath. "Just what we needed."

Jared stepped down the stairs, the white flames on the sword casting flickering shadows across his face. He walked as if he was the king of the basement and ready to show his disapproval by removing heads from shoulders.

It wasn't until he was at the bottom of the steps that his eyes shifted from the warlocks' to me and Morgana. "I thought you were strictly forbidden from investigating the warlocks." It wasn't a question.

"And I thought you had an internal neutral investigation team," I offered back.

"The Church has kindly provided such assistance. It just happens to be me." Jared gave me a grin like he'd won. "I can't wait to hang you out to dry for being here."

"Funny, I thought you would have noticed the trolls in the lobby? The same trolls Morgana and I have been hired to manage as they migrate." I smiled back. "Just doing our jobs. It's a small world."

He narrowed his eyes at me and Morgana, but Morgana was ignoring him and watching Sabrina aid the old man in the magical circle instead.

"Well, this looks like a very serious problem. One you must be incapable of handling since the barrier still stands. Let me show you how it's done." Jared hefted the sword off his shoulder, ready to charge the warlocks' magic circle.

I really wanted to watch him fry, but I decided to try to rise above the pettiness. "Charging it doesn't work."

"What do you know about magic?" Jared bit back with a snort.

Internally, I responded to him, letting him know that my kind made magic, so he should show a bit more gratitude. But I couldn't say that out loud.

So instead, I nodded over to the old man. "He seems to know enough to give Morgana pause. Far older than either of us."

"And still able to hear just fine." The old man turned to scowl at me, then glancing over and shaking his head as he took in Jared in his knight's templar getup.

Jared's eyes lit up as he registered the man. "Arch Magus Sir Benifolt." He said the name as if it had weight to it. "I didn't know you were here."

Sabrina's mentor looked up for a moment. "So you recognize me. And clearly you can see that I'm working. So remain silent so I can get back to my work."

Jared pursed his lips as if he had to forcibly keep them closed.

I smiled. I was starting to like the old man.

All the bluster seemed to fade from Jared. He let his sword swing down to the ground and he rested his hands on the pommel, sinking it an inch into the concrete. I tried not to show my reaction at the sword going right into concrete. It was weird to watch, but the white flames were a dead giveaway there was magic to the sword.

I turned to watch the old man, Benifolt, work his magic, holding my tongue.

Benifolt finished chalking on the ground, stepping back and looking it over again before drawing a final half circle that butted up against the warlocks' spell circle.

"It won't work," Charles sneered. "This is beyond even you, old man."

Benifolt slapped his knees and stood, groaning in the way only an old man could. He completely ignored his former disciple.

"It's done?" I asked Sabrina while checking my gun, readying for a fight.

She nodded. "The best we could do on short notice. The way the old coot wove force multipliers in with a rune complex is brilliant. He intends to siphon the mana from inside and create a feedback loop. I can't wait to watch it."

Sir Benifolt grunted at being called an old coot, but checked the diagram one last time with the precision of an expert tradesman. "I would hope I can outdo a petty warlock. But then again, I'm really testing my knowledge against a forgotten god." He paused, giving it one final look. "Yes, that's about the best I can do with what we have."

I hadn't thought about it like he'd said it. We weren't up against a cabal of warlocks; we were up against this god.

A term like that wasn't thrown around lightly, and it was the kind of thing to make you wonder if you weren't on the wrong side of the conflict.

Even as a legendary dragon, there were still beings above me in the food chain.

"Got it. No assurances," I responded, waiting for him to kick off the spell.

Benifolt bent down, and I could see a small trickle of magic flow into the diagram. But the magic wasn't the fuel for it. Instead, it was like just a bit of mana to prime the pump, like a trigger. Once that was done, the magical diagram took over.

Blinding, brilliant blue energy traveled along the chalk, lighting up the diagram he'd drawn on the floor. It filled itself with lots of raw energy as it started to draw from the environment. Under my dragon sight, it was even more brilliant. It was collecting mana and putting it to use, building up something at the edge of the barrier. Like clockwork, the magic diagram came to life.

I could see what the magic was becoming. It looked like a magical piston or maybe a battering ram, prepping to pierce the other magic circle.

The ground shook as it wound and struck. Cracks broke open in the cement foundation, and dust settled down on my shoulders from the unfinished ceiling above me as the hit resonated through the basement. This spell was powerful and complex magic, beyond what I had seen before or would understand anytime soon.

I stared at the magic as it worked, but as I used my other senses to watch it, a weird feeling came over me. A part of me felt like it could pick apart the magic.

There was a moment where the symbols leapt off the diagram and floated through my vision. It was almost as if my draconic supercomputer brain was processing the magic outside my conscious thought.

I couldn't make heads or tails of what I was seeing, and I certainly couldn't do anything with it if given a test. But somehow, it was being internalized. I smiled, knowing I was at least taking one baby step forward in my understanding of magic from watching the two enchantments interact.

Unfortunately, while I was gaining from watching the spell do its work, Sir Benifolt's magic wasn't effective enough on the barrier. The warlocks' magic circle was straining, but it wasn't breaking.

What was breaking was the basement. Another pulse from Sir Benifolt's enchantment had cracks propagating further across the basement, and the falling dust had turned into small chunks of debris. I was growing concerned that the magic was going to bring the hotel down.

I was about to say something, but Benifolt's enchantment lost its glow and it faded. The chalk on the ground had been scorched, and black marks ran through the enchantment, ruining what was once a beauty of magic.

"Is that it?" I asked Morgana.

She nodded, her face solemn. "Even enchantments have their limits. The problem isn't the magic itself, but the materials in which it's channeled through. Like other forms of energy, it has secondary outputs of heat and light. In the case here, you have the chalk burning and motes of dust scorching, like a circuit board that over-heats and the soldering losing its connec-tion. Given the environment, the enchant-ment was broken."

"Then how do enchantments sustain longer?"

"Because, like anything, with enough en-gineering, you can overcome the resource limitations. Also, I don't enchant some-thing with chalk if it was supposed to last more than a minute. Some of the greatest works of magic were made by dragons and still function today," she said the last bit pointedly to me.

While the short explanation from Mor-gana on magic had been interesting, we still had a rather large problem. Sir Benifolt's magic had failed and failed so spectacularly that the hotel may give way above us.

But it would seem that Jared was far less concerned. He strode forward, his powerful looking sword held high over his head. "If you can't solve this, I will!"

He threw his weight forward and swung the sword in an arc that left a trail of white fire in its wake.

I didn't know the power of that sword, but it glowed beyond just the flames. Given everything else I knew, my guess was that it was lent out from the Church's stash of weapons.

So I waited, watching as the sword came crashing down upon the edge of the war- locks' magic circle. To my surprise, it cut right through the barrier, causing blinding motes of red light to spill out. Against the harsh light, I could see the smug look of victory plastered across Jared's face.

That was, of course, before the ground shook and the very hotel beneath our feet cracked open with the same red light of the magic circle. Magic began to build in the air around us.

I jumped into action, grabbing Sabrina before the spell circle exploded. I protected her with my body as I let myself shift under my clothes, wrapping myself in a protective layer of gold scales.

Sir Benifolt shouted at Jared just before the ground shook. My back sprayed with hunks of concrete. I kept Sabrina covered, trying to keep myself wrapped around her as carefully as I could.

When the blast subsided, my ears rang as I got up off Sabrina, who was shaken, but okay. I was glad that I hadn't been the one to break that spell circle by force.

Chunks of the ceiling fell down on me as the building groaned and its weight shifted.

"Imbecile. Why is it that the young always feel the need to apply brute force to every fucking problem?" Sir Benifolt was raging at Jared as a blue eggshell of magic fell from around him. "Now I have to stabilize this building." He rolled up his sleeves and started quickly chalking out another diagram.

But, as he was bent over getting to work, Jared was leaning heavily on his sword. Blood dripped from a number of nasty looking cuts, but there was no sign of pain on Jared's face. Instead, there was a concentrated strain as his body twitched.

"Morgana?" I asked through the dust that filled the basement.

"Here." She came out of the dust, her neck bent at an odd angle and crackling as it righted itself.

A snorting noise came from deeper in the dust, where three figures now stood.

For a moment, I thought they were trolls. They had that same swampy green skin and smushed pig-like faces, complete with a pair of tusks.

But as I stared at them, trolls didn't quite fit. They weren't near big enough to be trolls, and they stood upright with the confidence of humans.

Their robes burned on their skin, giving off steam that stank up the crumbling basement.

"What the hell are those?" I asked no one in particular.

Sabrina didn't seem to care as her blasting rod pointed at the closest one and sprayed a jet of frost.

"Ha!" one shouted and stomped the ground. In response, as a pillar of earth rose up and blocked Sabrina's attack. "We are shamans. Future leaders of the trolls!"

One shaman caught Jared before he could raise his sword again and threw him through the dust, rushing after him.

"You two. Would you mind? I'm a little busy trying to keep the building from collapsing on all of us and the magi above." Sir Benifolt didn't even look up from his work.

Morgana's blades rang out as she unsheathed them, and I kept my scales covering me under my clothes. The beast roared in my chest, happy to fight.

CHAPTER 22

I checked out the two remaining shamans. They didn't seem especially tough.

"I'll split them with you," I called out to Morgana as I charged in, attacking the one I thought was once Charles.

My steps grew heavier as I shifted, adding more weight to the hit as I tackled Charles.

He held up well to the tackle, surprising me with the strength he had. His swampy green skin bulged with hidden muscle.

"Yes. See this muscle? I have real strength now." He wasn't even talking to me, calling over to Sir Benifolt.

I was somewhat offended that he wasn't paying more attention to me, instead seeking his former master's approval.

So I gave him something to write home about and swung a heavy right hook into his face, knocking him off his feet and smashing him into the wall. I smiled. That should get his attention.

Charles shook his head like a wet dog, his jaw cracking back into place. "Idiot. You dare challenge a shaman? Burn!" Flames leapt from his fingers, shooting a jet of fire straight at my face.

Trolls with magic? Okay, that might be a problem.

I let it wash over me, enjoying the warm sensation. I wondered what it would feel like to soak myself in fire. It honestly sounded relaxing, like a nice soak in a hot tub.

The flames cut out, and besides the collar of my clothes burning, I was completely untouched.

"What?" Charles looked at me, completely startled, like I was a freak. It was a little odd coming from a person that was green and had tusks sticking out of his mouth. Which, really, didn't even seem hygienic. I couldn't see a way for his mouth to be able to close around them—enough of that.

"I actually like fire." I smirked as I discreetly shifted my hand into golden claws, flashing them out in one swift move as I raked them across his gut.

Blood splattered to the floor, and his intestines threatened to spill out. Charles screamed and clutched at them, trying to stuff them back into his torso.

Charles was visibly healing like the trolls I'd fought, his skin closing tightly over the wound even as I watched. I moved to follow up my hit with another, but before I got to him, he'd muttered some quick chant. I was stopped; it was like someone blew a soap bubble around him. The barrier was solid and pushed me back as it expanded.

"Magic is far stronger than any paranormal talent," Charles said haughtily, straightening his back despite his bleeding stomach. "Nat'alet has gifted us his magic along with the attributes so that we can defeat those who dare push us back. Are you going to stand up to a god?"

"Apparently," I said, keeping my hand shifted. My dragon eyes could see the magic itself. There was a single point from where the magic was pouring out, and it wasn't within the shield. It was on the surface.

Slamming a fist into that point, the shield popped, and the force of my punch rippled out from the impact.

I'd expected Charles to look surprised, but he was unperturbed. Instead, he wove his hands through the air with the gleeful look of a child with a new toy. It made more sense when I was blasted with a beam of pure red energy.

I was lifted off the ground and hurtled through the air. I just barely managed to protect my torso with scales before I crunched into a concrete wall.

My body groaned from the impact, but the armor had protected me from most of the damage. That was definitely more effective than the fire.

"It would be nice if you didn't continue destroying the hotel foundation I am working to keep together," Sir Benifolt spoke, not even looking up from his work.

But his voice startled Charles out of his laser focus on me, pivoting it to his former mentor. Charles' face was lit with a red glow, casting wicked shadows across his face as he pooled more of the same red energy into his palm.

Not sure if the old man would be prepared for an attack, I jumped between Sir Benifolt and Charles to take the hit. Scales crept up my arms under my sleeves as I moved, and I smashed my feet into the concrete floor as I blocked Charles' attack.

The red beam broke up on my crossed arms, the red light spilling around me in beams too small to do significant damage. The concrete under my feet cracked as I used it to hold myself still and wait out the attack. But it didn't stop. The beam continued to pound into me.

I took a heavy step forward, pushing myself through the force and planting my foot once again into the concrete floor, anchoring myself before taking another step.

I slowly made my way across the concrete, pushing through Charles' attack. My sleeves had burned away, and the scales on my arms were starting to grow red hot under the pressure of his attack.

As I got close to Charles, another red beam shot out at me from my side. I couldn't react in time and still block Charles' hit. I braced for the impact.

But just before it hit me, it surprised me and bent to the side, nearly hitting Charles but breaking up his own attack for just a second.

I only needed the moment. My legs burned with exertion, but I ignored them, pushing forward. I launched myself, taking Charles to the ground.

He sputtered and slapped at my face to push me off. It became clear that he had put all of his eggs in the magic basket. He had no combat training.

Grabbing his chin, I lifted his head slightly, raising it six inches and slamming it into the concrete. A spray of stone shards and blood hit me as I buried his head a foot into the foundation.

He'd be down for a good while, if not longer, so I quickly pivoted to see if Morgana needed help.

She was standing with a feral smile as she slowly fileted her troll shaman. Based on where they were standing, I assumed that was the troll that had tried to blast me from the side.

Morgana's blades danced in the air like a pair of silver wings as they diced through the troll and its rapid healing. For a moment, I wondered if that's where her surname came from.

Morgana Silverwing. Honestly, she was more like Morgana Bloodybutcher, but who was I to judge an elven surname. It really did look like she was carving up the troll shaman like a butcher would a hog.

Morgana finished and flicked her blades clean, making eye contact with me. "I wonder how our templar friend has fared?"

But as she said that, Jared flew through the space between us on red beam propulsion. He'd been injured from cutting the magic circle, and it seemed those injuries were enough to make him lose his edge.

The troll shaman he'd taken stepped out of the dust and saw his two fellows. There wasn't a moment's hesitation before he drew a stone from his pocket. "We didn't finish, but we should have more than enough!"

He crushed the stone, and the red glow coming from below the foundation grew blindingly bright for a moment.

I had to shade my eyes given the intensity. When the light faded, the three troll shamans were gone. I stayed alert, scanning around, but they'd really vanished. "What was that?"

The glow beneath the hotel's foundation abated, and the only light remaining was Sir Benifolt's magic circle and Jared's burning blade.

Turning to Jared, I looked him over as he pushed himself into a standing position. He looked like a mess.

Jared scowled at me as he came out of the dust, covered in blood. He clearly hadn't held up his part of the burden, but at least it looked like he'd put forth a decent effort.

"It seems we failed," he declared, as if it had been a group failure.

"Na. Just you. We both killed our trolls." I brushed off his attempt to lump us into the responsibility of them getting away.

"I don't see them." He gestured broadly to the empty basement. "Looks like we can't confirm that."

Morgana scoffed. "Face it, templar, you lost to a troll. It seems templars aren't what they used to be."

Jared hefted his burning sword over his shoulder and tried to pretend like his wounds were merely flesh wounds; to me, it looked like his left arm had been nearly severed. "It isn't like Sir Benifolt has succeeded, either. And he's directly responsible for training them."

I turned, knowing the old wizard likely wasn't going to take that.

Sure enough, Sir Benifolt spoke up. "You had best curb your tongue, little boy. This was the machinations of an old forgotten god. It would appear my former disciple has been toyed with, and it went unnoticed by the Church."

Jared bristled at the accusation, pointing his sword at Sir Benifolt. "Or are you responsible for this whole thing? After all, it seems you've let yourself be deluded by demons. You think I didn't notice?"

Sir Benifolt stood up from his work, the runes he'd drawn glowing in the darkness. Luckily, whatever he had done seemed to be holding the building together. The basement had stopped shifting after the shamans had left.

Sir Benifolt stared down the burning long sword. "Jared, I think it is best that you be perfectly clear when you speak. What exactly are you accusing me of?"

I was curious as well. It was clear they were blaming each other for the mess, but I couldn't figure out where demons fit into the picture.

I turned to see if Morgana could clue me in, but I went quiet when I saw her face. She looked calm and collected on the surface, but I could tell she was just as clueless as I was. Always nice to be on the same page as your partner.

Jared stabbed his sword into the ground, sending a wave of bright light over our group. I braced for an attack, but nothing hit me. As the light dissipated, I looked around.

Morgana looked untouched as well, but Sabrina recoiled as her form wavered and then shattered. Or at least, the illusion that had been over her shattered.

Sabrina was not human. She was still wearing those loose robes that hid everything, but her sinful curves were trying to bulge through, regardless.

Now standing in the basement was a demoness. Polished black horns rose from the blush-colored skin of her forehead and curled back over purple hair that was so rich it might as well have been black.

Like a fountain of midnight, her hair cascaded down her back to her bottom, where her robes lifted in the back and a tail swayed. The tail's spade pointed tip flicking from side to side as she stood there in wide-eyed shock.

Sir Benifolt looked on with a neutral expression. "And your point is?" He didn't seem fazed at all by the sudden revelation.

Although, I had no doubt that, if Jared could see through the illusion, Sir Benifolt must be strong enough as well.

Sabrina turned her stunned expression to her mentor. "You knew?"

"Of course I knew. You think you could have walked into my workshop and I wouldn't have picked apart every magic on you? But I'll give you credit; your illusion is fantastic."

The demoness blushed an even darker red on her cheeks. "I just wanted to learn."

Jared sneered, "No, you worked to fool one of the greatest wizard minds for yourself. I bet this whole plot had you at the center of it." The way he spoke, it was clear that Jared was biased against any and all paranormal. He practically spat as he spoke.

I eyed her, replaying everything in our interactions. Adding it with the trust Sir Benifolt clearly had in her, I had no reason to think she was anything more than a bystander who tried to help.

Feeling firm in my opinion, I turned to Jared. "She had no involvement in the trolls."

As I said it, I leaned into my instincts to confirm, and they came back with a resounding confirmation that she couldn't have done this. "And those are strong allegations to be thrown around. I recommend you get more proof before trying again, because I'll fight you if you point that sword at anyone else in this basement."

Jared sighed dramatically. "You've all been fooled by this little demon hussy. I'm disappointed in all of you." His eyes raked over Morgana and Sir Benifolt, ignoring me.

The old wizard crossed his arms. "She's a fantastic student. That she's paranormal makes no difference. It was clear to me that she had the will and power to learn, so I taught her as I would any wizard."

Sabrina's eyes were wide, tears misting in the corners; for a moment, I thought she was going to cry. "I'm very young for a demon. They guard their knowledge. Since I had an opportunity, I took it. I wanted to learn all that I could."

"I could tell. The best students are those that understand the value of what they are learning." Sir Benifolt shifted to stand between Sabrina and Jared. "I've done my best to teach you regardless of the differences."

I nodded, stepping forward to stand alongside Sir Benifolt. "Jared, I think you should rethink your position. She's just another paranormal. That doesn't make her inherently dangerous or evil, just different. Judge her by her actions, not her existence."

Morgana joined us as well, putting her hands back on her blades as the three of us faced off against Jared.

I knew that Morgana and the Church had a truce, so that made her actions that much more important. If Jared pushed the issue, it could break that truce.

Jared paused, eyeing the three of us. I could see flickers of pride in his eyes. He didn't want to stand down, but he knew he was outmatched.

In the end, he sheathed the burning sword, putting out the flames and submerging the basement in near darkness. The only remaining light was the magic circle keeping the foundation together.

My eyes took only a moment to adjust, but after just a split second, I could see the basement in full detail. Jared seized what he believed was an opportunity and leapt forward towards Sabrina.

I wasn't going to let that happen. Jumping forward, I intercepted his movement and tackled him. We went down into a tussle.

The basement lit back up, one of the two wizards creating the light.

"Get the fuck off him," Morgana shouted, but I wasn't sure which one of us she was talking to.

Either way, I knew killing Jared wasn't the right move. It wasn't worth bringing the wrath of the magi and the Church down on us.

"This ends now. You need to get your shit together." I pushed off of him. "There's a bigger mess going on upstairs. We need to sort it out."

"I must agree with the youngster. And know that I won't tolerate you taking another go at my apprentice. Now, let's move upstairs; there still might be a troll problem." Sir Benifolt glowered down at Jared, who winced as he sat up.

I noticed that the tabard Jared wore was decked out in as much magic as his sword. It seemed to be passively healing his torn shoulder, which had gotten worse after our bout on the floor. His face had turned red, and he was glaring at me, his pride clearly wounded.

Ignoring him, I turned to head out. I heard Jared grumble behind me, "Fine."

But, as a light blossomed behind me, I knew Jared had drawn his sword again. The idiot really didn't know when to quit.

I spun my leg, sweeping out behind me without even looking. Morgana had ambushed me countless times in the name of training, and it looked like it hadn't been useless, because I caught his legs.

He fell as I spun full circle in a crouch. My legs burned as I pushed out of the crouch, using the strength of my entire body to slam him in the chest with the mother of all uppercuts.

He was no Morgana, that much was clear. Jared wasn't able to dodge or manipulate space. He simply flew through the air, back into the basement, his sword clattering to my feet.

I was fed up with him. He was so lucky that he had strong ties to the magi. "Really? I get ambushed by a drow vampire every time I try to take a shit. You might want to consider turning off your nightlight next time to be at least a bit stealthier."

Morgana covered her mouth and snickered into her hand.

I bent down to pick up his sword.

"Don't touch that!" he said through a cough.

I paused. His fear seemed more than just wanting to keep the obviously valuable weapon. "Why?"

"Because that is a sword blessed by Raguel, the archangel of justice. Only those deserving can wield it. The white fire it puts out when I hold it? That's a sign that I'm one of the most worthy to hold it. It would smite an unworthy monster like you."

I raised a brow at his words. Worthy wasn't the word I would use to describe him. Prick seemed more appropriate.

I stared at the sword, wanting to pick it up even more. If it lit up for me, that meant I wasn't a monster. Well, I might still be a monster, but a good one. Maybe even one that on the scale of an archangel's judgement was worthy to mete out justice.

And the beast inside me was pretty into the shiny sword. I was already planning a nice little spot for it in my hoard.

Reaching down, I clasped the hilt. My hand closed around the grip, and I braced. But nothing happened. I smiled, raising it up to eye level to check it out and sniffing it. "Is this silver?"

My comment was met with silence as Jared stared at me. "Impossible."

A moment later, prismatic flames burst out of the sword. They flooded the whole basement, scouring it but doing no damage because I intended no harm.

"Stop being so showy." I flicked it, and the flames went out in an instant. I looked back at Jared. "Looks like it likes me well enough."

Jared tried to get up, but his injuries had added up. He slumped to the floor, his mouth and eyes wide. "You can't. It—"

I cut him off. "Looks like I can. I'll leave you alone despite you ambushing me, which is more than you deserve. But I'm taking this as my prize." I turned to Morgana. "It's silver—I like it."

She rolled her eyes. "Heaven forbid we ever see a gold sword."

"There's gold ones?" I forgot about Jared for a moment.

"No. To the angelics, gold is gaudy, silver somehow is leagues better. Don't ask me; they have strange tastes."

I nodded. Gold was best, but silver would do. I stroked my new shiny sword.

"You can't do that. It's my sword. Gifted to me by the Church," Jared whined, pulling himself up.

Sir Benifolt laughed. "It seems he can and will. Maybe you aren't deserving of it anymore."

Either way, I didn't care. I could give it a test drive hacking apart trolls. I expected there would be more upstairs, ones we needed to deal with.

"Let's go. Attack me from behind again, and I won't be as lenient," I scowled at Jared, who stayed slumped against the wall.

"Lead on. But it sounds quiet upstairs," Morgana said, her pointy, blue ears tilted towards the exit.

"Quiet might be worse," I grumbled, throwing the sword over my shoulder and marching out of the basement.

CHAPTER 23

As we reached the lobby, the hotel was a wreck. It had been thoroughly destroyed. But the area was silent, except for the moans of several injured magi who were being tended to by paranormals.

I looked around. I'd expected to find trolls and magi fighting.

"Morgana, do you hear anything? Trolls make a lot of noise. We should be able to hear them."

"Nothing on this floor or the next. I can hear voices further up though." She tilted her head. "They sound panicked, but I don't hear any trolls."

At this point, outside the hotel, I could see a police blockade down the street, but they were letting through a truck and a few other vehicles. I had a feeling the council had been called in and was managing the crisis at the moment.

"Let's go see what's up." I headed over to the nearby doorway with the door torn away from the opening, taking the stairs two steps at a time.

Sabrina, Sir Benifolt, and Morgana followed me. Jared had never appeared from the basement. He was likely licking his wounds, but I knew that the tabard he'd been wearing would have him healed back up in no time.

Sabrina was back to her plain looking self, her demonic nature hidden back under wraps of an illusion.

We paused at each floor, listening for any sign of noise. It wasn't until the fourth floor that we found people. Or at least, partial people.

Magi were crowded around, and a handful of them had their lower halves mutated into swampy green flesh.

"Oh, thank mana. Can you help them?" A man ran up to me, looking at the sword over my shoulder.

The sword seemed to have a reputation. I wondered if they thought I was with the Church.

"I need you to take a deep breath and tell me what has happened." I tried to keep my voice calming, like I'd learned as an EMT. Being panicked never helped situations where lives were on the line.

"Okay." The mage breathed deeply, slowing himself down. "We woke up to screaming. When we went to investigate, we found trolls making a mess of the lobby. We tried to stop them, to fight back, but they just kept regenerating! Like, we'd hit them and seriously hurt them, and then before our eyes, they'd start reforming."

I held up my hand to stop him. "I know about the trolls. What I don't know is what has caused that."

I pointed to the girl laying on the ground in shock. Her legs stuck out far thicker than the rest of her, covered in swampy green troll flesh. It looked like somebody had split her and pieced her together with a troll.

"Right. Okay. So, we fought the trolls, but then some of the magi... they started to change, like the trolls were infecting them." He swallowed a lump. "We freaked out, and we couldn't figure out what to do. But then one of the infected people couldn't get out the front, so they ran up the stairs, and that's when we found out that if we went higher in the building, it would stop. So we've been trying to... to..." He was starting to break down, and he turned back to the girl.

I looked at Morgana, but she shook her head. She hadn't seen anything like this before.

I worked to triage the situation. It looked like whatever was causing the mutation was at least paused, so it was at least contained for the moment. I needed to make sure the troll issue was resolved.

"Everybody here seems partially mutated. Was anybody fully mutated? Where are the trolls?"

"They all disappeared. A big, red flash happened, and all the trolls and transmuted magi disappeared. Only those that were partially changed remained. Please, can you help her?" he begged.

"There's nothing I can do right now. But the Paranormal Council is down below, and I suspect the Order of the Magi will come out here soon enough. I have no doubt they'll put their heads together to see what they can do," I tried to console him. But I wasn't sure what could be done.

Sir Benifolt bent down and poked at the woman's lower half, his finger drawing a small enchantment on her leg. "I hope that will at least stabilize her for now. Take her to rest, and I'd like to see her later."

The young man's eyes went wide. "Sir Benifolt. It's an honor."

"No. It's a shame. What they did here tonight was despicable, and I'll do what I can to right that wrong."

He looked back at the girl, and I wondered if he blamed himself for what had happened. Charles might have been his former apprentice, but it seemed the old wizard had a weight on his conscience.

"There's nothing more for us to do here." Morgana put a hand on my shoulder. "Let's head back downstairs. I'm sure the council will be here already."

I turned my back on the young magi huddling together in fear, hating that we were at another dead end.

Morgana was right about the council. As we got to the bottom of the stairs, we found Rupert, Detective Fox, Sebastian, and the Summer Queen. The Summer Queen looked like she'd come straight from bed, dressed in a silver nightgown. But she stood comfortably with the others, talking with a few old magi.

Detective Fox looked up from the group and saw me over the Summer Queen's shoulder, his face shifting immediately to a scowl. "What are you doing here?"

The others paused, turning to see whom Detective Fox was speaking to. All eyes were on us.

"You hired us to deal with trolls. We've been tracking the troll attacks, and that led us here. We've done what we could to help contain the situation." Ignoring his continued glares, I continued, "Let me tell you what we know."

Florita, the sorceress from the convention, narrowed her eyes at me. "I thought you weren't supposed to be hunting magi."

"Like I said, I was hunting trolls. That happened to bring us here," I shot back. "How do you even know what happened here?" I was on edge, and her sudden accusation had me ready to fight.

"We received a message spell," the old wizard clarified. "It would seem your troll problem and our warlock problem are one and the same."

I could see the moment of realization on Detective Fox's face. He arched a brow as he looked between me and Morgana.

I focused on the old wizard, not wanting to deal with Detective Fox. "It would seem so. When we arrived, there were multiple trolls assaulting the lobby. We dealt with those that we could safely, but I detected a larger magic working in the basement and went to investigate." I paused. "Has anyone seen Jared?"

A few of their eyes fixed on the silver sword over my shoulder, questions burning in their eyes.

"Yeah, I borrowed the sword." I smiled, not going into further detail. "Jared was last in the basement, injured but safe. He fought alongside us to try to stop the warlocks-turned-shamans that were working magic down there. He was injured in the fight with one of them."

I left out the part about how he attacked me, and I took his sword in punishment and instead went into what we'd just seen. "Based on the accounts of those upstairs, it looks like the shaman triggered something that was able to convert the magi close to the basement into trolls. There's a number of partially changed magi up on the fourth floor, so any magi on the first three floors were at risk."

My short explanation was met with wide eyes and a few gasps.

"Where are these shamans?" The group was looking around, clearly on edge and wanting to attack something.

"Gone. Morgana and I killed two of the three warlocks involved, but Jared failed to kill the third. The third one used some enchantment and disappeared, taking the two that were dead."

"Impossible. Teleportation at that scale is impossible. This was a ploy by the paranormal to attack magi." Florita declared it loudly enough that I worried a few more ears outside this conversation might take up her accusation.

Luckily, Sir Benifolt spoke up from behind me. "The boy speaks the truth. Though, I'm unsure if Jared saved lives by preventing them from finishing their work, or if he doomed them by breaking the circle recklessly. We may never know. But the damage is done, and we need to move forward. Both of our communities are under siege by a cabal of warlocks and an old god. This is not the time to cast accusations and divide ourselves."

"Nat'alet," Sabrina provided. "That's the god they mentioned."

"Yes. That one." Sir Benifolt gestured dismissively. "These warlocks used his power to draw trolls to the hotel and were performing a great ritual in the basement."

Florita didn't seem pleased with that explanation. "It sounds like someone used a few stupid magi to attack their own," she reinterpreted.

Really, it was a paranormal using magi to attack paranormal. Sort of a stupid shell game if you asked me.

Either way, I could already see it was going to cause problems.

Rupert grabbed me by the shoulder and pulled me away as the others started bickering. "You look like shit. Go home and get cleaned up. There will be a council meeting in two hours. You and Morgana would be a welcome voice to discuss what you saw here tonight." He let me go before following up. "Oh, and call the girls. They were worried. And they keep bugging me for an update."

I frowned and fished into my pocket for my phone, finding that what had been my phone was now a crushed pile of electronics. Great.

"I'll get a hold of them," I promised, knowing that once I got my phone restored, it was going to be filled with missed messages.

Morgana fished hers out of her bra and handed it to me. "Go ahead. They're likely sitting around fretting and working themselves up right now."

"Thanks." I balanced the sword on my shoulder as I took her phone and started walking out to the car. The council was here. They could deal with the magi bullshit.

Using Morgana's phone, I tapped out a message to Scarlett. 'I'm fine. A troll crushed my phone. Heading back to my place in the Atrium to clean up.' I paused. What a weird life I lived.

After hitting send, the three dots popped up immediately as Scarlett texted back.

"So, two hours," Morgana repeated as we reached the van. "Rest up. We'll likely have to deal with council bullshit all night."

"Can we charge them more?" I joked, but Morgana looked like she was taking it seriously.

"This is going to take up the time I had planned for your bachelor party." Morgana angrily shifted the car into gear. "Your wedding is tomorrow."

To say it wasn't freaking me out would be a lie, but the draconic part of me was extremely content to lay a permanent claim to my mates. It felt right.

I nodded. "I'll have another wedding. Or we can push it back and do it before the ceremony her family is going to plan. This is just a private affair."

Morgana hummed to herself as she drove. "Sure. We can do that. Not like I can't use some strippers for other things."

"Really?" I asked. "Strippers?"

"With silver hair wigs even." Morgana smiled. "Don't worry, it'll be great when it does actually happen."

I wasn't too concerned. There were enough beautiful women in my life that strippers didn't spark much of an appeal. Though, a distraction from the growing nerves in my gut would be nice. Between the wedding and the fallout from tonight's event, I had a lot of tension riding on my shoulders.

"What do you think is going to happen with the troll situation?" I changed the subject.

"The council and the magi are going to come to an agreement to hunt down this Nat'alet. Of course, that will only be after tedious hours of arguing about who does what," Morgana grumbled.

"Who do they send to take on a god?" I knew we had some heavy hitters, but somehow the Faeries didn't seem like the types

to involve themselves in these types of af-
fairs.

Morgana was quiet a moment. Just a hum
of her engine and the wind rushing past
provided any noise. "No one will go after
the god himself, just his warlocks. Unless
you want to volunteer. Do you want to try
your hand at a god? He's no longer worshiped and just a powerful paranormal."

I swallowed. That sounded like a big leap.
"What do you think our odds are?"

"Depends. If he's really forgotten, he's going to be weak. In which case, he's not outside the realm of possibility for you, but it
isn't going to be easy."

"When is it ever easy?" I chuckled, pressing myself back into the seat. Going up
against a god didn't sound like a great idea,
but he also couldn't be let to continue attacks like what we'd just witnessed. "If I say
no, who takes care of it?"

"The council can't. Or at least, they
won't risk enough to go head-to-head with
Nat'alet. They will probably struggle with
him for a short period of time and then
they enter some sort of negotiations. He
hasn't gone after any of the big groups, so
it will be hard for the council to rally the
support and resources they'd need. If he
had hit that elven gated community, we'd
be having a different conversation."

"The Faerie?" I asked, hoping they might do something.

"Not unless he goes after them, which he won't unless he's just as stupid as a swamp troll." Morgana stared out the front window as the streetlights strobed over us. "Sometimes there are entities in the paranormal world that you don't just get rid of. You have to work with them."

I thought about what she'd said. Despite the trouble that this Nat'alet had been causing, Morgana seemed hesitant to go after him.

But that didn't sit well with me.

He'd attacked my city, harassed my mate, and now he had just terrorized a hotel of magi. No doubt that would have larger ramifications. Even if we stopped his followers, he could just regrow in power and influence. I liked to crush problems, not let them fester in a weakened state.

"If we have the option, we go after him. Nat'alet mucked around in Philly. I won't let his status cow me." People threw around the term 'god', but that was just a paranormal that had been worshiped. There had to be a weakness; not to mention, from what I'd gathered, he had lost much of his power in his obscurity.

"Good. I was hoping you'd step up. And hey, at least now we know you won't run out of big bad guys to go up against now that you've figured out your shifting." Morgana turned the van into her garage.

"The way I see it, what's the point of having all this power if I don't use it for a good cause?" I looked at the sword in my hand. It had believed me worthy. I needed to live up to that. "Besides, I want to keep pushing myself. You suspected that I might be more than just a dragon. Gotta live up to my family name."

Morgana smiled and patted my thigh. "Rest up and I'll meet you at the council meeting."

"Thanks. First stop: figuring out the perfect spot in my hoard for this baby." I held out the sword as I got out of the car, careful not to scratch the neighboring Ferrari.

"Are you really not giving it back? That could cause issues."

I understood what she was saying, but the possessive dragon within me clamped down. I felt my knuckles pop as I held tightly to the sword. "No. I think it belongs in the hoard."

Morgana laughed, her hips swaying as she led the way through the club, which was thumping with people. We walked past them and into the quiet Atrium.

As soon as we entered the Atrium, I noticed Scarlett leaning against the wall by Morgana's personal wing.

"I'll see you later." Morgana winked, walking on ahead. Few people had access to her wing, but she had extended that access to me, giving the stone door a bit of my blood to recognize me.

Scarlett jumped into my arms the moment Morgana was gone, peppering my face with kisses. "We were so worried. First there was the report of the massive troll attack, then we couldn't reach you." She grabbed my face and pulled it to face her before she pressed her lips to mine.

I pushed her up against the wall, her legs wrapping around me and her hands digging into my hair. The sword clattered to ground—Scarlett was the greater prize.

Growling, I pushed her back against the wall. "I thought we were on a sex break. Don't rev me up like that."

"I'm a big girl." She kissed my neck. "But maybe we should go into your place."

Snagging the sword and stepping through the stone door, I looked down the branch that went to Morgana's quarters, but she was already gone. I took the other direction and found the room that Morgana had given me when we had first started working together.

It was ornate, and almost everything in the room was decorated with a dragon motif. It was Morgana's idea of a joke.

Propping the sword inside the door, I focused back on the lovely fox wrapped around my chest.

I plopped Scarlett down on the bed and nuzzled her neck, kissing her and getting a nose full of her cinnamon and clove scent. "I love you. I'm sorry we haven't spent much time together the last few days."

She stretched out her neck, offering it to me as she held my head. "I know. It's been a busy couple of days. I haven't had much time for anything except security around the convention."

I nodded, pulling back slightly to look into her eyes. We hadn't talked much since I'd met her and Jadelyn's moms, and a lot had developed since then. I knew it was a conversation we should have before I devoured her.

She looked up at me, heat in her eyes, waiting to see what I had to say.

Running my hand through her hair, I asked, "You gave me the all-clear with Jadelyn, but that was before my relationship with her progressed so quickly. So I need to hear it again."

I stared into her eyes and let my dragon instincts pick her apart.

"Yes." Her voice sounded certain, but I saw a flicker in her eyes as she looked away and then looked back. She was hiding something.

"No, you aren't." I pushed off of her and sat back.

Scarlett glared at me, clearly wanting me to drop it. But I wasn't going to let anything come between us. She reached out, trying to pull me back to her. "It's not that big of a deal."

"But..."

She rolled her eyes. "But I'm a little jealous that you are taking a step forward with her before me. I— I worry that I'm going to be left behind."

"No." I pinned her to the bed. "Mine. Forever." A growl slipped out.

She heard the possessiveness in my voice and gave me a heartfelt smile. "I know. Just..."

I pushed off the bed and lifted my mattress to the side, my hand reaching and searching through the spatial vault Morgana had made for my hoard. I searched around, pulling out a bar of gold bullion.

"What are you doing?" she asked, sitting up and watching me.

"Hold on." I looked around the room for something I could use for what I needed, finally spotting it. Snatching a little kitschy ceramic bowl—I wasn't sure what it was meant for, probably for keys or something—I brought it back over to the bed, pleased with it.

Hunkering over the clay bowl, I cupped the small hunk of gold in my hands, but kept an opening between them. The beast rumbled in my chest, liking what I was about to do.

Scarlett crawled over, leaning over my back and shoulder to see what I was doing. I felt her chest press into me, the beast rumbling harder.

"Might not want to get too close. It's about to get very hot."

She still clung to my back, peeking over, and I knew her curiosity wouldn't be stopped, so I continued onwards, careful about how I started it.

Breathing deeply, I let out a small, tight jet of flame into my hand. I had melted concrete with my breath; I was pretty sure I could melt gold.

Sure enough, the gold glowed bright red as it turned into the consistency of clay in my hand, and I upped the heat until it was pooling between my fingers. I used the little ceramic bowl to catch the liquid gold as it spilled out.

Something about firing it in my dragon's breath felt right instead of leaving it in its original state.

Scarlett sighed into my back, and I felt little kisses along the back of my neck. She knew exactly what I was doing. There were very few things a man would do with gold to show his dedication to a woman he loved.

The hunk of gold melted into the bowl, and I stood. Scarlett clung tight enough to my back to hold on. Her weight didn't bother me as I took the bowl into the bathroom and put the plug into the sink drain before filling it with water.

The ceramic was a dull red from the gold. Thankfully, the trinket hadn't been secretly made of plastic and was able to withstand the heat. It melting would have made a mess.

With the sink full, I dipped the ceramic in, not letting water come up over the edge.

The sink water hissed angrily, and my bathroom suddenly steamed up like I'd just taken a long shower. But I could see the gold rapidly dim back down to a more manageable temperature.

Going back to the bed, I cracked the ceramic and picked away the pieces until I was holding a disk of gold. "Finger please."

Scarlett's hand shot out, her left ring finger extended. "Is it still too hot?"

I prodded it, trying to get a sense of how hot it was, but to me it just felt slightly warm. "Can you feel the heat coming off of it?" I held it up to her hand, but didn't touch it to her.

"Yeah, shit. Don't put that on my finger." Her hand hesitated for a moment before she pulled it back. She actually had considered if it would be worth it. I tried not to laugh.

Taking the disk, I shifted my pointer finger into a razor-sharp claw, and with some application of force, I peeled off a strip from the outer edge. It curled off as a thin wire.

"Finger again," I said, waving the wire in the air to cool off far faster than the disk of gold.

This time Scarlett put her hand back out without hesitation, and I curled the wire around her finger to size it, twisting the two ends into a loop before setting the wire down on the disk and using that razor sharp claw of mine to carve out an engagement ring.

She waited, eagerly giving me her ring finger each time I asked for it to size the ring just right. It took some time for me to slowly and carefully cut away the gold into a smooth ring. But I couldn't have it be just a plain band. I used my claw to carefully etch a scaly pattern.

Finally satisfied, I pulled Scarlett off of me and got down on one knee, but she didn't even let me say the words.

"Yes!" she squealed and tore the ring out of my finger, shoving it on her hand and admiring it. It was like a tiny gold dragon wrapped around her finger.

I was stunned as she stood there, admiring it for a moment. Her face shone with happiness, and she was even more radiant than usual.

But I didn't have long to admire her before she was latched back onto me, kissing me passionately and then fumbling with my pants. I glanced at the clock and cringed. We didn't have time.

"Scar... there's a council meeting."

She looked at me, determination showing on her face as she leaned down. "Then I guess we'll have to make this quick. Jadelyn told me it was different, and I want to see for myself."

Before I could ask what she meant, two illusion Scarletts were kissing me, and I felt Scarlett take me in a mouthful.

CHAPTER 24

I was almost a little embarrassed at how well Scarlett worked me over in just fifteen minutes.

"Is it really different?"

She licked at her fingers. "Oh yeah. I wonder if it has anything to do with you unlocking your shifting?"

I remembered what Morgana had said the other night at the club. "Morgana mentioned that my blood smelled better afterwards."

"Good enough for me." She scratched at her thigh. "Damn, I think it might even be healing me."

I raised a brow in question, wondering where she was injured.

"Down there, the reason we are on a pause. I can feel it doing the whole itchy healing thing that potions do sometimes." She wiggled uncomfortably in her skintight jeans before settling down. "But we need to go."

I opened the door, finding Morgana lounging against the wall outside of my room.

"Hope you two had a nice chance to relax," she grumbled. "If I'd had time for a proper bachelor party, you could have had the best relaxation."

"I don't think you're supposed to have sex at a bachelor party," I mentioned, now becoming a bit more concerned about what she had planned.

"Not if you do them wrong," Morgana scoffed, whipping her ponytail around as she kicked off the wall. "Come on, before someone throws a hissy fit that we are late."

Scarlett clung to my arm, folding her hands so the ring would be noticeably on display. It didn't have a gemstone in it, but I'd need more than fire breath and sharp claws to make a delicate setting for a ring. Maybe one day.

We entered the door that brought us to the council chamber, and Scarlett gave me a peck on the cheek before flitting off to go take her spot up in the onlooker area. Morgana and I weren't as lucky, taking the main hallway into the pit. I wasn't sure what it was officially called, but I liked to call it the pit.

We were a few minutes late, but I wasn't one bit sorry after my time with Scarlett.

The space we walked into was like the floor of an arena. It was a flat circular space, and above us, sitting around the lip, was the council. Although at the moment, they were in a less domineering lighting than before when I'd been forced to come and duel an elf I'd apparently offended. This time, the pit even had an array of chairs.

I took a seat and looked around. More than a few familiar faces were here. Sir Benifolt and Sabrina sat together, the Order of the Magi leadership minus Jared were present, and a few vaguely familiar magi that I might have seen at the hotel were in attendance.

Up above the council, I spotted some heavy hitters. Rupert, Sebastian and the Summer Queen dominated the lesser members, and I looked to where I remember Brent, Kelly's father, had sat. His seat lay empty.

Sebastian rose as Morgana and I sat down. "Will Jared Nashner be present?" he asked the magi in general.

"I'm here." Jared strode in, looking in perfect health and wearing a new pinstripe suit. "Thanks for waiting."

"Good. It seems everyone is here, and I'm sure we are all aware of why this session was called," Sebastian started the meeting. "A rogue agent has been attacking paranormal and magi in the city for the last few days.

Tonight, there was a large-scale attack, one that we thought it best to discuss as a larger group."

Florita the sorceress snorted. "A discussion is between equals, which I can say this setting is not very conducive to. Generally, equals don't sit far above the others."

She eyed the position of the council. Despite the comfortable chairs that had been laid out in the pit, it was still a very domineering position.

Leaning back in my own chair, I laced my fingers behind my head and relaxed.

"Apologies, but this is for our protection. Magi have been behind the attacks on paranormals in our city," Rupert supplied as a small commotion of high squeals sounded behind him, cutting him off.

I didn't know what had caused the commotion until Detective Fox looked like he wanted to kill me.

Ah, Scarlett had shown off her ring.

"Magi have done nothing of the sort. Trolls killed dozens of magi tonight. Some other paranormal was behind it all." Jared crossed his arms, not taking a seat. "You should be explaining to us why the paranormal have decided to attack the magi."

What little respect I had for Jared vanished. He clearly came meaning to further divide the group, working to shift the blame to the paranormals.

For his own goals, it made sense. But, in order to resolve this situation, it was downright counterproductive. But maybe to him, the resolution and peace between the groups didn't matter.

His words sparked discussion among the other magi present.

"Hardly," Sir Benifolt spoke up, and people quieted to listen. "I, along with several others working for the Paranormal Council AND Jared himself, witnessed three warlocks behind the attack tonight. They created a magic circle that lured the trolls, causing the transmutation and translocation spells that occurred at the hotel tonight."

Jared stood straight. "A Native American myth was behind all of that. Three warlocks were manipulated into believing they were doing what was right."

"Are you also being manipulated by your patron, warlock?" Sir Benifolt threw that down like a gauntlet. "Tonight I saw you bearing the templar's cross and a blessed sword. You serve the angelics and are a warlock, the same as those you fought tonight. The only differences between you are the choices you yourself make as a magi."

"Is this true? Do you work for the Church now?" Sebastian asked with a poker face. "That would make me question our prior discussion where you stepped in to assure us that the magi had a group to look into the issue. Was that you intervening on the Church's behalf?"

"Yes," Jared said proudly. "I was within my right as a templar of Raguel to mete out justice as I saw fit. Two of the three warlocks responsible were killed. Unfortunately, the third managed to complete their workings."

I nearly fell out of my chair. He seemed to have forgotten some key details.

Morgana wasn't nearly as tactful. The drow vampire burst into laughter so hard her chair wobbled.

"Morgana Silverwing, is there something you'd like to add?" Sebastian turned towards her. He didn't seem as annoyed at the outburst as I would have expected.

Given she had protected me when I had killed Simon, I would have thought he'd still be an ass.

"Sorry. It's just that Jared left out a few details. My partner and I killed two warlocks after Jared set off the spell despite warnings. He failed to kill the third, who then was able to trigger the spell."

Eyes around the room pivoted to Jared, who stood looking calm, although I saw his fingers twitching in a sign of his annoyance.

Sebastian spoke again, "Ah. Those are a few details. Sir Benifolt, I am told you were also present. Are there additional details that would make the situation clearer to everyone?"

"While Jared did set the spell off early, that was after my own failed attempt to disarm it safely. Setting it off early might be the only thing that saved those further up the hotel. As for the merits of combat, Morgana spoke true." The old man's words seemed to shift the opinion of the magi on the floor.

Sebastian paused to collect his thoughts and then pushed the conversation forward. "It would seem that both the magi and paranormal communities have some blame in the matter at hand, and both the communities at large were working in an effort to resolve the conflict. A few rogue agents caused strife and are to blame. Does anybody object?"

No one spoke up, the room falling silent.

I decided to move the conversation along. Blame did us little good, and I was ready to figure out the actions we could take. "If we are done with pointing fingers, what are we going to do about this? We have some magi partially converted into trolls and others fully transformed and kidnapped. They need our help."

"A cure needs to be found for the magi," Florita spoke up for the Order. "That must be a priority."

"What about those who were taken?" a young magi spoke up.

Both of them had addressed the council with their questions, clearly thinking the council needed to step up.

"The best cure would likely be killing Nat'alet who is behind this all. This appears to have been a forced shape-change; unfortunately, the Faerie are familiar with such magics. A spell like this takes time to set, their bodies will be trying to revert for the next twenty-four to forty-eight hours," the Summer Queen spoke for the first time. "Would the magi like to try their hand at killing him?"

The room was quiet.

"How about you, templar? Will the Church come and deal with this old Native American god to save two hundred magi?" she asked.

"No," Jared said resolutely. "They would not actively seek a battle of that scale. A group of templars would need to be assembled to even hope of taking care of it."

"Then I would propose those here in the city with a stake in this band together to deal with the old god," the Summer Queen declared. "Before it is too late. I shudder to think what will happen once he has an army."

It went against Morgana's expectations that the Faerie would want to intervene.

"Who'll deal with the god himself?" I asked.

There was a pause in the crowd as no one volunteered.

The Summer Queen put her chin against her knuckles. "I cannot. I'm out of season and it is the mortal world. It would be a danger to the Faerie Realm. I could, however, seek the Winter Queen's assistance, but I would need the workings of a number of magi."

"What form would this assistance take?" Morgana seemed interested.

"A barrier spell and cutting him off from his power, that is the best I could offer."

"We'll take it, for the right price." Morgana grinned wide enough for her fangs to show.

"By yourself?" Florita scoffed. "Impossible."

"Oh no. Not me. My partner." Morgana hooked a thumb at me. "He's more of the god killing type. Look at how broody he looks."

An unprofessional sigh escaped me. "I'm not broody."

Rupert leaned down from his seat. "Are you sure you want to take this on?" But Jadelyn appeared at his side and whispered into his ear. He did a double take. "Absolutely not."

She whispered into his ear again insistently.

"Never mind. It would seem my daughter has all the confidence that you can handle this."

His comment aroused more than curiosity in the magi around me and the Paranormal Council above.

"Then this assistance from the Winter Queen? What do we need?" I asked the Summer Queen.

"The help of at least a dozen wizards and time." She looked at the magi. "Can you commit to that?"

Sir Benifolt spoke for the magi. "I'll make sure you have two dozen—time is of the essence if we are to save these magi. How long do you need them?"

She waffled her head back and forth, shaking out her long, green hair. "All of tomorrow. This is not a small working. We will be summoning a piece of the Faerie Realm temporarily to cut him off and let the Winter Queen exert power over him. Moreover, it will need to be mobile. I doubt we'll be lucky enough to spend twenty hours setting up a ritual and just having him walk into it."

"It can be done." Sir Benifolt bowed. "I'm honored to be involved in a working this complex with you."

"So tomorrow night," I clarified. "We need to know where he is."

"A translocation spell like was used at the hotel is only good for about a dozen miles," Sir Benifolt explained. "Any farther and it becomes unpredictable. Meaning all the magi and trolls from tonight are still in the city. It also needs an endpoint with someone powerful enough to draw all of them at once."

"Which would have been Nat'alet himself," I finished.

"Rightly so," the old wizard agreed. "So he's here."

I looked at the council. "While the wizards prepare for the Winter Queen, can the Paranormal Council provide men to figure out where Nat'alet is holed up in our city?"

"We will do our part," Rupert agreed. "I would like a moment to speak with you after this."

"Of course." I did a small, polite nod. "Father."

The way he almost choked was priceless.

"There is still another matter before we conclude." Jared scowled at me. "My sword."

Morgana came to my aid. "You attacked Zach. He disarmed you and took your weapon. That is neither a matter for the council nor something unfair."

"I agree," Rupert said from above. "You two can work out your personal matter. It would seem, though, that the Church has rescinded their support in the problem we are facing. As far as I'm concerned, you've dismissed yourself."

Jared did a slow turn, noticing more than a few hostile expressions around him. He had denied support when the other factions had come together. He'd become the outsider. "I see. Like the other magi, I have canceled my travel for tomorrow. I do hope I won't be needed."

With that, he stormed out, and I wondered if that was the last I was going to see of him for this, or if he'd manage to rear his ugly head once again.

"Morgana, I thought they weren't going directly for Nat'alet?" This had been outside her earlier predictions.

She shrugged. "Everyone is taking a back seat in this one, and if I had to guess, the Faerie know him. Otherwise, Summer couldn't offer up Winter's power so readily."

"Anything we need to be worried about?" I asked, not wanting more surprises.

"No use wasting worries on it now. Come on." Morgana stood. "I need to go get my beauty rest if we're going to go up against a god."

"I thought you said I was fighting him."

"Just making you look good in front of everyone. Of course I'm going to help. This isn't some silly training exercise. This is the real deal, and we are partners." Morgana clapped me on the shoulder. "Besides,

I haven't tasted god blood in quite some time."

She strolled off with that comment, leaving me a little confused. Was that just a joke, or had Morgana gone up against this sort of thing before?

Oh well, I would soon learn if she was up to this sort of task. For now, I had a soon to be father-in-law to talk to.

Taking the stairs I'd seen Scarlett take before, I was stopped by two tough looking guards before being waved through.

Up here, the main council seats around the ring each had several more fanning out behind them, confidants, and seconds, along with a small troop of guards that seemed to be mixed from all the present species of paranormal.

"Zach." Jadelyn was first to get up and greet me, grabbing my hand and pulling me through the crowd. "Welcome to the council." She smiled so wide that it forced her eyes into a squint.

"Fancy digs," I joked. They all had modern comforts. I had half-expected them to be sitting on stone thrones carved ten thousand years ago, or something otherwise overly ostentatious.

"No, while some of us might be old enough to remember sitting on stone seats"—Rupert looked over at the elves and the Faerie—"some of us grew up with nice upholstery for our furniture. How are you?"

I took his hand and shook it. "Good enough. A few tussles tonight, but otherwise, I came out just fine."

"A few trolls and a templar shouldn't be impossible if you think you can take on this Nat'alet. Even if he's weakened and further weakened by the Winter Queen." Rupert fixed me with a look that would have chilled lesser men. "Are you sure you can do this?"

"There are no guarantees in life. But I have solid odds. Not to mention Morgana will be there as backup." I couldn't say that I'd walk away tomorrow night without lying. Anything could happen.

"At least you aren't stupid. I think we should cancel your and Jadelyn's arrangement tomorrow." Rupert said it with the sort of finality that it wasn't really a suggestion.

Jadelyn jumped at him. "Absolutely not. I have no doubt he'll be back tomorrow night and I'm willing to stake myself as collateral."

Rupert's brows shot up in surprise. "Daughter, I think I might have spoiled you too many times. Stop for a moment and consider what you are risking."

"I'm risking nothing, father. You don't understand—Zach will be fine." She smiled at me. "Won't you?"

"How could I not come back if someone like you is waiting for me?" Then I saw Scarlett. Scarlett had a worried look on her face. So instead of being realistic, I decided to reassure them all. "Both of you. I'm clearly too lucky. I'll be fine."

Sometimes comforting them, even if in only a small way, was worth tempting fate.

Rupert grunted, still not convinced. "I'll be discussing this with your mother."

Jadelyn smiled as if she'd already won and grabbed my arm, pulling me away before I and her father broke out into another conflict.

"Are you really going to fight this god?" she asked.

Scarlett came up and grabbed my other arm and we meandered around the area, just enjoying being with each other.

"Morgana is going to help, and it sounds like the Winter Queen is even going to pitch in. By the way, what's with that?" I looked to make sure no Faerie were around me.

"I'm almost positive there's at least a few attacks we don't know about," Scarlett spoke up. "They hit the Faerie—I'd bet money on it."

I gave a soft whistle. That was a stupid move.

"You don't get off that easy. Are you sure you can handle this?"

"No?" It came out as a question. "But if Morgana has confidence in it, then I'm willing to try. I'll never know what I'm capable of if I don't push myself."

"But a god?" Scarlett tried again.

"A heavily weakened god with the support of two other powerful paranormals. Besides, there's got to be precedent. How scary is one of my kind known to be?"

"Not sure." Jadelyn bit her lip. "Most of your kind stay hidden. Obviously, the bronze in Dubai is tough enough. He's not worried about anyone."

Scarlett added, "Dragons were killed early in the 18th century conflict. The Church threw everything at them. They didn't want to send down angelics until the dragons were gone. So I guess pretty fucking scary—still, I can't help but worry."

"Baah. Enough of that." I wanted to push past the worry. "What can I expect tomorrow? What do I wear?"

"Cheap suit," Jadelyn answered quickly. "Don't wear anything you want to use again. Otherwise, just come ready." She blushed at the final part. I knew that was at least involved.

"Not going to let me in on the big secret, are you?"

"It's more fun to surprise you."

Scarlett broke the two of us up before we could kiss. "It's midnight, and I'm afraid your pumpkin is about to expire, Jade. Not to mention you shouldn't see the bride on your wedding day. Bad luck and we certainly don't want to accrue any of that for you."

Scarlett had a smirk on her face as she pulled Jadelyn off, who looked at me wistfully.

I was looking forward to tomorrow.

"Young love," the Summer Queen said behind me. "Like blossoms in spring. Beautiful, short and something to be savored."

"Hello, we haven't formally met." I extended my hand. "I'm Zach."

"Charmed." She took my hand daintily. "We don't often need Morgana's assistance, but we do keep track of her for when we do. Pleasure to meet you. Though I must admit that I am vexed. What are you?"

Those gold eyes of hers bore into me with almost a physical weight.

"I'd prefer to keep that close for now." Figuring honesty was the best policy when it came to Faerie. Maybe it was just a myth, but I wasn't about to get into a war of words with her.

She gave a soft, thoughtful hum. "I can't even see past the veil put over you. Incredibly strong. We like strong, and the Faerie Courts aren't stupid enough to make an enemy out of you off the start. I heard about your tussle with the elves."

Ah. Now it made sense. This was a recruitment conversation. "I'll keep that in mind."

"That's all I can ask. But I'd mention that the Spring and Summer Courts make for some of the most beautiful getaways, and word is you might be honeymooning soon." She let go of my hand. "Think about it, and all you have to do is ask."

With that, the Summer Queen turned and left without waiting for a reply.

What strange people. There was just an oddness and alien quality to the interaction with the Faerie Queen.

But that was behind me. I had a great day to look forward to tomorrow.

CHAPTER 25

The next morning, I found myself trying to figure out how I'd ended up with the day I had planned. It was Monday, so I had classes, but I was also getting married. And then I had to figure out how to take down a god. Just your typical day.

Wanting a bit of normalcy, I found myself back at my apartment, pushing cereal around my bowl as I tried to figure out how I was going to fight off a god, but it was hard to focus on that when I was about to get married.

"Morning, stranger." My roommate Frank emerged from his room, Maddie trailing out behind him.

"Morning, guys. You look decently rested, almost like you two slept some last night," I teased. When I'd gotten to the apartment after the council meeting, it was late, and our shared wall had been suspiciously quiet.

Maddie rolled her eyes, moving around Frank and towards the kitchen, fishing through the fridge.

Frank plopped himself down across from me. "Everything okay? You are normally in class by now."

"Yeah, I'm fine. I just have a few things that came up on the new job last night, went late, and are going to carry over into today. Well, that and I have a date this afternoon that has me nervous."

"Which girlfriend?" Frank seemed to enjoy asking the question, a teasing look in his eye. He'd pestered me about all the women he'd seen in my life, thinking I'd become a player. Between my actual girlfriends and Kelly and Morgana, I had to admit I was surrounded by a lot of beautiful women.

Not sure how he'd take me confirming his theory, I decided to just go for it.

"Jadelyn."

"Wait, I don't think I've met that one." Frank looked at Maddie for help.

She squinted for a moment before recognition dawned on her face, her eyes filling with questions. "Wait, that was Chad's girlfriend before he died, wasn't it?"

"Yep." I tried to sound casual as I ate my cereal.

Frank paused what he was doing. "Wait, that girl from the club? The one you got in a fight with Chad over? Damn, man, well done."

Maddie raised an eyebrow at Frank, who walked over and squeezed her against him to placate her while keeping his eyes on me as we talked.

"So, let me get this straight. You have Scarlett, who is a lovely girl. And you're also dating Jadelyn? Let's not forget the mysterious boss of yours, the one in all the fancy cars. And I've also seen you with that cheerleader." Frank tried to wrap his head around it all. "Where is the dude I used to live with?" he teased.

"Cheerleader?" Maddie asked.

"Kelly," Frank clarified.

I laughed. Of course, he'd recognize the cheerleader on sight; before Maddie had tamed him, he had been quite the aspiring playboy.

"And they all know about each other?" he asked.

"First off, I'm only dating Scarlett and Jadelyn. They are sorority sisters. And yes, they know."

Frank leaned back and whistled as something started sizzling in the skillet. "Damn. I hate you a little. Maddie, think I can get another girlfr—?"

A wooden spoon thwacked him on the back of his head before he could finish his sentence. "Like you could handle more than me."

Frank recovered quickly and gave an innocent whistle, but from behind Maddie, he gave me a thumbs up and mouthed, 'How?'

I played out what my advice would look like. Step one, be a dragon. Pretty sure that one would be a non-starter.

Step two, bumble into the paranormal world and somehow manage to woo the women. I smiled to myself, happy it had happened to me.

No matter how I had managed to ensnare these girls in my life, I had been blessed. My heart warmed as I thought about it.

"Where'd you go off to?" Maddie asked, catching me lost in thought. A knowing smile played on her face.

But before I had to figure out what to say, my phone buzzed on the table.

"I'll bet that thing buzzes all the time. I'm sure having that many women keeps you busy." She finished up what she was cooking. "I can't imagine the hassle of running about with all of them."

Ignoring her, I looked at my phone. It was a text from Kelly. 'Zach, we have a problem at the football stadium. Get here ASAP.'

I was surprised by her text. She'd told me to avoid the football team until they figured out their alpha problem. It should have been the last place she wanted me. 'I thought it was off-limits.'

'Hurry, this is big,' she texted right after.

Frank sighed. "I know that look. You are going to rush off again. I swear, it's like you think it's life or death situations all the time."

I tried to fake offense, but I knew it was likely true. After all, I was often running off to save lives. "Best to get things done and not procrastinate."

"See, that's the kind of attitude you need if you want another girlfriend," Maddie said to Frank. "Can't laze about with more than one. They keep him on his toes."

Frank sighed, and I grabbed the suit from my closet for later. It was the only one I had. It was a nice classic black and would have to do.

"You two stay out of trouble," I joked as I left the suit hanging over my shoulder.

The stadium wasn't a far walk from my apartment, and since I'd become a dragon, it would take a lot more than walking to tire me out.

Listening to the snippets of conversation of students walking by was less amusing than usual. What excited them was no longer exciting compared to what I'd experienced. It only reminded me how much I didn't really fit into my old life anymore. That life had been dull compared to what I'd experienced in the paranormal world.

Which made me wonder what I was doing spending any time in classes anymore. Was that a life I wanted to pursue?

The part of me that had spent my entire life up until recently wanting to be a doctor said yes. But I didn't need it financially. I made more money working for Morgana. Even if I quit now, I could take a job or two a year and be perfectly content slowly building my hoard.

And it wasn't like I had a ton of time to spare. I was about to be committed to two women, and our current jobs and god problem had my schedule filled. School just didn't fit, despite how much I wanted it to.

As I walked towards the football stadium, I paused. Kelly and the wolf pack had decided to still pursue college. Continuing forward, I tried to piece together what they got from attending the university. The most rational answer I could get to was using it to build a bond between them as they formed a new pack, maybe even build a bit of independence away from their parents.

Jadelyn attended, but I assumed that, to run the family business, a college degree would be helpful. And she seemed genuinely interested in learning. And Scarlett was just tagging along to play bodyguard.

But my role in the paranormal community didn't really need college. Morgana's lessons had been far more valuable.

My musings ground to a halt as I neared the football stadium.

The school's stadium was like many colleges, their prized possession. A massive parking lot surrounded it, though at the moment it was mostly empty. A small huddle of cars for those who commuted in sat to one side, another set ringing the stadium. Those were no doubt the players' cars.

Shouting spilled out of the stadium before I even reached it. Over the shouting, I could also make out angry growls like there was — well, exactly what there was — a pack of werewolves fighting inside the stadium.

The short tunnel into the stadium proper opened up into a literal bloodbath. I knew Kelly had commented on the fighting before, but seeing it was an entirely different thing. The fight for alpha had gotten bloody.

The football team had over a hundred players, and the field was filled with werewolves tearing each other apart. It looked like the line of scrimmage had turned into a brutal assault, and those on the sideline had piled on.

Cheerleaders were sitting along the bleachers, boredom on most of their faces, except for one that was eyeing me as I walked in. I was surprised they weren't more freaked, given Kelly's tone in the text.

I stood there, not sure what I was supposed to do, when Kelly shouted my name. I turned, ready to help her with whatever she needed, but then I caught her face and paused. She was pissed.

"What the hell are you doing here, Zach? I told you to stay away." Her frown deepened.

I pulled out my phone and showed her the texts. "You're the one that asked me to come, Kelly. And what the hell is happening out there? This is insane."

Kelly ignored the second part of my statement, instead grumbling as she patted down her tight jeans and came up empty. She whirled on the girls in the bleachers. "Who the fuck has my phone."

That angry yell from Kelly suddenly put the two of us in the center of everybody's attention. Not only for the cheerleaders, but the brawling wolves nearest us paused and turned, hearing her tone. And the others picked up on the momentary pause, also growing curious.

A blonde-haired girl that looked like she could've been straight out of a mean girl stereotype meme stood up on the bleachers and cupped her hands over her mouth. "It is time we put an end to all of this." She gestured out towards the field. "Boys, this is the man that killed Chad."

Shit.

All the wolves were paying attention now as the last growling and tussling on the field died off, and I found myself the focus of attention for over a hundred glaring male werewolves.

Kelly shifted herself between the blonde and me, and the flicker of fear on her face told me that this was going in the direction it felt like. These wolves were about to pull me into their mess.

"Tiff. You have no idea what the fuck you are doing." She glared at Tiff, but the other wolf didn't back down.

Quickly, Kelly pivoted to speak to the wolves on the field. "And, boys, this is not a fight you want to pick. Chad had the power that corrupted him and three wolf packs to draw from, yet he lost to Zach. Do not do this."

"What happens if we kill him, Tiff?" Number 72 had his torn jersey still clinging to his chest.

Tiff, still on the bleachers, ignored Kelly's plea. "The bitches are in agreement. We'll support whoever can bring me the heart of the shifter that killed Chad. Full support for them to become alpha. Full backing from the girls, isn't that right?" She turned to the rest of the girls, who pointedly turned away from Kelly.

Kelly's back straightened at being ignored, and I was glad I wasn't on the other end of the look she was giving Tiff.

Grumbling and grunts started to pick up across the wolves on the field, a few starting to move around where they stood. I had a feeling I'd need to put my suit down if I didn't want to ruin it.

"Kelly, this is a problem."

"Let me handle this." Kelly covered the ground between her and the bleachers in just a few strides as she shifted, leaping up and catching Tiff in the face with her claws. She tore the blonde off the bleachers and was on her in an instant.

Tiff shifted as well, but by the time she was ready to fight, she'd already lost. She was torn up, her fur matted in enough blood that I knew she wasn't getting up any time soon. Kelly apparently didn't fuck around.

"Calm down, boys. Tiff doesn't speak for the girls. Does she?" Kelly asserted herself, but the girls on the bleachers turned away, awkwardly not making eye contact.

72 stepped forward, a leader among the fractured pack. "You've been out of it ever since your father died. Tiff is the new head bitch. Her word goes. Besides, we are all tired of fighting. We need a leader. You've been too distracted with this boy-toy, any-

way. I don't mind giving him a good thrashing."

The wolves on the field howled and barked in my direction.

While they couldn't decide who should be alpha, they seemed to at least be able to unite around attacking me. It looked like I might unite them after all for Kelly. Although, I wasn't sure how effective it would be without getting my heart ripped out, and I was pretty happy with where my heart was right now.

I was planning to give it to Jadelyn today, after all.

I warned Kelly one last time, "If they come, I'm not holding back. There's too many of them for me to not go all out." Eyeing the size of the pack arrayed out before me, I had a problem. A very lethal problem if I wasn't careful.

Kelly cursed under her breath and dove into the men.

But she wasn't going to be able to stop it. Two wolves jumped me.

Golden scales wrapped my body as I towered over the wolves, shifting into my two-ton hybrid form. I wasn't playing. There wasn't time to worry about my secret.

Most of them paused, but the two would-be-alphas full of bluster came at me. They became the first two victims.

My claws tore apart the first wolf, and I tossed the second into the air only for him to become a short-lived chew toy. His blood and flesh showered the ground below me. The sudden violence froze the wolf pack just as much as my shift.

I had noticed that they didn't fight to the death on the field, instead submitting, but if they expected the same from me when I was facing a hundred of them, they were crazy. As far as I knew, they were coming for my heart. This was a battle to the death for any who attacked me.

They were shocked as I opened my maw, snatching up the next closest wolf and spinning, my tail flinging back another dozen wolves.

The smack of my tail seemed to snap them out of their daze, and the wolf pack rushed me.

I plowed through the pack on all fours, flinging them aside and using my claws to tear through them in swaths.

Wolves leapt onto my back, but I rolled over and through the pack, crushing those on my back.

Spinning around, I reared up and stomped the ground with my front claws, bellowing a roar that made the thin metal bleachers vibrate. I worked to intimidate them with my power, hoping to avoid needing to kill more than necessary.

The wolves trembled at my roar, looking at their fallen pack mates littered around me. Those that could still move fell to their knees. I could smell fear and a hint of piss as many of them rolled onto their backs and put their limbs in the air.

I looked over and noticed that Kelly was the only one still standing on the field. Even the bitches off the field had rolled over onto their backs.

Shifting back to my dragon knight form in case someone had the wise idea to try to surprise me, I asked Kelly, "What the hell just happened?"

"They submitted," she said simply, her eyes registering only shock.

I used my dragon sight, cringing at what I found. Tethers of amber magic rose out of each of them, weaving a massive tapestry that tried to center itself on me. "No," I growled. "Remember what I said."

Already, images of the bitches going back to the betas riled me up, and I could feel the beast inside of me excited at the prospect and ready to kill all the betas to make it happen and claim all those women.

But the part of me that was still human firmly rejected it.

The pack magic slid off of me, failing to find purchase. I wasn't sure if it was my reluctance, or if I was actually not able to accept the pack magic as a dragon, but it didn't lock on me. Tentatively, I focused and pushed on the focal point of the magic, willing it to move to my desire.

I quickly glanced around. 72 had seemed to be a leader. Maybe he would make the best alpha? But as I searched the field, I couldn't find him. Giving up, I tried to push the magic into the nearest wolf, but it rejected him.

Frustrated, I wondered if I was going to have to try wolf after wolf until it accepted one, when my eyes locked on Kelly. A smile split my face as I imagined how pissed she would be if this worked.

Pushing the magic's focus onto her, it was like the final puzzle piece snapping into place as the pack magic eagerly joined with her. It poured into her without end as she sucked it up in what seemed like an endless moment.

Kelly gasped, her eyes wide and glowing amber with the pack magic.

There was a moment of disappointment as I felt the power leave me, but it wasn't meant for me.

I had just been lured here because of Tiff. The beast still wanted me to take the power and all the women that came with it, but I pushed it back down. Sometimes, it wasn't right.

"What the hell did you just do?" Kelly came out of it. "You can't. That's not possible. They accepted you as alpha, not me."

"Seems the pack magic was more than eager to accept you," I pointed out.

Her body swelled with power before my eyes. She wasn't so much bigger, but she seemed... denser.

She just kept shaking her head, muttering to herself and then to me. "This can't be. This shouldn't be. Do you have any idea what you've just done?"

"Sure, I made you alpha." I didn't give a fuck about their rules. There was no reason it needed to be a man. I'd just seen Kelly tear apart several wolves for disagreeing with her. And she'd learned from her father. She was the best one for the job.

But I didn't get a chance to say that before Kelly jumped me.

She took me by surprise, and we went down in a tumble. Her claws were out, and I grabbed her by the wrists before she could do harm that she would regret later.

"What are you doing?" I rolled us both, ending up on top. "You're alpha now. I can see the magic solidifying, even now."

The pack was coming out of their stupor, clearly not entirely pleased with the new development.

72 reared his ugly head. "No way. A bitch is a bitch. She can't be alpha." He strode

over, clearly about to make some sort of move.

I popped up off Kelly, grabbing 72 by the throat and throttling him back into the field, my knee landing on his chest. "She's alpha if I say she is. You've already seen what happens to those that come up against me. Would you like to join them?"

Another wolf tried to tackle Kelly, but she jumped, spinning and kicking out with a clawed foot. She caught him in the neck and sent him spinning away without a throat. "Anyone else have a problem with me?"

It seemed her display of violence reminded them exactly who they were dealing with, and no one stepped forward.

"See, you can do this," I said with a smile of self-satisfaction. Kindly, I had omitted the 'I was right'. Oh, how I was tempted to say those words.

"You." Kelly whirled on me, poking me in the chest and forcing me to take a step back. "Have messed this all up. What's going to happen to the pack now? Huh? Who's going to breed with the girls, or are we just going to be a barren pack? A pack destined to have no little pups?" Her voice broke a little at the end.

But fierceness returned to her eyes as she stalked closer. "You had the right to alpha, yet you gave it to me. I expect you to take responsibility."

"There's a whole world of science and magic," I countered. "A solution for this exists, even if I don't know it off-hand."

Kelly punched me. "This isn't a joke! This is two hundred people's lives." She gestured to the wolf pack around us. "They are my pack, my responsibility. The last thing I want is for them to look forward to a childless life."

I smiled. "Your pack. Already sounding like an alpha."

"This isn't a joke!" She pressed me back again.

A wolf spoke up from the field, sounding a little hopeful. "You could always give it up."

Thankfully, he distracted Kelly's ire from me. Poor guy.

"And let you fucking idiots tear each other up every day? No, beat me now if you have a problem with it. I'm not putting up with this every day anymore," Kelly snapped.

None of the men stepped forward, eyeing 72, who was still on the ground gurgling blood through his impromptu tracheotomy.

As the moment passed, whispers started up among the men, and I caught the couple mentions of the dragon.

The battle fury left me, and I realized we had a huge problem. "Fuck. Don't let any of them leave." I pressed a hand to my face. "I need to impress upon them my secret before this goes any further."

Kelly winced. "Shit. I don't know. They might stay quiet for now, but... there's two hundred of them."

The momentary idea of killing them all flitted through my mind before I squelched the idea. This was Kelly's pack now.

"Alright. Listen up," I bellowed over the field, getting their attention. "What I am stays a secret. Do all of you understand?"

A few of the wolves gave half-hearted nods, and Kelly stepped in. "Get on your feet and listen up."

I could see the web of pack magic pulling at each of them as they did what they were told. Even those that limped on a single leg took the shoulder of another and stood up.

"All of you fucked up today. This is the price. If you utter a word about what Zach is, you don't have to worry about him coming back to kill you. You're out of the pack, omega for life. And that's only if I don't tear your throat out too many times before then. Is that understood?"

Her words reverberated on the pack magic, and they all nodded quickly in understanding.

"Now, where's Tiff?" Kelly fumed.

The crowd jostled, and they threw a bloodied Tiff out in front of the rest of the women. They seemed to have changed sides pretty quickly once Kelly had won.

"Look on the bright side?" Tiff tried.

Kelly's palm was fast as it slapped Tiff hard enough for her to reel back, stumbling to a knee. "What bright side? We lost a dozen wolves today because of your idiocy. Their blood is on your hands."

"But I solved the alpha problem, and I got you him," Tiff pointed at me.

"Got me him?" Kelly looked back at me, confused.

"Think about it, Kelly. The alpha gets to date outside the pack. Think about Chad's engagement. It just makes sense for the alpha to have ties outside the pack, political shit and all. And it isn't like any of the betas will be good for an alpha bitch," Tiff groveled.

Kelly's lips quirked up at the idea, and she rubbed a hand on her chin as she eyed me up and down hungrily. "Girls, take her away. I'll deal with her later."

I didn't have a moment to react as Kelly jumped on me, looping her arms around the back of my neck and planting a kiss on my lips. Catching her on instinct, I held onto her ass and pulled her up for just a moment longer before putting her back down.

"Clean up your pack and we can talk later. I need to get going. There's my wedding and then I'm taking on the god that has been behind the troll attacks. I need to focus."

I'd expected more questions from her, but all she said was, "Can I help?"

I wanted to say no, but in reality, I could really use the help. "Sync up with Rupert and Detective Fox. I have a wedding to go to."

She gave a growl that wasn't unfriendly, but I couldn't quite place what it meant before she slapped my ass. "Will do." Then she said louder, "Get the hell out of my field. I apparently have a practice to run."

Kelly whirled away from me. "Get your gear back on, boys. Line up. Girls, stop loitering around. Meg, take my spot on the pyramid. Set thirteen in five minutes."

The pack became a buzz of activity, and I felt good leaving her in charge. She had taken on the alpha role quickly, and I grinned, still holding back my I-told-you-so.

Grabbing my suit, I decided it might be best if I headed over to Jadelyn's directly and avoided any other conflict before the wedding. If I didn't make it there on time, I'd have to face Jadelyn and the mothers. A shiver went up my spine at the thought, and I booked it, before turning back around because I was naked as the day I was born.

Couldn't show up to the Scalewrights like that.

CHAPTER 26

I'd been so focused on getting myself to Jadelyn's without further conflict that I paused as I stood outside the manor, realizing I was barefoot, wearing sweatpants and a sweatshirt one of the wolves had lent me. My suit was over my shoulder, but I didn't feel entirely presentable to enter.

"Zach." Claire, Jadelyn's mother, stood in the doorway.

Too late to turn back or clean up at that point, I moved into the doorway. Claire greeted me with open arms, grabbing me and pulling me into a hug.

Behind her, Ruby shadowed her, much like Scarlett often did to Jadelyn. "Morning, Zach! You're early."

I scratched the back of my head. "I ran into a little trouble with the college pack. Lost my clothes in the tumble. So I decided to just come over here before I got roped into something else. I would hate to be late or have something pull me away from today."

Claire made a cute noise. "That's so romantic. Ah, my daughter is too lucky. I'm happy you are putting our girls first."

"They are my world. Nothing would dare come between us." I flashed a charming smile at the mothers, working to reassure them.

"With what you are, once that secret is out, I doubt many people would want to get between you and your women." Claire paused. "Well, except for other women. That'll happen, but I've already talked to my daughter about it."

"Mine as well," Ruby agreed. "Taking charge of it will certainly benefit them in the long run."

The way they talked was as if they had experience curtailing their husbands into place. Jadelyn and Scarlett had at least made it clear they were cognizant of my needs and would work to ensure they were met.

Clearing my throat, I looked around the place. "Is there anything I can do to help set up?"

"No, we have it all under control. Besides, I wouldn't want to ruin the surprise. Jadelyn told me she has left you to your imagination in that regard. So our lips are sealed."

Jadelyn had enjoyed keeping details secret. I had no idea what a siren's wedding was going to be like, but I trusted my mate.

All I was told was to wear a suit that I didn't want to wear again, which of course had set my imagination off. That I'd bought this during the school year after my body had changed meant this would be the first and last time I wore this suit.

"Do you guys have shoes I could borrow?" My toes wiggled free; my shoes hadn't survived the transformation.

"Oh, barefoot is preferred." Claire waved off my concern. "Would you like to go talk to our husbands? They are currently planning up in their 'war room.'" She said the word with the same attitude a wife would about a man cave.

"That sounds great." I was feeling a bit out of place and useless among the women and the decorating. The servants walking by with bunches of flowers only made it worse. If they weren't going to put me to work, I'd rather go hang out with the men.

Claire rattled off enough directions that you would have thought I was going across town rather than through a home. But maybe their home was large enough to give off the same feeling.

I almost passed by the room, but luckily the door was open. As I passed it, I could see a room that could be nothing other than a man cave. It was like someone had transplanted a hunting lodge into the middle of the palatial manor. Stag and boar heads were mounted on the rough wood walls overlooking red leather couches.

Pushing open the door, I found Rupert and Detective Fox lounging on worn leather seats with tablets in their hands as they discussed plans for the evening. I knocked on the doorframe to announce myself. "Your wives sent me up here."

Rupert stood. "You're early."

"Nerves. Waiting around wasn't doing me any favors." I tried to keep the explanation short. "Seemed easier to come over now rather than wait around."

Rupert grunted in understanding. "Well, welcome then. We were just going over some of the texts that elves pulled from their archives."

Detective Fox eyed me up and down in my sweats, his eyes locking on my bare feet. "What happened to you?"

"Got in a tussle with the college pack. They are a few wolves short as a result, but at least they figured out their alpha situation." I grinned, wondering if he was going to add that to his investigation board he kept on me.

"You didn't," he scowled, clearly getting the wrong idea.

"No. Kelly is the new alpha," I said quickly, knowing the man wouldn't love his daughter being committed to somebody who also had responsibility for a hundred female wolves.

But my statement didn't seem to calm him very much.

"Kelly? As in Brent's daughter?" Detective Fox asked, surprised.

"Yup, turns out a female can be an alpha." I'd noticed how he emphasized daughter.

Rupert shook his head. "Strange times we live in. But she's competent enough. I don't care as long as it doesn't cause problems in the city."

I nodded, moving closer. "Tell me about what the elves pulled up."

Detective Fox held up his tablet. "Old journals from Spanish Missionaries. The elves had agents in place among them, making sure that any who got too close to mentioning the paranormal disappeared. As you can see, Nat'alet comes up only a few times, and the elves are even arguing over the translation. Look here."

He pointed to a spot on the screen. It had the original handwritten text from the missionary's journal, and below each line was a typed translation.

"They aren't sure what he's the god of. Bear men, or boar men. It might be a tribe, or a title for hunters."

"Or ManBearPig," I laughed.

Neither of them did, though. That was okay; they just weren't cultured enough.

"Never mind. He's the god of trolls," I pointed out.

"What? How did you get that?" Detective Fox looked at the transcript again as if that would reveal something I'd seen. But he was taking it all so literally; both of them were.

"If you were a Native American hundreds of years ago and you saw a troll transform before your eyes, what are the two first things you'd fixate on?" I asked my soon to be fathers-in-law.

Rupert got it instantly. "Tusks and size. The only things they'd have to compare them to would be a boar or a bear."

"Bingo. So it makes sense then why he's using the trolls to do all the work. Here, with the Order of the Magi convention and the swamp troll migration happening at the same time, he has both of his forces in place. Trolls and warlocks are rarely ever in the same space." Maybe it was my dragon brain doing all the work, but it suddenly made much more sense. "But what I really need to know is what his weakness is. Does it say anything?"

"It depends on what he once was." Rupert put the tablet down, no longer focused on the text. "God is just a term. Technically, the Faerie are gods, and so are more than a few other big name paranormals. Think of it this way, when numerous people worship a paranormal, it is like a collective spell. It pushes mana into them, forcing growth upon them beyond what they might have normally accomplished in their lifetime."

"So he's just a super-charged paranormal?" I had to admit, that made me feel better about my chances. "Could anything become a god? What about how the magi seem to worship dragons?"

Rupert snorted. "They very carefully don't worship living dragons, or yes, they would push one into what we'd consider godhood."

Interesting. I filed that away and focused back on Nat'alet. "Do you think it is as simple as him being a powered-up swamp troll?"

"Maybe." Rupert rubbed his chin. "This is a fairly stupid plan he has, but something tells me he's too smart to be a troll."

"At least you bargained for help from the Faerie," Detective Fox threw out.

As much as I wanted to claim the praise, I hadn't bargained with the Faerie. "Huh? I didn't bargain with them. Neither did Morgana."

Both of the men looked at each other in confusion. "You're sure? We figured you must have given that the Winter Queen came out to help," Rupert finished for his friend.

"Hate to disappoint you, but no. Morgana and I thought maybe the trolls hit too close to the Faerie Realm," I offered.

"No. We have a detailed accounting of the troll attacks. Wissahickon Park has been clear, almost as if they had been avoiding it. For good reason," Detective Fox refuted.

"Huh," I said as we all paused to think that over. "That means there's something we don't know, and she does."

Rupert sighed and rubbed his temples. "That's always the way with the Faerie. Walking headaches, the lot of them."

Rather than focus on trying to untangle a Faerie's logic, I focused on the information I was still missing to figure out my plan. "Do you have a final count on how many trolls we can expect?"

"Two hundred," Detective Fox said quickly, and I admit I'd been hoping for a lower number. He must have seen it in my face as he added, "Or more. Second guessing going in with Morgana?"

I'd lie if two hundred trolls didn't scare the shit out of me. Even if I could tear apart a dozen of them in my hybrid form, all it would take was being overwhelmed by them. Two hundred were a lot of trolls.

"Two hundred," I repeated barely keeping the smile off my face as I said the next part. "That's a lot for me to swallow."

"You can still back out. Nothing has happened yet," Rupert hedged.

"Oh, yeah. Definitely no small number. But I meant literally. I'm not quite sure my stomach is big enough to swallow them. The five that attacked Jadelyn were a tasty snack, but two hundred might be like forcing myself for that extra plate full of bacon at the buffet."

Part of me wondered just how big I would get if I managed to go full dragon. Logic said I'd be bigger than my hybrid form, but just what was the upper limit? That was something I needed to talk to Morgana about. I had a feeling I'd have some serious size on my side.

"You ate them?" Detective Fox said, bringing me back to the conversation at hand. Both men were looking at me a little warily. Good.

"Yup. They attacked Jadelyn—I wasn't going to let them live." My voice rumbled as the beast tried to get in on the conversation.

The men paused, clearly hoping I'd go on. When I went quiet, Rupert grumbled, then tried to play it off like he didn't care. "Keep your secrets."

The gleam in his eye said that he desperately wanted to figure it out, but he added, "As long as you take care of my daughter, I don't much care what you eat. Glad you aren't too concerned about going up against two hundred trolls."

Rupert paused. "Since we've gone this far, you should know. The skinwalker that attacked Jadelyn was part of a plot to replace her and other paranormal leadership with skinwalkers."

"What?" I growled. "Why would they do that?"

"We can only guess as to why they'd want to try and replace our leadership given what we know." Detective Fox answered shaking his head. "The skinwalker didn't know anything beyond his simple mission. We didn't want to anger you based on what little we knew."

I ground my teeth, wanting to tear a chunk out of Nat'alet and those who served him. How dare they go after my mate like that.

But it made sense if his plan so far seemed to be to cause chaos, weakening both the paranormal and magi, then it only made sense for him to take what power he could in the resulting confusion.

"Hello, boys," Morgana's voice surprised me from the doorway, jerking me out of my thoughts.

"What are you doing here?" I asked in surprise before realizing that it came out wrong.

But if it bothered Morgana, she didn't show it. The drow vampire was wearing her standard black leather getup. Although, no blades swung from her hips, and she had a cape hanging off her shoulders that was covered in markings that I felt contained her history.

"Morgana. Glad you could make it," Rupert said. "Zach, as her ward, we extended an invitation to her. And we wanted to talk with her about the plans for tonight."

"Ah." That made sense.

Morgana came over and pinched my cheeks. "It feels like just yesterday that I took you in. Just a little lost one." She gave off a wistful sigh.

"It was three months ago, Morgana," I reminded her.

"How time flies." She sat down in front of me. I still hadn't taken a seat. "Rub my shoulders, would you?"

Not seeing any reason not to, I did. She moaned, making me cringe. She knew how awkward that would make me feel in front of the fathers, and I knew she was enjoying every minute of messing with me.

"So, what's the plan?" she asked, taking control of the room.

The fathers looked a little shaken, and I smiled to myself as I realized she often liked to throw people off balance, only to take command of the situation. Kelly had hinted that, when I wasn't around, Morgana was far fiercer, and this felt like just a little hint of the control she could exhibit.

"Zach here had the idea that Nat'alet is the god of trolls. It seems like a sound theory given what we know," Detective Fox summarized.

I kept at rubbing her tense shoulders, and Morgana melted into the chair, speaking lazily.

"He's good like that." She groaned as I found a particularly tight spot on her right shoulder. "Who worships him?"

"Nobody, except three warlocks as far as we can tell. It seems he's been forgotten to time," Rupert clarified.

She nodded. "So he's still weak. This might just be his play to come back into the limelight, despite what those warlocks believed."

"Killing paranormal and magi to help the world heal," I clarified for the two men.

"Stupid," Rupert muttered. "If he's so concerned with the decline in mana, then maybe he shouldn't be throwing around so much magic. Couldn't have been easy to transform the magi."

"It makes a sort of sick sense," I added. "Though, I wonder if there's something else that we could do to further the same goal."

Rupert shrugged. "Too big of a goal to tackle in a single lifetime, and the decline is extremely slow. A problem for another day."

How Rupert shrugged it off bothered me, but I didn't let it show. Without a better understanding of the full situation, I decided to curb any judgment.

"But even if he's relatively weak for a god, he still has amassed an army of two hundred trolls. That's a problem," Rupert pointedly laid that out for Morgana. "Any ideas?"

She looked up over the chair at me. "How hungry are you?" The corner of her lips twitched as she tried to ask that with a straight face. No doubt her pointy ears had heard what I said earlier.

I, however, failed to keep myself from laughing. "Might be too much for me."

"Pity," she pouted. "Well then, given they are swamp trolls and we already have the Winter Queen's assistance, I suggest we use that to our fullest advantage. If she can make the gathering place cold enough, then we might just be able to freeze them out."

"About that." Detective Fox paused. "Did you bargain for their help?"

"No." Morgana grew serious for a moment. "That concerns me as well, but there is little that can be done. Her help will be invaluable. And I'm not in a place to turn it down."

"Agreed," Rupert scratched at his beard.

"But less fretting. Don't we have a siren's wedding to prepare for?" Morgana picked up the mood of the room and flipped it inside out with her own excitement. She looked up at me. "Can't say I've ever prepared to give someone away at a wedding..." She looked like she was about to start down some long reflection on giving me away, but Rupert jumped in.

"Ah. It is getting late." Rupert nodded towards the clock on the wall. "Why don't you go get dressed. I'm sure the girls will descend on us soon."

I knew when I'd been dismissed. Besides, if they wanted privacy to discuss it, then who was I to stick around?

Grabbing my suit, I wandered through the manor looking for a room I could change in. But I quickly became lost.

"Excuse me." I stopped a maid carrying a pot of flowers. "Where can I change?"

"Oh." She looked at me wide-eyed. "You're Zach!"

"That would be me." I gave her my best patient smile. "Anywhere is fine; I just need to get changed."

"Zach?" Scarlett's bright orange hair poked out of a door down the hall, her fox ears twitching. "You aren't supposed to be here. It's bad luck to see the bride."

I held up my suit. "I'm lost, and I need a place to change."

"Elda, I'll take care of my wayward man. Thank you for helping with the flowers." Scarlett popped out of the room, carefully closing the door behind her.

Jadelyn must have been inside getting ready.

Scarlett looked beautiful. She was wearing a tight green dress that reminded me of spring. Her hair was up and curled tightly in a bun with a few artful wisps of hair escaping.

"Come on." She caught up to me and grabbed my arm.

I couldn't help but notice my ring still on her finger and smiled in satisfaction.

"Yes. I'm yours." She smiled at me and paused to give me a peck on the cheek. "And I'd love to thank you again for the ring. But today is Jadelyn's day, and I think if we are to get this larger family to work out, I need to respect that as best as I can. That means no tempting me."

"No promises," I replied.

She huffed in exasperation. "Men only want one thing, don't they?"

"Hey."

"I'm kidding. Under that big, tough guy exterior, I know my man is a big softy. That's what makes you great." She clung tightly to me as she wound through the manor. "Here we go. You can change in my room."

She opened it up, and I wasn't quite sure what to expect.

It was warm. Orange walls and light wood tones set the tone of the room. A massive four-poster bed dominated the center of the room, but what caught my eye was a yellow stuffed dragon laying on the pillows.

"Really?" I broke free from her and dashed over to pick it up before she could stop me.

"Fuck. It was a joke! Jadelyn gave it to me yesterday."

"Uh huh." I eyed her suspiciously.

She pulled it out of my hands and put it carefully on a chair in the corner. From the new angle of her room, I could see the various weapons that had been hidden from the entrance view. A sword was strapped to the back of the dresser, and a shotgun peeked out from behind the door.

That seemed more like Scarlett to me.

"Go on. Get dressed." She shooed me into her bathroom and closed the door.

It didn't take me long to slip on the suit. Thankfully, it still fit me perfectly. I'd only gotten it this fall. Part of me had worried it wouldn't with how much I'd been eating.

Using the mirror and a little water, I tamed my hair and dried it off enough that

I wouldn't drip on my suit before opening the door.

A small intake of breath sounded as I stepped through. "You really do clean up nicely." Scarlett's tails batted me playfully as she bit her lip. "But let me make it perfect."

Her hands neatly straightened my collar and fixed my tie, then she licked her finger and smoothed out my eyebrows. She did a few more minor adjustments before stepping back. "There, that'll make an impression. Though it won't last long."

"Oh? Care to enlighten me on what to expect?"

"Nope. It is better if you experience it. At least, that's what all the sirens say." She added the last part after a moment's pause. "Let me go check to see if Jadelyn's ready. Stay here." She glared back at me as if I were a wayward dog that might wander off if not watched.

"Got it. Staying put in your childhood bed." I sat down on the plush mattress with a grin.

"Down boy." She narrowed her eyes. "Not today."

"That wasn't a never." I smirked, laying back and spreading myself across her bed.

She gave a huff of frustration, staring at me and fidgeting before she groaned and turned, heading out of her room.

CHAPTER 27

I amused myself in Scarlett's room, waiting for somebody to come get me. I was starting to wonder if they had forgotten about the groom when the door handle finally turned.

"Change your mind? We can do a quick roll in your childhood bed," I joked from the bed before Morgana's head popped in.

Fuck.

She grinned wide. "My childhood bed is on the other side of the world. Though the offer is tempting."

"Shit. I thought you were Scarlett." I could feel my face heating up.

Morgana lifted an eyebrow. "Is that you retracting your offer?"

"Not now, Morgana. I'm nervous enough as it is," I groaned, grinding my palms into my brow.

She pulled herself through the doorway and came to my side. "Cheer up. You're about to get your princess. Honestly, I'm a little jealous. Jadelyn is quite the catch."

While she said it like she was interested in Jadelyn, I got the impression she was talking about me. I might be pushing Morgana's comments aside, but I wasn't stupid.

"Thanks. You have been my rock since my life changed. I don't know what I'd do without you." I meant it. Since the whole you're-a-dragon deal, Morgana had been there for me every step of the way.

"Flail helplessly," Morgana supplied. "Or maybe just be dead in a ditch somewhere." She paused, dramatically making a show of pondering it. "Yeah, that last bit most likely."

I rolled my eyes. "Your perspective is uplifting."

"I'm not exactly known for being the bearer of good news. But this time I am. Jadelyn is all set up in her tent, and as my ward, I get to bring you down and throw you to the shark—I mean—siren."

"They're ready?" I perked up.

"Yep, so come on. Let's go get rid of those nerves. Not like you have a big bad you are fighting tonight."

"Somehow, this is scarier."

She rolled her eyes. "Maybe one day I'll know what it's like."

I paused. Morgana never touched on her personal life.

"You've never been married? In all your long years?" I asked. Given she was a vampire for at least four hundred years, and I expected that old again as an elf, I had just assumed there had been somebody at some point.

"I was a priestess before I became a vampire."

Now that shocked me. Trying to picture it, I ended up with Morgana in a leather nun outfit. It just didn't quite fit.

"Please tell me what that little fantasy was." She smirked, totally calling me on it.

"Just having trouble imagining you being any sort of holy."

"Priestesses look after their tribe's root tree, not any sort of god. But my life was dedicated to nurturing and protecting my clan's root tree. I couldn't marry and put a man before the tree. Then, my clan was burned down, and I was turned." She sighed.

There was no way that she hadn't gotten hundreds, if not thousands, of suitors, since becoming a vampire. Her magic alone likely tempted more than a few paranormal.

"Why not now?"

She forcefully pushed me through a doorway. "Oh look. Your wedding." She less than expertly forced us into another topic.

Outside the manor, the Scalewright and Fox family waited for me. Servants had taken time off their tasks to come outside and watch. Of course, what took up the most space was the tent. A white tent of heavy and enchanted cloth was erected over a pool in the lagoon.

"Welcome, Zach Pendragon," Rupert announced as I walked outside. "It is an exciting day."

Claire was standing beside him, vibrating with energy. "Today you join my daughter and our family. Though you don't have family to speak of, you have friends and others that enrich your life that will in turn enrich ours."

Morgana pulled me by the elbow. "I offer up my ward, Zach Pendragon, to join your family. I give this union here today my full support."

Scarlett rushed forward and took my other elbow. "I accept on behalf of Jadelyn, who is my sister in so many ways. Come with me?"

The two girls traded me off, and I got a look at Claire, wiping tears from her eyes.

"Any last words of advice?" I asked as Scarlett led me to the large white tent.

"Just go with the flow." She smiled, pecking me on the cheek. "See you after. Oh, and the tent won't let any sound out, so knock yourself out."

Nodding, I stepped forward, taking a deep breath at the big step I was about to take.

I reached forward, parting the tent flaps. It was dark enough inside that I couldn't see anything at first.

The tent flap rustled closed behind me, and my eyes adjusted to the dim lighting. Lanterns floated in the water, giving off just enough light to see by and setting the mood.

I looked up, and I couldn't take my eyes off of Jadelyn. She was mesmerizing. Her eyes smoldered as she sat on a rock in the lagoon, a thin white wedding dress pooling off of her and floating on the surface of the water.

I stood there stunned, breathlessly admiring her as her eyes twinkled with delight.

She wanted me to look, to soak up this moment. Jadelyn was immaculate as always, and just for me, she had styled her otherwise straight hair. And she'd worn enough gold and jewels, perfectly placed, drawing attention to her curves. It made my dragon want to pounce on her. She knew exactly what she was doing.

The smirk on her lips told me so. Then she opened them, and the sweet dulcet notes of her voice rang through the tent.

A chill ran down my back; the song felt almost physical as it swept through me. It was filled with such love and adoration that it pulled at my heartstrings and nearly brought me to my knees.

My feet splashed into the water before I even realized I'd taken a step. I hesitated, not wanting to mess up however the ceremony was supposed to go. But she reached out a hand towards me, beckoning me closer. The slight motion made her ample chest jiggle in the otherwise tight dress.

I had a feeling this was why I was told I shouldn't wear a suit I cared about. I waded through the water, drawn by her song, until I reached the rock. She pulled me up, but instead of kissing me, she pulled me into the crook of her neck and put her lips to my ear.

Images filled my head as she sang, dreams of her and me together. We were conquering the world, standing atop a mountain of gold. The love between us was clear. I sank one hand into her hair and held the small of her back with the other.

It was a blissful moment filled with dreams of us together, happy. She was showing me all she wanted for us, all she dreamed that we could be. And damn if it wasn't also turning me on. My pants were becoming unbearably constricting.

Kissing along her neck, my lips touched the soft scales that appeared when she was wet. I had expected a somewhat rough texture, but they were soft and pliant to the touch.

She held my head and pushed it down her neck to her breasts.

I greedily accepted the invitation. Dipping low, I peppered her soft chest with kisses and fished out a nipple from her strapless dress, taking it into my mouth like I was savoring the last piece of chocolate.

Her song changed. Rather than a blissful future, it turned lewd.

Images of her and me wrapped in pink silk replaced the previous thoughts in my head. Visions of us making tender love to one another filled my mind. She screamed in ecstasy in those images, and it stirred something inside of me.

Lust and love like I'd never known poured over me, filling every crevice of my mind.

I pushed her down on the rock and tore open her wedding dress, only a moment of pause, hoping she wouldn't kill me for destroying the beautiful garment.

Now. I needed her now.

Jadelyn smiled below me, stretching out on the rock and opening her legs. There were no panties in my way.

My hand turned into a claw, and I tore out the crotch in my suit, too excited to take time to unbutton my pants.

Her song faltered for just a moment as she looked at my erect member with wide eyes.

But the stunned look turned to hunger as her song picked up again with a much faster tempo.

There was no preamble, no coaxing her. I needed to be inside of her so badly that I thrust in without another thought.

I completely forgot that Jadelyn was still a virgin. I tore her hymen, and she arched her back as she hit a note that wavered in the air, changing slightly, like someone tuning a string.

She came back and grabbed my head as I felt her sex clench and quiver around my cock.

I paused, trying to figure out if she'd just orgasmed with the first thrust. No, that wasn't quite it, but I could feel it shift and move until her sex fit me like a glove.

At the same time, the note struck a pitch that resonated with me, filling me with a warm vibration of pleasure that made me feel like I was melting.

The vibrations of the note went straight through me to my soul, and I felt a harmony with her that blew my mind. The resonation coursed through me and shook me from head to toe as my body reacted.

I pumped stroke after stroke of semen into her. It was like she had just hit a switch, triggering a mind-blowing orgasm so hard that my vision spotted and I braced myself against the rock, lest I crush her under me.

I'd never come so quickly before, but I'd also never had an orgasm last so long.

"What was that?" I panted as the moment finally came to an end.

Jadelyn answered me with a kiss, stopping her song for the first time.

I savored her lips and pushed her harder against the rock. I could already feel myself ready for another round.

Pushing off her, I pulled down the top of her dress and took handfuls of her soft breasts.

"What did you do to me?" I asked, still struggling for air.

Jadelyn smirked and hit that note again.

My entire body shook with pleasure, though it wasn't as explosive as the first time.

"I gave you my song. During a siren's first union, they have a unique opportunity to tune their song and their body to another." She smirked, letting out another one of those notes for emphasis.

I nearly came again.

"Your body?" I asked, realizing she wasn't just a fantastic fit—she was a perfect fit for me now. "Sing for me." I smiled.

She grabbed my head and sang into my ear once again as I lost myself pumping inside of her. Reveling in her wet warmth.

It was pure ecstasy as I stroked inside of her.

I came another two times before she had her first release.

Her orgasm made her hit that perfect note again, and I nearly blacked out with how hard I came inside of her. Ripples of pleasure spread from my scalp down my back as I pressed myself deeper, just wanting to feel her wet warmth wrapped around me as I came undone.

I let out a deep breath as I came down, happiness coursing through my veins.

"Join me for a swim?" Jadelyn offered.

I blinked away the black spots from my vision. "Water and sex don't normally work together," I said before I realized how stupid that might sound to a siren.

She only laughed. "I think you'll be surprised."

I grabbed onto her tightly and rolled us both off the rock and into the water with a splash.

Jadelyn laughed, batting me on the chest. "Be delicate, you big brute."

I realized I could understand her perfectly under water.

Claiming her plump pink lips, I let us both sink down deeper into the lagoon as she breathed air into my mouth while we kissed.

I was still firmly inside of her and started thrusting slowly, cautious of lost lubricant. But it didn't seem to matter. If anything, she felt slicker than before, like fresh- ly poured oil. Nearly too slick for any sort of friction.

Jadelyn clung to me as I tried to relearn the mechanics of sex. Rather than thrusting with my hips, I had to use my arms to pull and push her along with the sway of my hips.

She was insatiable as she hungrily de- voured my lips. Bubbles exited out the cor- ner of our kiss and tickled my cheeks. Her nails raked along my scalp as she refused to let the kiss end. And I wasn't complaining.

It was amazing. Her overly lubricated sex made me hungry for friction, pounding harder into her as I chased after another release. I ground my hips into hers and let a hand slip between us so I could rub her clit.

"Fuck me, harder," Jadelyn broke the kiss to scream before reclaiming my lips.

Fast and hard. This time, I focused on trying to get her off. I needed to even the score.

My aggressive fingers worked their mag- ic, and Jadelyn broke the kiss to let loose another one of those orgasmic notes that rippled through me, pulling out another one of my peaks.

My mate had her eyes closed and mouth open in pleasure; her veil and dress flut- tered in the surrounding water.

Mine.

The beast made himself known, pushing forward, demanding that I take her again.

The white lines of the scar I'd marked on her shoulder stood out, and then began glowing iridescently in the water.

Jadelyn gasped, her eyes shooting open and a torrent of bubbles escaping her mouth as she pulled me close again. "I love you so much. I'm yours, now and forever."

My feet touched the bottom of the lagoon, and she wrapped her legs around me, hooking her ankles and forcing me to sit on the bottom.

We kissed like that again. Jadelyn provided me with air to breathe as she squirmed in my lap. I knew she was trying to bounce on me, but the logistics underwater were making it difficult.

When she pushed off, I pulled her back down hard, impaling her once again.

I could feel her lips quirk up in a smile as we kissed. Playfully, she pushed off the ground again, only for me to slam her back down.

It became a game as she shot up as hard as she could each time, almost trying to escape me, and I'd slam her back down as she moaned into our kiss. Apparently, not only was she a screamer, but she enjoyed it rough.

That I could do.

"Yes," she screamed as I slammed her down hard enough to make my hips ache.

Time lost all meaning as we traded off. I repeatedly impaled her on my cock, her sex squeezing me for all I was worth as we shared the longest kiss of my life.

By the time Jadelyn finally stopped, the water was thick with new white sediment on the bottom of the lagoon.

Coming down from our sex craze, we lingered there, kissing and petting each other. I refused to pull myself out of her snug sex.

Jadelyn patted me on the chest and stood up, kicking her legs and pulling me back to the surface.

I gasped for air, wondering how long I'd just used Jadelyn's breathing while we were underwater.

My skin was wrinkly enough to tell me it had been hours. "That was... amazing." I could hardly believe what had just happened.

"Worth the surprise?" she asked, pulling herself up onto the shore and opening a trunk that I hadn't noticed when I'd entered.

"Well worth it. Will you always be able to sing that note?" I asked, trying to say it casually but somewhat desperately, hoping that it didn't go away. After experiencing it, I wasn't sure I could give it up.

She chuckled, clearly hearing the bit of desperation in my voice. "Yes. You stole my song. When I'm aroused, it will always be your note. It also means I can't tempt other men like I used to be able to." Her sopping wet dress dropped to the floor.

"Good," I growled, coming up behind her and wrapping my arms around her. I kissed her neck possessively.

She slapped away my hands as they wandered to her chest and her sex. I shrugged at her, giving her a look to tell her I wasn't sorry for trying. I just couldn't get enough of her. That song had thoroughly changed me, and I craved more of it.

"Stop it," she moaned as I continued touching her. But her body said differently as she pressed herself back into me.

I let my hands play down between her legs again as she turned her head, and we kissed. She let loose one more of those blissful notes as she came over my fingers.

"Enough," she said breathlessly. "I understand Scarlett's plight better than I thought I would after just one session."

"Not sorry," I growled.

She patted my hand and pulled it out of her sex. "Never be. I think I'm going to enjoy that stamina of yours."

She bent over and reached into the trunk. I let my hand run along the curve of her tight ass as she bent over. My mind was already coming up with all kinds of ideas, but she popped back up and inched her butt away from me.

"Towel." She handed it to me, putting it between us; I nearly growled at the slight separation. She rolled her eyes a bit, continuing on. "There's a robe in there when you are dry. I'm not quite ready for that yet."

She covered her waist with another towel. I pulled her back to me and fluffed her with my towel. She smiled, doing as I did. We dried each other off.

I barely managed to hold myself back from going again with her, but I had a feeling that it had gotten late.

When we finally emerged from the tent in white fluffy robes, Scarlett was the only one still waiting for us. The sun was setting.

"Wow. You're still walking." She eyed Jadelyn skeptically.

"Barely." Jadelyn sprang from my grasp and ducked behind Scarlett. "I think I might need my bodyguard though."

"He's a savage, isn't he?" Scarlett narrowed her eyes at me. "Why are you still hard?"

I looked down to see my stiff member trying to poke up between the folds of my robe. "It's like she did something to me."

Jadelyn blushed. "I'll have to be more careful with your song. You seem to have quite the reaction."

"Think of something else," Scarlett scolded me. "Because we are going to have to present the two of you to our parents, who are waiting just inside."

I took a deep breath and tried to tense my thighs while not looking at my two lovely mates. Thankfully, that trick always worked. It took a moment, but I was able to be more presentable.

"Okay. I think I'm ready."

CHAPTER 28

I felt awkward walking into a room with Jadelyn's parents in just a robe, them knowing full well what we'd been doing. The way the wind brushed my balls was a constant reminder that I had to be careful, or I might end up flashing my new in-laws.

"They're back," Scarlett announced to the room, entering first. Her tails playfully swatted the air behind her.

"Welcome back," Rupert said from a loveseat.

Claire was sitting beside him, resting her head on his shoulder. The Fox parents were on another loveseat. I got the feeling from how comfortable they were that those were each of their preferred seats.

Morgana was on her lonesome, sitting in a large, red leather chair that could have been a throne. That left a couch open in the sitting area, so I headed that way.

I settled in, only for Scarlett and Jadelyn to come sit next to me like bookends and keep me from sprawling out. While I liked having them nearby, I'd been planning to sprawl out on the couch. I was more than a little tired and could use some sleep before heading off to battle.

"Do you need food?" Ruby asked.

"Yes, he does. Half a dozen steaks for him, and I'd love one too," Jadelyn said on my behalf. "So, how is operation troll extermination going?"

"We aren't calling it that," her father sighed. "The Summer Queen and the magi have upheld their end, but we haven't been able to locate the missing swamp trolls."

I wondered where Kelly was in her progress. "Have Kelly and her pack started looking?"

"Kelly?" Rupert frowned.

"Brent's daughter," Jadelyn filled in for him.

Before Rupert could comment further, I had my phone in hand and was texting her. Clearly, she hadn't gotten in touch with the council.

After a short back and forth, I called her, putting her on speaker.

"Hello?"

"Hey, Kelly, you are on speaker with the Scalewrights, Foxes, and Morgana. We have a problem."

"The trolls? Yeah, you mentioned something before you zoomed out of the stadium, but you didn't say much." She sounded tired.

"I seem to remember it as you kicking me out," I teased, but pivoted quickly to the time sensitive task. "So we need to find a big gathering of swamp trolls, and we need to find them tonight. I can't think of a better group for the job than a pack that probably needs to get some energy out."

She seemed to agree because she perked right up just as I heard something heavy crash to the floor in the background. "Yeah. Okay. I'll get the pack going. Any chance I can get paid for this?"

I looked to Rupert to see if he'd ante up, but it was Morgana that spoke first. "Kelly, I think I can come up with something for you. If you find them, that is."

"Can do. Make it worth my time, Morgana." There was shouting in the background before Kelly hung up.

"Well, then let's see if we can't get you two fed and find some clothes that'll fit Zach," Claire offered. "He might even want to keep a few things in your room, Jadelyn."

She did a double take. "What?"

"I assume that's where he'll be staying if he comes over, or I guess he would trade off with Scarlett's room?" Claire tapped her chin in thought as Jadelyn stared wide-eyed. "Don't be so shocked. You two are together now. I'm not going to make you sleep in separate rooms."

Rupert huffed loudly.

"Maybe we should just put that aside for now," I tried to play peacekeeper. No use stepping on Rupert's toes, and we hadn't figured out what we wanted yet.

"Yes, later. For now, we celebrate your union." Morgana raised a glass, helping wrap the conversation.

***

Things had settled down at the Scalewright manor by the time Kelly called me back. I was hopeful as I answered the call.

"Zach, I think we found them," she said as soon as I answered, a bit out of breath.

"Where are they?" Morgana's pointy ears picked up what she had said from across the room.

"Where, Kelly?" I put her on speaker so everyone could hear.

"An abandoned mall just outside of town. It reeks of swamp trolls. None of us went inside, but we could hear a hell of a lot of them thumping around inside." She rattled off an address.

I turned to look at Detective Fox, who was hurriedly jotting down the address and putting it into his tablet. "We'll have people out there within minutes to verify. Kelly, do not engage. There are likely over two hundred swamp trolls in that mall."

"Got it. I'm not about to jump at the chance to tango with that many trolls." I could practically hear her roll her eyes. "My pack will circle up and keep an eye out until you get here."

The house immediately descended into a flurry of activity as everyone got ready to leave at the same time. Rupert and Detective Fox sent a barrage of calls out to the council and their subordinates to coordinate.

It was actually fascinating to watch just how many people they had working for them. You think of the rich and powerful as fat cats leaning back, admiring their empire, but this made it clear just how much work it took to keep it all together.

"You ready?" Morgana asked, coming and leaning over the back of the couch.

"Ready as I'm going to be." I pulled at the nice shirt and jeans that the Scalewrights had wrangled up for me, feeling bad that the clothes weren't going to last the night.

I had never gone through so many clothes before. I'd have to let the girls go on another shopping spree with me at the rate I was tearing them with my shifts.

Scarlett came back into the room decked out in leather pants and a biker jacket, complete with knives strapped along her thigh and peeking out from inside her jacket.

"Odd. You look like you are ready for a fight," I commented dryly.

"I'm coming with." She crossed her arms, daring me to revoke that privilege.

Really, compared to Morgana or me, she wasn't a heavy hitter. But she was still a highly skilled fighter. And stealth could have its value; her illusions could serve a number of roles in battle.

"Fine. But against Nat'alet, you stay back." I wasn't about to see her get hurt in a collision of that size.

"Deal." Her ears bounced as she nodded happily.

My eyes raked over Jadelyn. "You aren't about to try to get in on this, are you?"

"Nope." Jadelyn crossed her arms. "I know what my strengths are, and fighting isn't one of them. And Scarlett would never let me get that close to trouble; she treats me like a glass sculpture."

"Damn right!" Scarlett agreed, pulling out and inspecting the sharpness on one of her knives.

"I'll stay with the council and help coordinate things in the command center. I've got your back if something goes wrong." Jadelyn nodded.

Detective Fox came back into the room, straightening the collar of his ugly beige detective jacket. "Come on. We have confirmation the trolls are there."

We all got up and headed out.

A caravan of black SUVs pulled up, and everyone piled in. I found myself smushed in the middle of the backseat, with Morgana and Jadelyn on either side of me while Scarlett sat in my lap, her tails fluffing me.

"Zach." Jadelyn looked down at her feet as she started to talk to me. "You'll come back, right?"

"He will," Morgana interjected. "I promise." The way she said it to Jadelyn seemed to carry more meaning than I expected.

"On your word then." Jadelyn breathed a sigh of relief. "I trust you both, but I can't help but worry."

I wrapped an arm around her and rubbed her back. "This isn't without its risks, but you know that. We'll be careful. It will take a hell of a lot to take me down and keep me from you."

She leaned into me, fragile and vulnerable. For the first time, the danger I was in put an extra pressure on me. It wasn't just my life that hung in the balance. The ripples that my death would cause were evident, and just the thought of it was heartbreaking in its own right.

My hand wandered down to her hips and pulled her tightly against me, squeezing her with all the reassurance I could muster as we drove.

Morgana, Scarlett and I shared a loaded look. We all knew the stakes of this battle, and we weren't about to lose it.

When the car finally rolled to a stop, we all hopped out, and I checked out our surroundings.

We were down a side street at a mall that had once likely been a little hideaway. The area had a bit of privacy from the surrounding large pines. Windows were boarded up, and the exterior was tagged with spray paint. The place looked like no one had been there for ages; the turned over dumpsters were empty.

The only thing that gave away the swamp troll's presence was the swampy stench that lingered in the air. It was like being downwind from a sewer plant.

"This is horrible. No wonder Kelly's pack was able to find it so quickly." I choked on the air.

Hundreds of people had been waiting when we arrived, filling the parking lot. I recognized Kelly's pack among them, and then there were also a number of elves ready to fight. The paranormal groups were rather separate, but if they could come together, they'd be a hard army to take down.

"Imagine what it's like for us wolves with our sense of smell. Most of the pack is going to be nose blind for the rest of the week," Kelly greeted us, clearly overhearing what I'd said. "We saw two trolls come out and poke around, but otherwise there's been no activity."

The squeal of tires sounded as pickups poured into the parking lot, each of them sporting a large stone slab in the bed, propped up and leaning against the cab.

Sir Benifolt was driving one of the pickups and pulled up next to us. "We have the magic circle ready. It won't be perfect, but making it mobile was the hard part."

I let my eyes shift and stared at the stone slabs; each of them radiated powerful magic. "What do we need to do with those?"

"Get them in a circle around the mall," Sir Benifolt said, but it looked like the plan had already been communicated. The other pickups spread out around the parking lot, getting into position.

Sabrina slid out of Sir Benifolt's pickup and came up to me as her mentor pulled his truck forward, getting it into position. "Here. I thought you could use this."

She handed me the enchanted broken broom handle. It looked like it had now been sealed in some sort of wax, or maybe polyurethane, to preserve the enchantment better.

"Thanks." I wasn't sure if I was going to use it, but I liked the idea of Scarlett having it.

It would help her more than it would help me. I'd get it to her later; I wasn't about to hand it off in front of Sabrina.

So I tucked it into the back of my jeans for later. "So, how does this big spell work?"

"The stones are acting as resonators, and the Winter Queen has a similar setup in the Faerie Realm. She won't actually be here, but these stones and the ones with her are in sync, so she can cast something and affect the world here. It is sort of a variant on translocation, along with illusion and convocation. Really, it's quite brilliant."

She was geeking out, clearly in her element as she talked with large hand gestures and excited squeals. I nodded, smiling at her enthusiasm.

"So these just copy what the Winter Queen is doing at her set and create it here?"

"Basically." She pushed up her glasses, and I wondered if she really needed those. They looked almost too thin to be for her vision. Maybe they were part of her cover. It seemed like, as a succubus and a wizard, if she needed her sight fixed, she could have found somebody to do it.

"But it won't just mirror her spells; it will also mirror that section of the Faerie Realm, meaning that it's going to get downright frosty here," she continued with a smile.

"Good for dealing with swamp trolls," I realized. "Maybe we can do this without killing all of them."

She smiled. "That sounds like a noble goal given that they didn't really do anything wrong. But it will also cut off the space inside, creating a barrier inside the region."

Morgana, who had been listening at my side the entire time, spoke up, "So no support once this starts. But that also means he isn't escaping anywhere."

There was a vicious grin on her face. I almost felt bad for the god who would be trapped in a space with her and me with no escape.

At that moment, half a dozen trolls ambled out of the mall entrance. They must have sensed something going on outside. I'd expected them to look at least somewhat human, but there was nothing recognizable about them. They were pure troll.

"How much longer do you need to set up?" I shouted to Sir Benifolt.

"Ten minutes," he said, eyeing the trolls as they sniffed around. Their beady black eyes tracked our group in the parking lot.

Guns were being checked and loaded around us as sirens and elves alike propped guns over the hoods of cars and checked their equipment. We were ready for a hell of a fight.

But I knew guns wouldn't stop a swamp troll; they would only delay them. And that was if you got them in the right spots. If you hit center mass on a troll, the bullets were worthless.

I watched the trolls as they studied us. There was a tense moment of standoff as everyone held their breath to see if the trolls would make a move.

While we waited to see what would happen, I noticed that one of them was smaller than the rest. At this distance, it didn't register immediately, but when the first spark of red light gathered in that troll's hands, I was already running forward.

I coated my arms in scales under my sleeves as I braced against the blast. My forward momentum ground to a halt as I took the force on my crossed arms.

Not wanting to shift in front of everyone, I reverted my arms back to normal after the blast.

After I took the hit, I ducked down. Gunfire erupted behind me, and I watched more than one hit the trolls in the torso.

"Aim for the ankles!" I shouted over the gunfire, and I watched as they adjusted their shots. The gunfire began tearing out the meat of the trolls' ankles and calves until a red barrier snapped into place to cover them.

The gunfire stopped as the shooters realized the bullets weren't getting through the barrier.

Kelly howled and two dozen wolves leapt forward, taking the chance to move into the fight while the gunfire ceased. I knew they could handle the trolls, but I wanted a piece of that shaman.

I charged with the wolves. As we streamed around the barrier, the trolls were getting back onto their feet, wobbling as their legs stitched back together.

A wolf, one I had a feeling was Kelly, leapt up on a troll and knocked him out of the way as three more dog-piled onto it with her. Just like that, the wolves used their numbers to take down and keep down the trolls. I could see why they had been used in the past to help guide the swamp troll migration.

Red flashed, and I saw a wolf soar through the air, letting out a yelp. I pivoted to the shaman.

If he was the warlock from before, he looked different now. I had no hope of picking him out from any other trolls. Their swampy green skin and those expressionless black eyes gave nothing away.

The shaman struck out with a glowing red palm, but I caught his forearm and spun away, carrying him up and over my shoulder before hammering him back down onto the concrete. Two werewolves were on him in a heartbeat.

Their claws raked across the shaman's body, tearing muscle and ligament free and preventing him from doing anything but healing to stay alive.

We had vastly outnumbered this small band of trolls, but as I looked through the mall entrance, I could see dozens of hulking forms lurking in the darkness. Something about it made it hard for me to judge how far away they were.

"Kelly. Hold the ground outside the mall. Spread out your pack in case they come out another entrance."

"What about you?" Kelly asked in her hybrid form, looking up with a bloody muzzle.

But before I could respond, a wolf shifter growled at me. "Don't order around our alpha."

Kelly's claw hooked his face and forced his head around to look at her. "Don't get in a dick measuring contest with him. I'm sure if he really wanted to, he could flatten you with that giant golden rod of his." She not so subtly reminded him of what I was.

I ignored them both, not wanting to waste time. "We are going to push inward." I noticed Morgana and Scarlett had caught up with me. "We need your pack to protect the magi, so they can finish summoning the

Winter Queen. Get out once that has been done."

Kelly grumbled something under her breath before looking at me again. "You got it." She started barking orders and jerking her head as she worked to get her pack to do as I had asked.

I handed off Sabrina's blasting rod to Scarlett, and she looked at it with a raised brow. I answered the unspoken question. "It sprays mist that freezes things. Sabrina made it."

Scarlett shifted it back and forth in her hands, giving me an odd look. "That's the one that is actually a succubus?"

"And a friend." I realized Scarlett was hesitant to use it.

"Right," she said slowly, tucking it into her leather jacket. "Because it's entirely possible to just be a friend with a succubus."

Morgana snorted. "Maybe she could actually give him a run for his horniness."

"Hey," I protested, trying to peer through the mall entrance for a better look, but there were no lights on inside and those forms didn't seem any closer. "Enough. No time to deal with my sex life. We have a god to kill."

Crouching low, I led the two into the abandoned mall, hating that I couldn't make out anything in the dark.

CHAPTER 29

As we walked into the dark, my mind began playing tricks on me. I could have sworn I saw trolls looming not far from the entrance, but the mall entrance was quiet.

The smell of rot mixed with algae filled the air, highlighting the swamp trolls' presence. And occasionally, there would be the heavy thud and grunting that sounded like trolls fighting. But we had yet to come across any. It was like they were always around the next corner, but we never saw any.

I didn't like that Nat'alet's goal was unknown. It was a missing piece that would have helped us with our strategy. But regardless, he'd forcefully recruited a standing army in our city. We couldn't leave that alone, and we couldn't leave all those magi to their current fate.

The god seemed to have no qualms about hurting and killing paranormal and magi alike. From our discussion, I had a feeling this was more than just the desire to replenish mana in the world. It had to be about more than that, some sort of power grab, perhaps. He'd planned this out, waiting for the perfect moment when swamp trolls and magi overlapped.

I swallowed, not loving the idea of a god that had planned out his takeover for years when I'd had a few days to prepare. But I had a feeling he hadn't planned for a dragon to be in the mix.

Regardless, he'd committed a paranormal crime in my city, and I was duty bound to get justice. My path was becoming clearer to me. Working with Morgana felt right. Protecting my women felt right. This god had to be stopped.

We stalked through the mall. The once pristine white tiles were now marred by a lack of care and thousand-pound trolls traipsing through the place.

"What was the plan again?" Scarlett frowned as she followed behind me, clearly anxious.

"Once we find them, we need to contain them. We can't have them spilling out into the parking lot. We need to buy the magi time," I answered. We were the distraction.

Passing a few storefronts, the space opened up into a large two-story circular area that must have once been the beating heart of the mall. Now trolls lumbered about where shoppers had once walked.

Filtering through the noise of the trolls, I caught voices up on the second floor. We ducked to the side, avoiding their line of sight, and listened.

"—the fuck does he think he is. I'm going to fry his ass the second he comes out."

"Calm down, Ty. No, you aren't. None of us can do anything like that," another voice spoke up.

Angling myself so I could see better, I spotted two Shamans arguing in what appeared to have been an ice cream parlor.

I tapped Morgana on the shoulder and pointed to her ear, then up to the two arguing. "Hear anything?"

She rolled her eyes. "Bitching about Nat'alet. Seems he didn't earn any favors in converting them."

"I wouldn't want to have ugly, green skin either." Scarlett smiled. "But I'm more interested in them being unable to do anything about it."

Nodding, I braced myself against a corner and peered around. The grout on the tiles must have seriously needed replacing, because just my weight against the wall cracked the grout and a tile fell to the floor.

Shit, I cursed to myself.

My entire body tensed, and it was like the entire world went silent for a moment as I strained to listen for any reaction.

The shuffling of trolls quickly moving towards us indicated that my fumble had not gone unnoticed.

"Seems the time for stealth is over," I whispered to the two ladies, not wanting to give away more than I already had. "Do me a favor and hang back. I'll be the big distraction."

"Okay. I'll go on ahead and see if I can't find this Nat'alet's hideout." Morgana ghosted away.

I glanced at Scarlett to get her agreement, but I found her with her hands on her hips.

"Like hell I'm leaving you here alone." She fished out that blasting rod. "Plus, I want to ride a dragon."

"Pretty sure you've ridden a dragon more than a few times." I didn't have time to argue with her. The best I could do was keep her safe. She saw my reluctant agreement in my eyes and beamed.

Rolling my eyes, I shifted into my hybrid form, becoming a sixteen-foot-tall, hunched over, wingless dragon. My new form was tall enough to see over the lip of the second floor, my head rising to see the two shamans.

"Holy shit." One leapt to his feet and backed away. His friend had his back to me, but jumped around to see my big scaly head.

"That's... a dragon?"

My mouth opened, a jet of flame tearing out of my throat, the air vibrating and rumbling with the heat.

The ice cream shop was instantly filled with bright orange dragon fire as I tested if shamans were also fire resistant. The flames cut off, and I felt Scarlett scurry up my back and grab onto the horns on my head.

"Wow," she gasped. "Never seen you really let loose with the fire before."

I puffed out a stream of smoke from my nose. When the air cleared, the two shamans came back into view. Their skin peeled and sloughed off as if they had second-degree burns, but their troll nature was healing them faster than I had done damage.

"Ha! We survived the dragon's fire. This change might not be so bad," one of them was shouting as his hands glowed red.

I closed my eyes and ducked my chin, taking the blast on the crown of my head. My claws tore at the second floor of the mall, holding myself otherwise still under the force of their attack.

When it abated I didn't hesitate, snapping my neck forward and sinking my teeth into him. I readied to tear him apart as two trolls tackled my lower legs.

Toppling from my position, I found myself hanging over the second story. I took one shaman with me as trolls swarmed me.

A cooling sensation ran down my back as Scarlett blasted the shaman with Sabrina's rod. She let out an exclamation of pleasure as it hit, readily firing off more and more shots. She seemed to enjoy her new weapon.

At that point, there were a dozen trolls trying to get a handhold on me and pin me down. I could not let that happen.

I thrashed, using my massive weight to knock a leg free as I tossed up the screaming shaman in the air, biting him in half on the way down. My claws lashed out at the trolls, cutting vast swaths of flesh out of their bulk.

Scarlett whooped on the top of my head as she hung on for dear life.

I tore through the trolls with my claws before I body checked one into the wall. A spray of frost hit the pinned troll's head, making it easy for me to shatter it with a second press.

"Ty!" the other shaman screamed, turning to me. "You killed, Ty!"

He fired a shot, but I realized too late that he hadn't been aiming for me. He'd aimed for Scarlett. His blast hit her, and she flew off of my back.

Time slowed as I watched her face twist in pain from the blast. She fell in between two trolls, landing in a crumpled ball.

My beast roared inside of me, and I didn't hold it back. I let the draconic rage consume me.

I moved to where she'd landed, instantly attacking the two trolls before they had a chance to attack her. I pinned one down beneath my claws and ripped the other off its feet with my jaws before I severed its shoulder from the rest of it with a powerful bite.

My back legs curled forward, and I raked my claws along the pinned troll's chest and legs, tearing it to bloody ribbons.

Another blast hit my side as I hunkered over Scarlett protectively.

"Ha. You aren't an actual dragon," the shaman said. "Just something that looks like one. Trying to protect your rider?"

With the loss of mobility I had in order to keep Scarlett sheltered, the trolls closed in around us. Meanwhile, the shaman continued to pepper me with those annoying red beams of force.

I screamed in rage as the trolls rushed me. There were two or three for each of my legs and another two for my tail. Thrashing could only do so much as they worked together to immobilize me.

My claws sank into a few of them, but the trolls ignored the pain, their swampy green skin bulging with muscle as they all strained against my exertion.

Damn them, I cursed internally.

A thud announced the presence of the shaman as he jumped from the second story.

"Ty really is dead." He bent over the other shaman's remaining body. "Guess we can't heal from everything. But what the fuck are you doing here?" he asked, standing back up straight and appraising me.

I huffed. I still hadn't figured out how to talk.

"Doesn't matter. Nat'alet will want to meet with you. Goons, hoist him up. We are going to meet the boss."

The trolls seemed to follow his orders. They kept me stretched out as they put me up on their shoulders.

The shaman picked up Scarlett, tossing her over his shoulder. "I'll take your pretty little kitsune if you don't mind."

As he touched her, the dragon in me roared, wanting to slowly remove every limb from his body, letting him regrow them so I could do it again.

I drove towards him, managing to power through a few struggled steps before the trolls were able to corral me. Even with my bulk, a dozen trolls were too much for me to overcome.

"Don't worry. I'll take good care of her. I'm told once you get a green dicking, women don't go back." He sneered. "And I've always loved anime with fox girls."

The rage inside me turned more deadly, quieter. He needed to die. And to do that, I needed to focus. I used the enhanced focus my dragon was giving me to run back through my options.

There had to be something. I was a shifter, and while I was still learning how to properly use it, I could take some from the wolves' strategy. I'd seen them use their shifts when they fought, flowing between them, snapping out a kick only for it to become a claw.

I smiled a wicked smile at the shaman in my hybrid form. Enjoying the slight fear that spread on his face even as he stood his ground.

Focusing, I shifted back to my dragon knight form, surprise flickering on the shaman's face.

My body's sudden shrinkage allowed me to slip loose of the trolls. As they released their hold on me, I fell to my stomach and rolled up to my feet. I was still covered in golden scales, but I was also much smaller and more human in proportion.

The shaman threw Scarlett at me as his hands glowed red.

I had no choice. I grabbed her, wrapping my scaled arms around her as I turned and took the blast on my back. The beam had plenty of force behind it, so I jumped and let it carry me out of reach as trolls tried to recapture me.

Throwing Scarlett over my shoulder and jumping again, I latched onto the second story and pulled myself up. I gently laid Scarlett down as I turned back to the shaman.

I was beyond pissed. My beast was right on the surface, ready for a fight.

It wanted to blast the trolls with fire, but I knew it wouldn't work. That wasn't their weakness. The beast didn't seem to care, thrashing in my chest, demanding that I smoke the fuckers.

I glanced down at Scarlett, her chest still rose and fell; besides a few scrapes, she looked like she was just sleeping. But that didn't dim the protective urges in my chest. The shaman would die for harming my mate.

Jumping back down to the first floor, I landed in a crouch that shattered the tiles below me.

"So, you aren't just a beast." The shaman watched me. This time he had the trolls gathering before him. It looked like the safety net of trolls made him more chatty.

"You picked the wrong fight."

He snorted. "I didn't pick a fight, you did. Can I ask what you are?"

I ignored him. There was no reason to tell him. One of us would be dead soon, and I was betting on him. The beast thrashed in my chest once again, demanding I incinerate them with my breath.

Pushing it down, I ignored the instinct. I'd already seen that they were resistant to fire. Instead, I jerked to the side, my claws tearing at the first troll in my path.

The trolls tried to grab me and tangle me enough to pin me again, but this time I fought like Morgana had trained me rather than a wild animal.

Weaving between the heavy troll limbs, I inflicted any damage I could as the trolls pressed forward in a tight, jumbled knot. The whole thing was comical; they tripped and scrambled over each other trying to get me.

Unfortunately, the mass of trolls was too dangerous to get close enough to do lasting damage. They would easily be able to overwhelm me if I got too close. All I could do was injure an arm enough for it to fall limp for a few seconds before the troll's healing brought it back into the fight.

The beast still demanded I wash them with fire, and I realized that if nothing else, it would serve as a nice smoke screen between the shaman and me.

If I could get him, that would remove the biggest threat.

Breathing deeply, I was surprised when I felt a slight shift in my body.

Normally, it felt like my chest was filled with lava, like a volcano on the verge of erupting. This time, it felt cold. Icy cold, like when you grab meat straight out of the freezer and your fingers feel like they are going to fall off. Excitement spread through me, and I was glad I'd listened to my draconic instincts.

My scales rippled as I breathed out.

Blue frosty liquid spewed out of my breath like a fire hose. As soon as it hit the air, it vaporized into a freezing mist.

I was distracted as, in the corner of my vision, I saw my arms ripple. As the freezing mist passed, my gold scales became silver. I couldn't wait to experiment with that later and figure out what it meant. But for now, I had some trolls to freeze.

My breath was like a supercharged version of Sabrina's blasting rod.

The troll's skin frosted over as the ground grew slick with ice, and icicles formed off their bodies. It was incredible to watch.

The mass of trolls ground to a halt, the first few toppling over and shattering into pieces. It only took a few crumbling before the rest of the trolls tried to turn and run.

My breath washed over them, catching as many as I could and managing to hit the shaman as well. They all turned into pop-sicles.

My breath cut off only a few seconds after it started, the freezing power strong enough to freeze them in just moments.

"W-w-what-t-t-t." The shaman's teeth chattered as he tried to speak.

Apparently, he'd survived thanks to the trolls taking the brunt of my breath. But he could barely move, his body already curling in on itself in an attempt to preserve what heat was left.

I pushed aside the trolls, letting them shatter on the hard ground. I cringed, knowing they likely had been manipulated. But I needed to dwindle the god's forces, and they'd seen my secret.

My steps echoed in the abandoned mall as I continued towards the shaman, letting him watch as the frozen trolls crumpled. "Where is Nat'alet? And what's the end goal?"

The shaman gave me a brittle smile, his frostbitten cheeks cracking when stretched. "We were forced. He has power over us now."

I had a small blossom of sympathy for the man. Being controlled by another wasn't something I'd wish on most. But he'd touched Scarlett, and his fate had already been sealed.

His hand filled with red light, so I quickly stepped forward, tipping him over. His lower half shattered into shards of ice. He screamed, but it was short-lived as the light faded from his eyes.

I looked around, trying to figure out my next move.

If we finished Nat'alet soon, there would be hope of reverting the trolls back to their former selves. The clock was ticking, but the Summer Queen had given us hope that, if we killed Nat'alet before twenty-four hours, then the magi would regain their humanity.

Unfortunately, I knew that I'd have to kill many of them in the process. I hoped none were Sabrina's friends, though she did seem like a loner.

Leaping back up to where I'd left Scarlett, I took the moment to look her over and make sure she was okay. I found a solid goose egg forming on her head. Touching it caused her to wince and hiss as she squinted her eyes.

"Zach?" She looked up at me in a daze. "What happened to your scales?"

I glanced down at myself. The silver scales still covered me rather than my normal gold. "I'm not sure. But it is still me. Apparently, my dragon has some extra kickass abilities."

Scarlett touched my arm and frowned as she looked at the color. "So, I'm not seeing things? Those are actually silver?"

"Yeah. I got a little pissed when he took you out. He didn't see it coming."

She laughed. "Neither did you." She snickered at some joke that I didn't understand.

I figured she must still be loopy.

Hoisting her up in my arms, I padded down the steps and picked up Sabrina's blasting rod. I handed it to Scarlett for safe keeping. "We need to move. The fact that we aren't already swarming with trolls has me worried."

"Why?"

"Because what the heck are two hundred trolls doing here if they aren't coming to the sound of a large fight. I'm not exactly quiet when I'm angry."

She cuddled into my arms, and I started to look around to pick a direction. But, as I took a few steps, a change began to spread across the mall.

One moment it felt like a chilly November afternoon, and the next it was like someone had stuffed the whole place inside a polar vortex. The air changed too, from the dirty city air to a clean, crisp air filled with vibrance.

"What was that?" I asked, looking around for a new threat.

Scarlett took a deep breath. "It feels like we are in the Faerie Realm."

I settled down, placing what we were feeling. "They must have finished the spell."

Glancing up through the skylight that dominated the wide-open area of the mall, high above the building, blue wind swirled in the air, wrapping around us.

"And it would seem that we are now officially trapped here with Nat'alet. Come on, we need to find Morgana and see what she's learned."

I looked around for something to wear. Ducking into a shop, I grabbed a curtain still hanging up and tore the worn cloth from its hooks, wrapping it around myself and taking one hook. I stabbed the hook through the cloth and bent it to clip my makeshift toga tight. I had kept my size, but I retracted my scales for the moment, concerned about meeting with the Winter Queen.

"You okay?" I asked Scarlett, noticing she was shivering in my arms.

"For a little while. You're pretty warm, but it is freezing in here."

I didn't really seem to notice. Then again, I wasn't really a thick coat kind of person, and my draconic constitution had only made temperature extremes more comfortable. Or maybe my silver scales came with other benefits.

The mall was eerily silent for a place with hundreds of trolls. The only noise was my puffing breath as we moved forward to find a god.

CHAPTER 30

As we moved through the mall, it seemed bigger than it should have been. It had been ten minutes, and we had yet to see another sign of trolls.

A hand wrapped around my mouth, even as vigilant as I'd been, and I yelped into it.

"Shhh. What the fuck happened to your scales?" Morgana asked over my shoulder. I could feel her breath on the back of my neck.

I made a muffled noise into her hand, reminding her she needed to let go for me to speak. "Not sure myself. They hurt Scarlett and... and I got really pissed. My breath became frosty and my scales changed."

"Before or after the Winter Queen's spell came?"

"Before," I clarified.

Morgana bit into a nail, and she watched me. "Pendragon. Is this what it means?" Morgana had a theory about my last name being more than just a name, but a title that was once held by the king of dragons.

"Badass is what it means," Scarlett said, still sounding loopy from her concussion.

"Give me one of T's potions. I know you have at least one stuffed in your bra."

"Why don't you fish it out yourself. No hands though." Morgana opened her chest to me and damn, did that have an effect on me.

Scarlett ruined it. "Just fuck him already. God, you two are obnoxious."

Morgana's smile stayed as she quickly dug her hand into the small pocket space I knew she kept in her bra. A little red vial came out with her hand, and she shoved it unceremoniously into Scarlett's mouth, maybe even a little vindictive.

Scarlett choked on it. I knew from experience they tasted disgusting. Why T couldn't make them taste better, I wasn't sure.

"Better?" Morgana asked.

The kitsune in my arms curled into me, wrinkling her nose. "Better laying in his arms. You should think about it sometime. Or do you already?" She glared back at my partner as tension started to crackle between the two of them.

"Why don't you two cut the shit. Now isn't the time for it."

"Sorry." Scarlett was quick to apologize. Morgana just frowned, grudgingly nodding her own acceptance of a truce.

"Okay. What did you learn, Morgana?"

"That this isn't a mall. Or at least, it's not just a mall. Notice how big it is?" she asked.

I nodded, having started to piece it together in our walk. "So then what is it? Is this like your bar?"

"Don't know. It isn't spatial magic. Or at least, not directly. But we are in a different space than just the mall we walked into. The place goes on for a long while. Eventually, it empties into a space where hundreds of trolls are building something." She scowled. "But then the Winter Bitch came, and I wasn't about to get any closer without you there."

"She's here?" I was surprised. I thought she was staying in the Faerie Realm.

"An avatar of her is here. Come on. If he hasn't already, Nat'alet is going to have to show himself; otherwise, I'm pretty sure she could waste him."

"Why doesn't she?" I asked, lowering Scarlett down now that she was healed. But she protested, clinging to my neck.

I gave in. She wasn't slowing me down, so I kept her cradled in my arms.

Scarlett spoke, "Because she's a bitch, and she isn't here to help."

"As much as I hate to agree, she's right. We knew the Faerie had an ulterior motive. Question is, how much help will we get once they get whatever it is they want from this." Morgana picked up the pace as we ran through the too big mall.

My feet slapped with what might as well have been gunshots. Stealth was definitely not my strong suit.

**

We entered a large space, and now I was convinced something was wrong with the mall. Someone had built a small quarry in the middle of the mall. It was like the space had stretched.

I rubbed my eyes and tried to comprehend a quarry being inside the mall. Tiles were ripped up, and the trolls were hauling cut stone out of the quarry. It was being brought over to a large stone tower being erected to the side. The tower must have been four stories tall; my brain failed to compute how it was inside the mall.

But what was most odd about the scene was that the trolls seemed frozen in time. They were hunkered over their stone as if they'd gone to sleep right there.

"It's the cold," Morgana explained. "Even if they don't freeze, they huddle up like that for warmth if they get too cold."

I smiled. That made this all much easier.

Morgana's ears twitched. "Seems like the Winter Queen just found Nat'alet." She

moved quickly to the partially construct-
ed stone building. Inside, the building was
bare stone. Two figures stood inside.

The Winter Queen's back was to me, but
her rich lavender hair and frost blue skin
wrapped in white furs made it easy to pick
her out.

Nat'alet was a surprise. He was sitting
on an oversized stone throne, which only
made him seem deathly thin. His skin hung
off his skeletal frame like it was ready to
slough right off with a breeze. He was old,
and surprisingly, his skin was the same
frosty blue as the Winter Queen's, though
his hair was a dull grey.

"It seems your guests have finally arrived."
The Winter Queen turned to look at us, and
her silver eyes swept over me like a pair of
knives scraping the scales off a fish.

Her form wavered slightly, reminding me
that she wasn't there in the flesh.

"Merely pests," Nat'alet's voice boomed
with a rich, deep power that belayed his
otherwise fragile looking body. "I shall deal
with them after we discuss why you are
here."

A growl rose out of my throat at being
dismissed. I had a feeling he wouldn't call
my hybrid form a pest.

The Winter Queen gave a brittle laugh.
"Doesn't seem like he agrees. He's the one
they think will kill you, and I have to say,

with the current state of your trolls, he might even stand a chance."

But when she looked at me, there was a question in her eyes. She wasn't sure what I was, either.

"No matter. You came here to speak to me. Speak," Nat'alet demanded from his throne.

"Don't speak to me that way, Merville." The Winter Queen glowered.

The blood drained from Nat'alet's face at the name, but he pulled himself back together in a snap. "I have no idea what you are talking about," his voice boomed, but it sounded hollow, like a man hiding behind something.

"You failed. When you used old magic that we have since scoured from the world, you showed your hand, Merville." The Winter Queen glared with such intensity that, even without being the recipient of the glare, I could feel the weight of it. "That magic has been stripped since we opened this portal in North America. But you predate that and the surrounding area. How could I not recognize this?"

"I didn't touch the Faerie. Why are you here?" Nat'alet's voice cracked as he scrambled to talk himself out of being in trouble with the Winter Queen.

Turning to Morgana, I raised an eyebrow. "What's happening?"

"I think I know why the space inside the mall is distorted." Her gaze hardened. "We are in the Faerie Realm. Or at least, we are in a piece of it."

Without turning, the Winter Queen addressed Morgana, "See, she's even figured it out Merville. You stole a piece of the Faerie Realm." Her tone sent shivers up my spine.

"I— I—" He stumbled two times, almost like he couldn't speak the following words. "Eat brownie shit. I have ruled this small piece of the Faerie Realm for over four hundred years, ever since I was tossed aside. Do you think just because you are a stuck-up queen bitch that you can take it away from me?!" Nat'alet lost it. Spittle flew out of his mouth as he screamed at the Winter Queen.

The Faerie Queen was unperturbed by his outburst, a slight smile dancing on her lips. "There's another option, of course. You could return this piece of the Faerie Realm to me. If you do that, I will withdraw my presence from this. Otherwise..." Her eyes lingered on me. "The council's candidates to kill you will receive my support. They look quite dangerous, don't they?"

Scarlett nearly jumped forward; Morgana holding her shoulder was the only thing stopping her. "The Summer Queen said you were here to help."

"She said I would provide a barrier and remove him from his source of power. That is precisely what I'm doing. The barrier around this drab building will not fall for hours, and taking back a piece of my realm will take part of his power. I am doing exactly what the Summer Queen promised. I'm just not doing it exactly as you wanted."

She looked over her shoulder at Scarlett as if she were a petulant child. The Winter Queen then focused back on Nat'alet. "And in your case, you get to survive on your own merit without my interference."

Nat'alet's eyes wandered over to Morgana and me before focusing back on the Winter Queen. "You damned bitch."

"He's going to do it," Morgana whispered.

"She betrayed us." I felt a hate boiling in my gut for the Winter Queen. She might have stuck to the letter of her agreement, but she wasn't here to help. She was here to use us as pressure to get what she wanted.

I spoke up louder, "Whether you think you are in the right, you are crossing me." My tone was harsh to the Winter Queen. "You will regret that."

"Morgana, would you put a leash on your little man? He doesn't know to whom he's talking."

"Oh, he's more than capable of making his own decisions," Morgana backed me up.

I stepped forward, the beast hammering in my chest and my palms itching for a fight.

The Winter Queen snapped out her wrist in my direction, and a frosty blue magic washed over me.

It was frigid. I assumed it was what she'd done to the frozen trolls outside, but it slid off me. Cold didn't bother me one bit.

For just a moment, there was a flicker of hesitation in her eyes. The fact that her magic hadn't affected me gave her pause.

"It is unfortunate that you have to be caught up in this, but I have made a deal with Summer, and I cannot go back on my end either." She softened. "If he gives me the piece of the Faerie Realm, my hands are tied, but I will do what I can."

I paused, realizing that my anger wasn't just with her. The Summer Queen had negotiated with the council and then the Winter Queen. She had a role in this.

Where was the piece of the Faerie Realm going after this? Had Summer traded more, and the Winter Queen was just a middleman broker?

There were layers to this that I'd have to peel back.

"Fine. If he accepts, you pull back. I don't want you or anyone on your behalf to observe the fight." The least I could do was try to protect my secret a little longer.

Her pale blue skin wrinkled slightly as she frowned. "So be it. No one outside those present will observe your fight."

"Zach, is that wise?" Scarlett turned to me in confusion.

"Yeah. I don't want anything holding me back from letting loose." My voice rumbled with a growl as I focused back on Nat'alet. I needed something to sink my claws into and tear apart.

"So, what do you say Merville?" The Winter Queen held out her hand, already knowing what he was going to do. She hadn't left him any options.

The skin-and-bones god on the throne sighed. "You'll leave?"

"Yes. And the barrier will remain for four hours, or until one of your groups is defeated," the Winter Queen clarified.

Nat'alet spat on the floor before magic gathered into his hands, drawing from the world around us.

The mall walls around us started to shrink, collapsing inward, even as the stone structure we were in continued to stand tall. Walls crunched against the stone structure as the four-story stone tower shoved its way back into reality.

Ceiling tiles crashed to the floor as the stone held. Light fixtures shattered and cords tore, dangling down around the stone walls as it ripped through the ceiling of the mall.

The shifting stopped, and Nat'alet held out a glowing sphere. "Take it, but we are not even. I will plan my revenge." He didn't budge from his throne, and the Winter Queen didn't either. They both seemed to wait for the other to make a move.

It was a game of dominance, one my dragon was quickly growing tired of watching.

But before I could move, the Winter Queen flicked her hand and the orb shot over to her. "With that, the deal is done." She turned to leave.

"What about defrosting all of my people?" Nat'alet stood up for the first time. His legs were as thick as toothpicks and wobbled slightly.

"I said I would remove myself and not interfere. I never said I would undo what I'd already done." She winked at me, trying to earn a measure of my goodwill. "They will thaw on their own in time."

Nat'alet's eyes glowed red. He looked like he was about to fight, but the Winter Queen was done. The avatar she had brought wavered, disappearing with the piece of the Faerie Realm that had been the center of their bargain.

With her departure, the mall was already rapidly climbing in temperature. She might have not undone what she had done to the trolls, but I estimated we had less than ten minutes before they started to regain enough body heat to be a problem.

"So, you're here to kill me." Nat'alet swung those glowing red eyes back at me and my group. "Poor choice."

With the Winter Queen gone, I let my scales come out, taking on my dragon knight form. I was still silver. Figuring out how to change that would come another day.

"A shifter?" Nat'alet smiled. "Two can play at that game."

His skin and bones pumped like someone was inflating him. As he grew, his legs grew stocky and his torso ballooned, taking on dark maroon scales. His neck split, and seven heads rose up before me. He almost had a draconic form, just distorted slightly, like a pale mimicry.

Well, now we knew. Nat'alet was a hydra. His massive form towered over us, his seven heads attached to a wingless lizard's body.

My brows pinched in confusion. "Morgana, are hydra's fae?" If he was once a Faerie, this couldn't be right.

"He's a changeling." Her blades rang out of their sheaths. "But he's a very powerful changeling."

Scarlett had a gun in one hand and Sabrina's blasting rod in the other. "Is he a hydra for all intents and purposes right now?" She grimaced at the creature before us.

"Ordinarily, a changeling can't mimic paranormal abilities. But in this case, I think we need to assume he's going to heal at least as fast as a troll."

"Cower before me!" Nat'alet's head spoke each word from a new mouth in a way that was rapid and alien. "I am no changeling. I am a god."

He roared, stomping his feet like a petulant child. I had a feeling we'd just touched a soft spot.

"Got it. Changeling. What, were you abandoned by your big Faerie mother?" I mocked him, hoping to anger him into attacking me. My shift to my hybrid form was an element of surprise that might just make this a short fight, and time was a factor with the trolls' defrosting.

Sure enough, I'd hit the mark. Nat'alet screamed in impotent rage, but instead of charging, spat streams of green liquid.

We all scattered as the acid hit the floor, bubbling and hissing as it ate away at the stone.

I had the urge to demand Scarlett sit this one out, but I knew asking her to do so would only end in an argument that would be a distraction. There was no time.

"Scarlett, I need illusions from you. We have seven heads and three of us. Make it harder for him to outnumber us. And be ready with that blasting rod; I want to see if it can't come in handy freezing his wounds open."

I hoped giving her those tasks would keep her at least a bit out of the way, while still providing us support.

"Morgana—"

"Wouldn't be the first time I killed a hydra," she cut me off. "Be careful of its blood. It's just as toxic as its breath. Fire works best for cauterizing a head, but frost might just do in a pinch." Her eyes wandered my scales before she shook her head. "We'll figure out how you can switch between them later."

Nat'alet hung around waiting for us. He wasn't in a rush. He was more than happy to wait for his troll army to weaken us.

I charged the massive beast, remaining in my dragon knight form for the moment. My fingers elongated to claws as I jumped over the first head.

The heads moved quickly, like seven co-ordinated, striking serpents. One after the other snapped forward, jaws full of fangs glistening with residual green acid from its spit.

But, as I moved over the head, two illusion versions of me moved as well. Scarlett was already at work.

The illusions and I danced, trading places like a ball and cup shuffle game as I ran along one of the necks, hoping to get to a place where I could do some damage.

Nat'alet's attention was split, his heads snapping in pairs of two while the last of his seven heads remained focused on the girls.

I leapt from the neck onto the hydra's back, thinking it was best to go for the heart. My claws slashed a deep cut, but on the body of the hydra, it was nothing but a scratch.

Instinct made the hairs on the back of my neck stand up, and I bolted from its back as it washed itself in acid. The acid appeared to do nothing to himself.

My claws smoked as the blood on my hand sizzled, trying to dissolve my scales.

Damn. The hydra had amazing defensive properties. I could only imagine the pain of biting it in my draconic form and having that blood pour into my mouth and throat.

"Careful, Zach," Morgana warned before she blurred forward. She used the moment of the hydra's distraction to attack, her blades dancing along its flank as she cut open a stream of small cuts.

When Nat'alet's head whirled on her, she disappeared, only to reappear on one of the heads. Her magic made an impossibly thin blade of spatial magic that tore through three of the heads at once.

I took the opportunity, picking up a torn metal electrical duct from the debris and sprinted forward, leveling it like a lance.

It pierced the hydra's hide, driving straight for its heart, but Nat'alet's body bubbled and shifted before I could reach the heart. His form darkened and shrank rapidly until a copy of Morgana rose from where the hydra used to be. I blinked, stepping back and trying to figure out what had just happened.

CHAPTER 31

Nat'alet wiggled his hips and pulled at the tight corset. "How in the hell do you wear this?" he asked with Morgana's body.

"Better than you, that's for sure." Morgana scowled as the fight simmered.

I braced, knowing this would be it. We weren't all going to make it through this battle, and I'd be damned if anybody on my side went down.

Two illusions of me squared up around Nat'alet as Scarlett's tails went to work. They moved first.

Nat'alet spun with Morgana's speed and grace, a blade slicing through the first illusion. I moved forward. I'd fought with Morgana, and I could only hope that he couldn't use her skills as well as she could.

As I moved in front of him, I swung, my scale-wrapped fist swinging for the fences. Unfortunately, Nat'alet blurred with vampiric speed, his leather-clad leg wrapping around both my shoulder and head as he twisted and threw me into the real Morgana.

We went down in a tumble as Morgana caught me.

Nat'alet was on us in an instant, but I was able to get on my back and coil my legs before he reached me. I snapped them out, catching him in the chest and launching him backwards.

Morgana rolled off me and back to her feet, shooting forward a moment later. Her blades were like hummingbird wings; they struck faster than my eyes could track. But Nat'alet kept up with her in his Morgana form. Their blades rang out in the partially collapsed mall.

This wasn't right. Had Morgana been holding back this much in all our sparring?

Either way, they were equally matched. Given his relation to the Winter Queen, it was likely he was old enough to have learned to fight with swords and practiced as long as Morgana. Based on the slightest furrow in the real Morgana's brow, she was coming to the same conclusion. I needed to do something to break this stalemate.

Think. I had to find a way for my brute force to help make a difference in the delicate dance they were doing.

If he had all of Morgana's skills, that meant he also had vampire speed and healing from near death. I needed to distract him and give Morgana an opening.

Picking up a chunk of concrete, I hurled it faster than a baseball pitch at Nat'alet, only to charge after him.

He dodged back, letting the chunk separate him and Morgana. And dodged right into my fist.

Or at least, I thought it would. Instead, my fist bent in space and nearly collided with the real Morgana as she came at him from the other side.

The spatial distortion snapped away, and I ducked into a roll, just barely avoiding my arm being severed as Nat'alet cut at me with a blade of spatial magic. The hairs on the back of my neck stood on end.

That had been too close.

"Zach, let me handle this one. My speed and spatial magic paired together are going to be too much for you." Morgana was short as she reengaged Nat'alet.

I stepped back, startling as Scarlett grabbed my shoulder. Jumpy as I was, I whirled on her with my fist up.

"Careful, big guy. We have another problem." She pulled me away from where the two Morganas were heating up. Spatial magic crackled through the air and large rents were torn in the floor as the magic went wild.

A shiver raced down my spine. I didn't like it, but Morgana was right. This was a fight above my level of skill. I might be a badass dragon, but I wasn't a match for Nat'alet when he was mimicking Morgana.

Scarlett pulled me away and pointed to the quarry which was still sticking out of the mall floor. Trolls were starting to twitch and wiggle; their blood was flowing once more.

"Shit," I swore.

I came up to the first troll. Reaching down, I wrapped my hands around its throat, about to pull its head off. But this felt different from when I'd killed in the heat of battle. These were innocent people, nothing more than a tool that Nat'alet used.

A growl of frustration escaped me as my claws opened and closed inches from the troll's head. "Scarlett, can you frost the area? Keep it cold enough that they don't become active?"

She looked at me funny, but then put the blasting rod to use. Given the size of the quarry, it felt like trying to put out a fire with a squirt gun.

I growled and grabbed the closest troll, pushing it off the ledge of the quarry to the bottom. He'd heal.

Then I grabbed the next troll, shoving him down. "Focus on frosting the inside lip of the quarry. If we can keep them down there, that's enough." It would also reduce the amount of area we needed to keep cold.

She continued to spray frost over them. "Zach, can you breathe frost again? I think we could use it about now."

Pushing another troll back down into the quarry, I stared at the pit. Even if I got them all in, Scarlett was right. She wasn't going to be able to cover the whole pit with just that blasting rod.

Her idea made sense, but I hadn't used the frost breath outside that one battle. My scales were still silver, but I had only purposefully breathed fire before. And, if I accidentally washed the place with fire, we were going to have hundreds of trolls snap awake.

Fuck. Risky was an understatement.

"Let me get them down into the pit first." I worked double time, pushing half-frozen trolls into the quarry pit as Morgana and Nat'alet fought so hard that the surrounding stone was cracking. Their spatial magic was running rampant from their battle.

Morgana had always held back her magic; I remembered now when she had told me that her magic essentially cost lives. Every time she used it, she'd have to replenish herself with more blood.

At times, I hadn't understood her reluctance to just drink more blood, but then again, Morgana was a complex woman. She had secrets that I still didn't know.

Pushing the last troll into the quarry, I looked over to check on Scarlett's progress. She was still hosing down the lip, angling the blasting rod upwards so it would freeze the air above the quarry and settle down into it.

I hoped that would keep the trolls inactive rather than outright kill them.

And now I had to do the same, but on a larger scale. Don't fail me now, beast, I told myself.

Taking a deep breath, I pulled on my body the same way I would to breathe fire, hoping that my breath had changed along with my scales.

Feeling the breath coming, I let it go.

Bright dragon fire exploded across the opening of the quarry. I knew the second I'd let it out that it was wrong. I quickly twisted away, melting the entrance to an old clothing store instead.

"Zach!" Scarlett admonished me.

I cursed inwardly. I didn't need the added admonishment. Just that bit of fire had warmed the quarry, removing the thin layer of frost that had settled down there.

Trolls and shamans rumbled as they moved and uncurl from their almost frozen states.

"Let me try again." I dug deep, trying to recall what it had felt like when Scarlett had been hurt. It wasn't a fiery, explosive rage. It was sharper, crisper.

Trying to resummon the image and emotions that had been raging through me when the shaman had hurt Scarlett, I drew on my breath again and let it loose.

This time, it worked.

Frosty blue fog sprayed out of my mouth, coating the ceiling in thick layers of ice. Confident I had used the right one, I pivoted and directed my blast downward, coating the lip of the quarry in ice so cold that wisps of fog rolled off of it as the warmer outside air came into contact.

I sprayed down the surroundings, feeling the temperature drop sharply and letting the peripheral spray sink down into the quarry.

When I let up, the trolls and shamans had hunkered back down, trying to preserve what little warmth they had left.

But, before I had time to pat myself on the back, two Morganas flew through the air, landing not far away. They seemed to have lost their swords, reverting to wrestling on the ground.

Both of them were torn up. Their healing appeared to have slowed, and one look with my shifted eyes told me they were nearly drained dry of mana. That meant their enhanced speed and healing were also nearly gone, not to mention their spatial magic.

"Gun." I held my hand out to Scarlett; she didn't hesitate, slapping a pistol into my hand. Checking the gun over, I racked the slide and pointed it at the two vampires. "Okay, enough."

The two looked at me, taking in my position and the gun. It was enough to make them pause.

"Don't worry, I have this," Morgana on the right said.

"Bullshit," the left one said, clawing at her eyes.

I fired off a test shot. When neither of them blurred away, I confirmed my suspicion. They were out of juice and susceptible to bullets.

"Cut it out. Now, which of you is actually Morgana?" I regretted saying that the moment it left my mouth.

"I am," they both spat with the same characteristic Morgana snark.

Shit, I cursed inwardly. I had to figure out how to tell them apart.

My eyes shifted between the two drow vampires, and I felt a headache coming on.

"What am I?"

"A dragon," they both said quickly.

Morgana on the right continued, "I mean, it is pretty obvious after what's happened. You're going to have to pick a harder question." She said it with the same typical Morgana characteristics. But it could have easily been Nat'alet.

"That's just what the fake Morgana would say." Left narrowed her eyes before her expression softened. "Zach, come on. Stop being stupid. It's me." Seeing me falter, she added, "I love you and trust you to do the right thing."

A shot rang out, and the Morgana who had told me that she loved me crumpled, the bullet lodging itself right between her eyes.

"Holy shit," Scarlett yelped. "You shot her!"

"That was one hundred percent Nat'alet." I turned to the real Morgana. "Like hell Morgana would ever profess her love for me. Even if she did feel that way."

Morgana rolled her eyes at me. "Remind me never to get mushy with you. Help me up?"

Her leather leggings and signature corset were torn, showing off more of her dark blue skin. Her corset was barely hanging on to keep her nipples covered, exposing more of her sinful curves. I wondered how it had held up in the first place.

"Had enough?" she asked.

"I was assessing your injuries," I grumbled. Reaching down, I offered her a hand, pulling her up. Then I went one step further and lifted her up, swinging her into a princess carry. Turning, I started walking to the exit. "Besides, you know you like me looking."

"Get a room. This is getting old. Either fuck each other's brains out or move on." Scarlett scoffed, but the way her tails moved energetically behind her gave away her excitement at the idea.

"Morgana would probably be all for it. What do you say?" I teased her, wondering if she'd finally open up.

"You'd like that, wouldn't you?" Her red eyes dripped with hidden meaning as she gazed into my eyes.

I couldn't help but let the moment linger. "Let's get out of here first, then we need to have a talk, Morgana."

Her cheeks turned a darker purple, and she looked away, a cute shyness coming over her.

Up above the torn roof, I looked at the barrier that the Winter Queen had erected. I was surprised it was still there. Based on what she'd said, it was supposed to fall when Nat'alet died.

I froze. The back of my neck prickled just as the area lit up bright red. "Dodge."

Curling down over Morgana, I watched in horror as Scarlett took the brunt of a red beam that hurled her across the open space and crashed through a boarded-up store.

I whirled. My chest felt like it was filled with enough anger to burn the world alive.

My mate. No one fucked with my mate.

Morgana pushed against my chest, rolling out of my grip. "I'll check on her."

With the need to carry her gone, I shifted into my hybrid dragon form. Mass packed onto me as I turned into a sixteen-foot-long dragon, pouncing on Nat'alet.

I wasn't sure what had possessed me into thinking I could kill a god with a bullet to the head. It had seemed straightforward at the time. And now Scarlett... If she...

I couldn't even think about it, flying into a blind rage.

Nat'alet smirked at my anger, shifting once again. This time, though, he grew even larger than the hydra we had faced. His skin bubbled a swampy green as he transformed into a twenty-foot-tall swamp troll.

He caught me mid pounce and slammed me into the mall floor, shattering it and sending a spray of concrete everywhere.

I coughed up blood; even my hybrid body didn't hold up against that level of damage. My rage had overpowered my better senses of combat, and I had paid the price. I wouldn't make that mistake again.

"If you were an adult dragon, this might have been a challenge. Little baby whelpling, it is a shame to kill you and remove your heart from helping heal the world."

Another one of those huge, green, meaty fists slammed into my flank, and I felt my ribs crackle dangerously.

I worked my jaw and tried to quip back, but even if I could speak, he didn't want me to.

A fist came and broke my jaw as he buried my head into the floor. Nat'alet punched as hard as a semi-truck flying down the highway.

"Maybe I'll skin you, wear it myself. I hear you married into the Scalewright family. That would make a wonderful cover for me as I establish my new religion. Despite the hitch the Winter Queen put into my plan, they will move forward."

Nat'alet's ugly mug smiled around his tusks as he huffed swampy breath in my face. It smelled like a sewer.

"The best part? I need to take off your skin while you are still alive. I think I'll do the same with your two ladies and find two lovely shamans to take them over. Have a beautiful drow vampire and kitsune to play with and do my bidding."

I thrashed under him, but even with my size and might, he had at least another several tons on me and was pressing me down with his full weight. If I tried to shift out of this, he'd flatten me like a pancake.

He was deliberately keeping my head and my mouth pointed away from him, forcing me to watch him out of the side of my eye.

Working slowly with my dragon tongue, I asked, "Why?"

Or at least, I made a noise that sounded somewhat like that. But I needed to keep him talking so that I had a chance to come up with a better plan.

He paused, trying to decipher what I had said before he guessed it. "We are tired of how the world is progressing. It was simpler back when humans had bows and spears, or even swords. Modern weapons are a problem, even for those of us who have been around long enough to amass power. So much sweeter were the days when a little magic brought tribes of man to their knees in worship."

There was a gleeful look on his face as he reminisced.

I snorted; he was an old man stuck in the past. Things changed. The world would always move forward. The only option was adapting to the changes, not trying to revert everything to what it used to be.

It didn't escape me that he spoke as if he wasn't alone in this endeavor.

I realized paranormals in general seemed more outdated. Maybe the shorter lifespan and turnover of generations among the humans had led to faster advancement.

Reading my face, Nat'alet continued, "You are too young. Far too young to understand. It was better back then and will be again."

His hand came off my chest and he hammered me again. This time, I could feel my ribs snap under the force.

"But you won't get to see that. I'll beat you until you can't move and then we'll see about that skin of yours."

But, before he could hit me again, the mall lit up with bright silver light. He turned to look, his eyes widening at whatever he saw.

Something hurtled into him, large, feathery, silver wings filling my vision as Nat'alet was ripped off me and thrown into the stone structure that pierced the mall's ceiling.

It came crashing down on top of him as my new feathered friend landed gracefully.

"Morgana?" I tried to say in disbelief as I pulled myself out of the hole Nat'alet had put me in.

Standing there was Morgana, battered and beaten, and with two silver angel wings sticking out of her back. They gave off a radiant light that even now I could see was burning her shoulders.

"I can't hold this for long." She punctuated the statement by coughing up blood that sizzled as it landed.

"Scarlett?" I tried to ask, wheezing the word out. But Morgana knew what I wanted.

"Safe. She'll live... if you can get your ass up and help me finish this."

My bulk rose from the ground, and I roared in answer. Despite my broken jaw, I was filled with enough determination to ignore the pain that coursed through my body.

Nat'alet pushed aside the stone wall that had collapsed on him, taking us in. "Ah. This is part of the secret between you and the Church."

His body was covered in wounds. I noticed they weren't healing quickly. It seemed all of us were on our last legs.

I opened my jaw and breathed out frost at him before he could get up. I wasn't about to let him recover if I could help it.

Nat'alet blocked it with his forearm and pushed it away with a blast of red energy.

"Please. It won't be that easy." He stood back up, his left arm partially blackened like it had been frostbitten. "Come on. I want to see the full power of the famous Morgana Silverwing."

CHAPTER 32

I glanced over at Morgana, still captivated by the silver wings spreading out of her back.

She pulled them back and, in a single flap, crossed the distance between her and Nat'alet, colliding with him. Nat'alet's colossal troll form took the hit, and they both went flying through the other side of the stone structure, collapsing the whole thing in on itself.

Stones slammed into the floor, raining down thuds that rivaled the intensity of thunder.

I paused, wanting to charge forward but being unsure. I was weak from the battle. One of those stones could put me down.

Anxiously, I watched as the dust cleared. Morgana and Nat'alet were in a tussle. She pushed him out into the parking lot, knocking him through walls and personally wrecking the whole mall.

Apparently, no wrecking ball was needed when you had Morgana and a five-ton troll.

I shot forward, ignoring the pain that coursed through my body in protest. When Nat'alet was positioned right, I jumped onto his back. My claws and teeth tore at his back, taking huge swaths of flesh from him. I smiled when they didn't immediately regenerate.

His arms reached back and got ahold of my neck, and he wrenched me back and forth, trying to pull me off.

I sank my claws deeper into the muscles of his back, using his own force to shred it to ribbons.

Morgana shot in again on her wings, smashing into his face and shattering his orbital bone, causing the lumbering changeling to stumble to the side.

But he still managed to get a firm grip on me and yank me off. Not being removed without a fight, I kept my claws dug in, taking a portion of his back with me as he flung me to the side. I smashed into the wreckage of the mall as he wavered on his feet.

"Neither of you are going to walk out of here alive." His eyes glowed red as he blasted me deeper into the mall with another hit of that red force magic.

To make matters worse, I watched as Morgana's wings blinked out of existence. One moment she was flying around like a superhero, and the next she was stalling in midair, arms flailing in surprise.

Nat'alet smacked her out of the air so hard that she bounced off the pavement and shot towards me.

Watching Morgana's body sail through the air, the world came into sharp focus. I had to catch her. My bruised and battered body felt like it tore in two as I darted to catch her.

Morgana's body collapsed into my arms. She was broken; blood and burns covered her body as she looked up at me, her eyes bleary and blood seeping from the corners.

"I'm all out," she coughed, her eyes fluttering closed.

As I stood there praying, her chest still rising and falling, something snapped inside of me.

This god's followers had come for Jadelyn. He had hurt Scarlett, and now had taken out Morgana. Nat'alet had to die. There was no other option.

The beast that had ridden with me my entire life seemed to swell, grow from depths I didn't know existed inside of me, a leviathan emerging from the dark depths inside of me. I laid Morgana's crumpled body down behind me, turning to face Nat'alet once more.

I pulled on that strength, trying to add more mass, more size to myself. It felt like trying to pull a boot out of muck. It was stuck, almost a suction holding me back.

I ripped hard, pulling that mass into me, empowering myself as much as I could. My scales rippled silver, then gold, then a flicker of something else before once again turning silver.

Nat'alet paused, his eyes wide with surprise for only a moment before he blasted more of that red force magic at me.

I ducked my head, the crown of horns catching the blast and withstanding it better than before. My claws sank into the pavement. I held my position.

More power, more mass, filled me. I felt like a balloon swelling past its limits. My skin and scales stretched painfully. With a roar of all the pain and frustration inside of me, I pushed against the force of the red beam. Slowly, I was able to take one step. Then one more.

Nat'alet's eyes grew even wider, and he tried to put more behind the blast, but he was running low.

I smiled, tossing off the red beam and charging Nat'alet, knocking him back and goring him with my horns.

In the same motion, I reared back, rising on my back legs as my claws whipped him across the face, carving out chunks of flesh.

Nat'alet stumbled, bending over and clutching his face as I towered over him.

It was at that moment that I realized just how large I'd become. Smiling, I stayed focused, hoping Morgana would live for me to show her this new form. The raw power that filled me felt amazing, and I wasn't about to waste it letting Nat'alet recover.

I leaned into him, taking him down to the pavement and crushing the asphalt beneath us both. My claws raked across his body once more, tearing him apart before my head reared back as I surveyed my victory.

Nat'alet coughed blood, shock spreading across his face. "It doesn't matter what you are. We will find a way. Then I'll skin you and wear you like a prize." He spat in my face.

My breath came up inside my chest in a confusing flurry of sensation, but it didn't matter which breath was coming. He would die.

To my surprise, I spat out fire and ice coiled together. They drilled into Nat'alet, freezing and burning him. The dichotomy didn't cancel each other out; instead, they ripped him apart on a molecular level as they caused rapid expansion and contraction, destroying everything that he was. He was pulverized into dust.

The chemist nerd in me marveled at the power. It was incredible.

I let out the last fumes of my breath as fog and smoke curled together. As it cleared, I waited to see what would remain of Nat'alet. His upper body was gone, and what remained began to shrink.

Given the previous two times he'd shifted, I was ready and waiting to squash whatever new form he took like a bug.

But instead, he became the same shriveled up icy blue Faerie changeling that I'd seen before the battle. But this time, he was missing his head and a good chunk of his chest.

Just to be sure, I snatched what was left of him and tossed it in the air, catching him with my teeth and chewing thoroughly before swallowing.

At that point, I wasn't taking any chances. Although he tasted like bitter cold coffee that had sat for so long that it had molded, I powered through, my nose wrinkling at the nasty taste.

As I swallowed, the barrier around the mall flickered in warning. It was about to collapse.

My mind snapped back to the present. I darted over to the collapsed mall and dug out the area around the stone tower until I came up with Scarlett. Carefully carrying her out of the rubble, I set her next to Morgana.

I was too big to provide any sort of careful nursing to them, so I tried to shift back. It took a few breaths before I was able to calm myself enough to be successful.

Injuries plagued me, but I ignored them to be with Morgana and Scarlett.

"What a sight to leave on," Morgana's voice cracked, drooping eyes looking up and down my naked form.

I didn't have time for her antics and checked on Scarlett. She had a pulse and was breathing. The beast in me calmed marginally, but was still on high alert. The Scalewrights would get her back on her feet, and I'd have my bouncy kitsune mate again. Although, her father might have a few things to say about her current state.

"Just going to ignore me?" Morgana coughed up blood.

"Hush. You aren't going anywhere. You just need a little blood. We'll pump you full as soon as we are out of here." I dismissed Morgana's injuries.

"Zach, that's what I'm trying to tell you. It's not going to work."

I gave her my full attention, laying Scarlett down to recover. "What do you mean?"

She coughed again, struggling to breathe. "At the risk of you shooting me in the head, there's something I want to tell you."

"Shut up. You aren't dying."

Morgana's ears wilted as her face pulled into a frown. "What I did here comes with consequences. I'm something that shouldn't exist in more ways than you know."

"The wings," I said quickly, understanding her and leaning over her.

The small smile she gave me in response was confirmation enough. "I've done some horrible things in order to keep my wings. Turns out, they were a little too much for me this time around, Zach." She grabbed my hand, her grip weak. "Will you hold me? I want to leave this world in your arms."

I didn't argue, picking her up and cradling her in my arms. "Can my blood help?"

"No. The damage is done. Celestial magic destroys vampires like nothing else. The only reason I didn't turn to dust long ago was because I've drunk so much of their blood to the point of becoming part celestial. Angel blood is the only thing that has been keeping the damage I once did to myself at bay. Even if I had more, I'd run into the same problem that has been chasing me for hundreds of years. It is only delaying the damage."

She felt so small in my arms.

Not sure what to say, I simply held her, stroking her hair. We were still for a long while as I did my best to comfort her.

I couldn't believe it. Morgana had always seemed invincible to me. A brilliant fighter, feared by most. And here she was, crumpled up in my arms.

Everything we'd been through, and this was how it ended? It didn't seem right.

I looked around, trying to come up with some miracle, some chance to help her.

The barrier that the Winter Queen had erected was slowly falling, but it would take another ten minutes by my best guess before we could leave. I would not get any help from the outside world in time.

"Morgana? Are you sure my blood won't help?" I looked down when she didn't reply.

She lay in my arms with a sweet smile on her face that was so unlike the badass drow vampire that it almost made me laugh. But the stillness on her face stopped, the laugh cold, my heart aching.

"Morgana?" I jostled her, but she was still unresponsive. I tried to check her pulse, but I realized that I had no idea if vampires even had one.

Cursing, I brought my wrist up to my mouth and bit until I drew blood. The pain didn't matter. If anything, it helped remind me that the moment was real. A moment I wished wasn't happening.

Blood welled up on my wrist and ran down the side of my hand as I made a fist and let a drop dribble off my knuckle and onto her blue lips. The blood pooled on her lips, overflowing and pouring down the side of her cheek.

I could feel warm tears leak from my eyes and run down my face.

"Morgana." My voice sounded distant and weak. I could fight a dozen trolls, tell a Faerie Queen to fuck off, and kill a god. But I couldn't save a woman who loved me?

I knew it. I'd known for a while if I was honest with myself. In her own way, she loved me. It defied her otherwise bold and independent attitude to make a move, but that didn't change the reality.

She'd been my rock and support in every way since joining the paranormal world. She'd become one of my closest friends. While I hated the thought of risking that to try for something more, now I might still be left with that nothingness, without giving it a chance.

I should have made a move, even if it had risked everything.

My hands curled into fists around her form, and I gritted my teeth, wondering if I'd been stupid to come up against Nat'alet. I'd been ready to put my life on the line, but not hers.

I closed my eyes, letting the pain wash over me. But, as I sank into the sadness, a small noise caught my attention. Opening my eyes, I watched as Morgana's lips moved just the slightest bit, her little blue tongue fluttering out and licking my blood off her lips.

I shifted her and grabbed her jaw tightly, forcing it open and letting more of my blood dribble down my arms into her mouth. Her lips and tongue moved as she savored my blood.

A warm smile spread across my face. It was working.

Time moved slowly as I waited, watching for more signs of life. I promised myself that, when she recovered, I was going to tie her to a bed if that's what it took to have a serious conversation. Things were going to change.

Her nose sniffed, a small moan escaping as she smelled the fresh blood flowing from my wound. Her mouth darted forward, her fangs sinking into my arm.

Sharp pain was followed by bliss, and I had to stumble down to sit as warm pleasure washed over me. I barely had enough cognizance to remember that vampire saliva was a powerful narcotic.

But she was alive and drinking my blood. I could only hope that it would be enough.

I let the warmth sink into me, and I was transported to the feeling of being barefoot on a warm summer, curling my toes in warm, loose dirt as the world displayed life all around me.

Smiling, I enjoyed the high. So much goodness was in the world; I should really pause and enjoy more of it. The narcotic saliva in my veins helped me see that goodness.

Bliss, pure unadulterated bliss, spread through me as my body relaxed.

My head lolled to the side, and I stared at the site of so much carnage and wreckage, but all that darkness slid off me, as if I was a bright shining star that darkness couldn't touch.

So. Good.

My eyes rolled into the back of my head as I reveled in the sensation. Only dimly was I aware that Morgana was still feasting on my wrist.

We stayed like that for a few moments before a sharp pain spread through me. Confused, I was pulled out of the haze, trying to figure out what was happening.

Suddenly, I felt like a fat kid's juice box as she sucked hard. I realized she was draining me dry.

I pulled as much as I could from my mass to replace the blood, but it wasn't going to be enough.

Reaching up, I tried to grab her head and pull her away. But my fingers missed her hair; my coordination was completely shot. I tried again, but that time my hand passed well beyond her ponytail as I tried to grab her.

Morgana's eyes were still closed as she sucked greedily away at my blood. She was killing me, and she didn't even realize it.

And, despite how hard I wanted to care, my body was still relaxed, sinking back into blissful thoughts. The feeling of peaceful meadows folded in on itself as darkness bled into the corners and my vision faded.

***

Jared saw the massive pillar of freezing fog collapse just as his phone rang.

"Hello." He hadn't recognized the number, but he had more than a few associates that liked to change their phones when contacting him.

"They succeeded. The god is dead," the voice on the other whispered through their receiver.

Jared smiled. It was always good to have contacts that were willing to provide up-to-date information.

"Who killed it?" He wanted to know if Morgana's partner was as dangerous as she was trying to goad everyone into believing.

"Don't know. Morgana walked out carrying two limp bodies, that partner of hers and a kitsune. Looks like she's been crying; they must have died."

Jared couldn't keep the grin off his face. After butting heads with her partner, there was a small measure of satisfaction at the news. Now he just needed to get his sword back. "Good work. Keep me updated."

He pocketed his phone and let out a satisfied whistle, turning back to the new hotel he'd booked.

Everything he had wanted had happened, even if it hadn't turned out exactly like he'd hoped. The Templars would want to hear the news of what had happened. They might even send backup to take out Morgana. It was a great opportunity. She was rarely ever so weak.

If not, he might be able to whip up a few magi to go after her, try to rekindle that spark of aggression between the two factions. If the Church ever wanted to position themselves to make another move, the first thing they needed was to get the magi back firmly on their side against the paranormal.

The stupid paranormal monsters were a menace to society. Case in point, an army of trolls almost got loose in the city. He couldn't imagine the destruction and loss of life that they would have caused. A weapon like that needed to be contained and controlled by those who stood for something. That, or removed altogether.

He hated paranormals, and he'd even grown up with one.

They didn't understand what it meant to work for power and ability. While he was sent off to train with the Templar, giving blood, sweat and tears for his prowess, his sister was powerful enough to crush him under her boot at only the age of ten. It wasn't right.

He walked into the hotel he was currently using. It had a wonderful view of the city. He found something comforting about being high up and watching the streets below buzz like an anthill. It separated him from the mundane and let him think analytically about what his next move would be.

As the elevator dinged to his floor and he made his way to his room, he paused.

Something wasn't right.

Putting a hand on the door handle, he summoned up a quick ball of light. He squeezed it in his hand, ready for whatever was on the other side. Flinging open the door, he paused halfway to releasing the ball of light.

Sitting in his dark hotel room, lit by the blue light of a computer screen, was his younger sister. Her hauntingly beautiful face glared at him and the spell he had prepared for her.

His eyes dipped down to her impressive chest, almost on instinct, and he flinched just before his head smashed through the TV stand, spraying wood chips everywhere.

"Do not look at me like that, pig," Helena spat as she kicked the door closed, suddenly on the other side of the room.

Jared had to wonder why she was more brutal on him than the door. He stared up at her as the cross tucked under his shirt worked to heal the fractured jaw he had just received.

"I don't know what you are talking about," he denied everything.

"Of course you do. You always look at my chest. Disgusting disgrace of a human. I'm your sister for crying out loud." The pure hatred she had for him stabbed into him like a dozen knives.

But this wasn't the first time. And it just wasn't fair. His half-sister was the most beautiful creature he'd ever seen, yet she nearly killed him anytime he looked at her.

There was a flap, and she reappeared on the couch for a moment, her massive white wings spanning the hotel room before they sank into her back.

His father had looked for a long time to find a paranormal to reinvigorate their family's sorcery. It had finally come from the most unlikely of places. The Church had offered an angel in return for the Nashner family's service. And Jared had been happily promised, sent to train with the Templars as soon as he was of age.

After that, he'd had the displeasure of being raised with a Nephilim.

"What are you doing here?" Jared kept his head down, fuming at having to show any deference to the beautiful bitch.

"The seraphim sensed something here tonight. Something big was here, like a blip on the radar before it disappeared." She looked out the window at where the pillar of fog had been.

Jared started to nod, but stopped as the pain in his jaw continued. He had to wait a few moments longer before his jaw was healed enough that he could manage to get out a few words.

"Morgana Silverwing fought a Native American god. Nat'alet. The Winter Queen was invoked into this world. There was a battle. Morgana is weakened." Jared spit to the side. "You could take her out. She's weak."

Jared knew about the truce, but he also knew that only mattered as long as Morgana had enough strength to be a pain to kill. His sister could easily out power Morgana at the moment.

But the world around him blurred as his sister pulled his face up to hers. "Do not fuck with Morgana Silverwing. Am I understood?"

He snorted. "She's just a vampire, no matter how special her magic is."

Helena looked at him, her eyes full of shock. "Do you really not know?"

"Of course I know. She killed Gregor, the head of the Templar. But you could take her out right now, no problem." He found himself back on his ass as he finished. He was thankful she hadn't hit him again, and that just made him angrier.

"That's not what really happened, brother. The Church just doesn't want to look weak." She sighed, looking out the window before deciding to tell him. "Morgana fought her way not only into Templar headquarters, but into the rift there between our world and the celestial plane."

"Wait. She went to the celestial plane? That's impossible," Jared squawked. "She's a vampire. Holy light should have killed her instantly."

"Yes." Helena's tone was somber. "She tore her way through the ranks of angels, devouring hundreds and ultimately draining Archangel Ramiel. The stories say she changed, that heaven's holy light was no longer able to harm her. That is why, no matter how many little cherubs she drains for that stupid champagned blood every year, the Church won't make a move. They are terrified she could barge back into the celestial plane and kill another archangel. They won't risk it."

Jared's face went slack and his mouth opened, but there were no words. She had killed an archangel.

"I see you understand the gravity of the situation. With my mixed heritage, I might be unfettered here on earth, but I'm no match for an archangel, nor do I have a reason to fight Morgana." Her eyes looked at him, pausing on his back before glancing around the room. "Where is your sword?"

Jared hesitated before changing the subject. Helena's mission was always her top priority. He'd distract her with that. "You said you were looking for something powerful that showed up. It had to have been Morgana, Nat'alet or the Winter Queen. Those were the only big powers here."

"All of those are known to us. This was something new, something hidden." Her brow furrowed. "I'll be staying here to see if it shows itself once again." She crossed her arms under her chest.

He couldn't help himself, checking out the reflection of her in the window.

"So, where did you lose your sword?" She turned back, staring him down.

Praying to the heavens above, he braced himself as he told her what had happened, knowing she wasn't going to like it, and he might need the healing of his cross again before he was done with the story.

CHAPTER 33

I woke up groggily to the beeps of hospital equipment.

"Where—?" My words stopped as I devolved into a coughing fit before I could finish the sentence.

"Zach." Jadelyn's lovely face appeared at my bedside in an instant, leaning in and crushing me with a hug.

Scarlett lingered over her shoulder with a big smile, her eyes strained from worry. I looked her over quickly. She had bandages wrapped around her head, but otherwise, she looked okay.

"Where am I?" I managed the second time. It didn't look like any hospital I'd seen before.

"Our house," Scarlett answered quickly. "Hospitals don't exactly work well for paranormals. But thankfully, you took to transfusions like anyone else."

"Transfusions?" I frowned. The last thing I remembered was Morgana sucking down on my blood. I played through what I could remember, panic hitting me as I remembered Morgana's crumpled form.

I tried to sit up, but Scarlett pushed Jadelyn aside, pinning me back to the bed and giving me a glare. "Stay put," she nearly growled.

I looked around. "Where's Morgana?" After what had happened, we needed to talk.

Scarlett and Jadelyn exchanged looks, seeming hesitant.

My stomach sank. No, she had to be okay. I had given her my blood. She'd moved more. She had to have healed.

When they still didn't say anything, I was barely able to squeeze out a command over my breaking heart. "Tell me."

Jadelyn was the first to speak. "Nobody has seen her since she dropped you off. She came out of the barrier once it fell. She was carrying you and Scarlett. When someone looked at you and they realized that you were near anemic... Well, several people, including my father, weren't happy. Zach, she nearly bled you dry. What happened in there?"

Grumbling, I realized they had it all wrong. And those accusations would have about broken Morgana. I knew she'd already be completely wracked with guilt over not having better control.

"Is my phone here?" I looked around.

"It was gone, but you can use mine." Jadelyn produced a phone and unlocked it.

I found Morgana's number and shot her a text, but it came up as one of those green bubbles that meant her phone was offline. Frowning, I called Bumps in the Night.

"Hello, Bumps in the Night. What can I help you with?" one of Morgana's workers answered.

"Hey. This is Zach. I need to speak to Morgana," I said quickly.

There was a pause on the other end of the line for a moment, and I heard the rustle of fabric as she called to someone on the other end.

"Hello?" a voice that was certainly not Morgana came over the phone.

"Who's this? I wanted to speak to Morgana." I was getting frustrated.

The woman on the other side of the phone paused. "This is Vivian. Morgana just promoted me to manager before she left."

"Left?" I nearly shouted into the phone. "Where'd she go?"

"Don't know. She came back yesterday morning, grabbed a few things, promoted me, and then walked out the door. I heard her calling for a cab to the airport, and she's been gone since. No word from her." Vivian sounded genuine.

I let out a frustrated sigh. "You said this happened yesterday?"

"Yeah. Early. She's never gone MIA like this." Her voice fell. "Anything I can help you with?"

It was all I could manage not to shout at her, but it wasn't her fault. My frustration was with Morgana for disappearing and myself for not being able to console her.

"No. Thank you." I hung up before I took my anger out on her.

"What day is it?" I asked the girls.

"Wednesday," Scarlett provided, stepping forward and grabbing my hand for support. "You were out for thirty hours."

"She's gone?" Jadelyn asked, only hearing my side of the conversation.

"She might think so, but she's not getting away from me," I growled. "Help me get this shit off me."

Scarlett put a hand on my chest. "Let a doctor come and check you out first."

"I'm fine." I tore the IV out of the back of my hand and started tearing off the sticky pads stuck to my chest. The hospital equipment started beeping loudly as if in complaint.

Apparently, that was enough to bring the doctor to the door.

"Hold on. We need to check you." He tried pushing me back down on the bed like Scarlett had, but I wasn't interested.

I grabbed him by his lapel and hoisted him into the air and off of me. "Feeling just fine, Doc."

His eyes bulged as he squirmed in my grip.

"Put him down." Jadelyn grabbed my arm, and I let her tug him back to his feet. "Zach. Let the doctor look at you. Please."

Growling at my mate for the delay, I fixed the doctor with an angry glare. "Do it quickly."

He had his stethoscope out in a whirl, looping a blood pressure cuff over my arm as he took my vitals. "I was only able to provide an intravenous solution to keep your blood pressure up while giving you as many nutrients as we could via your IV. Your natural healing took care of the majority of it. Though if you would be willing to disclose what you are, we could do more in the future."

The doctor gave Jadelyn a stink eye, no doubt for holding back that information from him earlier.

I put a hand on his shoulder and rooted him to the floor. "If you look at my mate like that again, I will eat you. What I am is big enough to follow through on that promise and still have room for the rest of your practice. Do I make myself clear?"

There was a good chance I was still in a bad mood and looking for places to blow off some steam. Maybe.

The doctor tore the blood pressure cuff off me. "Well then. Your vitals seem to be alright, but given the loss and recovery of blood that you've experienced, I recommend you don't exert yourself too much." He swallowed. "Try not to, um, eat too many people. Get plenty of food though."

Scarlett pushed her way between the doctor and me, turning him around and hurrying him out of my way. "He's normally quite nice. We'll make sure you are set up with payment for your help."

I finished pulling off all the monitoring devices and got out of bed, feeling the breeze of the hospital gown down my backside.

"Clothes?" I asked Jadelyn.

She produced a neat pile of clothes that I'd never seen before, but they fit perfectly. By the time I was dressed, Scarlett was back, and Ruby, her mother, was with her.

"Zach, I'm so glad you are okay." Ruby wrapped me in a soft, motherly embrace. Her hug smothered me in a way that made me feel small, despite being larger than her. "We were so worried."

I grunted, not sure how to answer at first before words came to me. "Nat'alet was more trouble than we expected, but in the end, I killed him and ate him to be sure."

My eyes wandered to Scarlett's bandaged head, her fox ear poking out of the wrapping. She looked particularly pathetic and adorable.

"You ate him?" a voice sounded from the doorway.

"Well, the first time I shot him in the forehead and failed to make sure he was fully dead. I wasn't going to make that mistake again." I sighed as Claire came in, knowing they were going to get the full story out of me before I could go anywhere. "Let me explain what happened with the Winter Queen. That's where it all started, and what took some of the odds out of our favor for the battle."

They reacted appropriately to my story, gasping at the details of the Winter Queen's agreement, and then gave appreciative sounds as I described the battle.

When I got to the part where Nat'alet reappeared after I shot him in the head, they winced. Ruby pulled her daughter close as if to confirm she was still alright. I left out the part where I shot fake Morgana because she told me she loved me.

I muddied the details as we got to Morgana's transformation, wanting to keep her secret safe. And I backed off on details of my surge in strength. I still wasn't entirely sure what that had been.

Finally, I ended with how I held Morgana and tried to revive her with my blood.

They looked guilty after I finished. "We didn't know what had happened. As you can imagine, we were quite angry when all we could see was that she'd fed on you nearly to your death."

I grimaced, knowing the damage was done. "I'll let her know when I find her. If you'll excuse me, I have to track her down."

"Of course." Claire patted me on the thigh. "Good luck."

Relieved of the motherly duo, I pulled Jadelyn with me. "Where is your entrance to the Atrium?"

"This way." My lovely blonde siren led the way, and I couldn't help but let my eyes wander over her shapely rear and long legs. There was still a hunger that our wedding night had stirred in me.

She looked over her shoulder, catching my appreciation. "We can take a detour if you need."

It was certainly tempting, but the longer I waited, the better Morgana could hide.

"No, but soon," I rumbled, leaning over her and tilting her head back for a kiss. I slowed down, also grabbing Scarlett for a kiss, careful of where her head was wrapped. "Both of you."

"Consider it a promise." Jadelyn patted me on the chest. "Come on, before we distract you too much."

Scarlett bit her lip and let her tails fan out behind her. They pulsed slowly, and I ran my fingers into those fluffy tails, eliciting a gasp from her as we walked.

I played with them as we moved through the hallways. Eventually, Jadelyn slowed down, nearing an otherwise unremarkable door and opening it.

As we entered, I found myself in the Atrium.

I took note of where the Scalewright manor door was and led them both down to Morgana's personal wing, opening the ominous stone door and stepping through quickly to my room.

Opening it, the first thing I noticed was that my bathroom had changed. Instead of a large but normal bathroom, it extended much further, looking more like the inside of a spa.

"Shit. This isn't the best time, but that was my father's gift to you. He had Morgana do it on our wedding day," Jadelyn explained before moving into the living area of my apartment.

My eyes scanned the kitchen table, and then I ducked into my bedroom.

Nothing.

I'd been hoping that Morgana had left something for me, a note of where she'd gone or what she was doing.

In my bedroom, I pulled up my mattress and stuck my head through the spatial vault she'd made there. Inside was my horde, completely intact. There was a pile of gold and jewels with the dagger Chad had used in a little stand to the side, and Jared's sword leaning against the wall next to it.

There was no sign of a note from Morgana there, either.

I growled in frustration.

"Not finding what you are looking for?" Scarlett asked.

"Morgana should have left me a note if she was leaving." I paced the room again, but I still found nothing.

Scarlett's tails drooped. "I hate to tell you this, but maybe she didn't want you to follow after her."

Bullshit. She...

It would be just like her to run away after what we shared.

I stormed out of my room and opened Morgana's, stepping inside for the first time since I'd lived there.

Inside her room, I froze. It was different from what I had expected.

The room was warm, covered in mosses and lichen, like a little underground cave. It was a vision of nature. The room spoke of an underground oasis. I'd always thought of elves that lived in trees, but this was the haven for an elf who lived under roots.

Trying to look past the decorations, I tried to find something that could point me in the right direction, but nothing stuck out.

I did, however, notice the plush gold dragon laying on her bed.

"Did you get Morgana one of those stuffed dragons too?" I asked Jadelyn.

"Yeah." She smirked. "Kind of a joke, but between us girls in your life."

I rolled my eyes, but the way it was carefully placed next to her pillow spoke of her treating it like a prized possession. I cursed internally. Why the hell did she have to run?

"There's one last place I'd like to look. Catch me up on what happened while I was out while we walk?" I headed back out of Morgana's wing and took the Atrium to Bumps in the Night.

"Uh, let me think. Well, the magi were pulled out of the collapsed mall. They had stayed safe down in the pit and thankfully, with Nat'alet dead, magi were able to help them shift back to humans. The council rounded up the remaining trolls and pushed them along on their way to Florida. Hopefully, we are done with the migration for the year," Jadelyn supplied a quick summary.

"How is the tension between the two groups?" The last thing we needed was magi being out for blood after everything.

"Not great, but everyone stood down thanks to your new friend Sir Benifolt."

I raised a brow. "My new friend?"

"He sang your praises. Since you had been badly injured, he used you as an example of just how far the paranormal community has gone to right everything. Jared showed up and tried to stir up shit, but I think he's out of the Order of the Magi. His connection to the Church and their reluctance to help has soured more than a few connections."

I was a bit surprised that Sir Benifolt had stood up for me. We'd fought side by side, but it wasn't like we'd built some sort of deep bond. I wondered if it had to do anything with his apprentice. "What about Sabrina?"

"You mean the succubus?" Jadelyn's manicured eyebrow arched as she gave me a judgmental look.

"I meant my friend, the wizard. But yes, she happens to be a succubus. Which is odd. I guess I'd always pictured a succubus as dressing a bit more like Morgana." Sabrina's plain illusion and that brown robe she wore were about the least tempting thing I'd ever seen.

"She's fine. She's still hanging around Sir Benifolt and asked after you. We talked, but I'm hesitant to pull a succubus into our relationship. I think she might be transferring to the school though." She looked to Scarlett for support, but I spoke up.

"It's fine. I'm not chasing her down. Right now, I need to find Morgana and have a pleasant talk with her." I growled, it wasn't going to be pleasant. "Scarlett, while you were unconscious, we chatted..."

"Don't tell me. She told you she loved you and also got a bullet to the head?" Scarlett giggled. "I still can't believe you did that."

Jadelyn looked between us, trying to catch up. Apparently, Scarlett hadn't shared that part of the story with her while I was out. So I told her about how I knew which Morgana was real and which was fake.

Jadelyn doubled over laughing as I plucked a set of keys at random in Morgana's garage and pushed the fob as I found which car it went to.

The silver Porsche would have to do.

I slid in with the girls and pulled out before I got the conversation back on track. "Morgana came about as close as she probably ever will to telling me she loved me. And she showed it too, sharing a secret as she protected me from death."

I explained what had transpired with her transformation, filling in the gaps I had left out when talking to their mothers.

"Angel wings," Scarlett murmured. "Hell if I know what that means. Jade?"

"Not a clue. But we do know she and the Church have a sordid history and a standing truce."

I nodded. "I'll bet my entire horde it has something to do with the wings. And she said something about the champagned blood she always drinks. I think it helps slow any ill effect the wings had on her. It sounded like she got it through means she wasn't proud of, but how, I don't exactly know."

"At least it's all over," Jadelyn said, running her hand along my arm, seeming to want to reassure herself that I was safe.

"For now," I cringed. Nat'alet had used his last words to indicate there were others working to the same ends he had been. And I had yet to solve the mystery of the skinwalker. While some worked with Nat'alet, I wondered if there were more.

"There might be more bad news." I shared what I was thinking.

Both of the girls settled into a comfortable silence as we mulled it over. But the silence was broken when I pulled into the nursing home parking lot and surprised them.

"Where's this?" Jadelyn asked, looking out the window, confused.

"We are going to see one of Morgana's oldest friends. If anyone in Philly has an idea where she went, it's T." I got out and checked in with the nurse who led me to his room.

T had played a major role in helping reverse the effects of a new drug introduced into the paranormal and human worlds, ultimately leading to Chad's death. Since then, I'd met him a few times when he supplied Morgana with magical ingredients.

T was an outcast from the elves, just like Morgana, and he seemed to have known her since she was a child. They'd shared a few stories of her antics back then.

I knocked on his door, opening it before he could respond.

The old elf lingered in the corner of his room. He was tall, even a few inches taller than me, but his hands and face were thin. The rest of him was hidden under a voluminous robe.

"Zach. In my old years, I've thought about becoming a personal hair stylist." he greeted me, plucking a pair of scissors and a comb from a shelf. "Give me a person to practice on?"

"I don't have time for this." I rolled my eyes at his attempts to get more pieces of me. The first time I had met him, he had wanted my nail clippings. Apparently, pieces of me would help power spells. Those nail clippings had gone into a jar labeled dragon claws and then into his secret ingredient cabinet he kept in the nursing home's kitchen.

"Oh, come on. Your hair looks much too long, and those nails! Don't get me started. You must let me trim them."

"T, Morgana is gone," I cut through his act.

His bushy eyebrows rose up, and the old man routine he kept up melted away, replaced by a focused elf.

"She's gone?"

"Well, fled is more like it. She nearly died, finally opened up, and then she ghosted me. Please tell me you know where she is. I'll let you take a lock of my hair if you can tell me where she is."

T grumbled for a moment. He turned to his bookshelf, plucking off a letter and holding it close. "She very likely went back home."

"Where's that T? I need to find her."

"The city in the shade," he sighed.

I glanced at the girls to see if they could translate for me.

"It's a paranormal city, hidden in the alps," Jadelyn supplied for me.

"Correct," T confirmed. "Sentarshaden, Switzerland."

"A whole city? T, you need to give me more than that."

With that, he held out the letter. "If you deliver a letter to my daughter, then she might be able to help. My daughter is in Sentarshaden. If Morgana went back there, she would have gotten in touch with her oldest friend."

I froze, knowing that T was trusting me with one of his deepest secrets. His daughter had remained hidden for her safety for years, keeping them cut off. To my knowledge, T and Morgana had been the only ones who knew where she was until he'd just told us.

"How do I get in contact with her?" I asked.

T smiled and pulled out a blank piece of paper, starting to jot down detailed instructions on how to communicate with his daughter. Apparently, she hid in the masses of the city, and they had developed secret drop methods for communication.

With a new goal in hand, I turned back to the girls.

"You know, I think we should go on a honeymoon." Jadelyn tapped her lips. "Where do you think we should go?" she asked Scarlett.

"I hear Switzerland is beautiful in the winter," Scarlett played along. "I'll bet your new hubby, the lost one, would absolutely love to see the hidden paranormal city there."

"That's such a great idea." Both of them smiled wide at me.

"Thank you both." I paused, my throat feeling tight. They were too good for me. "I have to go after her." I hoped they'd be able to understand.

There was no way in hell I was going to let Morgana slip through my fingertips. I couldn't believe she'd run, and we'd be talking about that when I got her back. But first, I had to find her.

The beast simmered my chest, agreeing that she was going to be pounced on and pinned for making us chase after her. Although I had to admit, a part of the beast in me liked the chase.

"Best of luck." T swiftly cut off a chunk of hair from the back of my head, and carefully coveting the hair, he sealed it in a baggie.

I rubbed the back of my head. A deal was a deal, but it probably looked terrible. "Alright, let's go girls. I think we should see if we can't take our finals early so we can get started on this honeymoon."

"Great idea," Jadelyn chirped. "I'll see if I can't pull any strings with the administration."

I kissed her on the cheek and pulled both of them lovingly out of the nursing home. I couldn't believe I'd found two beautiful women that supported me so much. Neither had hesitated in going after Morgana with me.

Even if we hadn't cemented that, Morgana was mine. She knew it, too. Her denial and flight wouldn't save her from my clutches.

I wasn't going to let her feel guilty about what I'd done willingly, although she might not even know that.

There had been regret in her tone for what she did to temper the effects of the wings. She'd once told me that we were the bad guys, that we were the monsters. I had a feeling she felt that way about herself, only reinforced by waking up with me nearly dead.

She had a darker past than I'd realized, but it didn't matter. I couldn't wait to rid her of the idea that she was a monster, or at least make her realize that she had a home with me, even if she was one.

"Zach, you're growling," Scarlett whispered as we passed through the lobby.

"So. I am what I am." I stuck my tongue out at her. "Growling is part of what I do."

The girls laughed as we walked back out to the car. Jadelyn was on the phone, already working to coordinate our honeymoon.

Morgana would be mine next time I met her.

Afterword

Phew. I am tempted to just go on and write straight into book 3 after that ending. Morgana might just bc the best potential waifu of the series.

But alas, I need to stick to the rotation. Dao 3 is on deck. I finished chapter 21 today, hopefully will have it finished on my end here before the end of next week. Going into the holidays for editing I expect some sort of delay, but I think I'll be able to still get Dao 3 out for Jan 9th.

I wanted to thank everyone for the review and support of Dragon's Justice Book 1. It blew my expectation out of the water and I'll do my best to keep this series going. Obviously, there'll be a book 3 after the way this ended. I hope to have that for you on March 9th.

Life is good. I'm dabbling with the start of a few new series trying to find the right tone and voice for the 2 new series I plan to start next year. Right now I have a Super Hero and a LitRPG planned. But I'm not allowing myself to play with my new ideas too much until I finish up what I've started, so for now, they are just dabblings. I have more ideas than I know what to do with. Sounds like I just need to keep on hammering the keyboard, doing what I love.

As always, reviews are the lifeblood of the system. Drop me a review if you can.

Leave a Review

If you want to follow my progress for future books I do monthly updates on my mailing list and Facebook page.

Mailing List Sign Up

Author Bruce Sentar on Facebook

Patreon

ALSO BY

Legendary Rule:
Ajax Demos finds himself lost in society.
Graduating shortly after artificial intelligence is allowed to enter the workforce;
he can't get his career off the ground.
But when one opportunity closes, another
opens. Ajax gets a chance to play a brand
new Immersive Reality game. Things aren't
as they seem. Mega Corps hover over what
appears to be a simple game. However,
what he does in the game seems to effect
his body outside.
But that isn't going to make Ajax pause
when he finally might just get that shot at
becoming a professional gamer. Join Ajax
and Company as they enter the world of
Legendary Rule.

Series Page

A Mage's Cultivation:
In a world where mages and monster grow
from cultivating mana. Isaac joins the class

of humans known as mages who absorb mana to grow more powerful. To become a mage he must bind a mana beast to himself to access and control mana. But when his mana beast is far more human than he expected; Isaac struggles with the budding relationship between the two of them as he prepares to enter his first dungeon. Unfortunately for Isaac, he doesn't have time to ponder the questions of his relationship with Aurora. Because his sleepy town of Locksprings is in for a rude awakening, and he has to decide which side of the war he is going to stand on.

Series Page

Dao Divinity: The First Immortal
Darius Yigg was a wanderer, someone who's never quite found his place in the world, but maybe he's not supposed to be here...Ripped from our world, Dar finds himself in his past life's world, where his destiny was cut short. Reignited, the wick of Dar's destiny burns again with the hope of him saving Grandterra.
To do that, he'll have to do something no other human of Grandterra has done before, walk the dao path. That path requires mastering and controlling attributes of the world and merging them to greater and greater entities. In theory, if he progressed

far enough, he could control all of reality and rival a god.

He won't be in this alone. As a beacon of hope for the world, those from the ancient races will rally around Dar to stave off the growing Devil horde.

Series Page

There are of course a number of communities where you can find similar books.

https://www.facebook.com/groups/haremlit

https://www.facebook.com/groups/HaremGamelit

And other non-harem specific communities for Cultivation and LitRPG.

https://www.facebook.com/groups/WesternWuxia

https://www.facebook.com/groups/LitRPGsociety

https://www.facebook.com/groups/cultivationnovels

Made in the USA
Monee, IL
12 January 2024

51638255R00312